hope larson

chiggers

lettered by
jason azzopardi

ginee seo books   atheneum books for young readers
new york   london   toronto   sydney

Atheneum Books for Young Readers * An imprint of Simon &
Schuster Children's Publishing Division * 1230 Avenue of the
Americas, New York, New York 10020 * This book is a work of
fiction. Any references to historical events, real people, or real
locales are used fictitiously. Other names, characters, places,
and incidents are products of the author's imagination, and any
resemblance to actual events or locales or persons, living or dead,
is entirely coincidental. * Copyright © 2008 by Hope Larson * All
rights reserved, including the right of reproduction in whole or
in part in any form. * Book design by Sonia Chaghatzbanian *
The text for this book is handlettered. * The illustrations for
this book are rendered in ink. * Manufactured in the United
States of America * First Edition * 10 9 8 7 6 5 4 3 2 1 * CIP
data for this book is available from the Library of Congress. *
ISBN-13: 978-1-4169-3584-1 * ISBN-10: 1-4169-3584-3

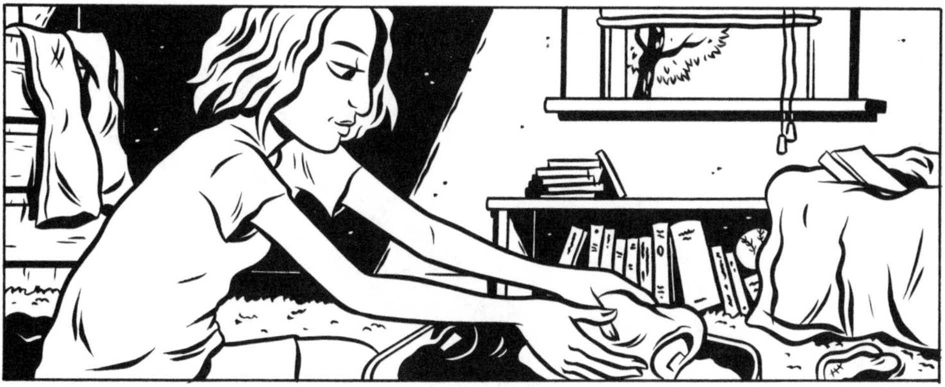

for Marcella

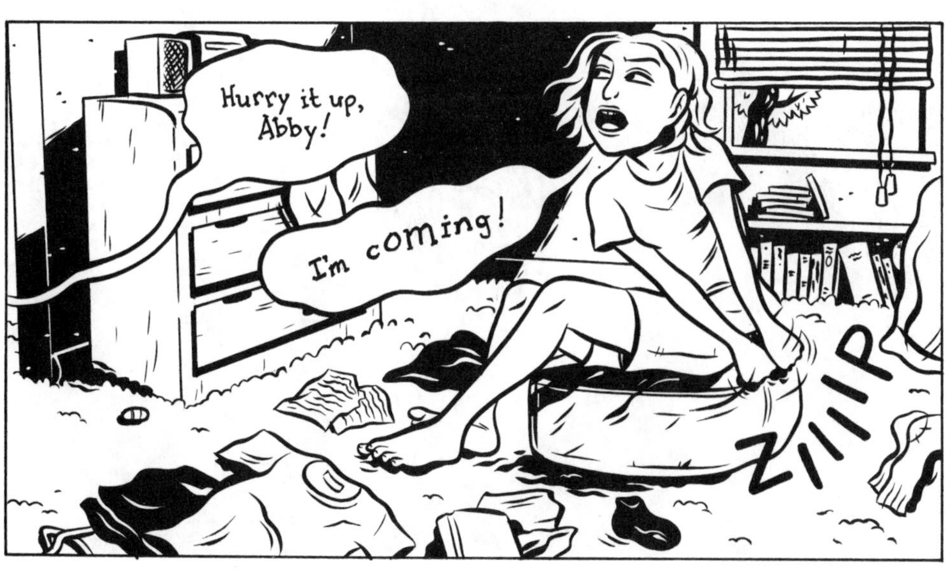
Hurry it up, Abby!
I'm coming!
ZIIIP

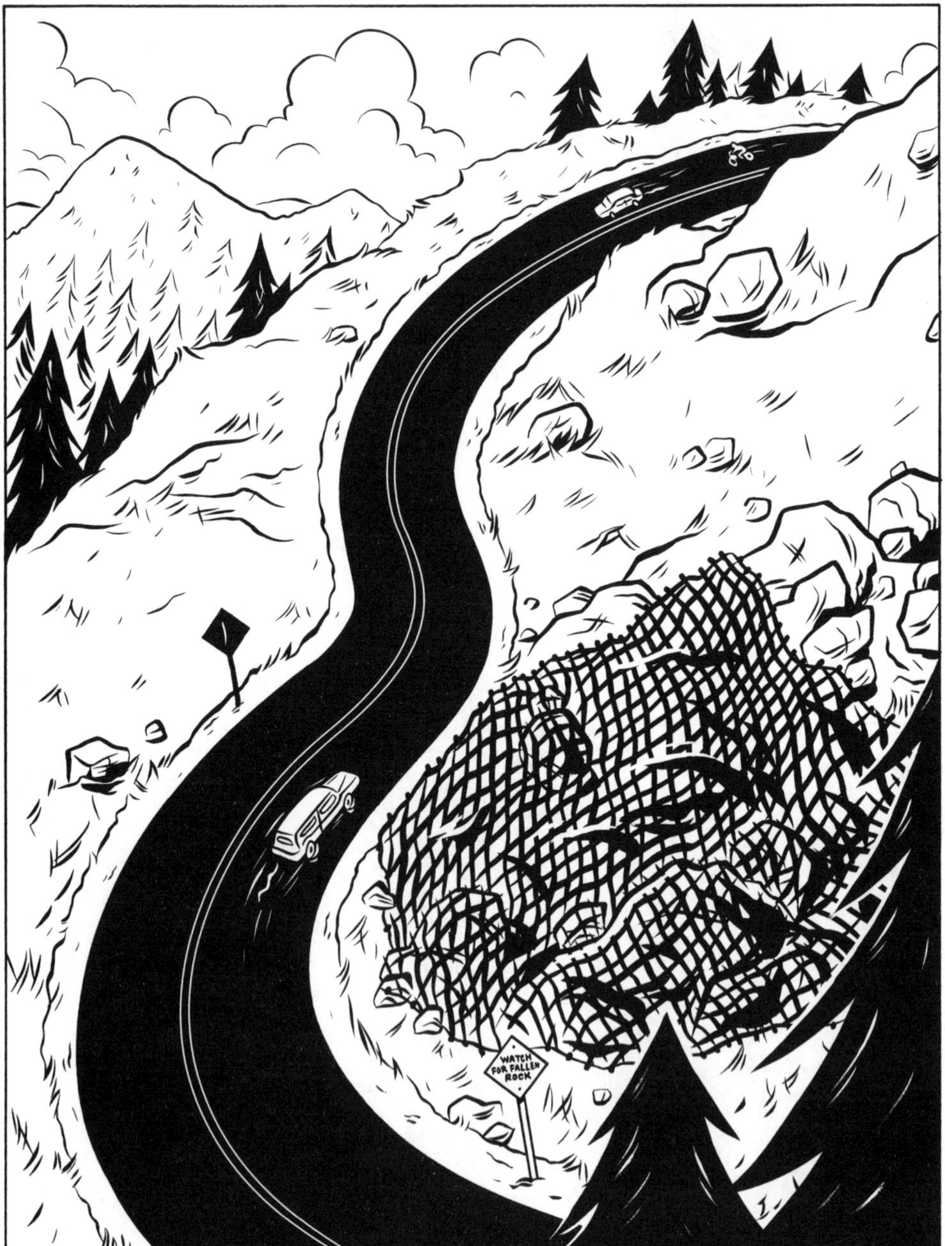
WATCH
FOR FALLEN
ROCK

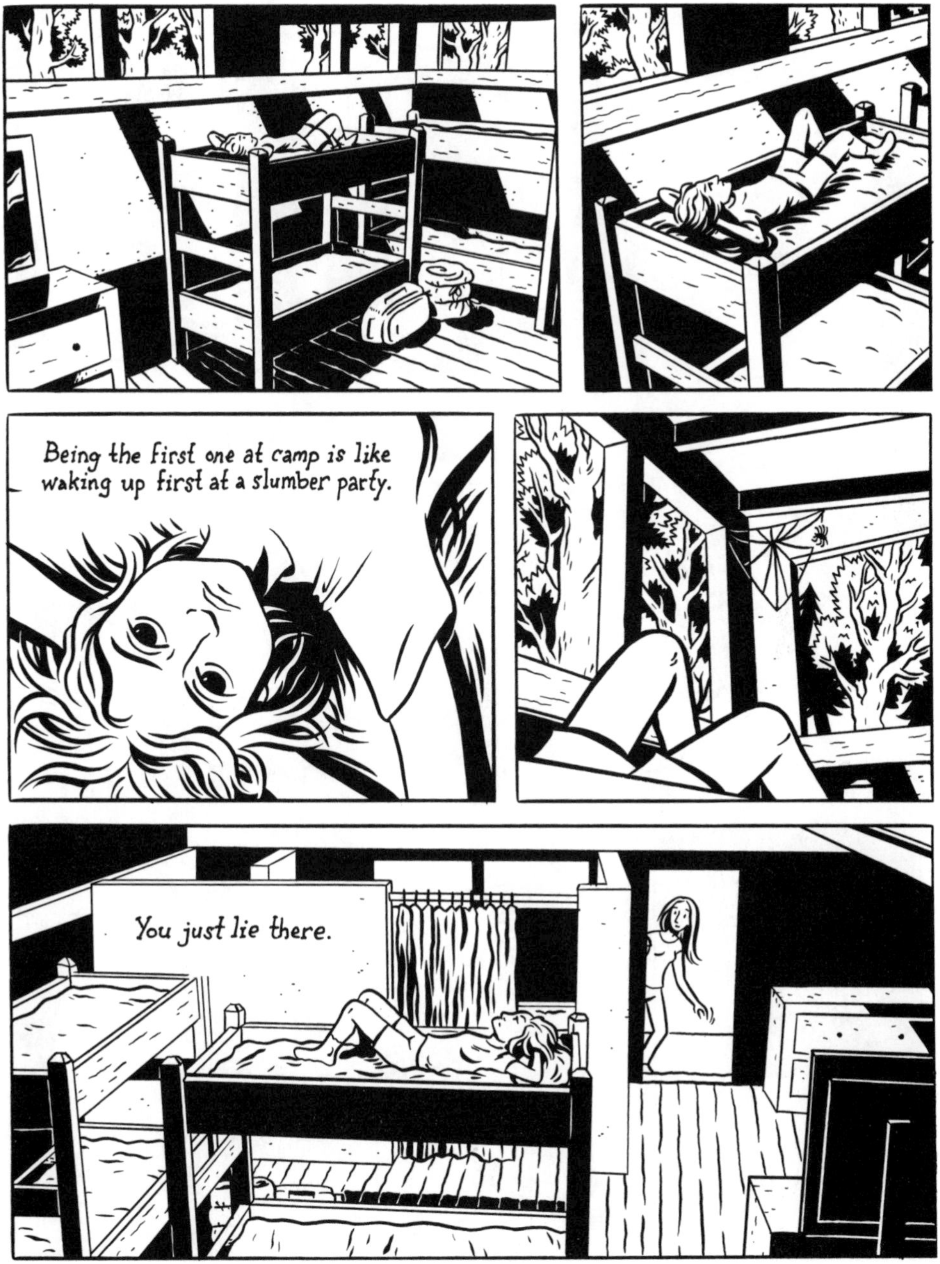
Being the first one at camp is like waking up first at a slumber party.
You just lie there.

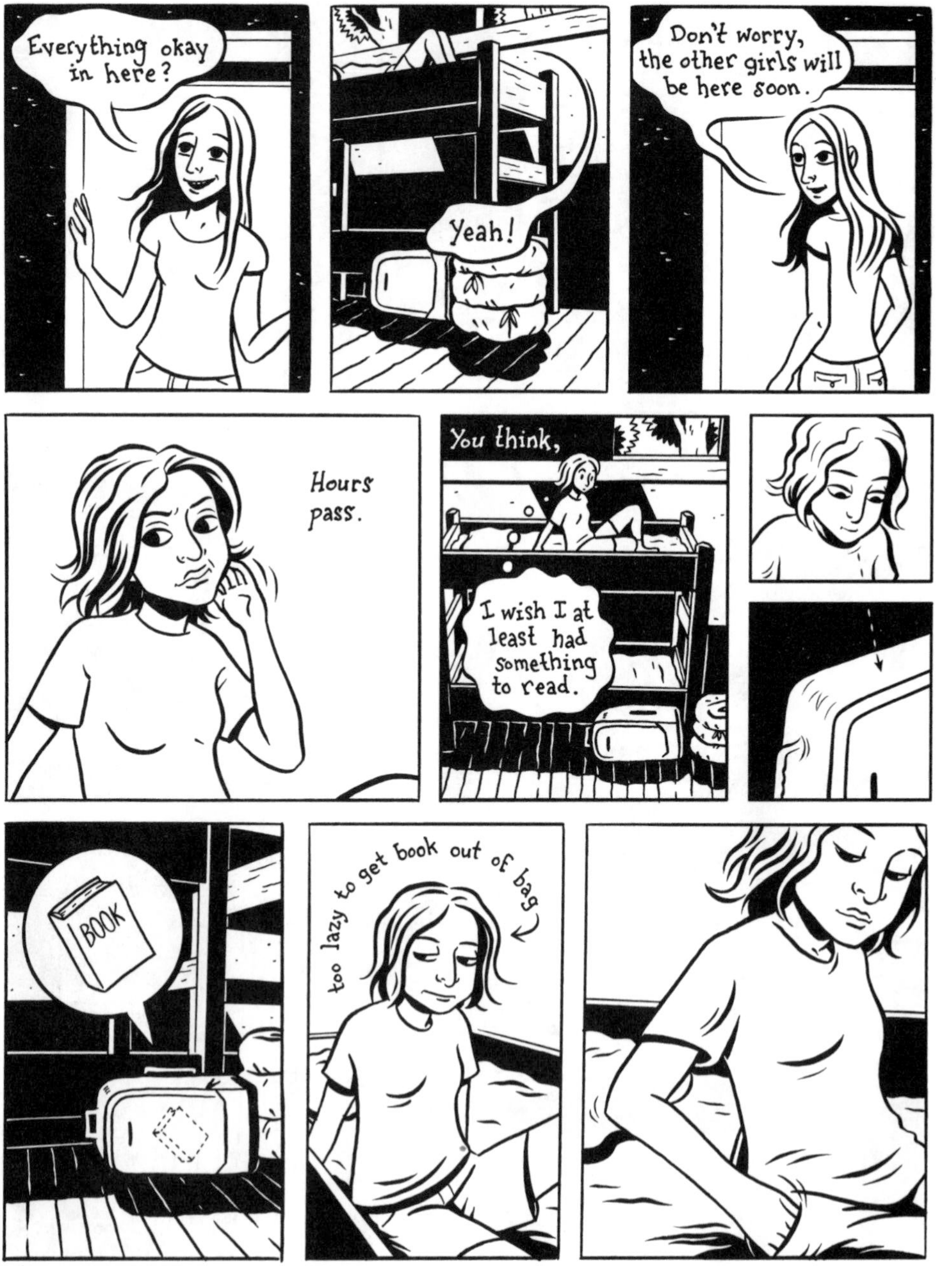
Everything okay in here?
Yeah!
Don't worry, the other girls will be here soon.
Hours pass.
You think,
I wish I at least had something to read.
BOOK
too lazy to get book out of bag

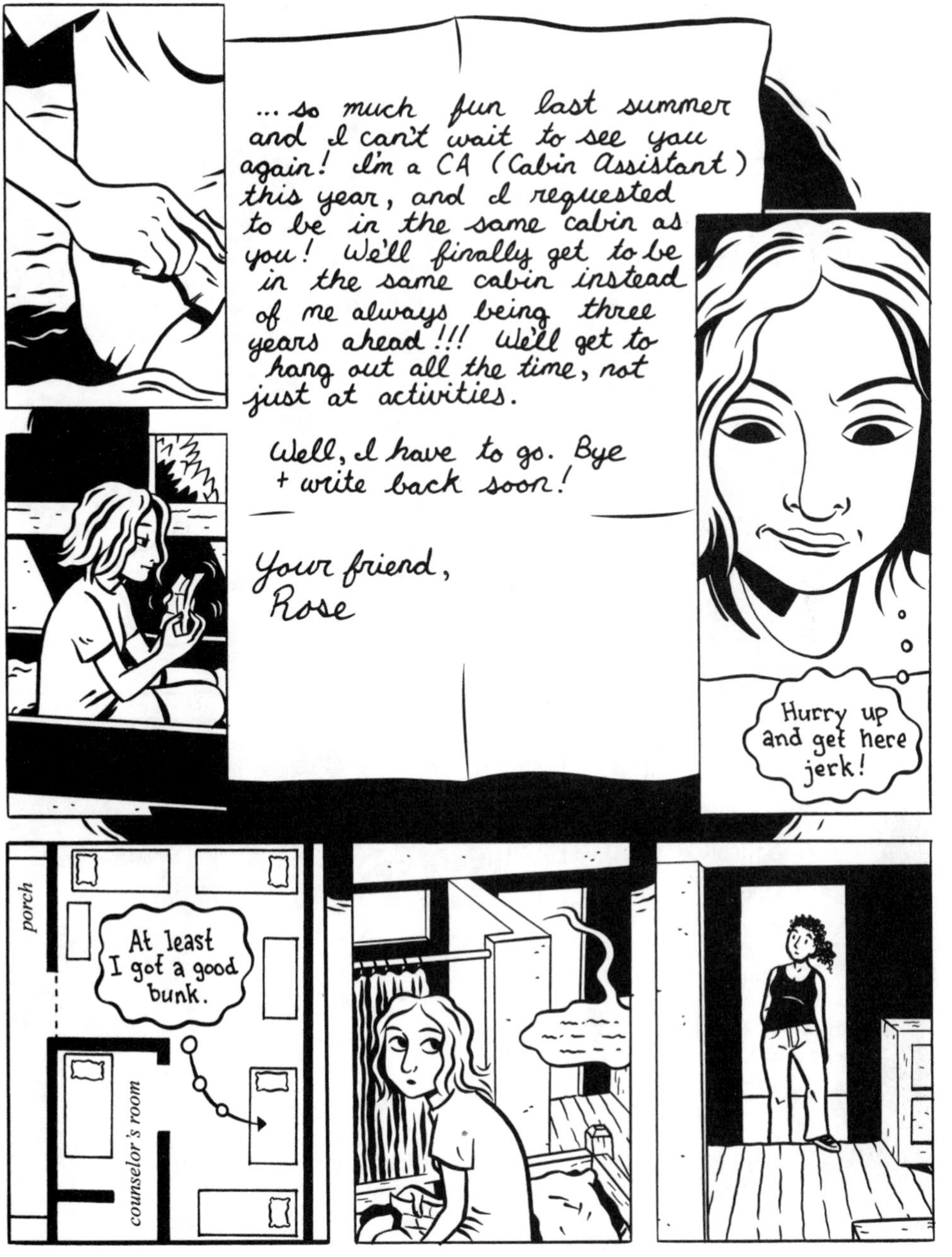
...so much fun last summer and I can't wait to see you again! I'm a CA (Cabin Assistant) this year, and I requested to be in the same cabin as you! We'll finally get to be in the same cabin instead of me always being three years ahead!!! We'll get to hang out all the time, not just at activities.
Well, I have to go. Bye + write back soon!
Your friend,
Rose
Hurry up and get here jerk!
porch
counselor's room
At least I got a good bunk.

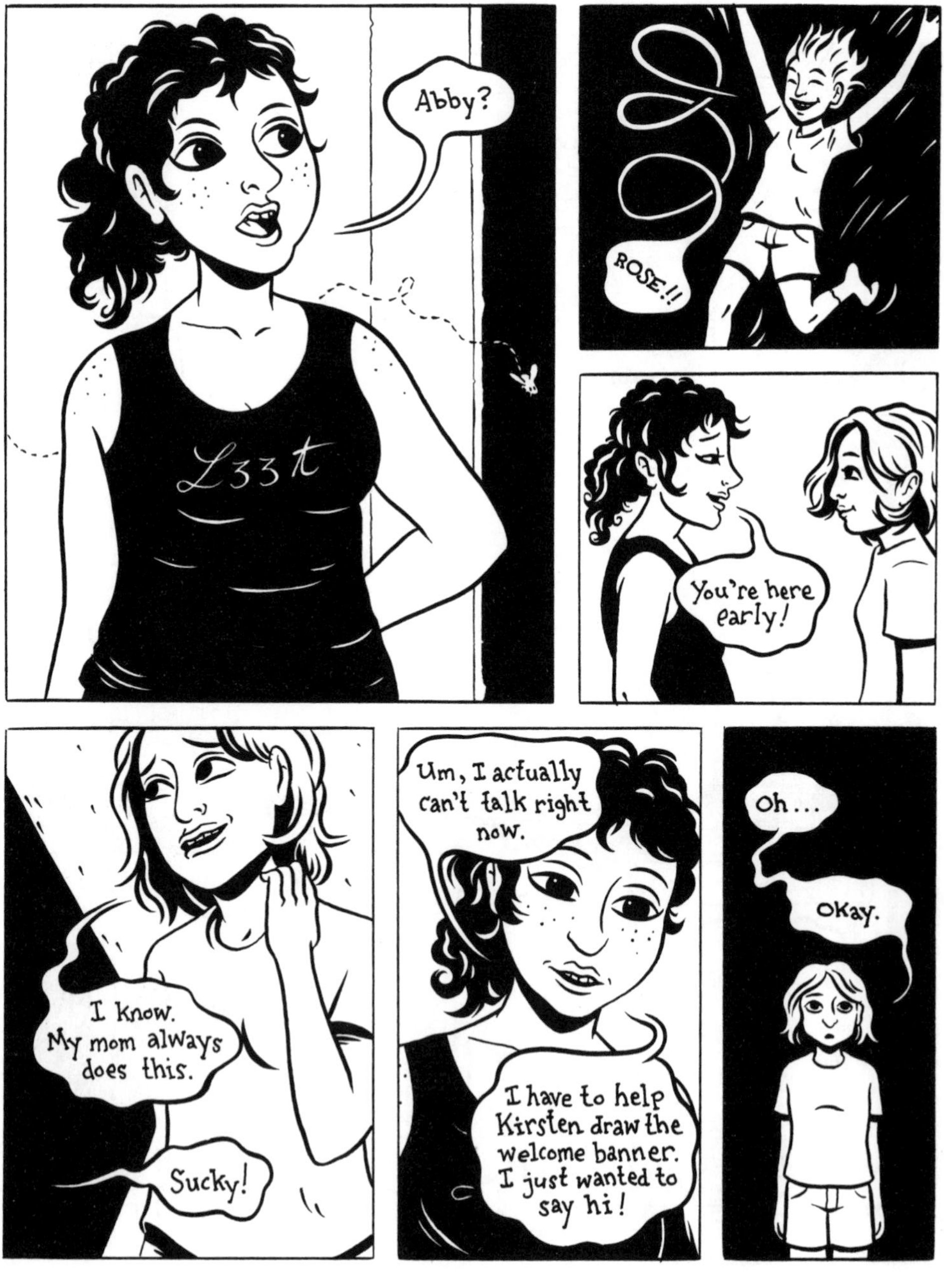
Abby?
L33t
ROSE!!
You're here early!
I know. My mom always does this.
Sucky!
Um, I actually can't talk right now.
I have to help Kirsten draw the welcome banner. I just wanted to say hi!
Oh...
Okay.

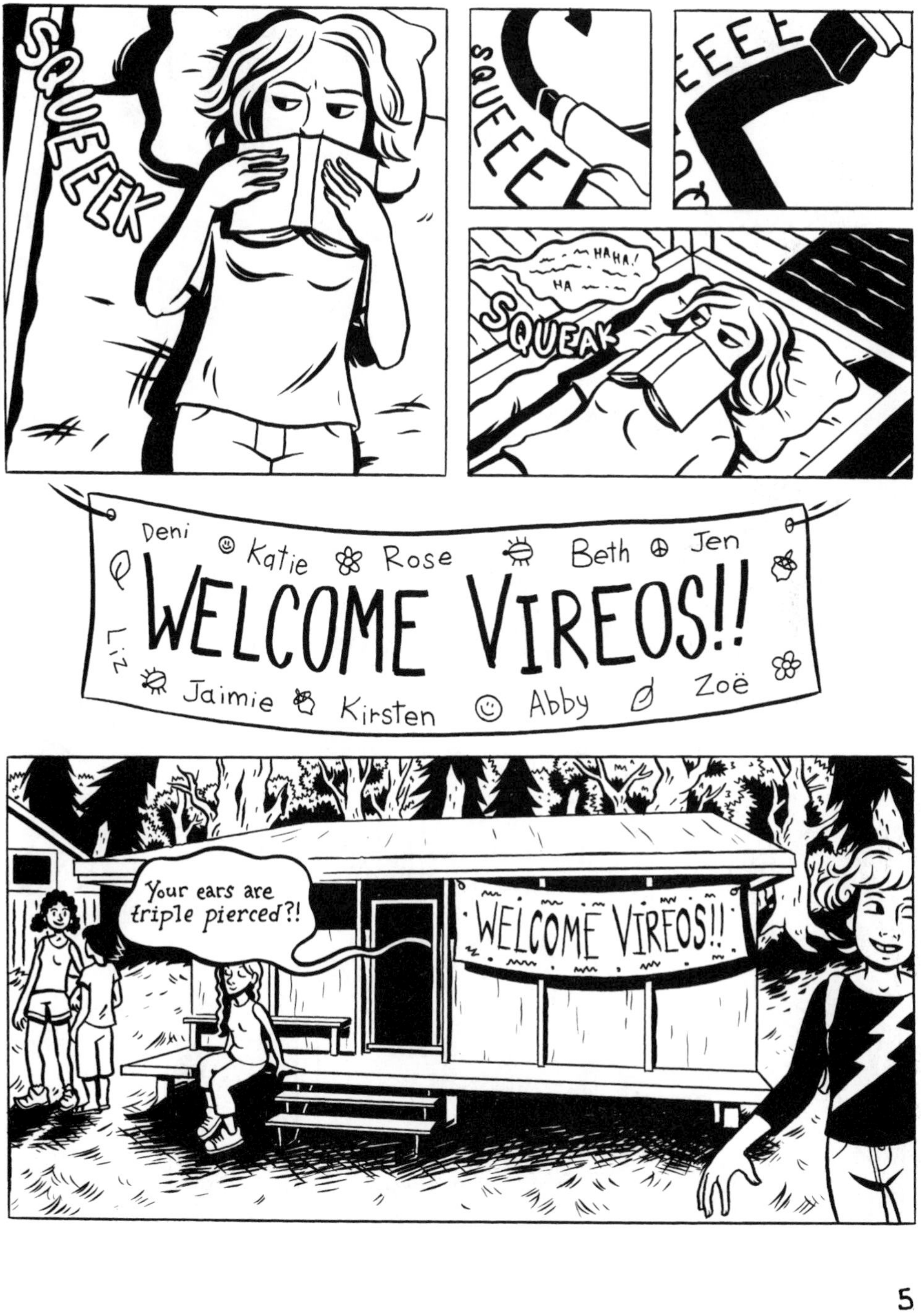
SQUEEEK
SQUEEEE
EEEE
HAHA!
HA
SQUEAK
Deni
Katie
Rose
Beth
Jen
WELCOME VIREOS!!
Liz
Jaimie
Kirsten
Abby
Zoë
Your ears are triple pierced?!
WELCOME VIREOS!!

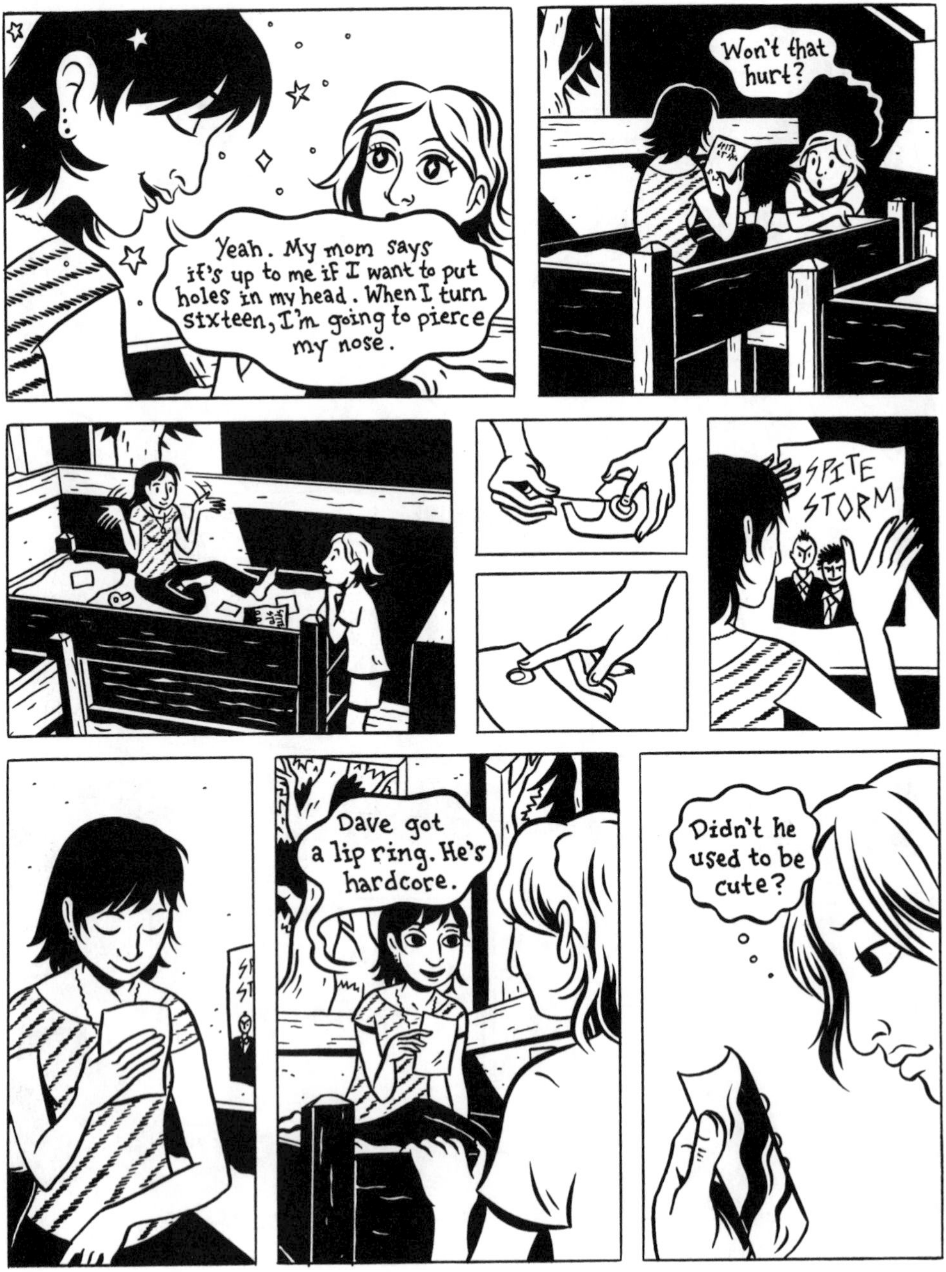

Yeah. My mom says it's up to me if I want to put holes in my head. When I turn sixteen, I'm going to pierce my nose.
Won't that hurt?
SPITE STORM
Dave got a lip ring. He's hardcore.
Didn't he used to be cute?

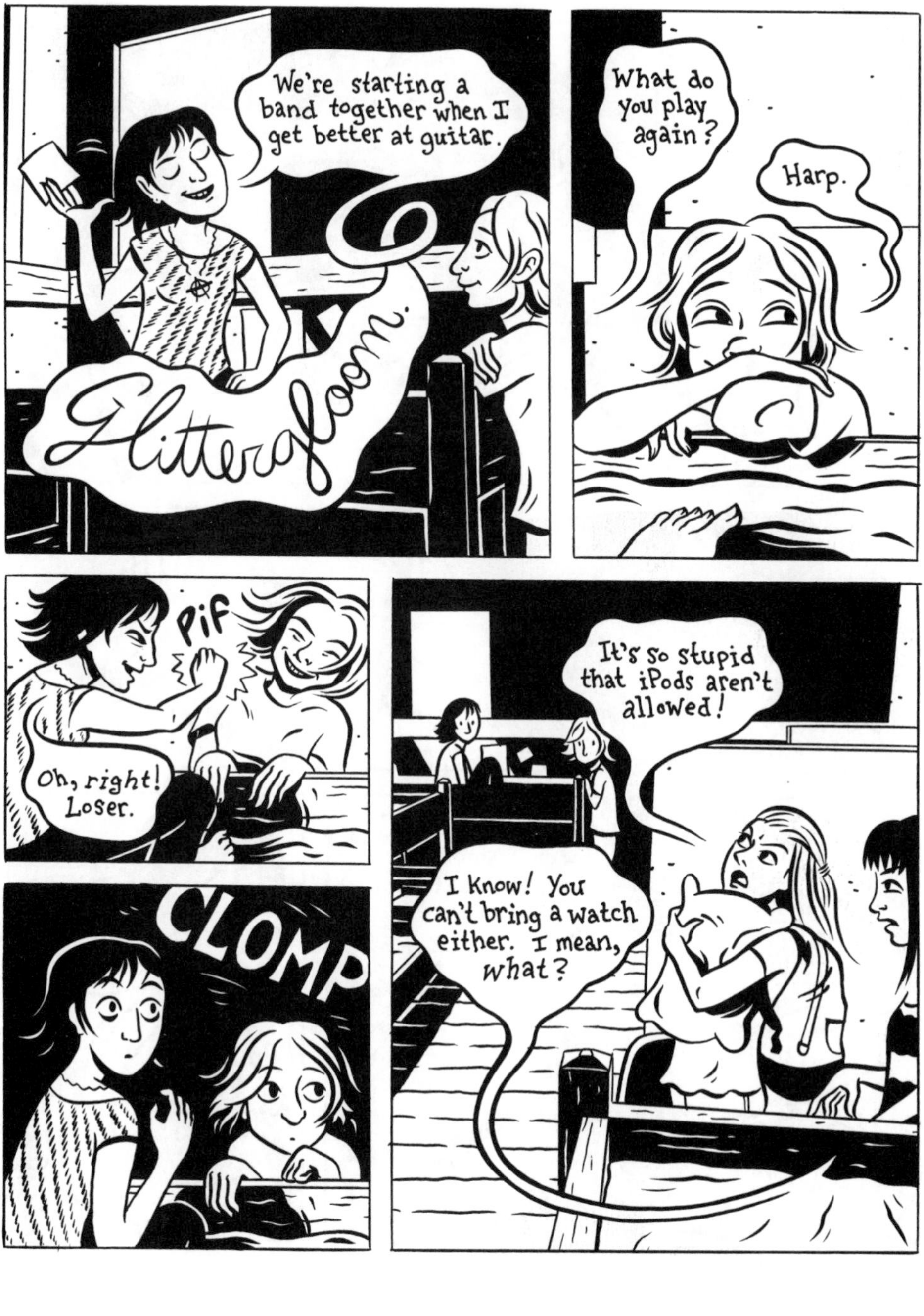
We're starting a band together when I get better at guitar.
Glitterfoam.
What do you play again?
Harp.
PIF
Oh, right! Loser.
CLOMP
It's so stupid that iPods aren't allowed!
I know! You can't bring a watch either. I mean, *what*?

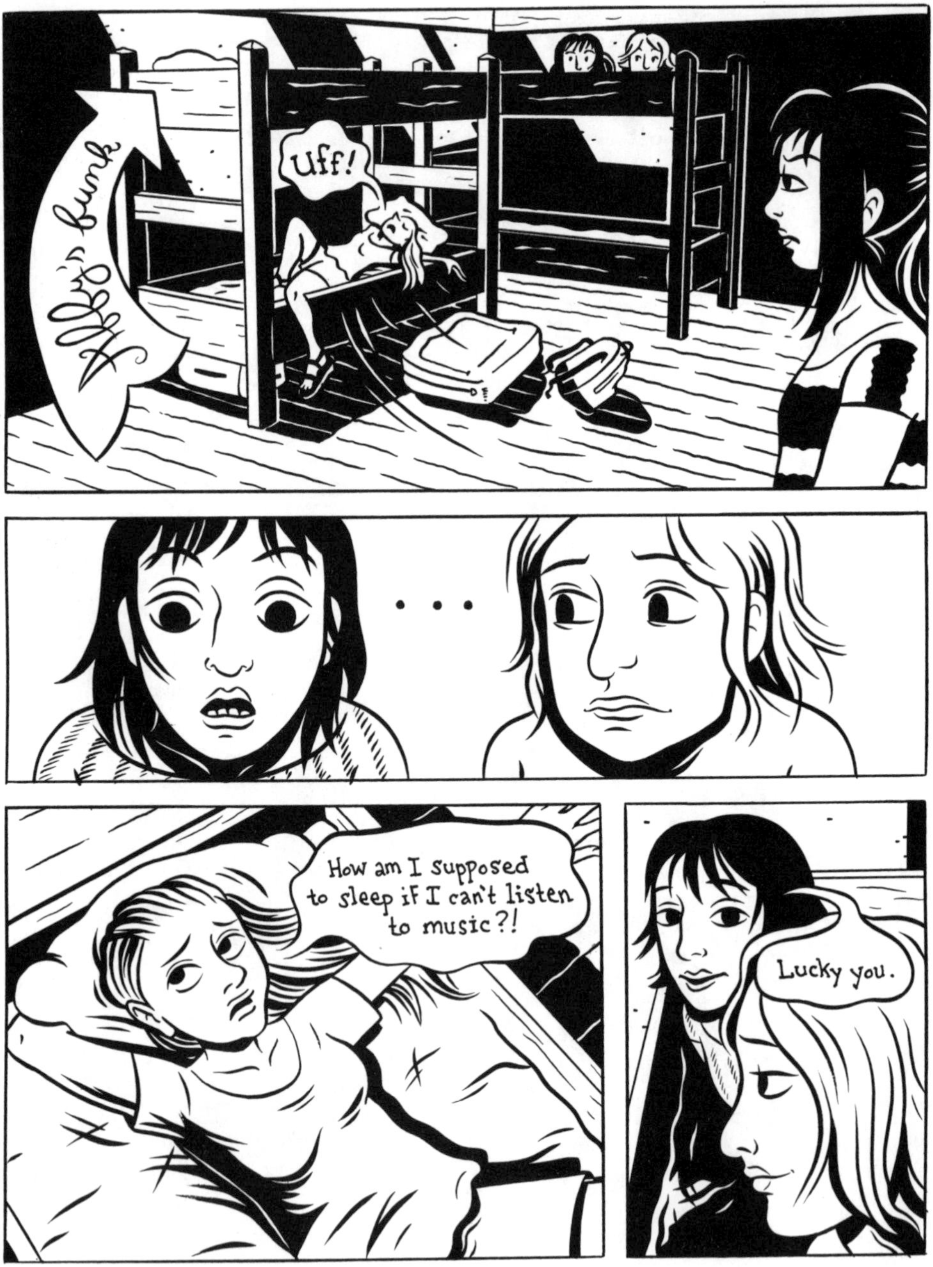
Ally's bunk
Uff!
. . .
How am I supposed to sleep if I can't listen to music?!
Lucky you.

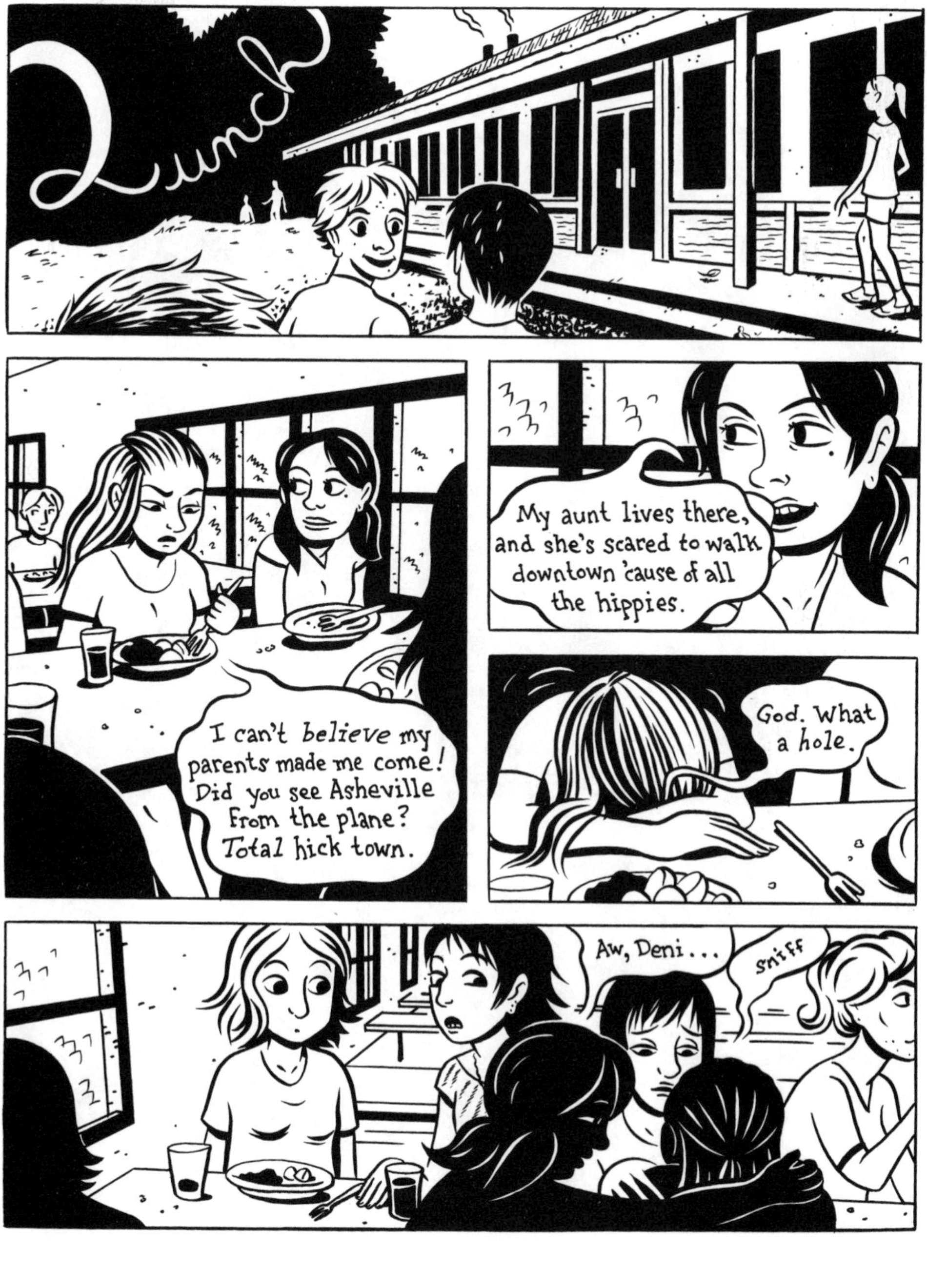
Lunch
I can't *believe* my parents made me come! Did you see Asheville from the plane? *Total* hick town.
My aunt lives there, and she's scared to walk downtown 'cause of all the hippies.
God. What a *hole*.
Aw, Deni...
sniff

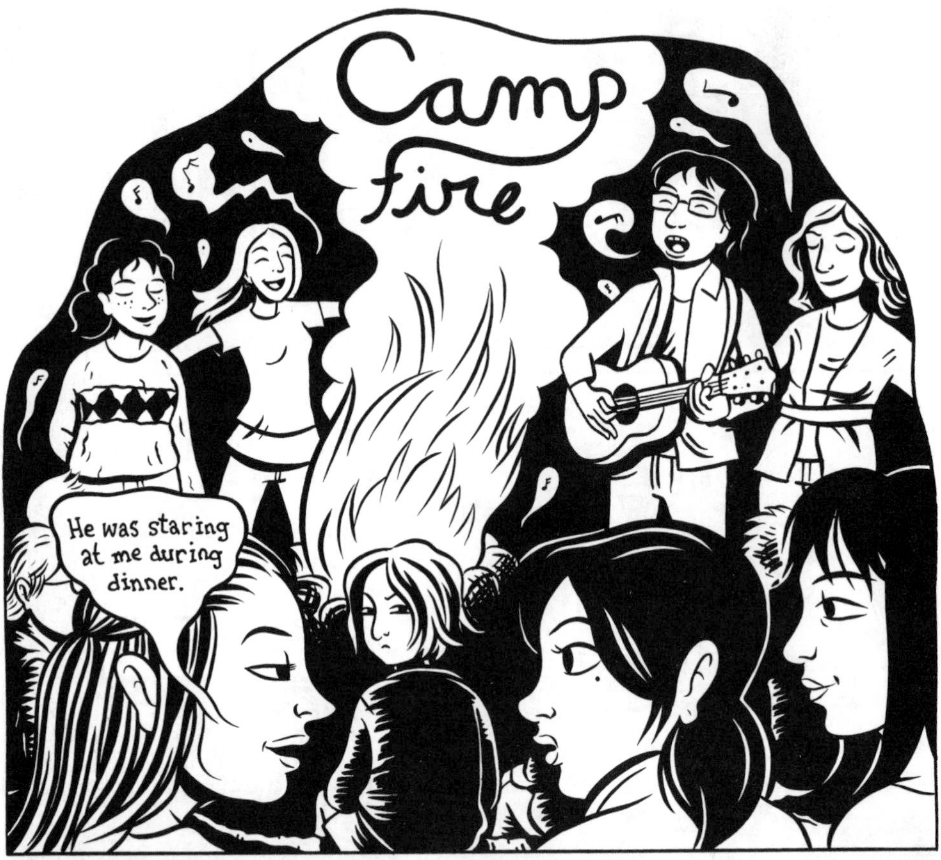
Camp fire
He was staring at me during dinner.

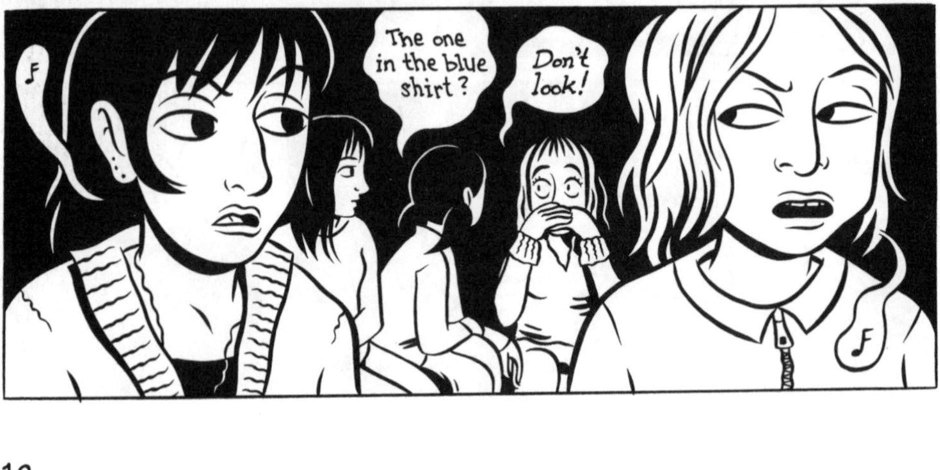
The one in the blue shirt?
Don't look!

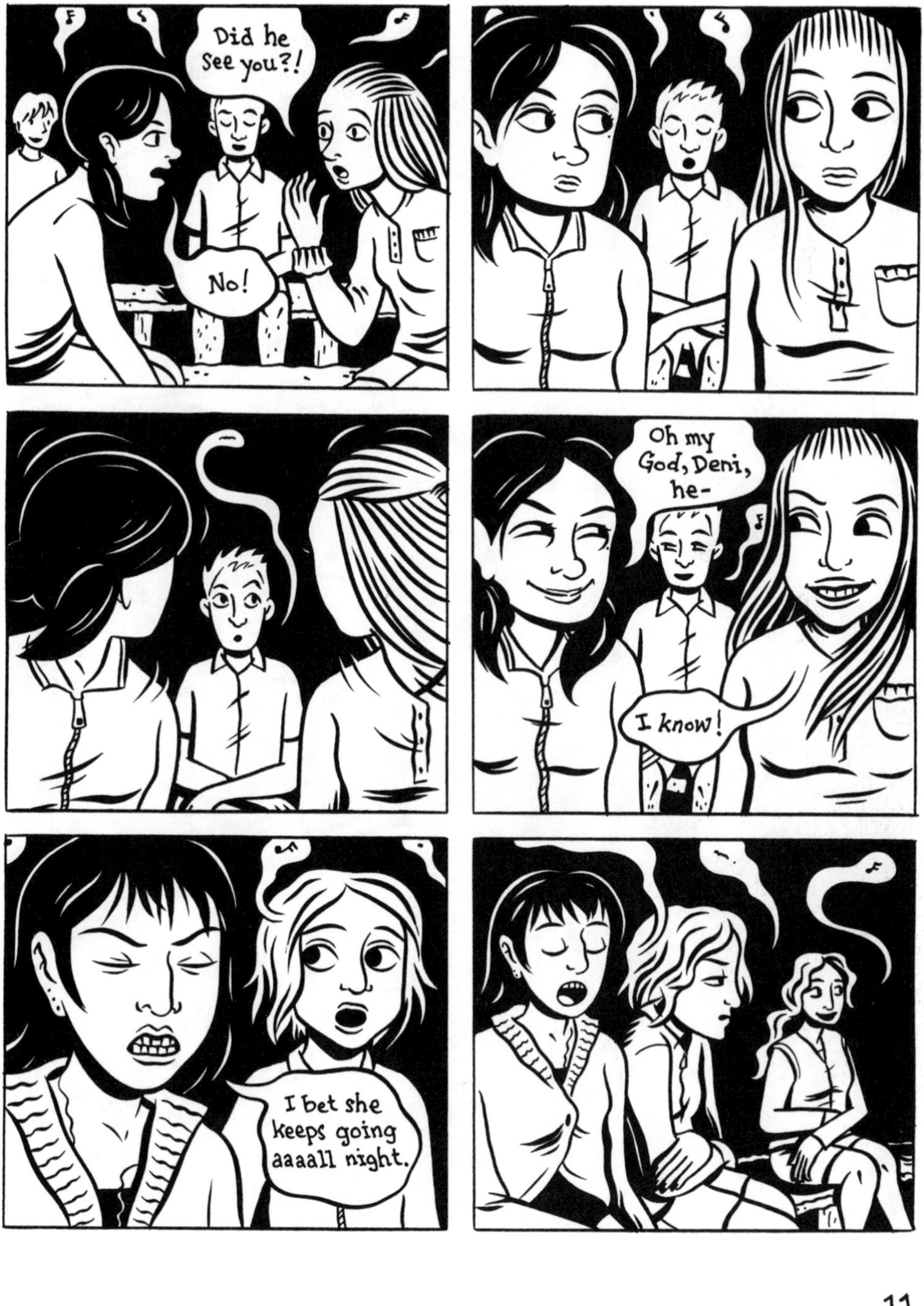
Did he see you?!
No!
Oh my God, Deni, he-
I know!
I bet she keeps going aaaall night.

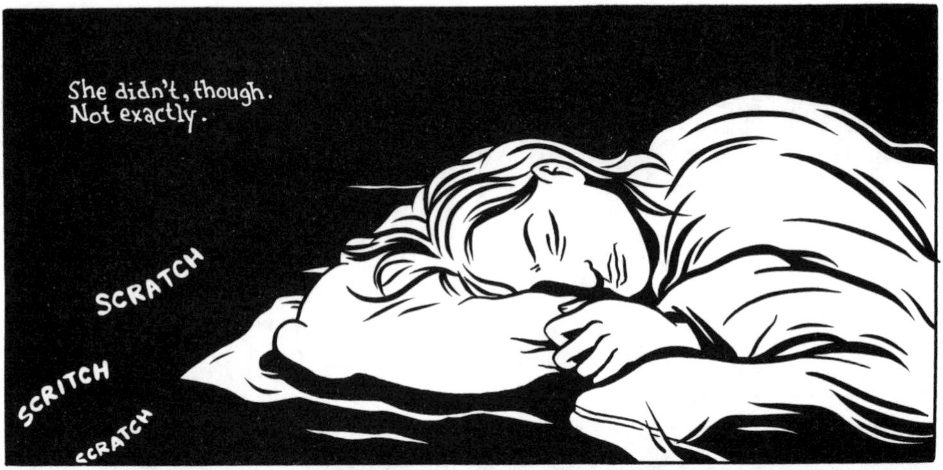
She didn't, though.
Not exactly.
SCRATCH
SCRITCH
SCRATCH

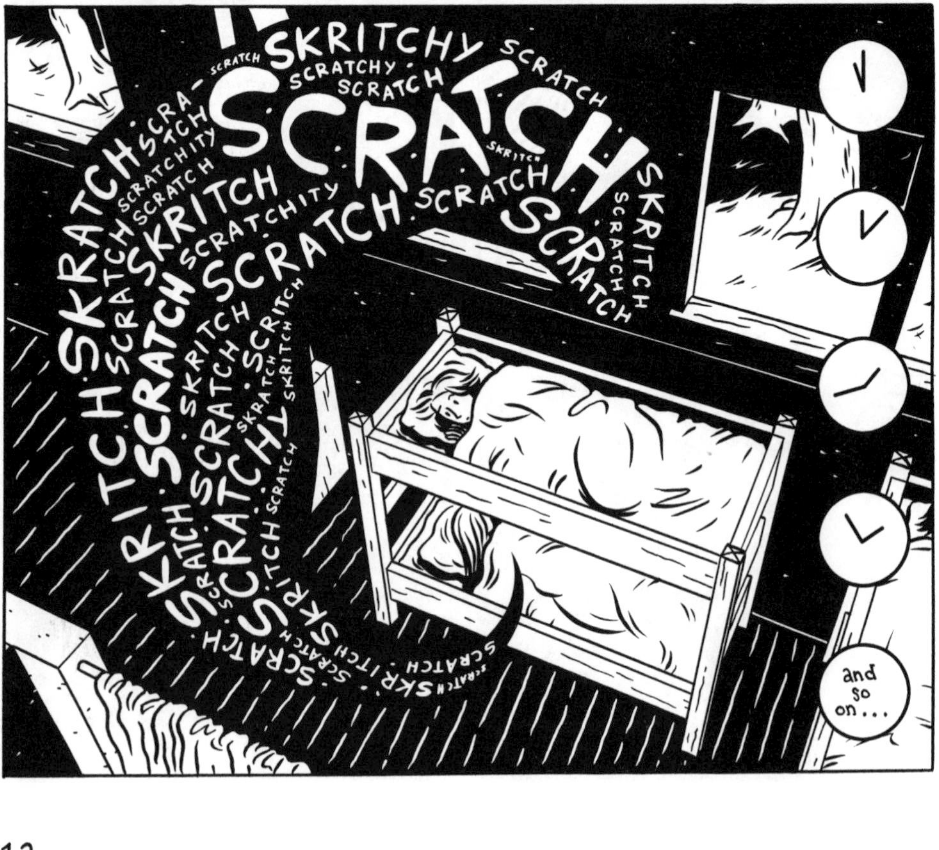
SKRITCHY
SCRATCHY
SCRATCH
SCRATCH
SCRATCH
SKRITCH
SCRATCHITY
SCRATCH
SCRATCH
SKRITCH
SCRATCH
and so on...

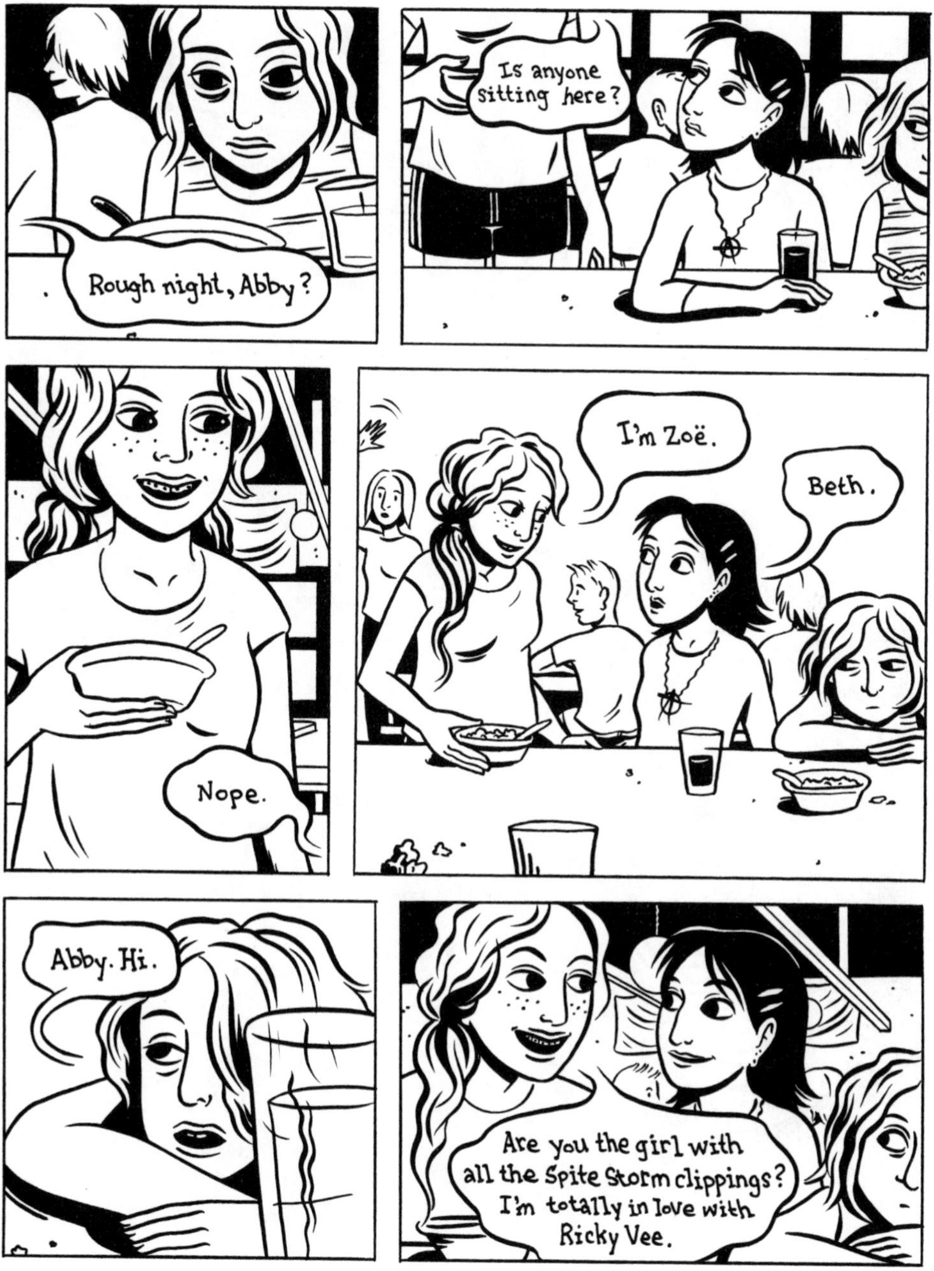
Rough night, Abby?
Is anyone sitting here?
Nope.
I'm Zoë.
Beth.
Abby. Hi.
Are you the girl with all the Spite Storm clippings? I'm totally in love with Ricky Vee.

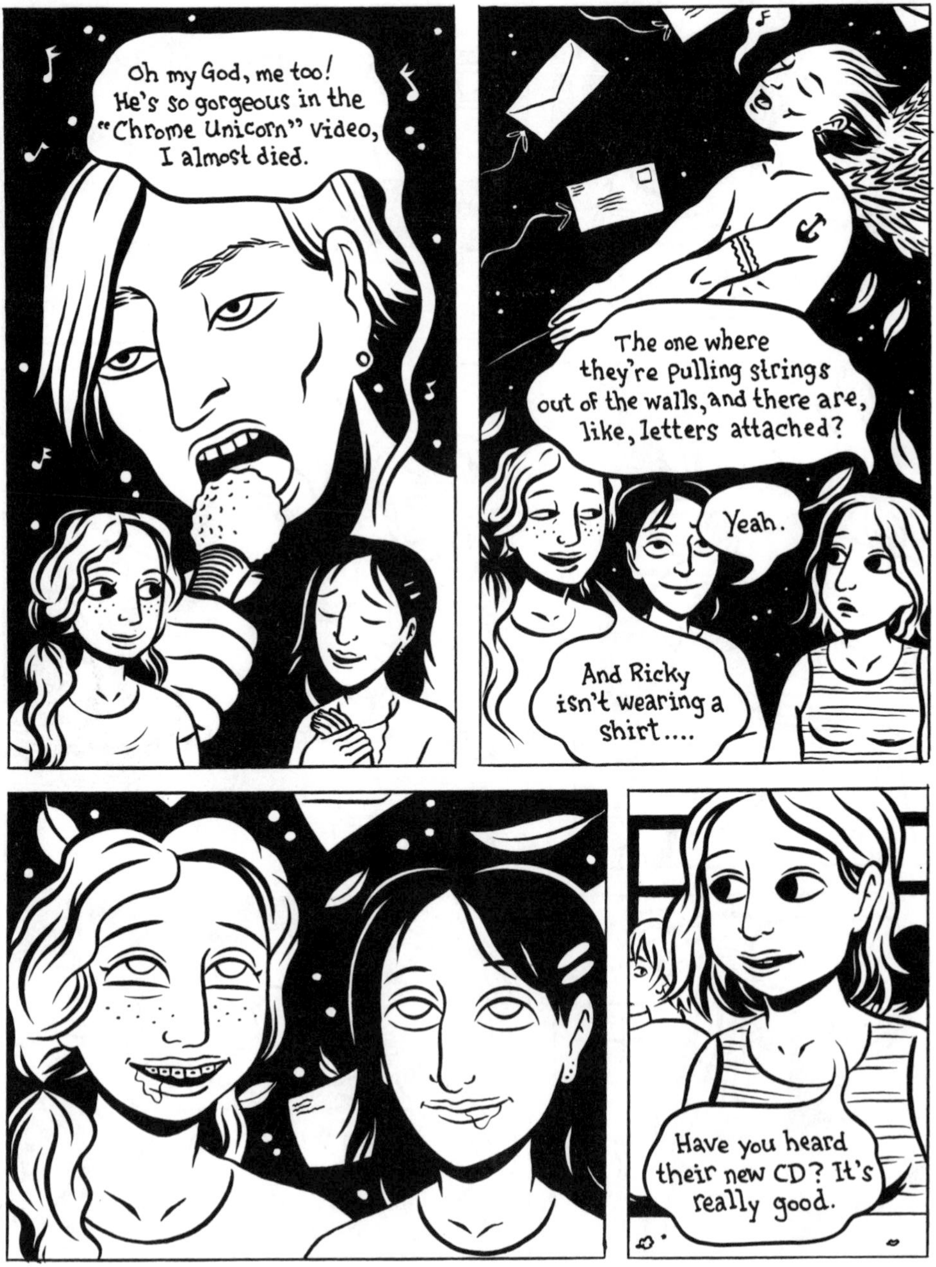
Oh my God, me too! He's so gorgeous in the "Chrome Unicorn" video, I almost died.
The one where they're pulling strings out of the walls, and there are, like, letters attached?
Yeah.
And Ricky isn't wearing a shirt....
Have you heard their new CD? It's really good.

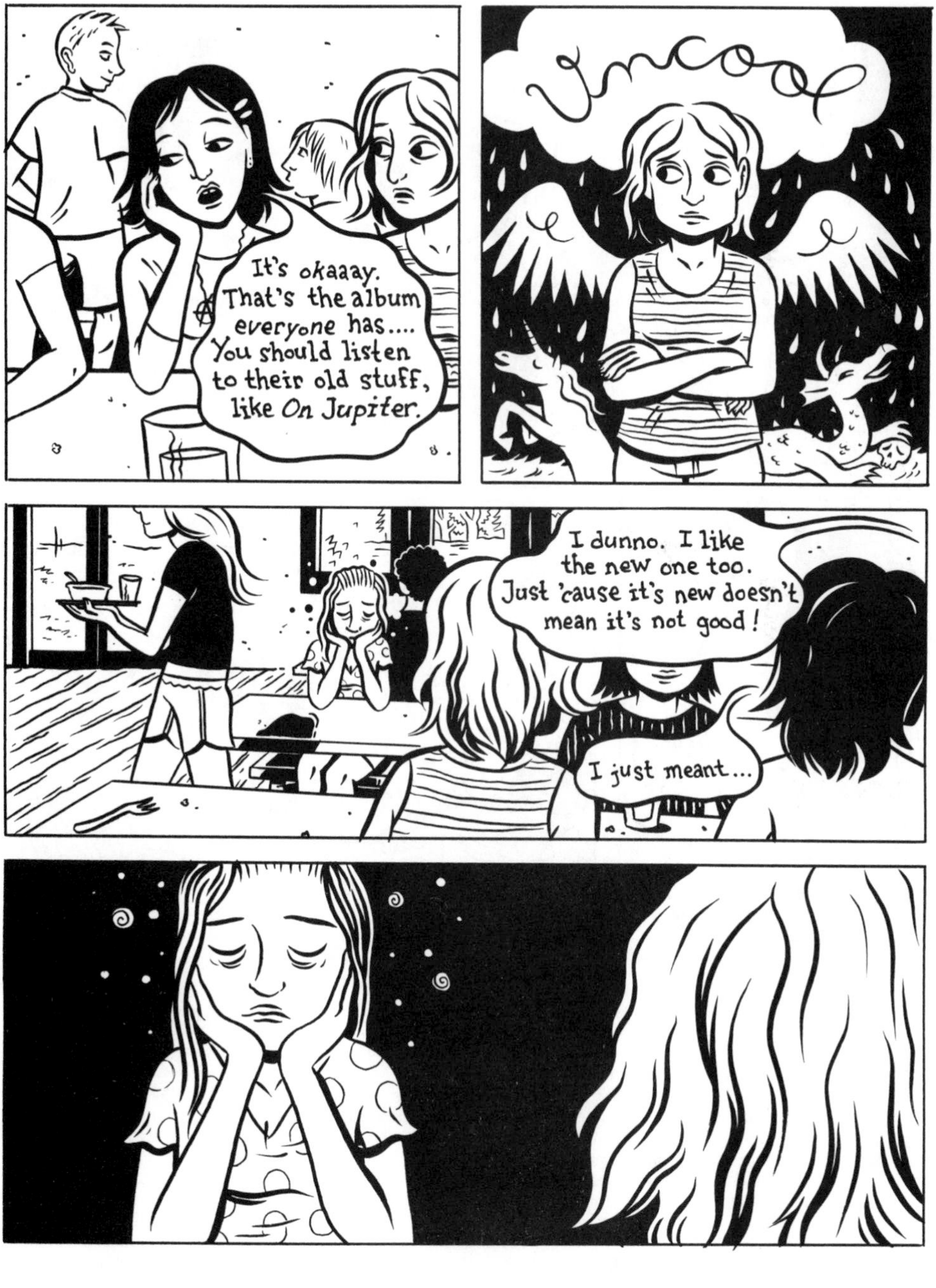
It's okaaay. That's the album everyone has.... You should listen to their old stuff, like On Jupiter.
Uncool
I dunno. I like the new one too. Just 'cause it's new doesn't mean it's not good!
I just meant...

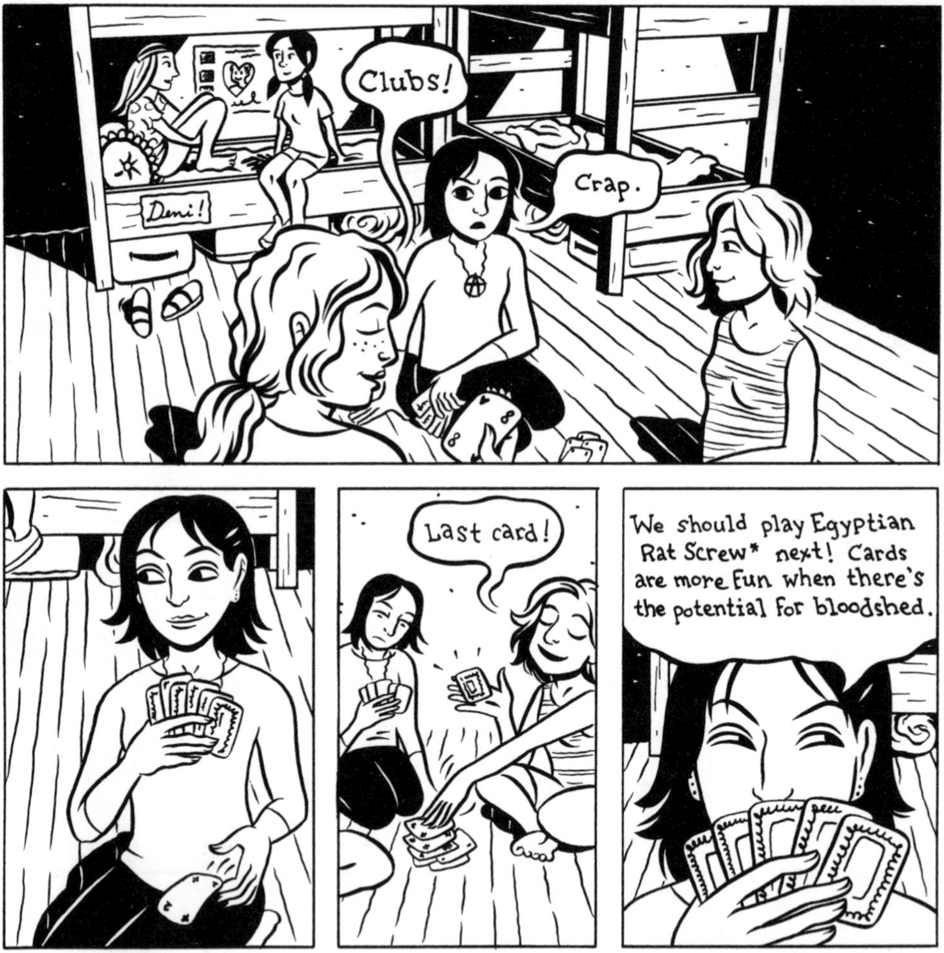
Demi!
Clubs!
Crap.
Last card!
We should play Egyptian Rat Screw* next! Cards are more fun when there's the potential for bloodshed.

***Egyptian Rat Screw**

You will need: A deck of cards with jokers removed, a sturdy table (or the floor), and two or more players.

Objective: The winner of ERS is the player who succeeds in taking all the cards.

The deal: Players sit in a circle. The dealer shuffles the deck several times and deals it evenly among all players who pick up their stacks of cards without looking at them.

Play: The first player, seated to the left of the dealer, takes the card from the top of her deck and plays it without checking to see what it is. Play continues clockwise, each participant playing one card until a face card (ace, king, queen, or jack) is played. In this case, the next player has a set number of chances to beat the face card: four chances for an ace, three for a king, two for a queen, and one for a jack.

- If she manages to play a face card, play passes to her left and the next player must try to beat it.
- If she doesn't, the player to her right takes the whole stack of cards and adds it to the bottom of her own.

If at any time two of the same card are played–if, for example, a 2 is played on top of a 2, or a jack is played on top of a jack–all players slap the cards, and the player who slaps first takes the stack. If you lost all your cards or weren't an original player, you can try to "slap in" on doubles. Be careful not to slap when there AREN'T doubles on the stack, though! If you do, you must pay the penalty: take the next card in your hand and place it, face up, on the bottom of the stack in play.

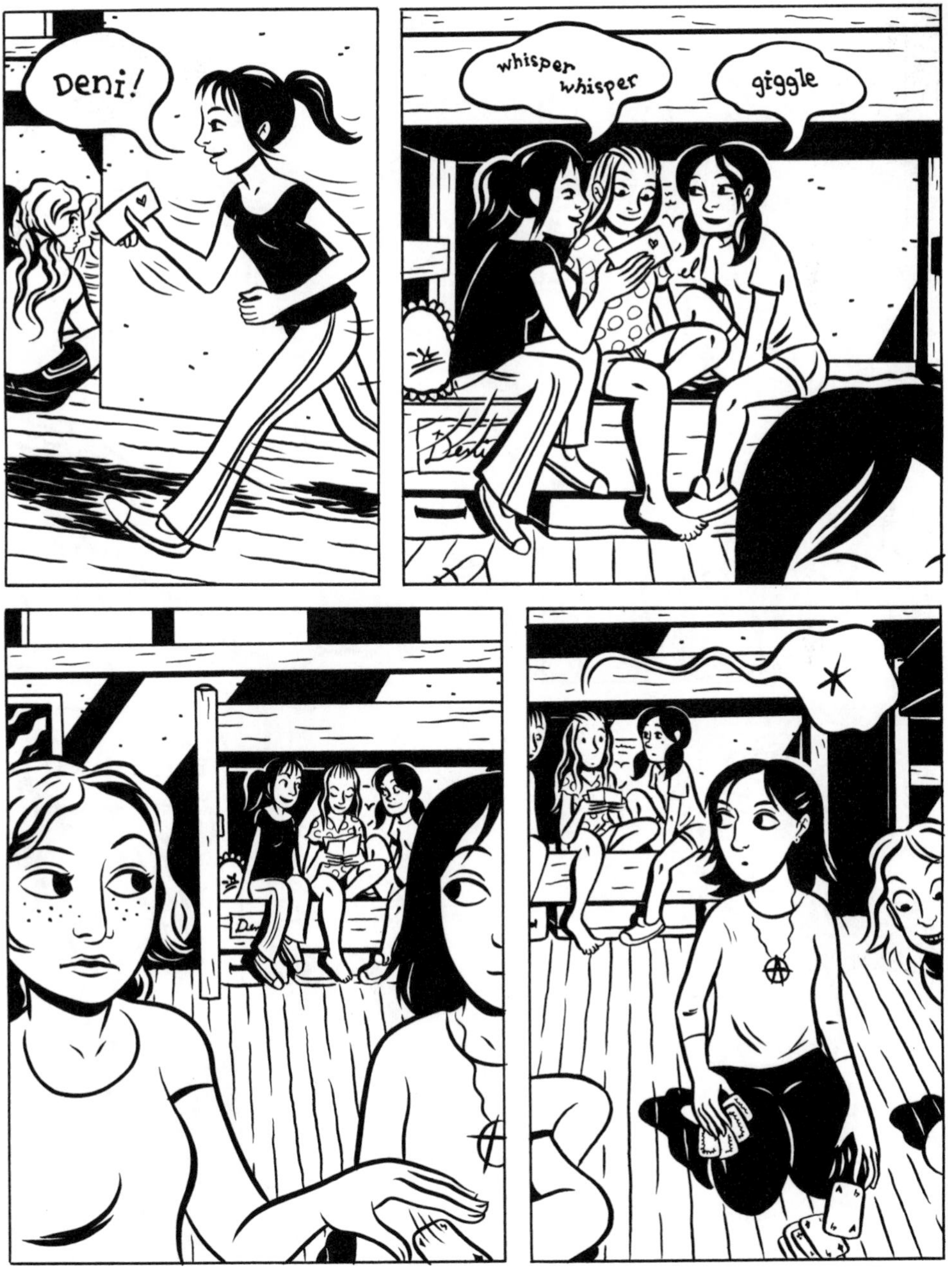
Deni!
whisper whisper
giggle

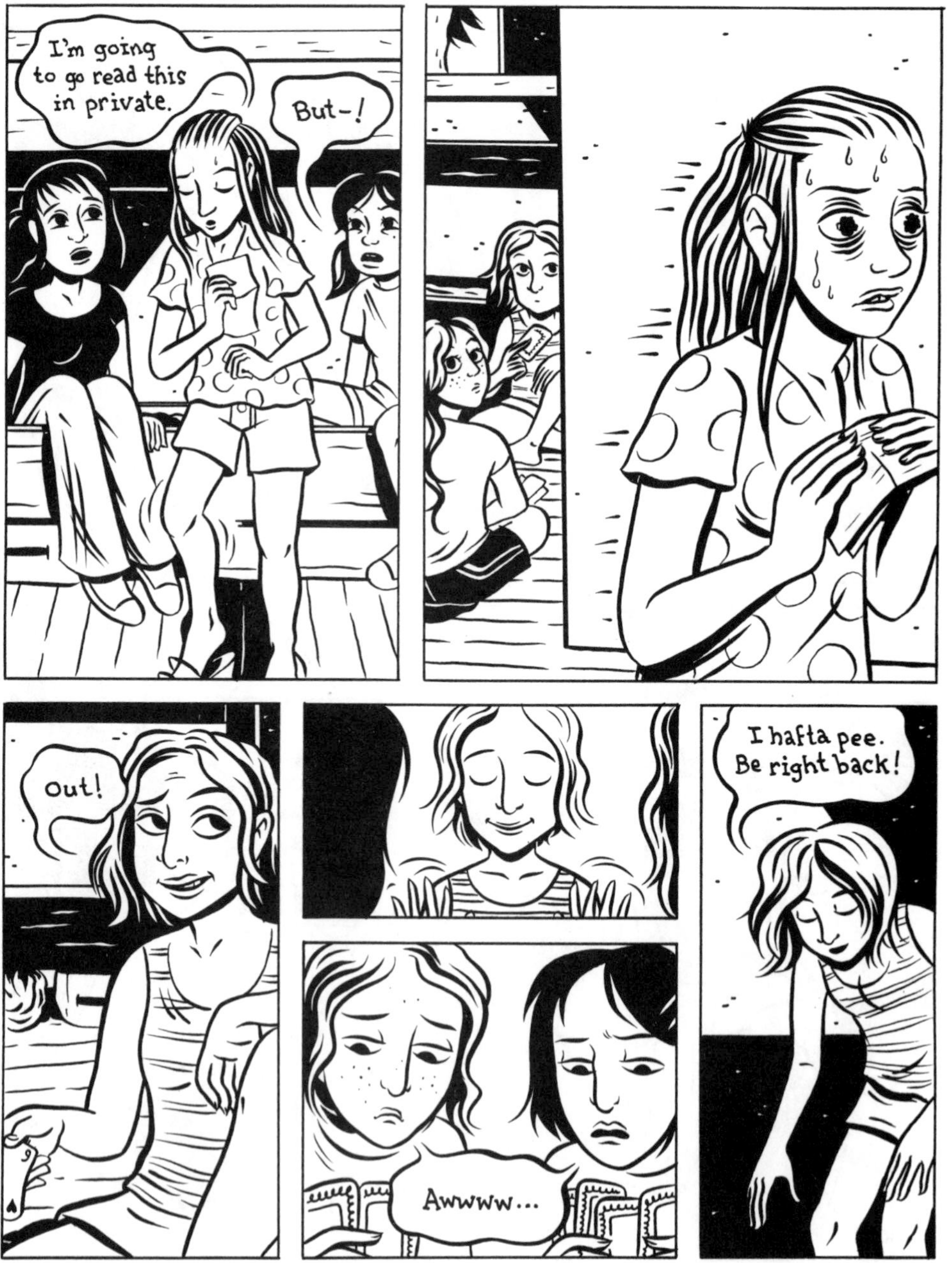
I'm going to go read this in private.
But-!
Out!
I hafta pee. Be right back!
Awwww...

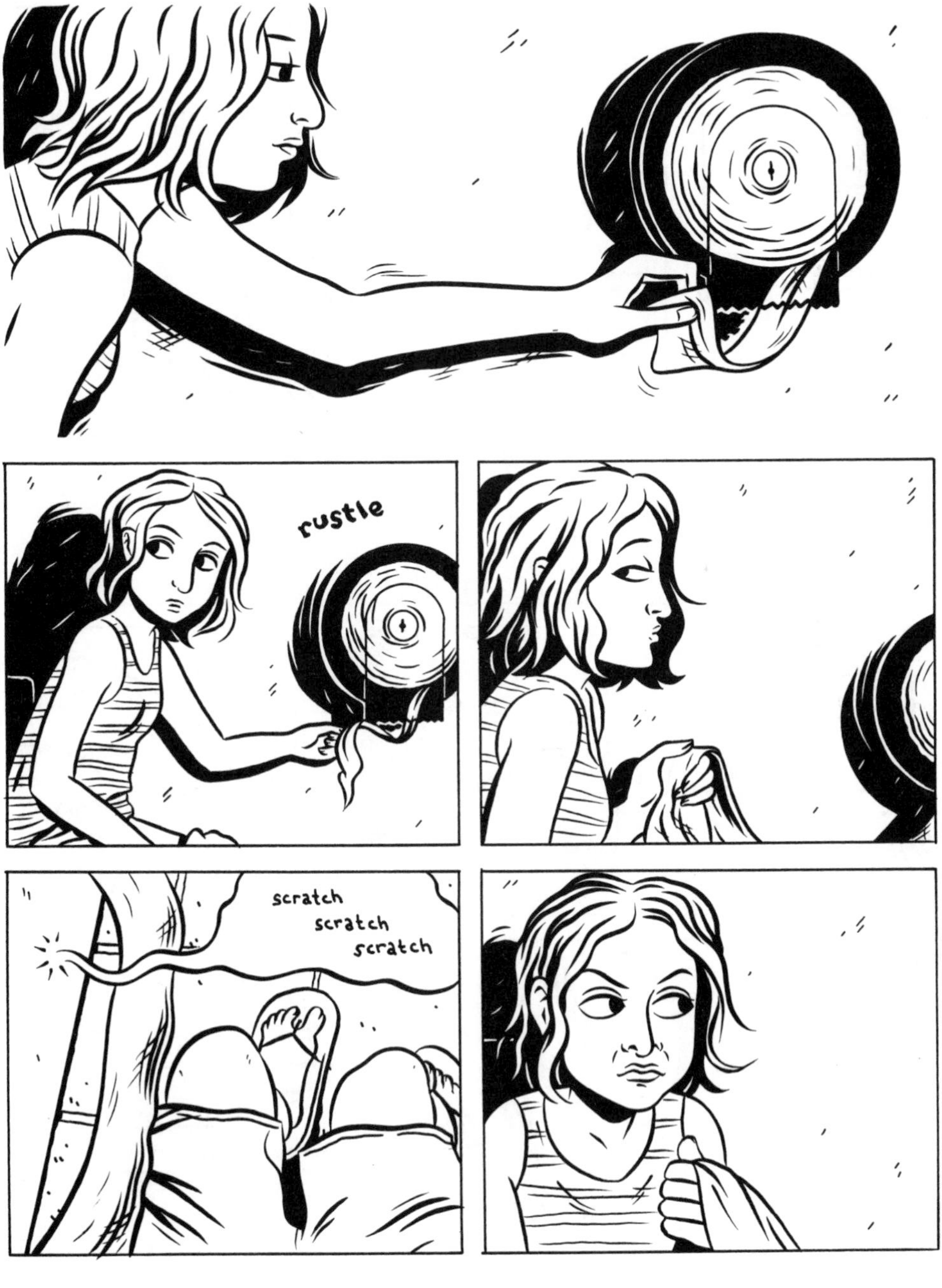
rustle
scratch
scratch
scratch

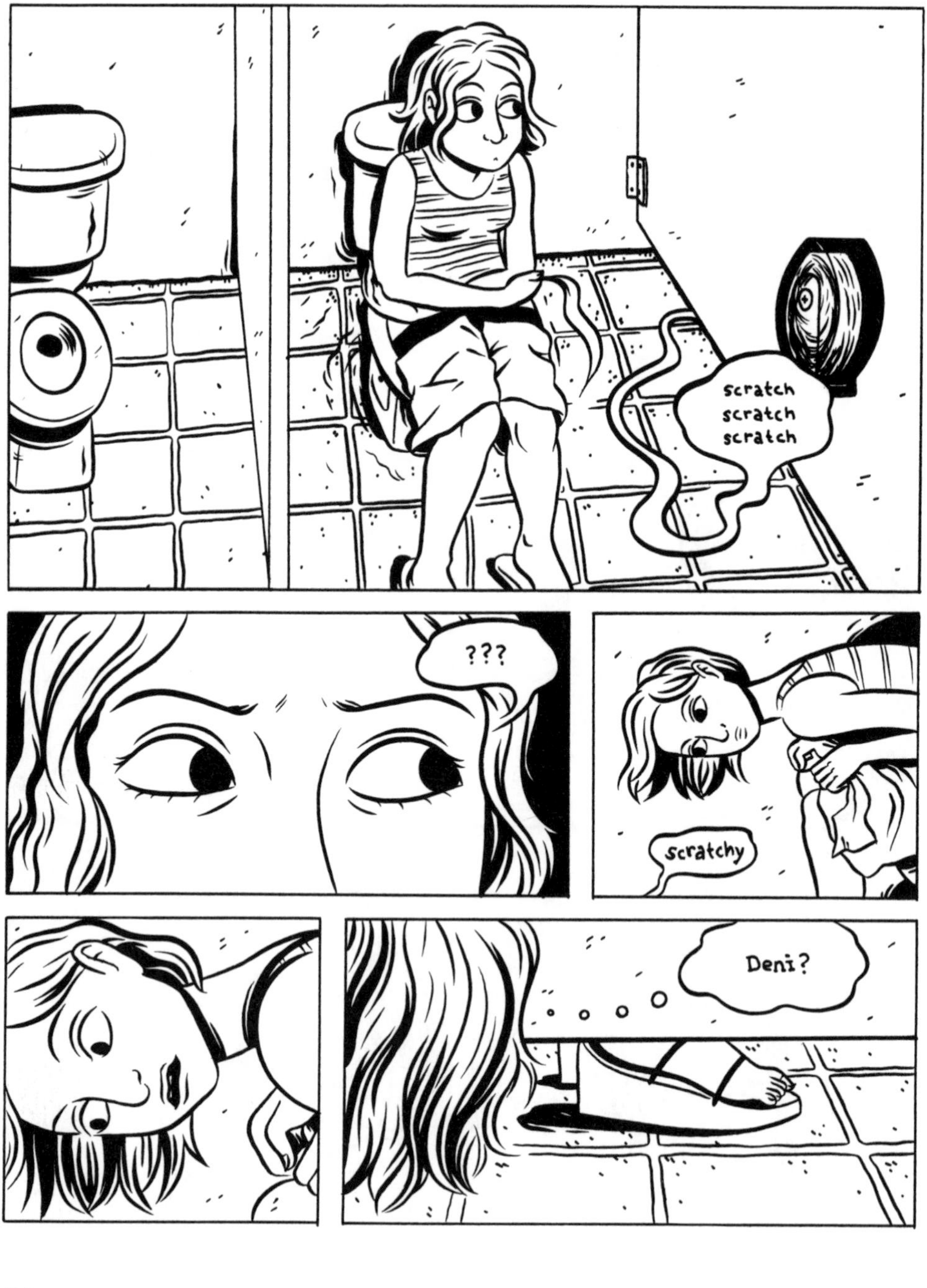
scratch
scratch
scratch
???
scratchy
Deni?

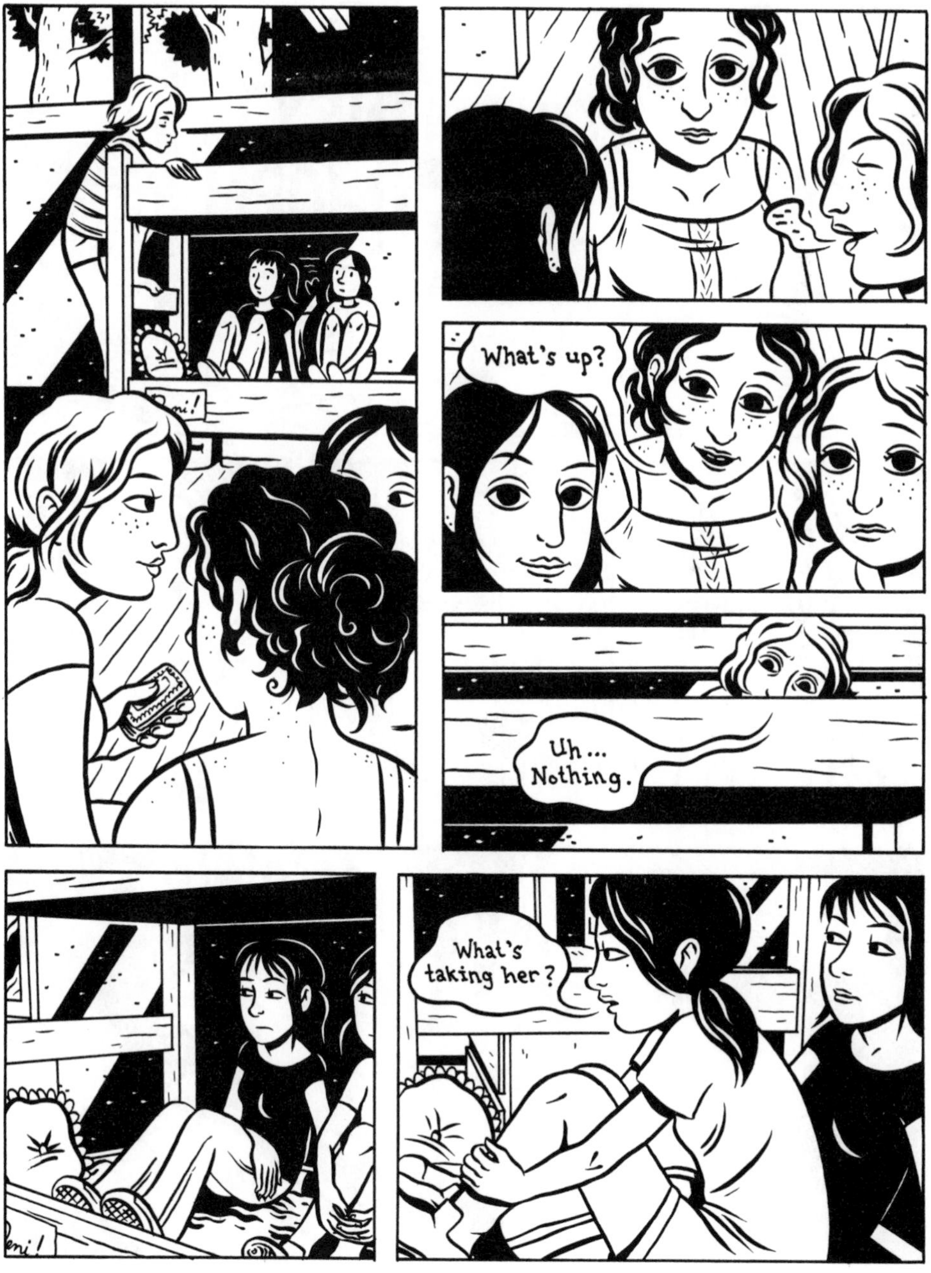
What's up?
Uh... Nothing.
What's taking her?

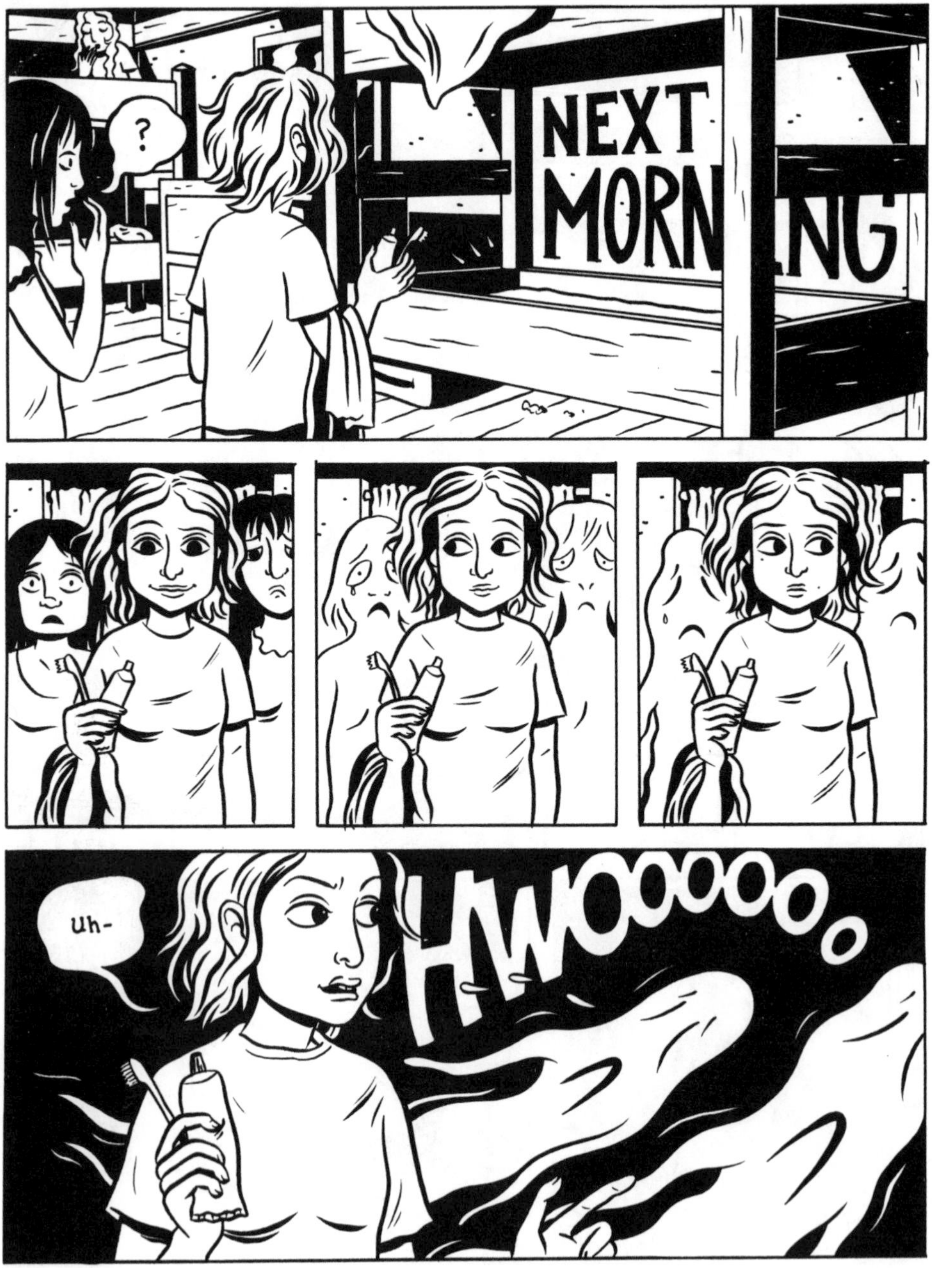
?
NEXT MORNING
Uh-
HWOOOOOo

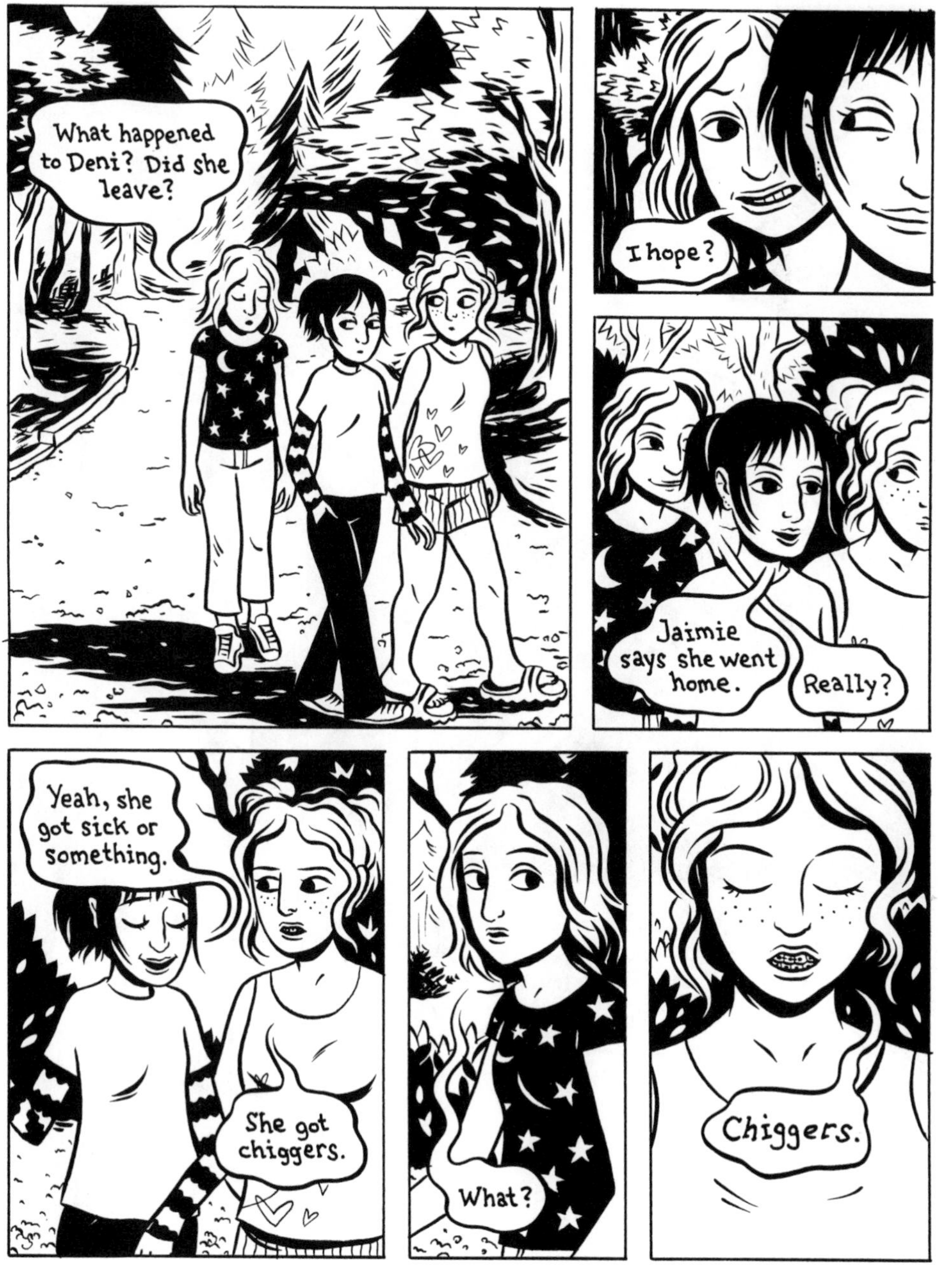
What happened to Deni? Did she leave?
I hope?
Jaimie says she went home.
Really?
Yeah, she got sick or something.
She got chiggers.
What?
Chiggers.

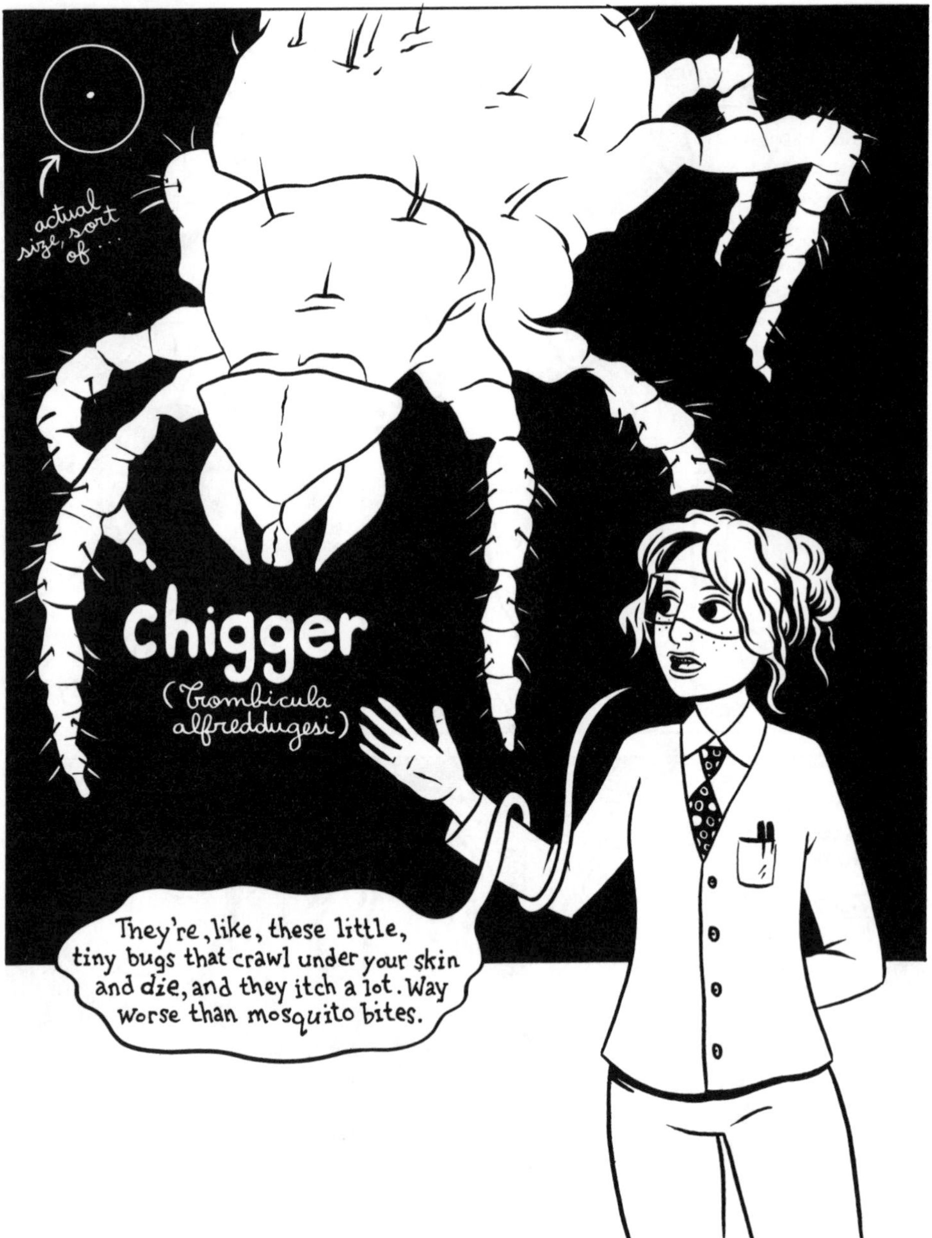
actual size, sort of...
chigger
(Trombicula alfreddugesi)
They're, like, these little, tiny bugs that crawl under your skin and die, and they itch a lot. Way worse than mosquito bites.

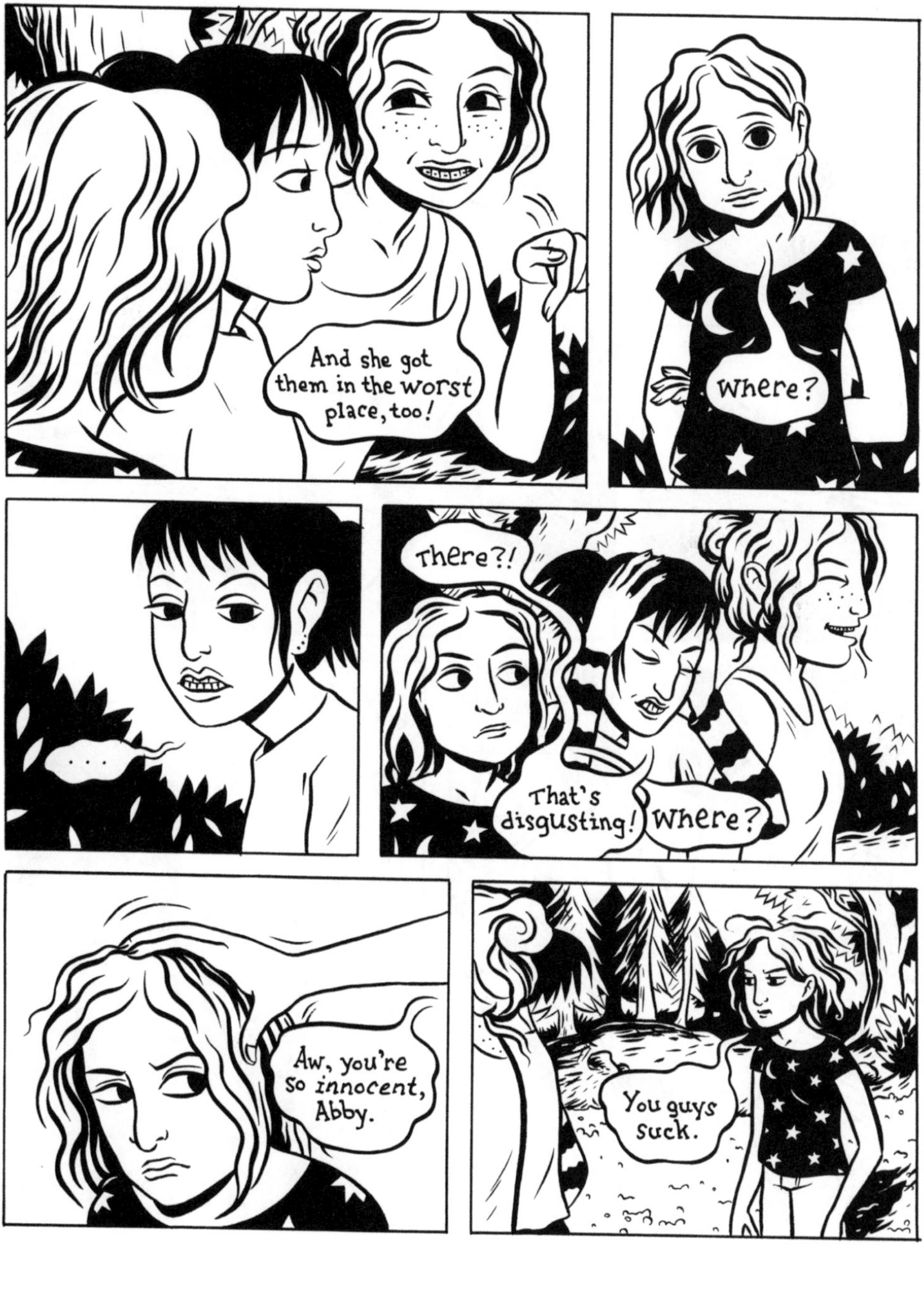

And she got them in the worst place, too!
Where?
. . .
There?!
That's disgusting!
Where?
Aw, you're so *innocent*, Abby.
You guys suck.

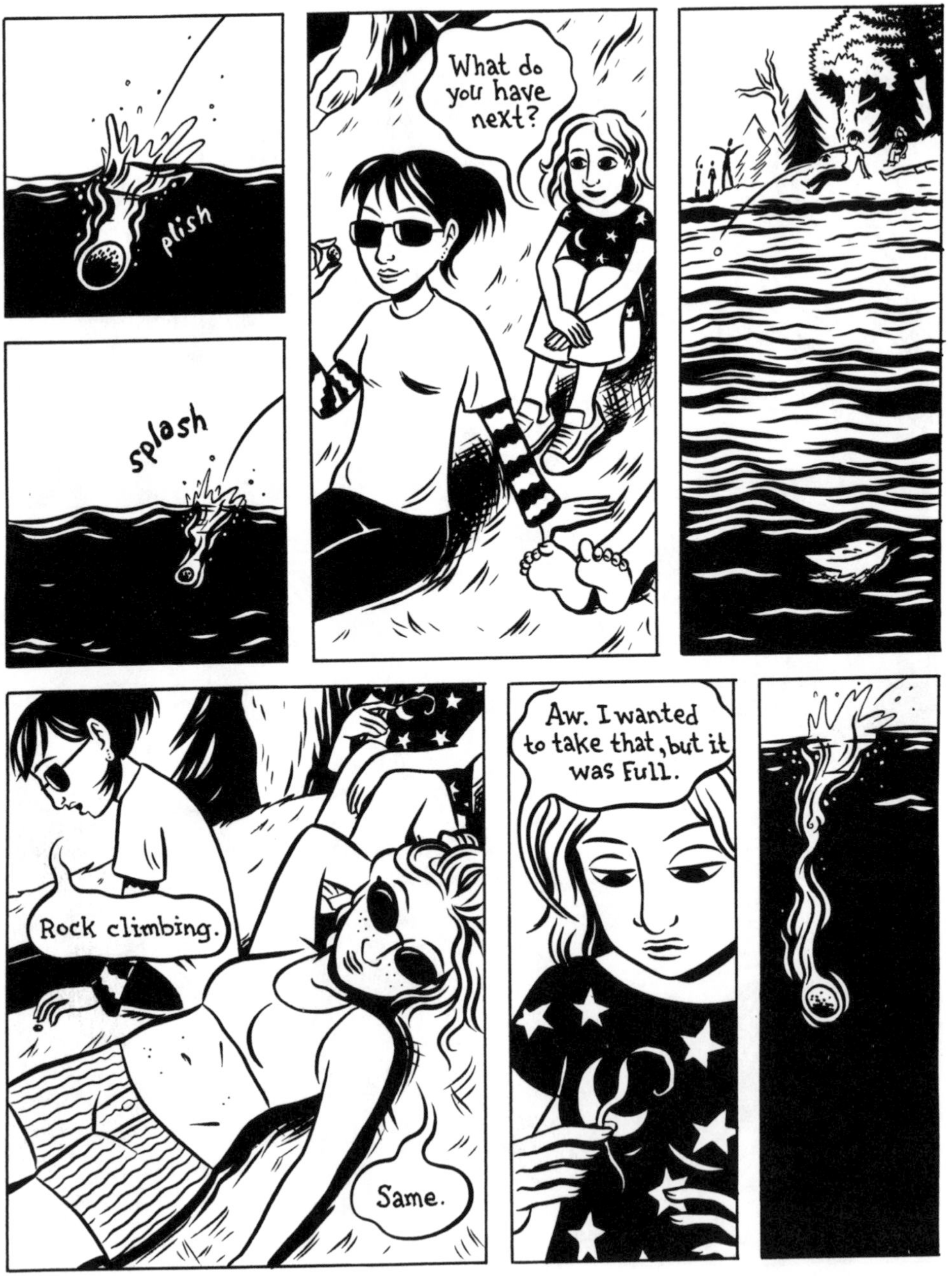
plish
splash
What do you have next?
Rock climbing.
Same.
Aw. I wanted to take that, but it was full.

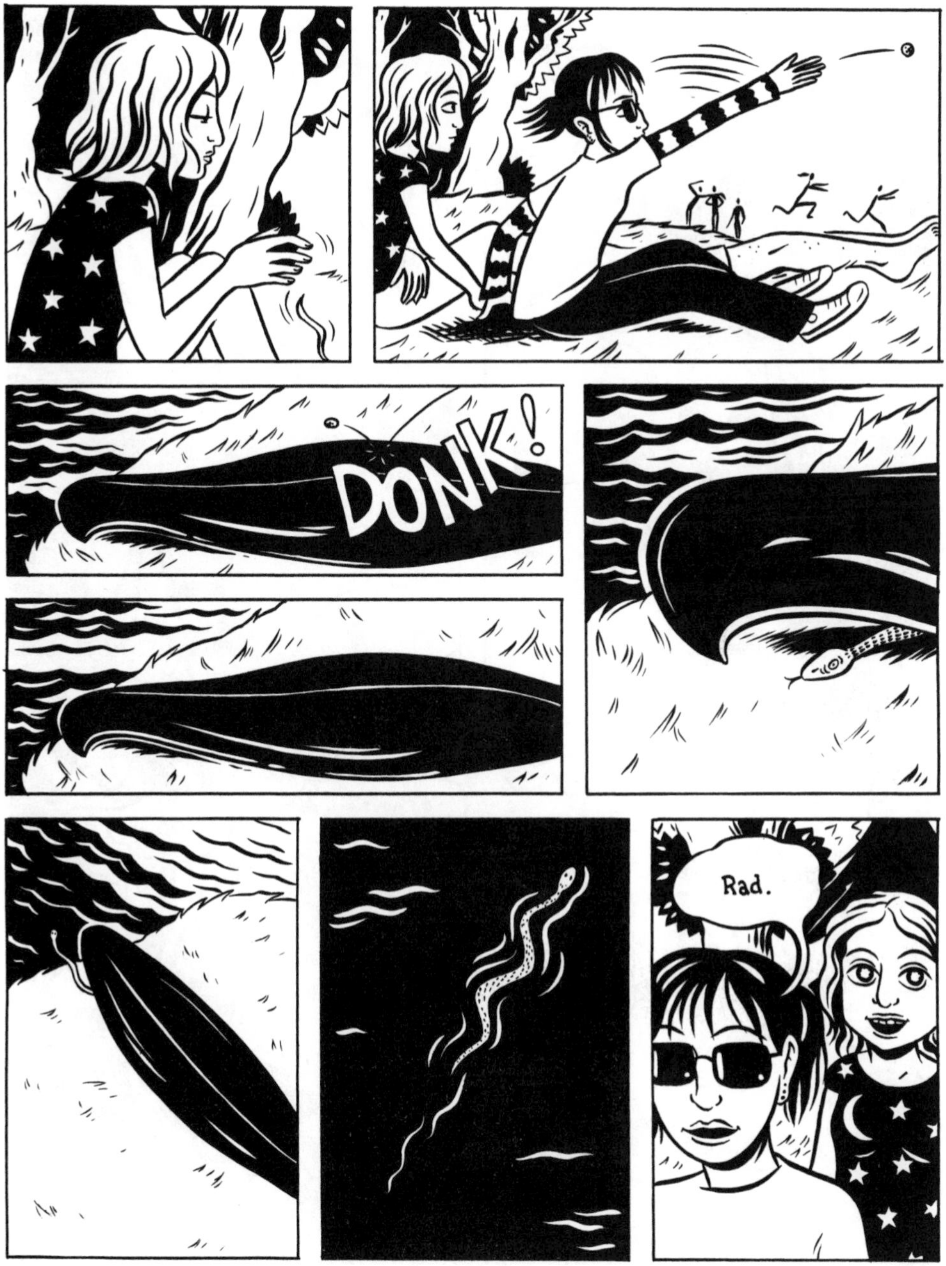
DONK!
Rad.

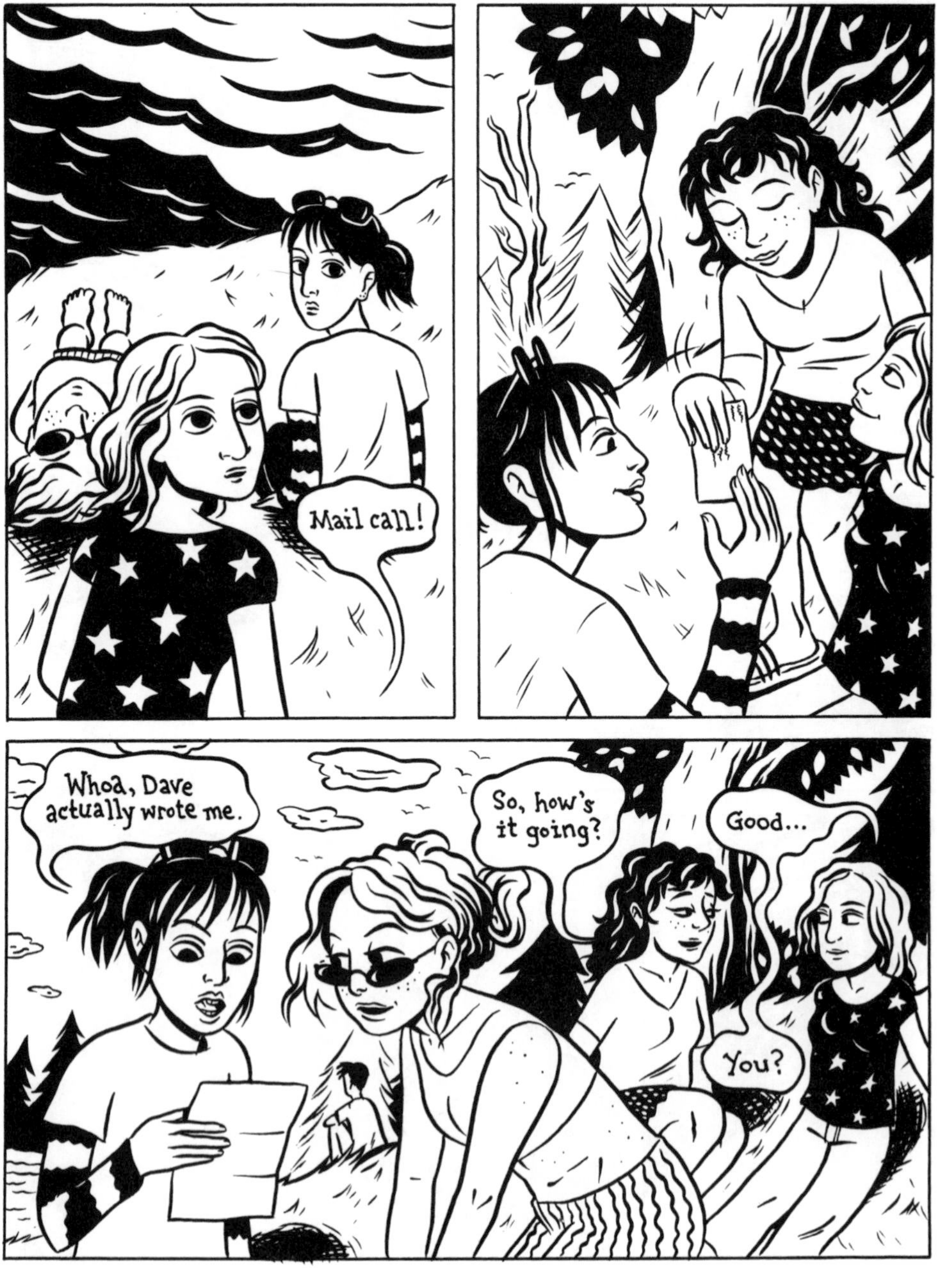
Mail call!
Whoa, Dave actually wrote me.
So, how's it going?
Good...
You?

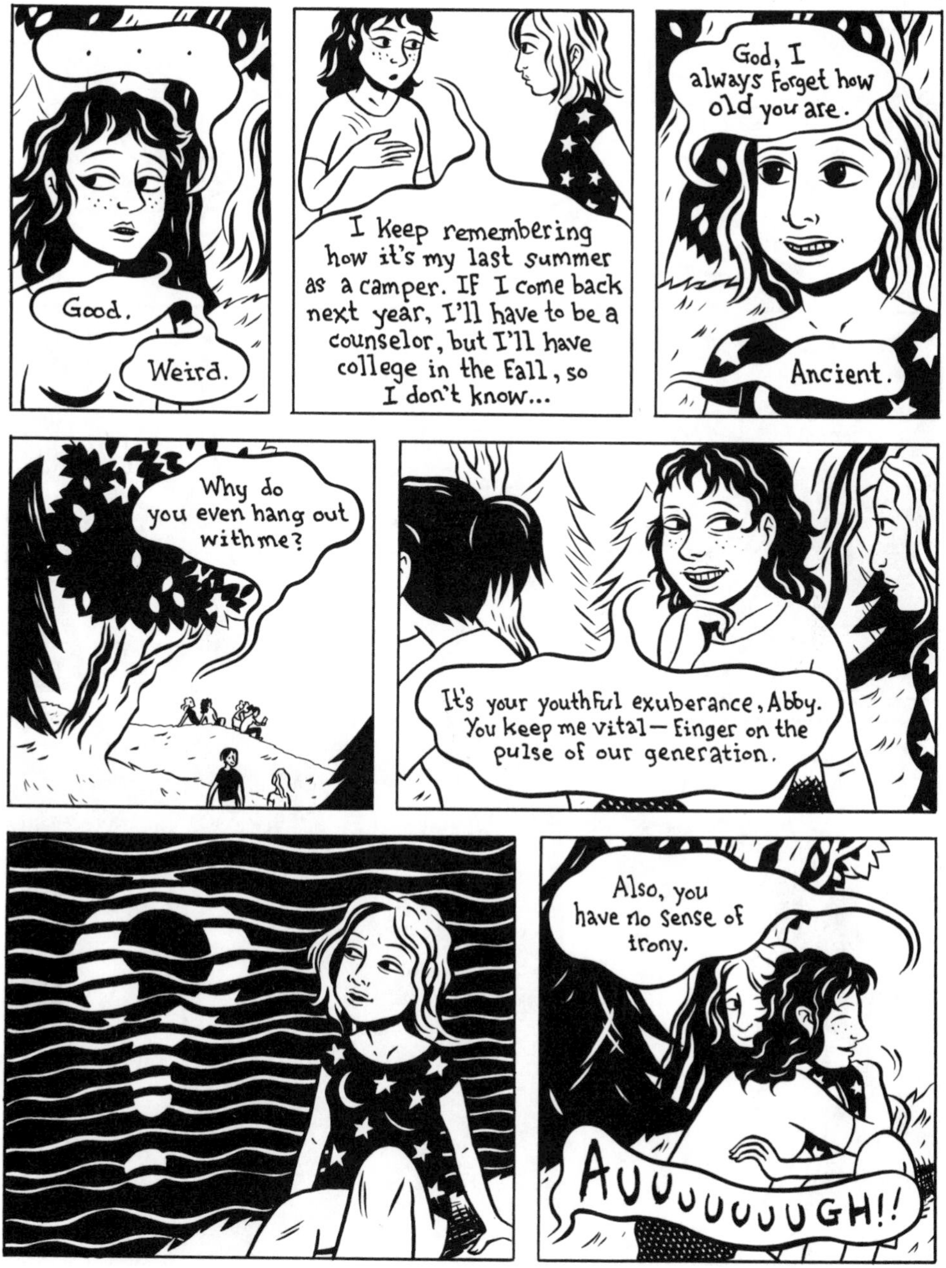
. . .
Good.
Weird.
I keep remembering how it's my last summer as a camper. If I come back next year, I'll have to be a counselor, but I'll have college in the Fall, so I don't know...
God, I always forget how old you are.
Ancient.
Why do you even hang out with me?
It's your youthful exuberance, Abby. You keep me vital — finger on the pulse of our generation.
Also, you have no sense of irony.
AUUUUUUUGH!!

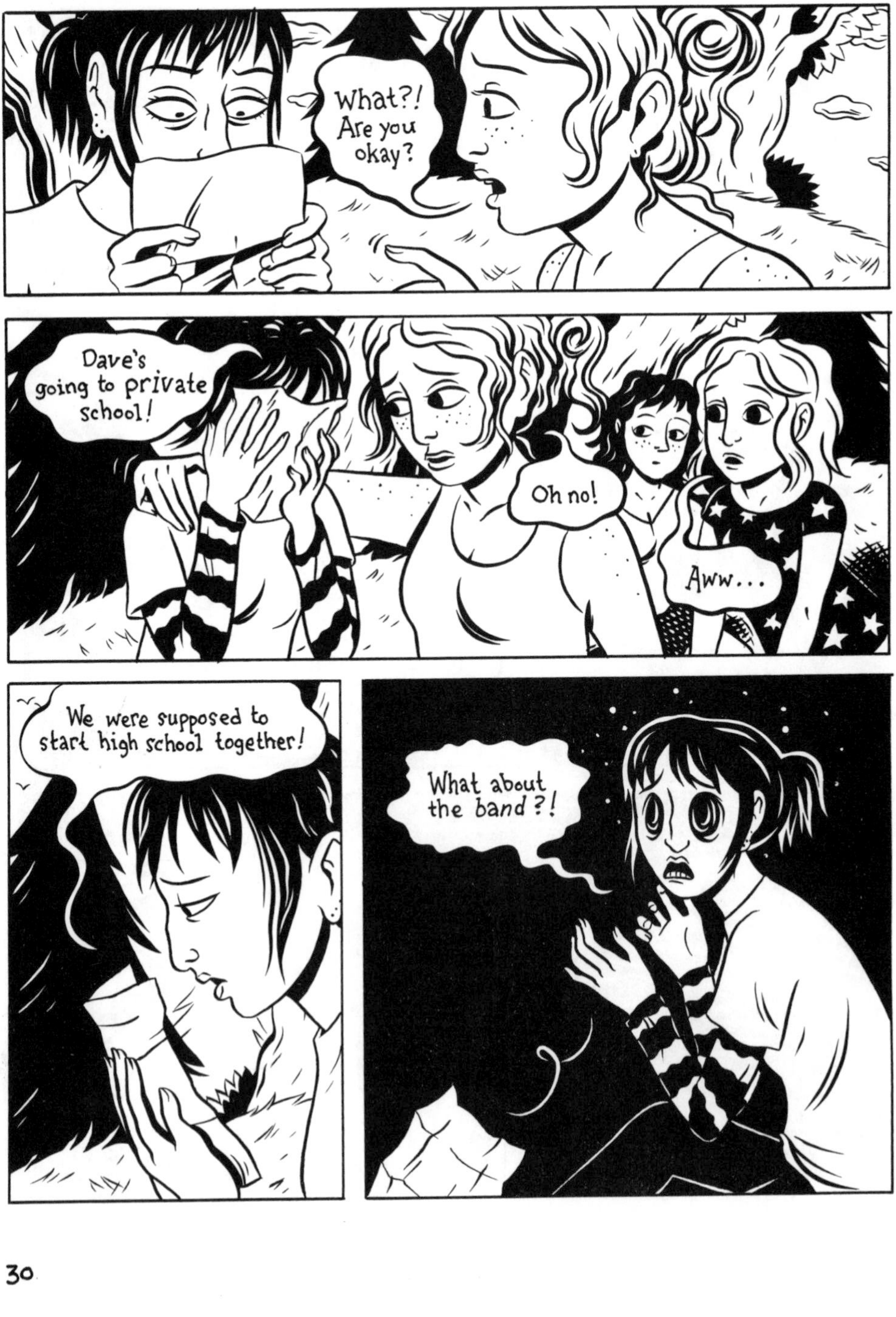
What?! Are you okay?
Dave's going to private school!
Oh no!
Aww...
We were supposed to start high school together!
What about the band?!

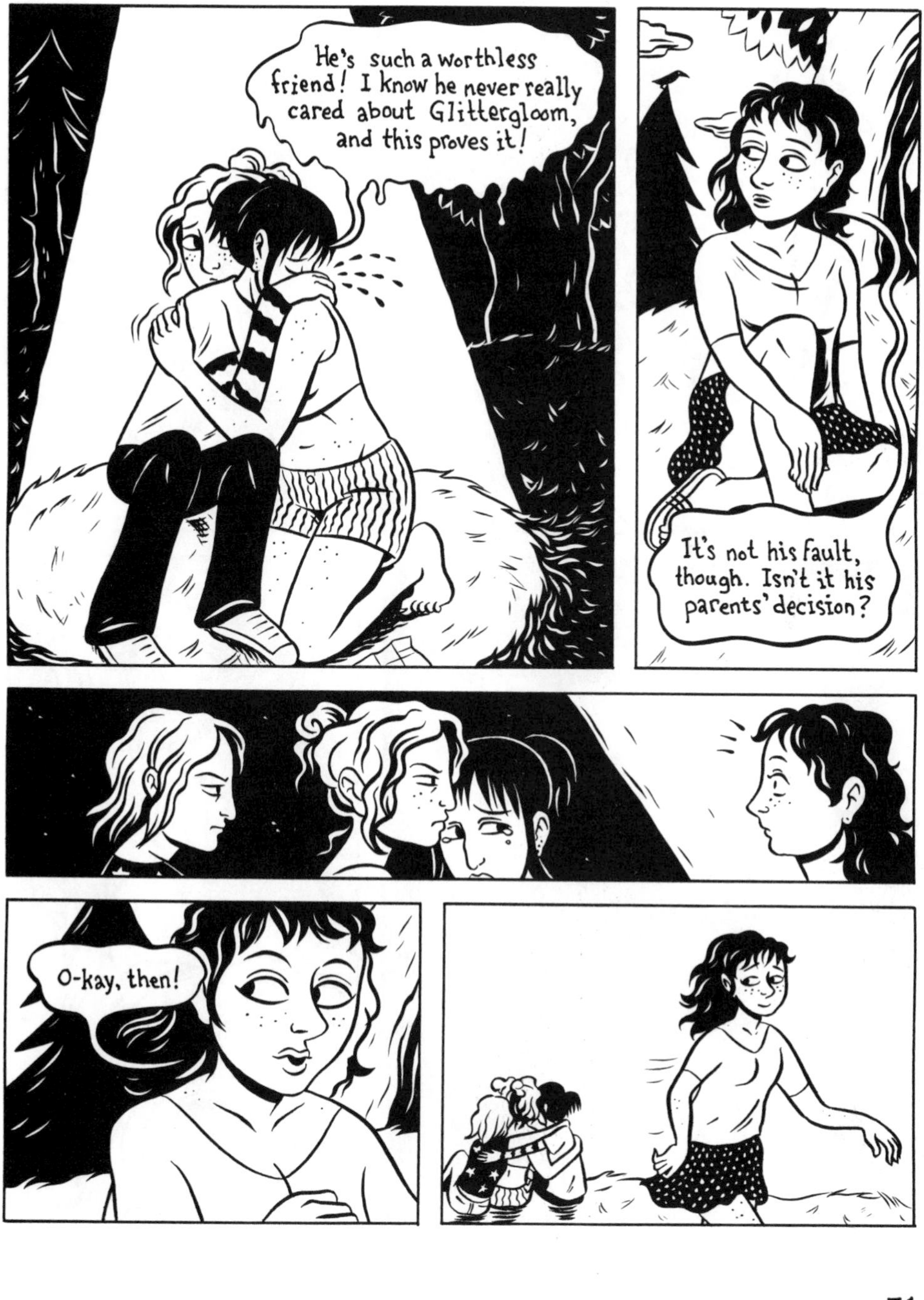
He's such a worthless friend! I know he never really cared about Glittergloom, and this proves it!
It's not his fault, though. Isn't it his parents' decision?
O-kay, then!

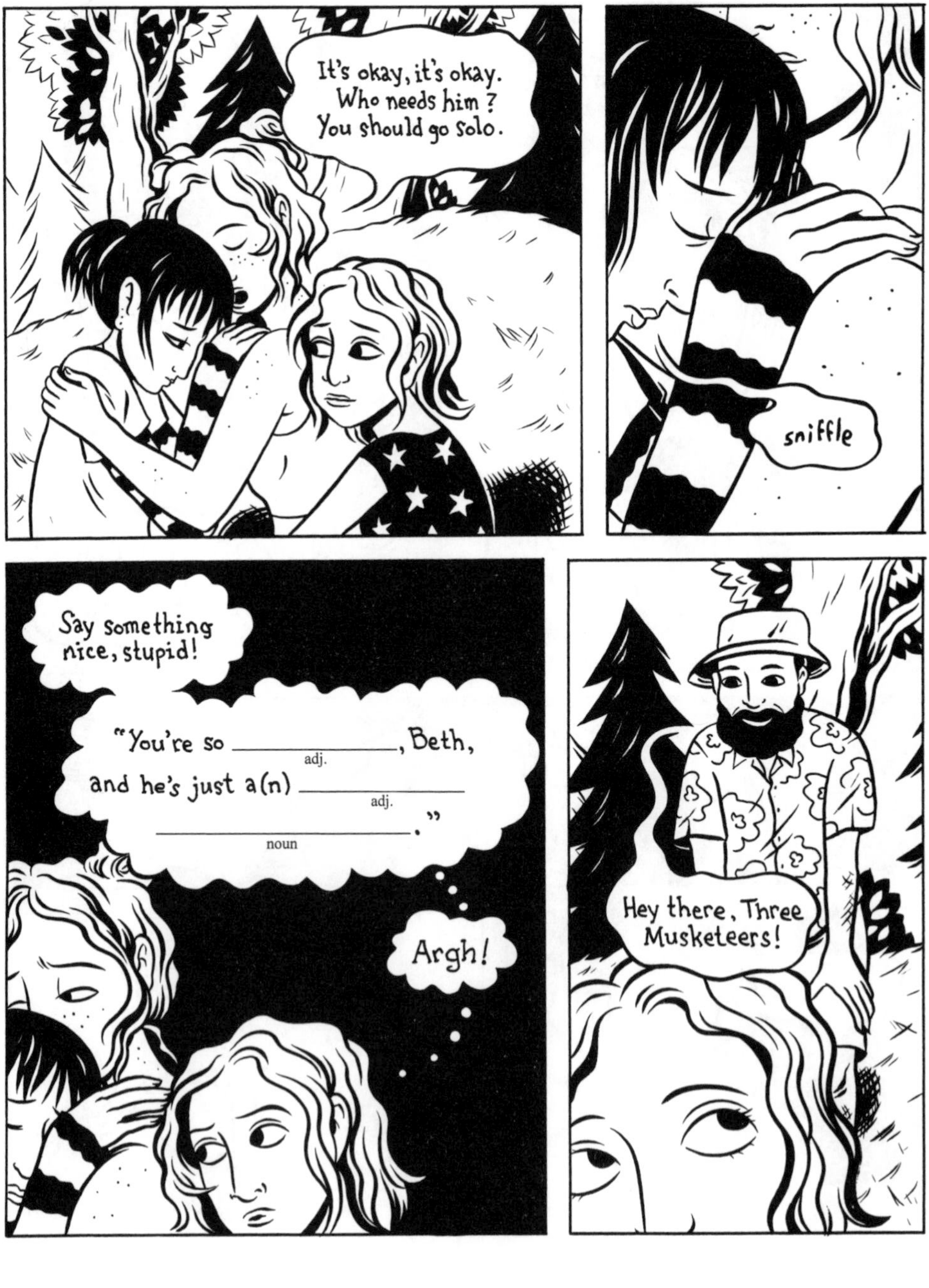
It's okay, it's okay. Who needs him? You should go solo.
sniffle
Say something nice, stupid!
"You're so ________, Beth,
adj.
and he's just a(n) ________
adj.
________."
noun
Argh!
Hey there, Three Musketeers!

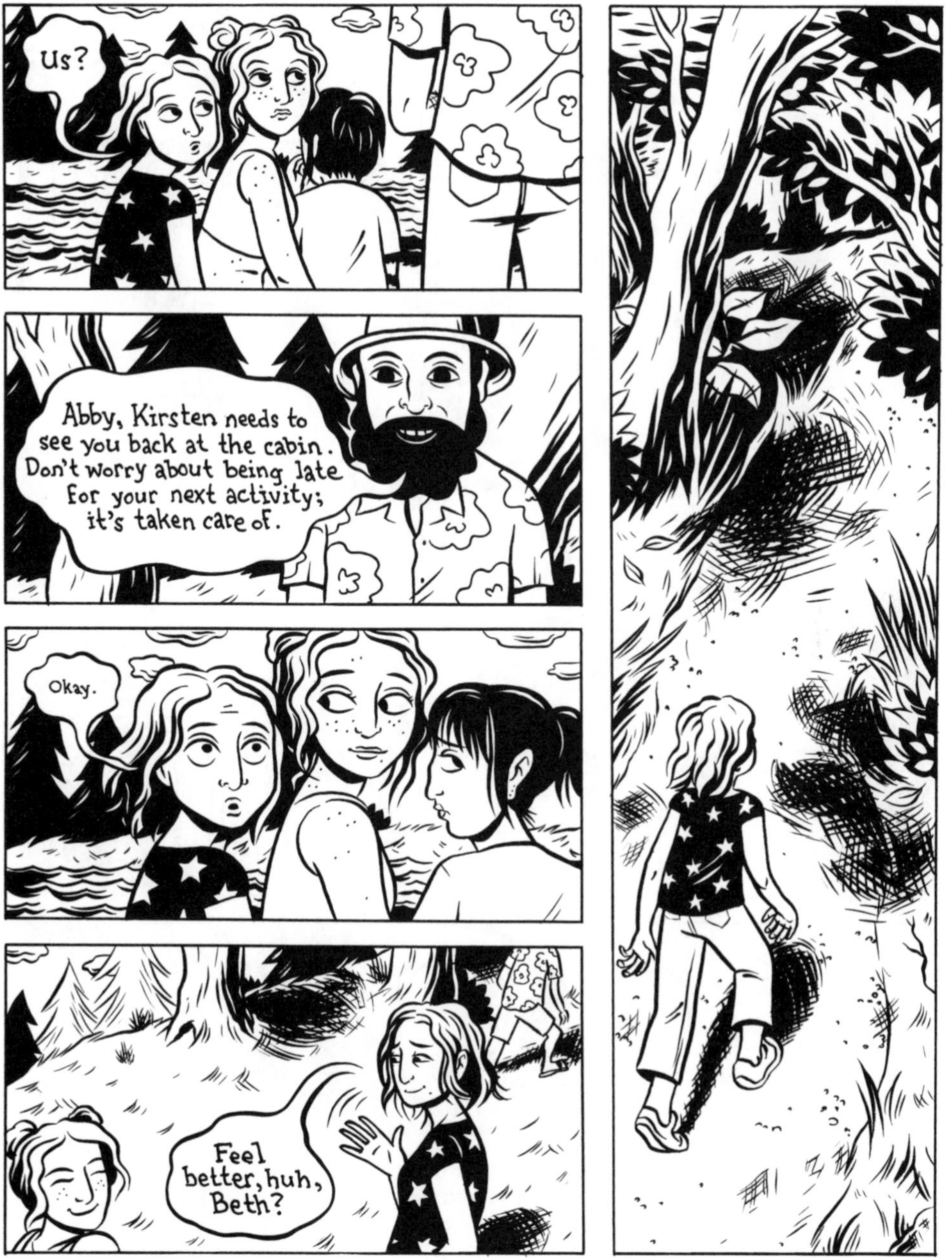
Us?
Abby, Kirsten needs to see you back at the cabin. Don't worry about being late for your next activity; it's taken care of.
Okay.
Feel better, huh, Beth?

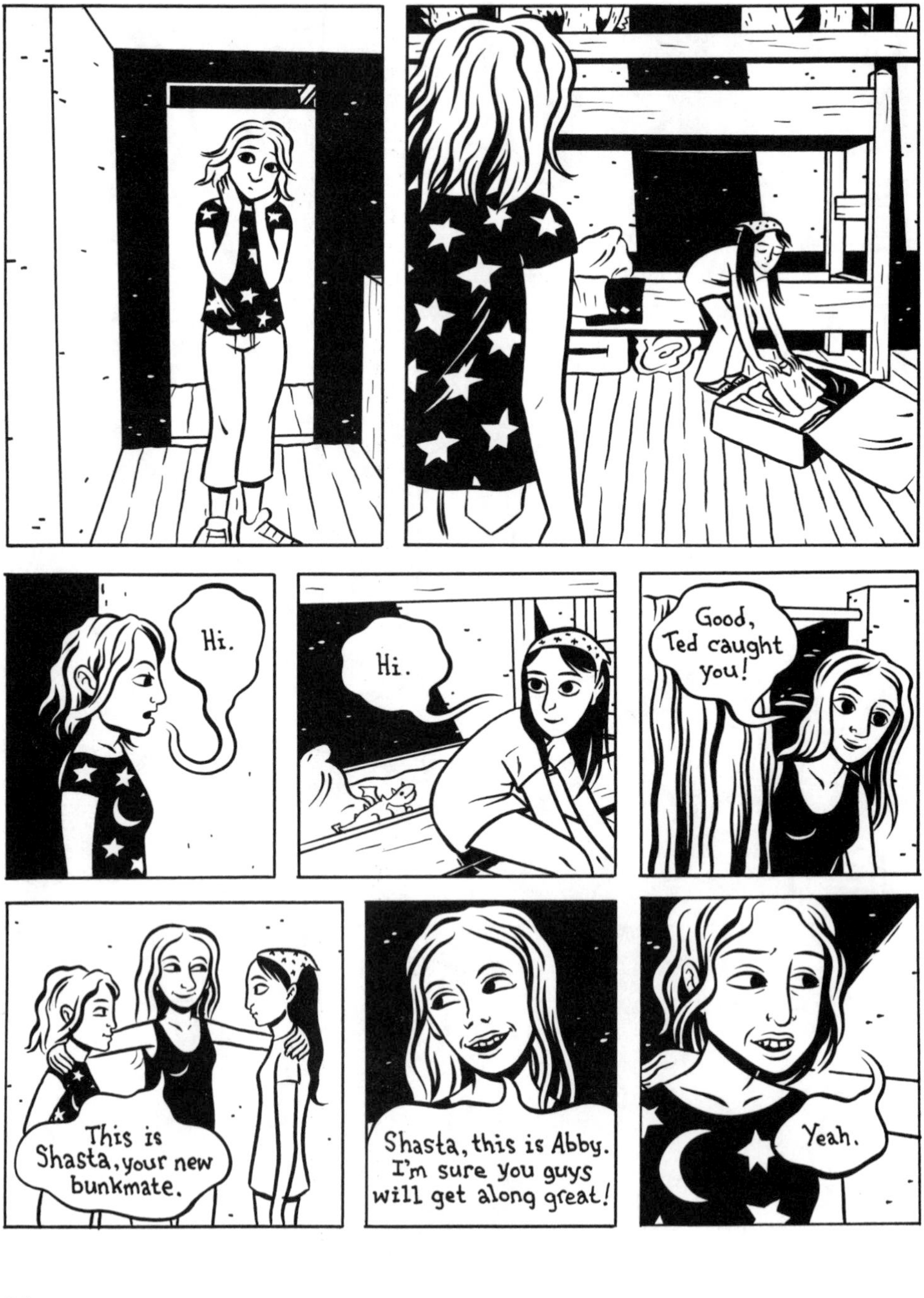
Hi.
Hi.
Good, Ted caught you!
This is Shasta, your new bunkmate.
Shasta, this is Abby. I'm sure you guys will get along great!
Yeah.

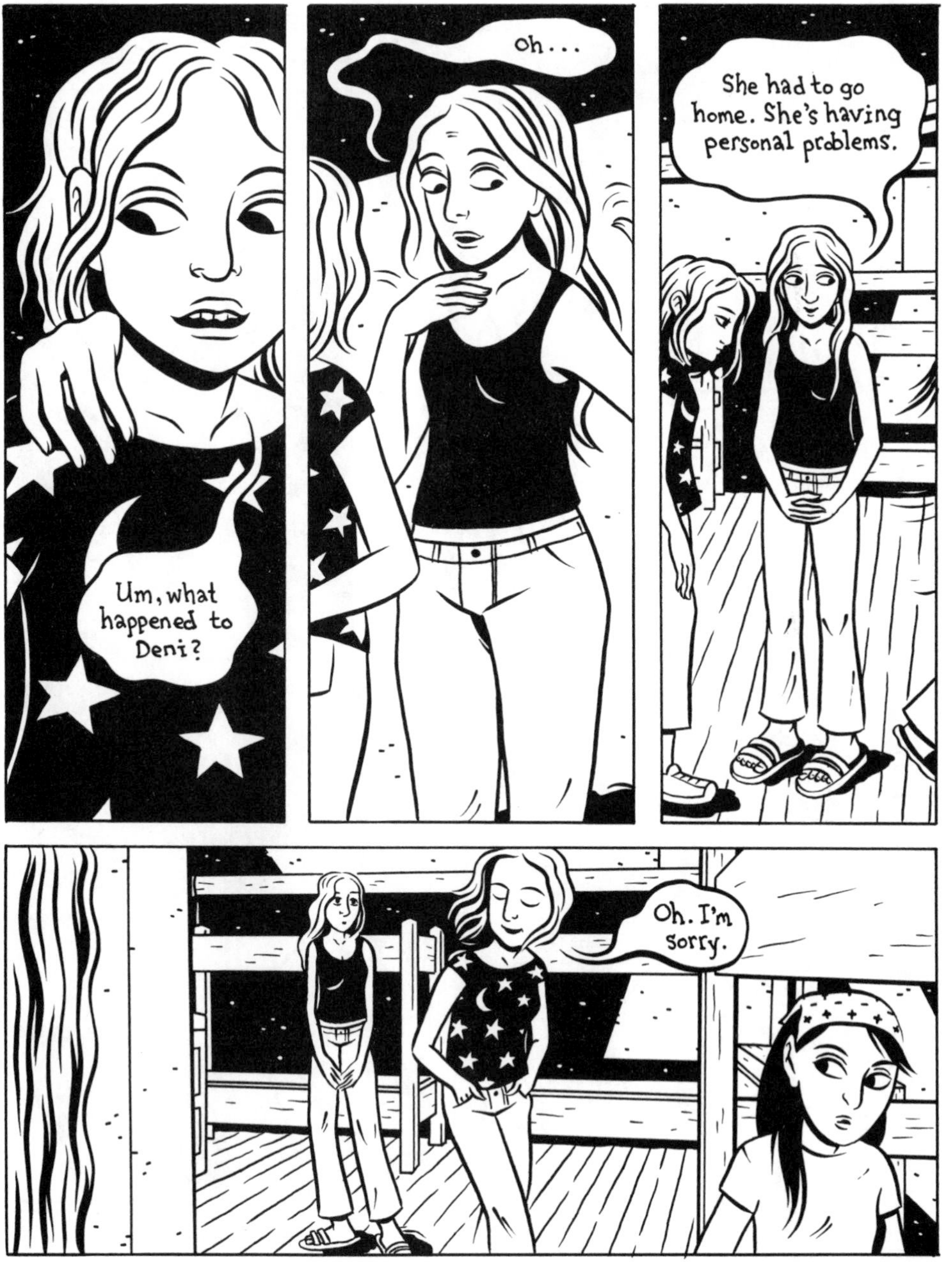
Um, what happened to Deni?
Oh...
She had to go home. She's having personal problems.
Oh. I'm sorry.

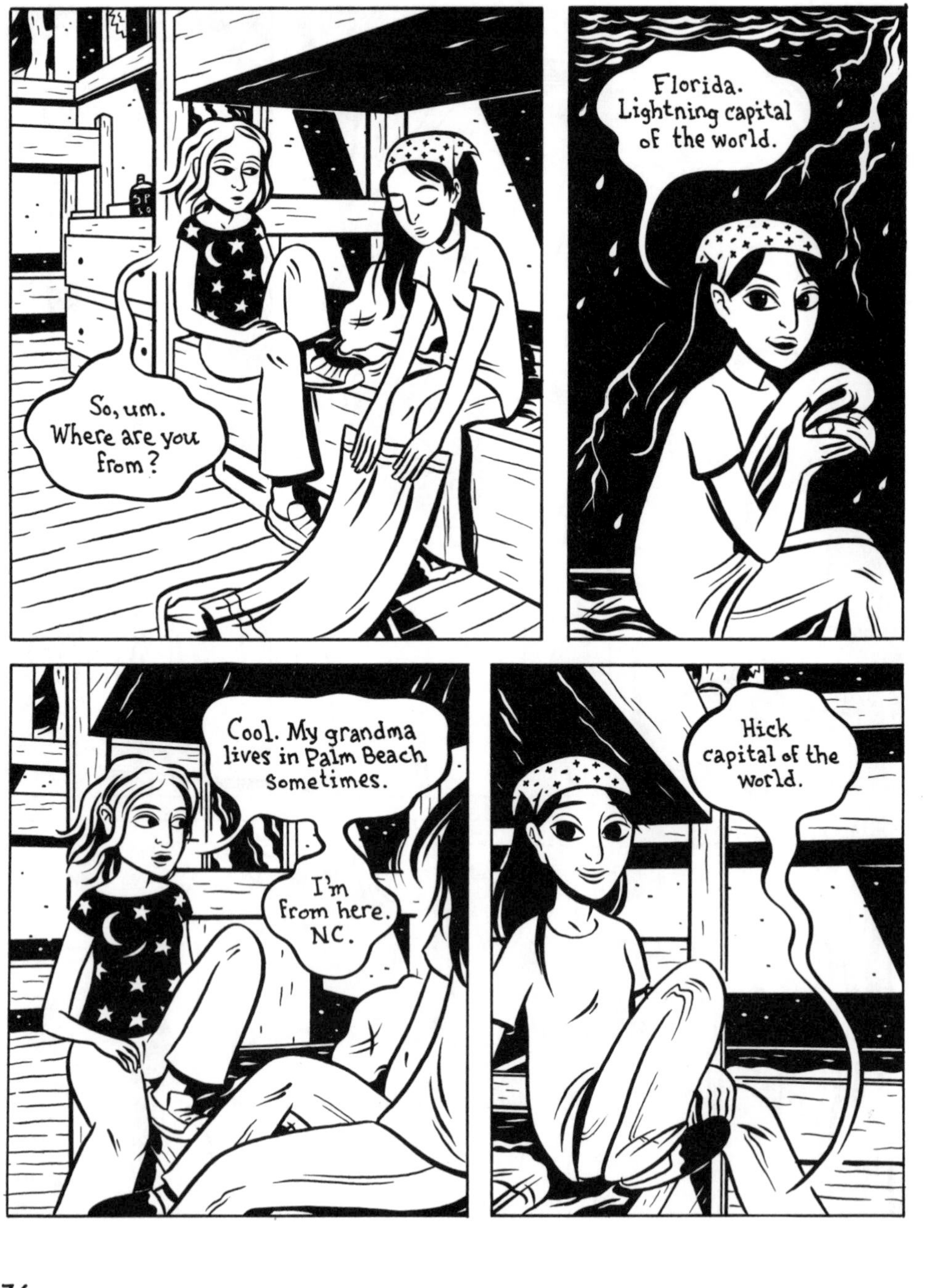
So, um. Where are you from?
Florida. Lightning capital of the world.
Cool. My grandma lives in Palm Beach sometimes.
I'm from here. NC.
Hick capital of the world.

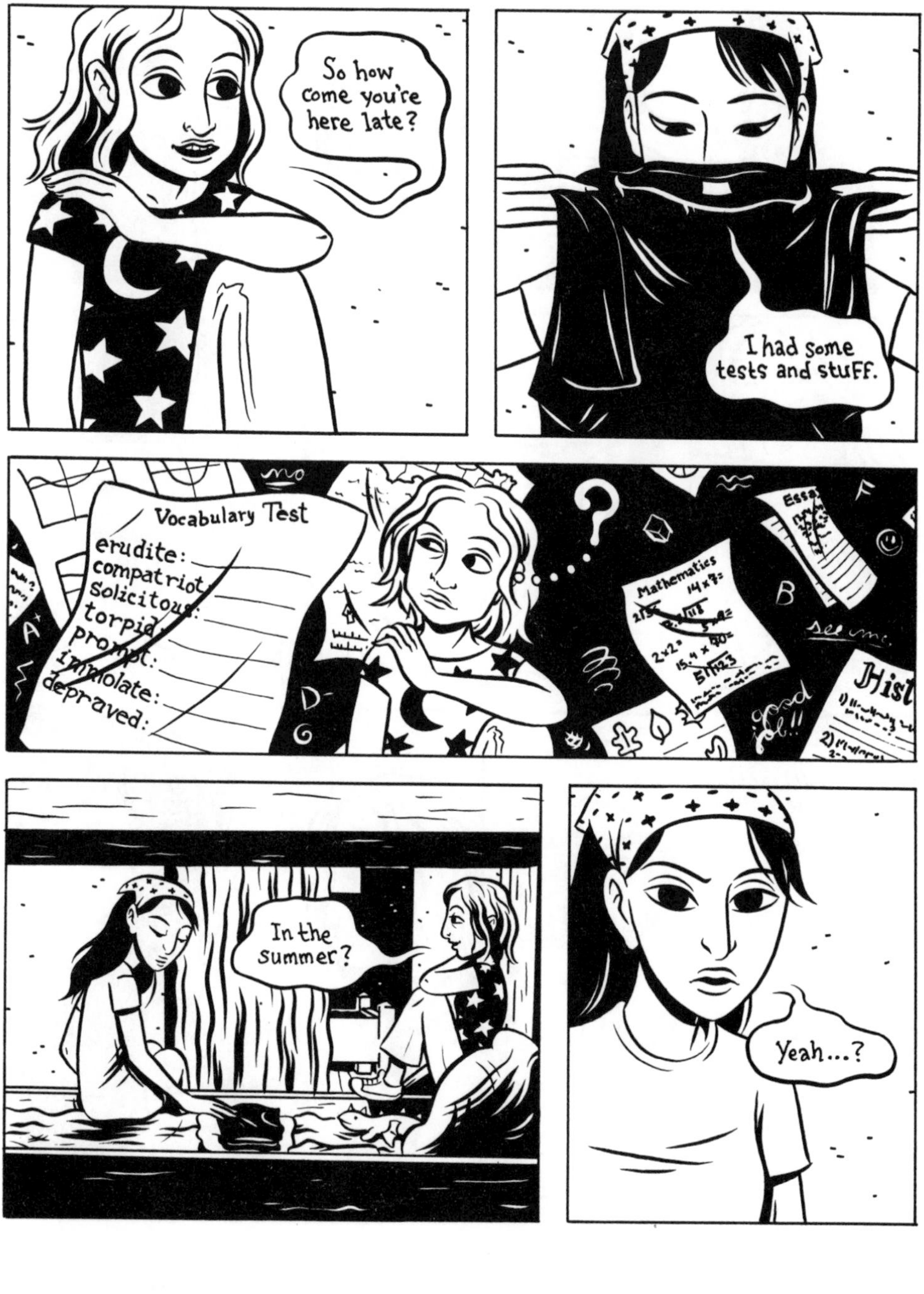

So how come you're here late?
I had some tests and stuff.
Vocabulary Test
erudite:
compatriot:
Solicitous:
torpid:
prompt:
immolate:
depraved:
Mathematics
Essay
Hist
see me.
In the summer?
Yeah...?

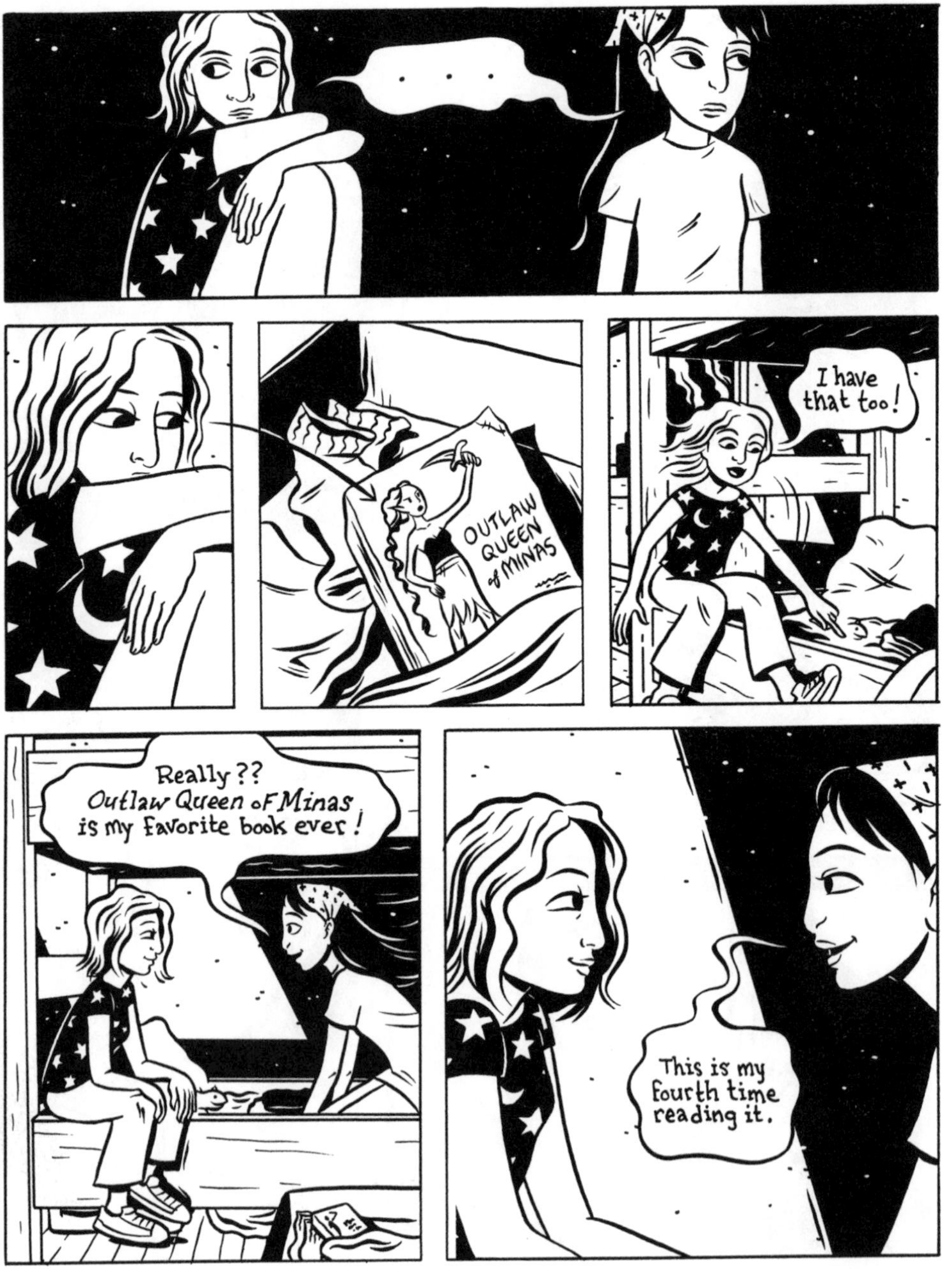
. . .
OUTLAW QUEEN of MINAS
I have that too!
Really?? Outlaw Queen of Minas is my favorite book ever!
This is my fourth time reading it.

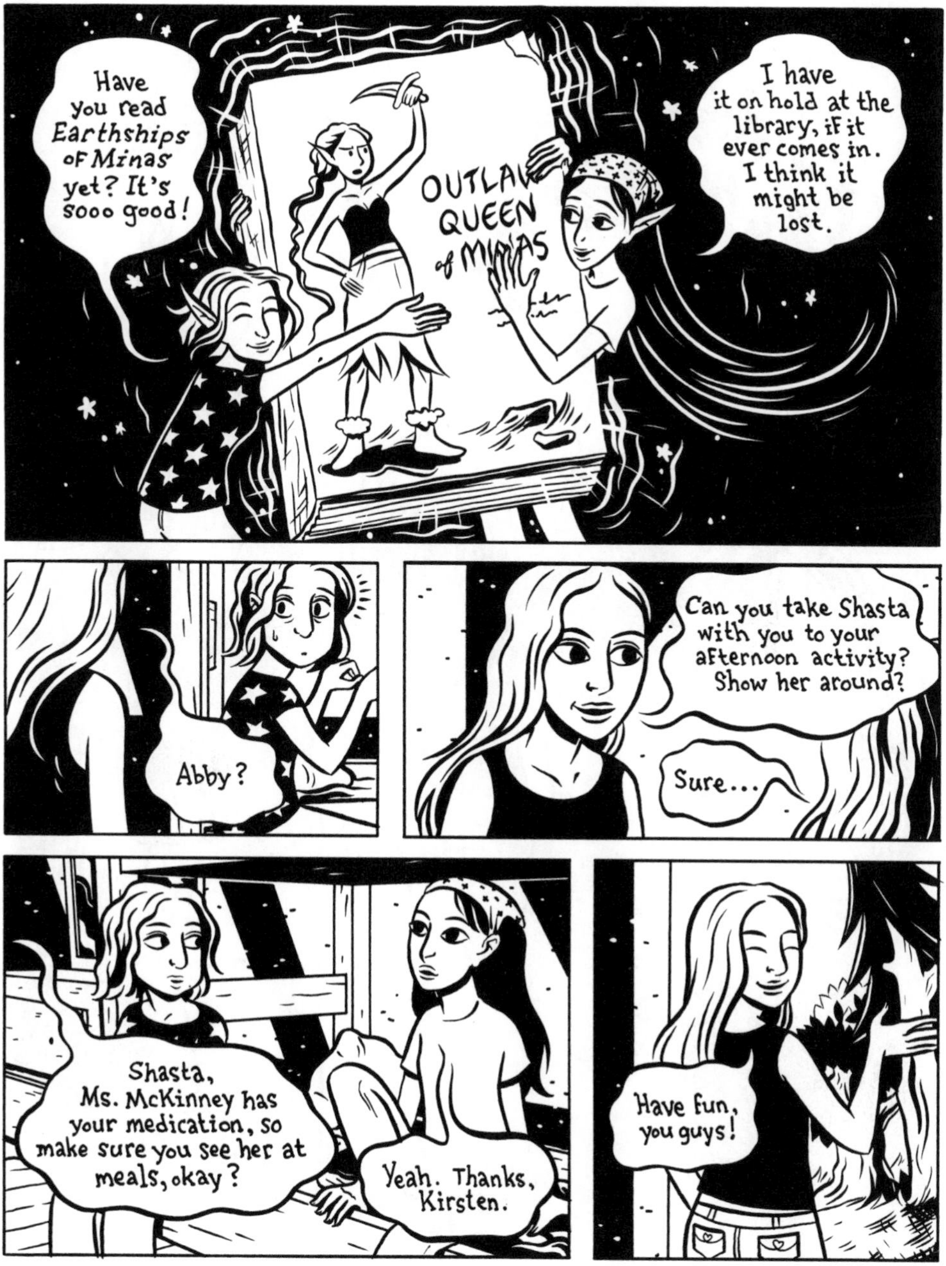
Have you read Earthships of Minas yet? It's sooo good!
OUTLAW QUEEN of MINAS
I have it on hold at the library, if it ever comes in. I think it might be lost.
Abby?
Can you take Shasta with you to your afternoon activity? Show her around?
Sure...
Shasta, Ms. McKinney has your medication, so make sure you see her at meals, okay?
Yeah. Thanks, Kirsten.
Have fun, you guys!

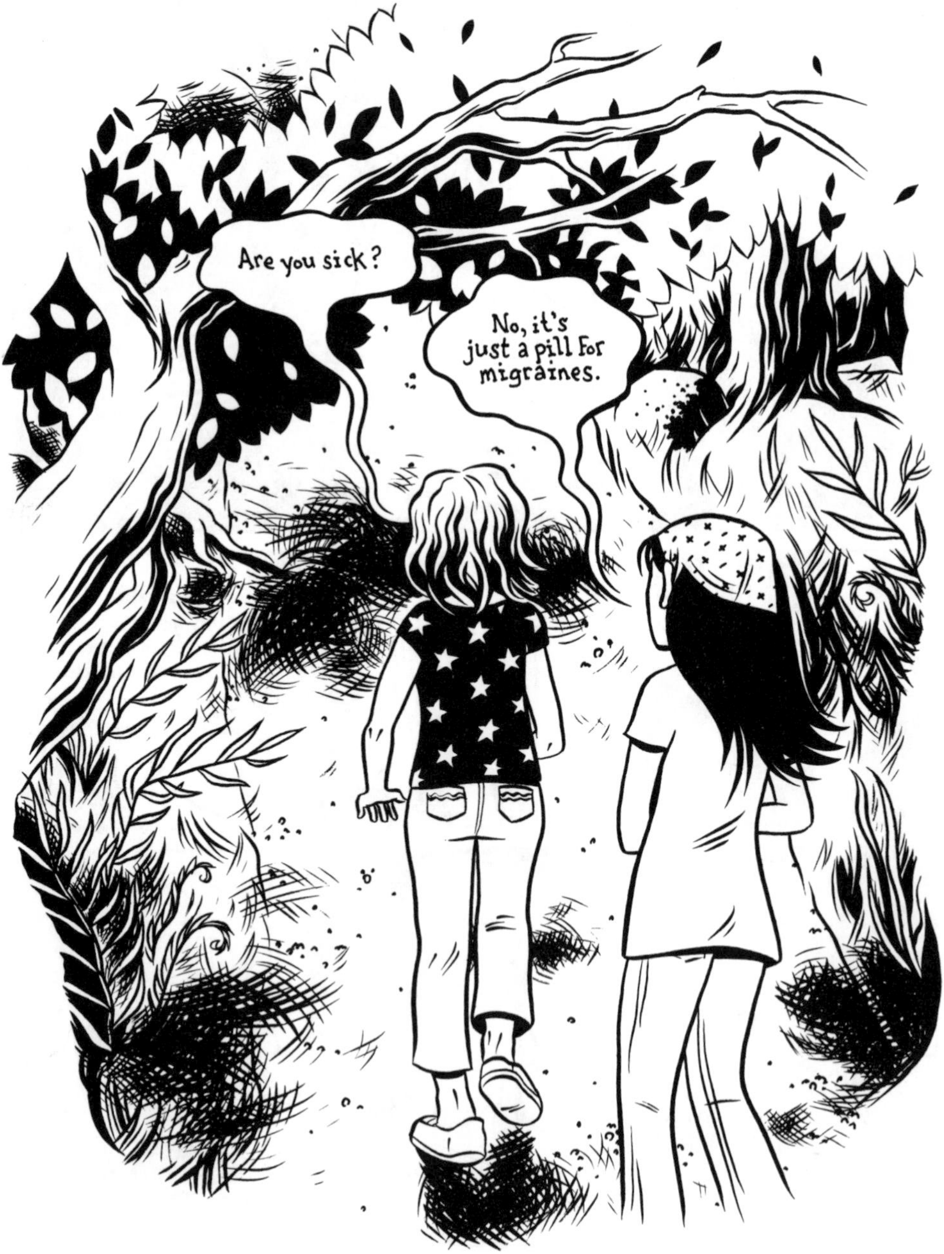
Are you sick?
No, it's just a pill for migraines.

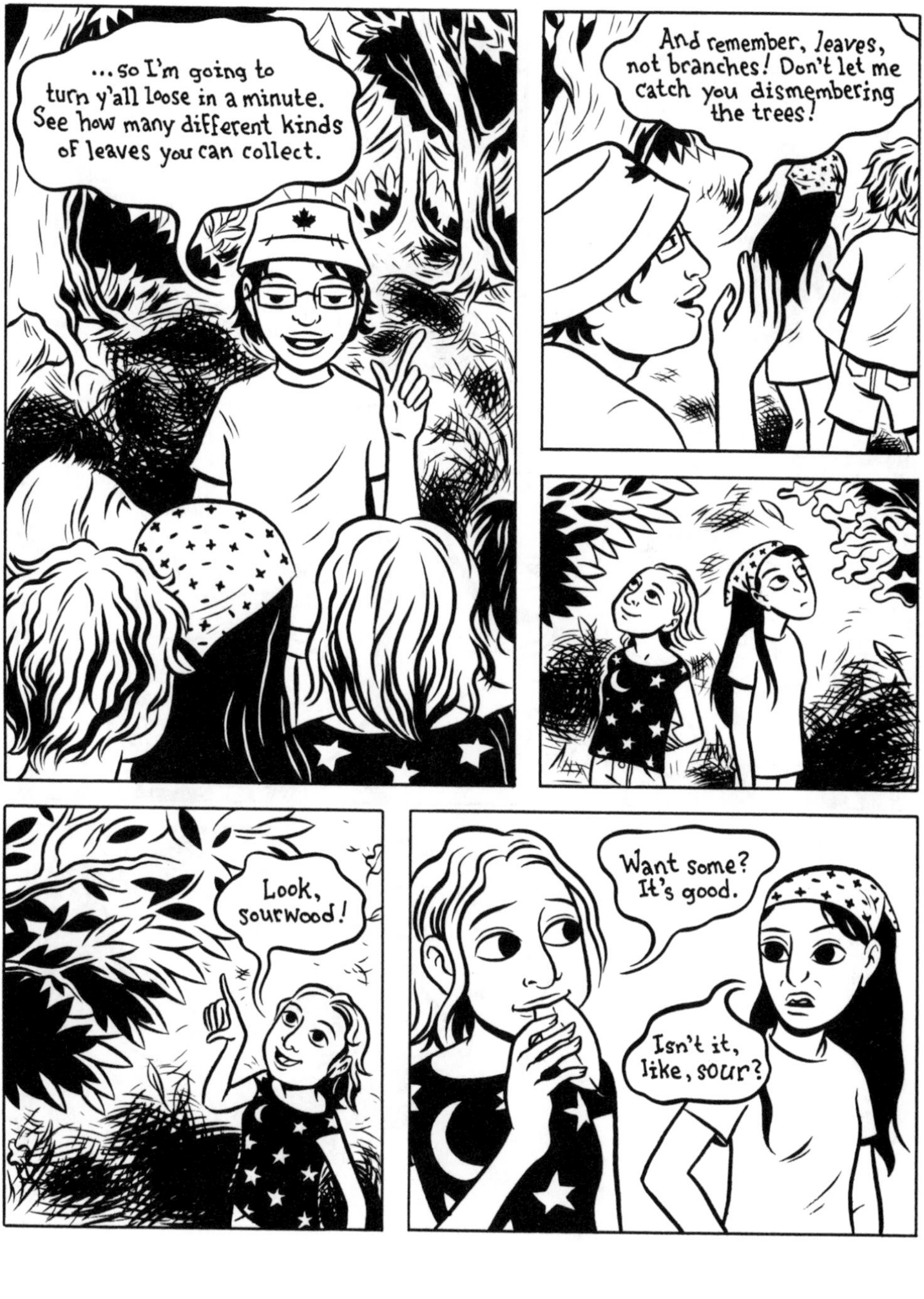
...so I'm going to turn y'all loose in a minute. See how many different kinds of leaves you can collect.
And remember, leaves, not branches! Don't let me catch you dismembering the trees!
Look, sourwood!
Want some? It's good.
Isn't it, like, sour?

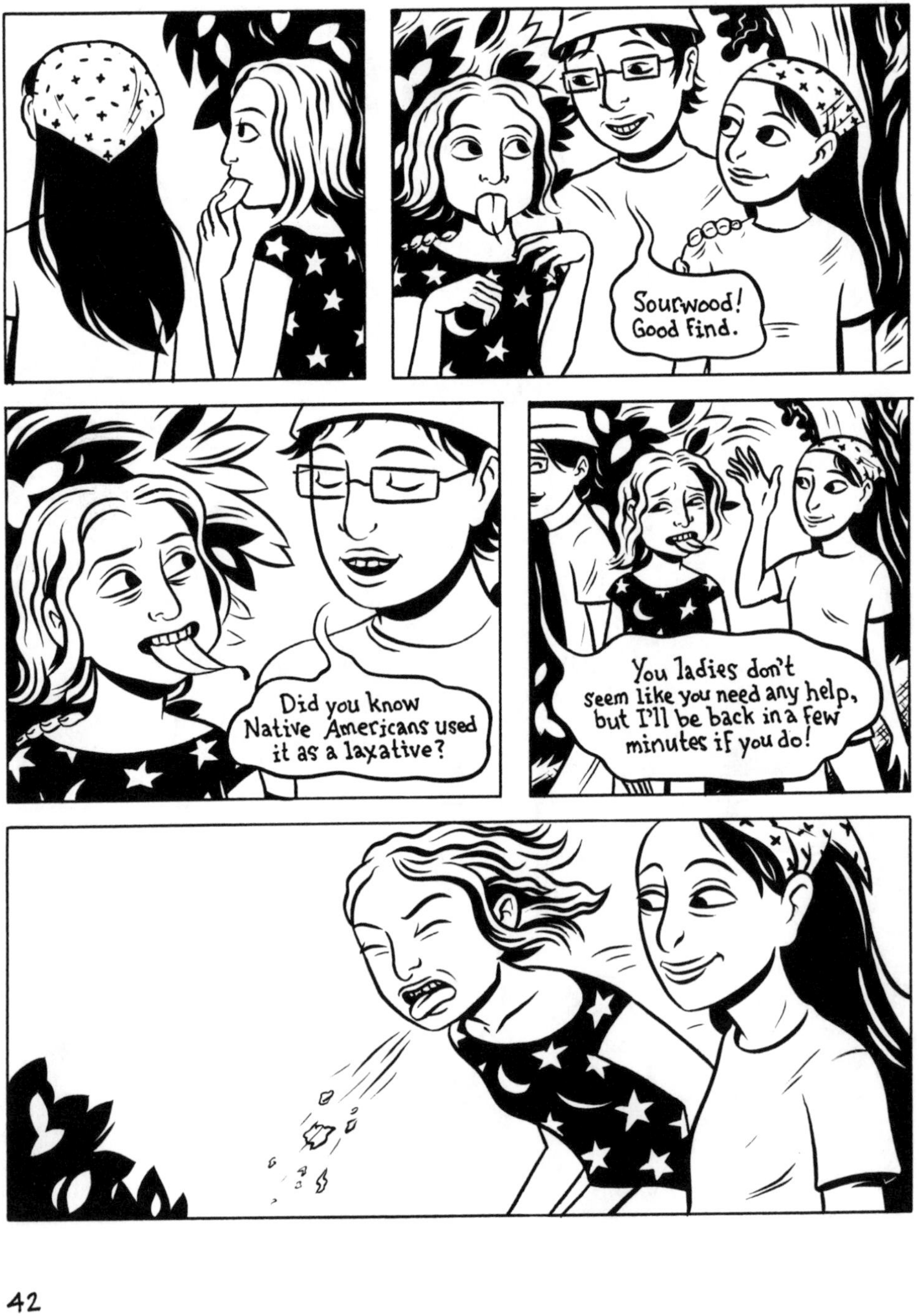
Sourwood! Good find.
Did you know Native Americans used it as a laxative?
You ladies don't seem like you need any help, but I'll be back in a few minutes if you do!

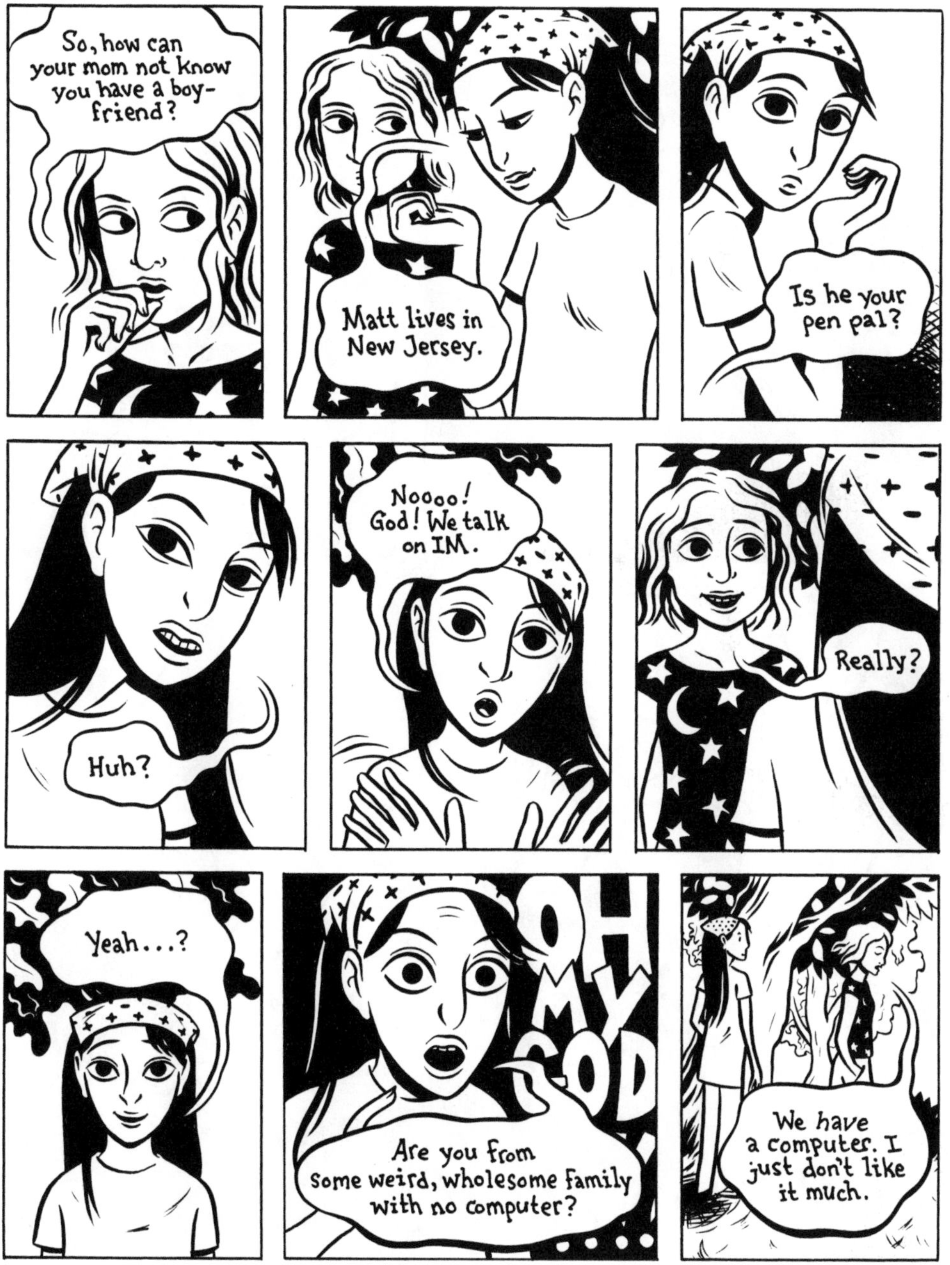

So, how can your mom not know you have a boy-friend?
Matt lives in New Jersey.
Is he your pen pal?
Huh?
Noooo! God! We talk on IM.
Really?
Yeah...?
OH MY GOD
Are you from some weird, wholesome family with no computer?
We *have* a computer. I just don't like it much.

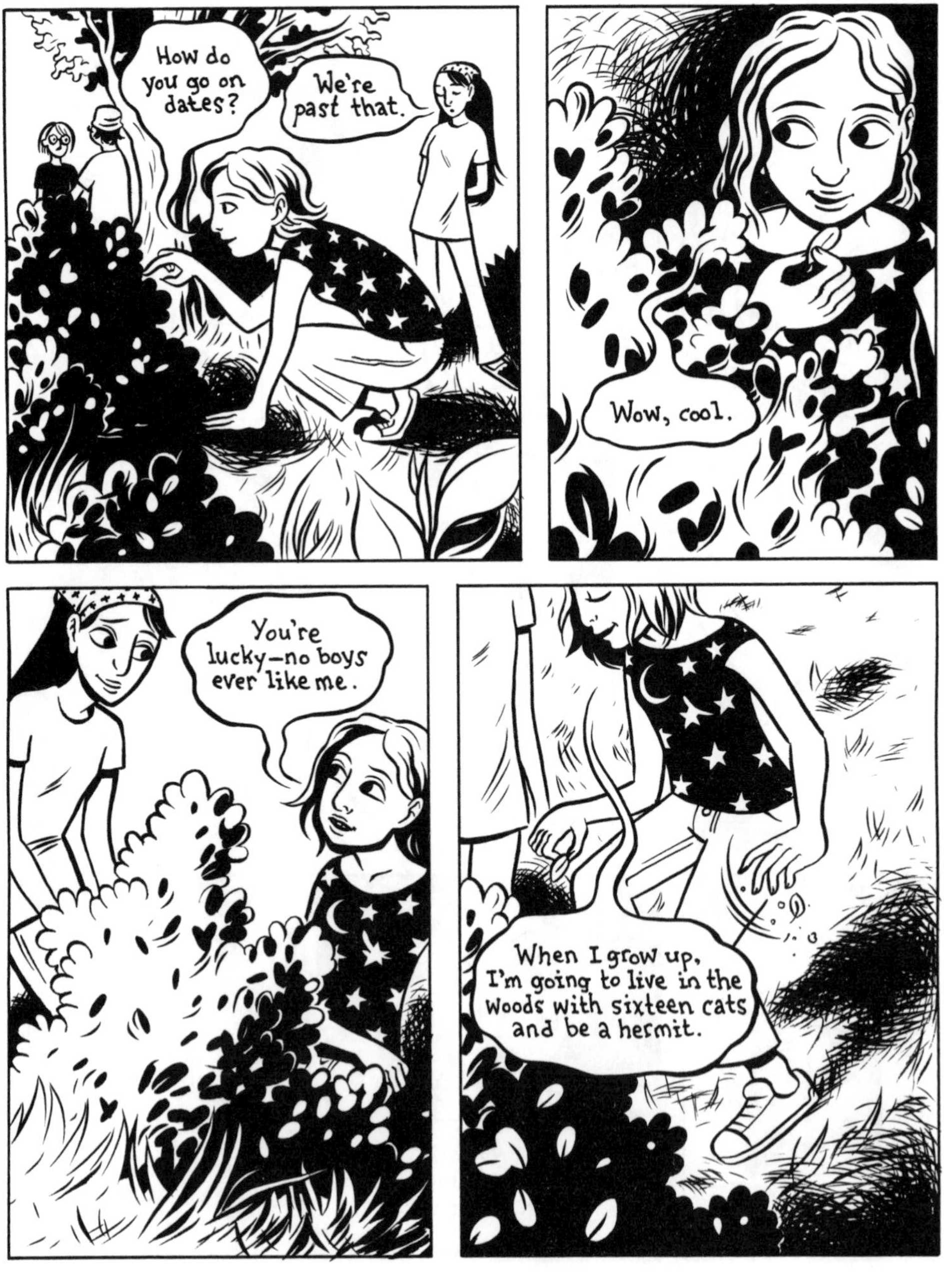
How do you go on dates?
We're past that.
Wow, cool.
You're lucky—no boys ever like me.
When I grow up, I'm going to live in the woods with sixteen cats and be a hermit.

Later

So, are you the new Deni?

?

I'm the new Shasta....

Like the cola?

Like the mountain.

?

In California?

Right. Cool.

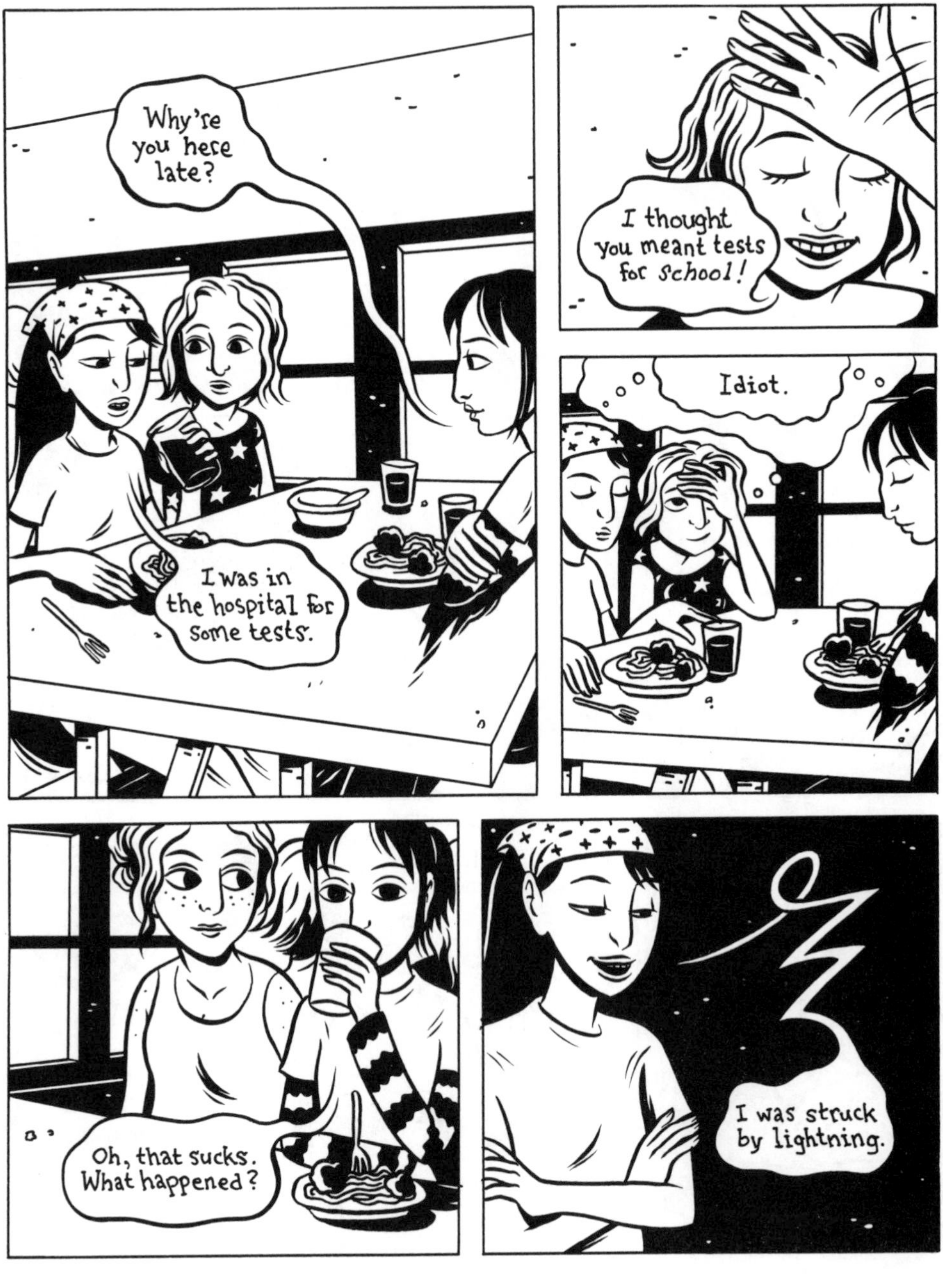
Why're you here late?
I was in the hospital for some tests.
I thought you meant tests for school!
Idiot.
Oh, that sucks. What happened?
I was struck by lightning.

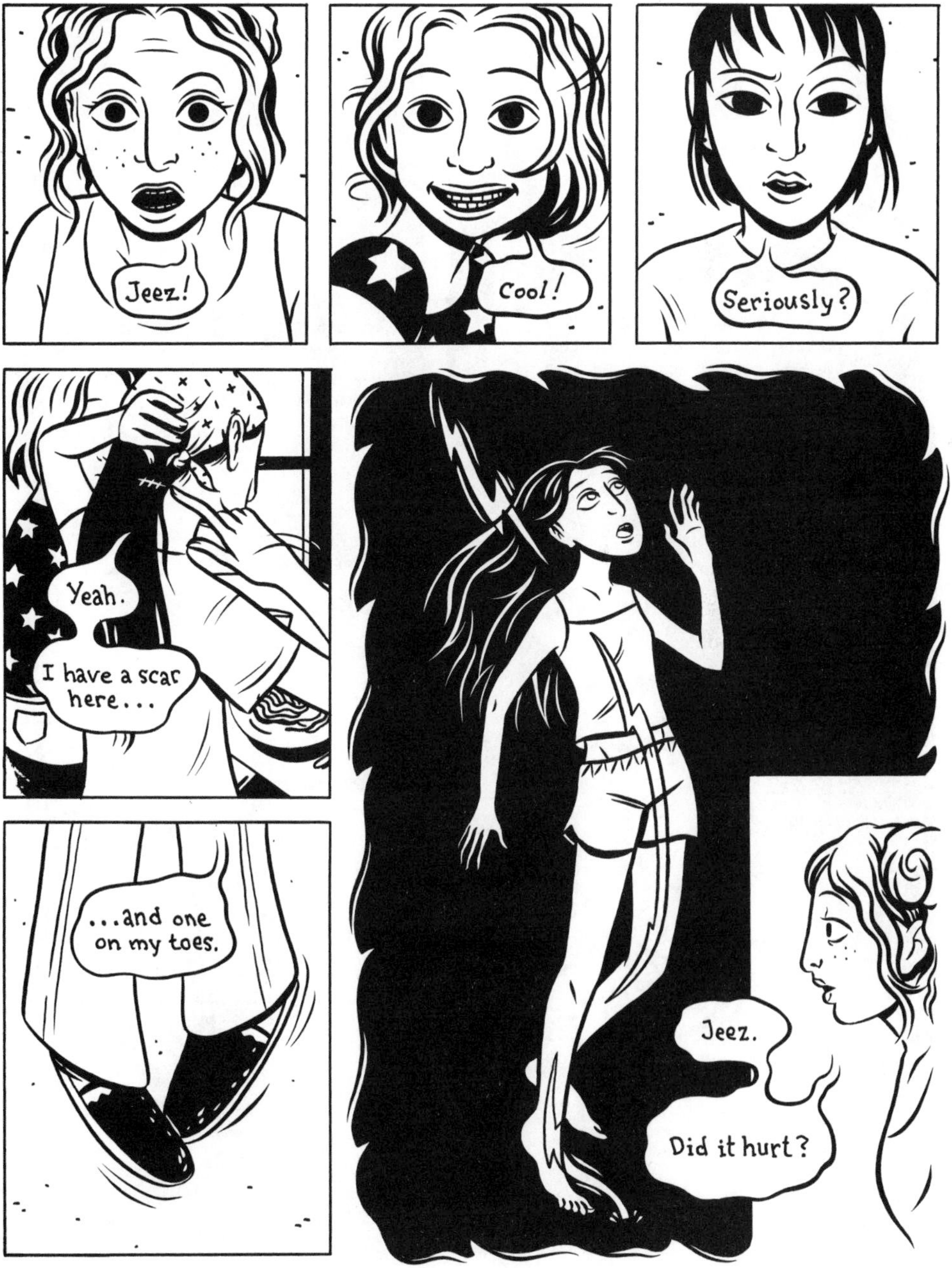
Jeez!
Cool!
Seriously?
Yeah.
I have a scar here...
...and one on my toes.
Jeez.
Did it hurt?

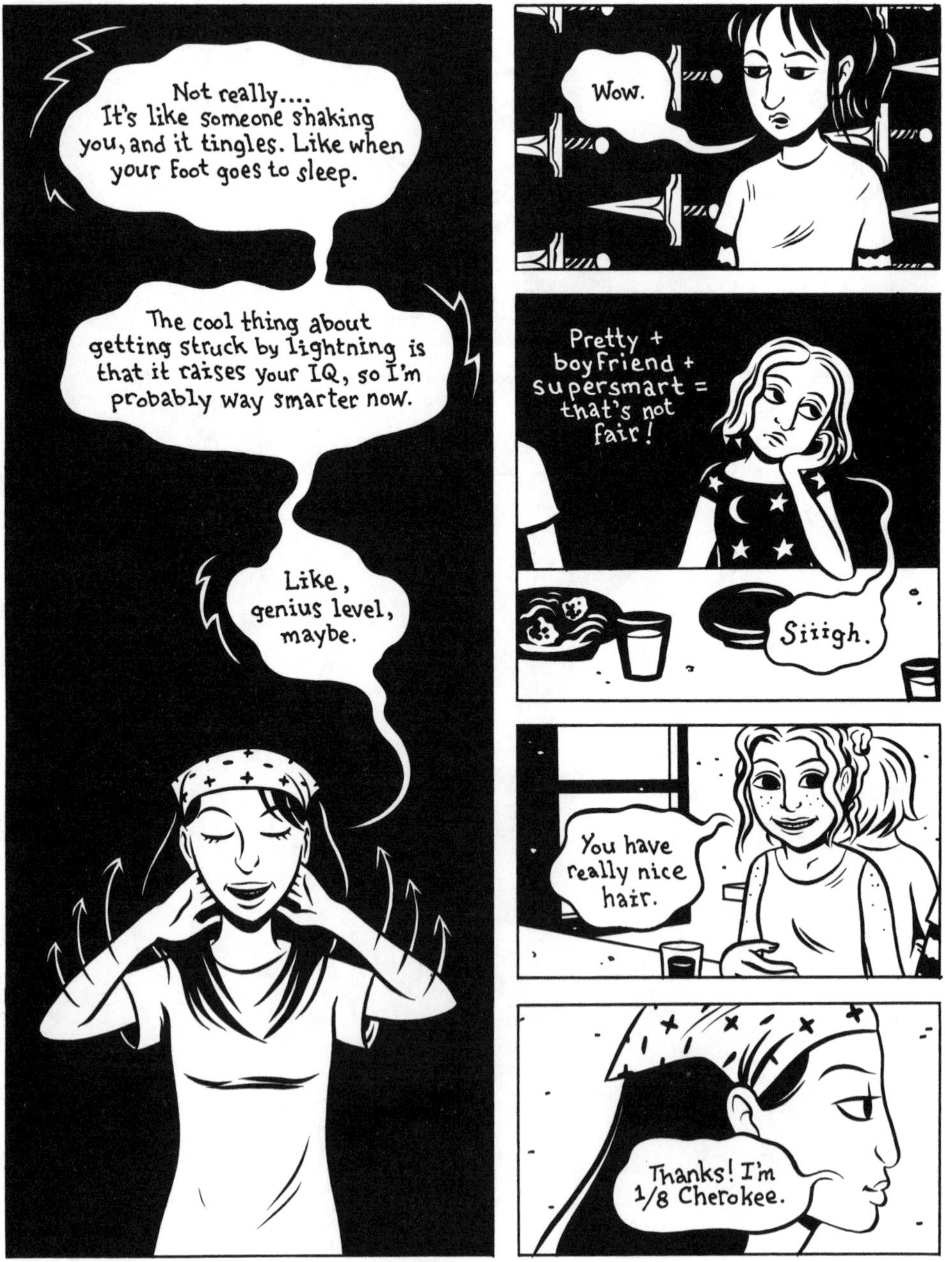
Not really....
It's like someone shaking you, and it tingles. Like when your foot goes to sleep.
The cool thing about getting struck by lightning is that it raises your IQ, so I'm probably way smarter now.
Like, genius level, maybe.
Wow.
Pretty + boyfriend + supersmart = that's not fair!
Siiigh.
You have really nice hair.
Thanks! I'm 1/8 Cherokee.

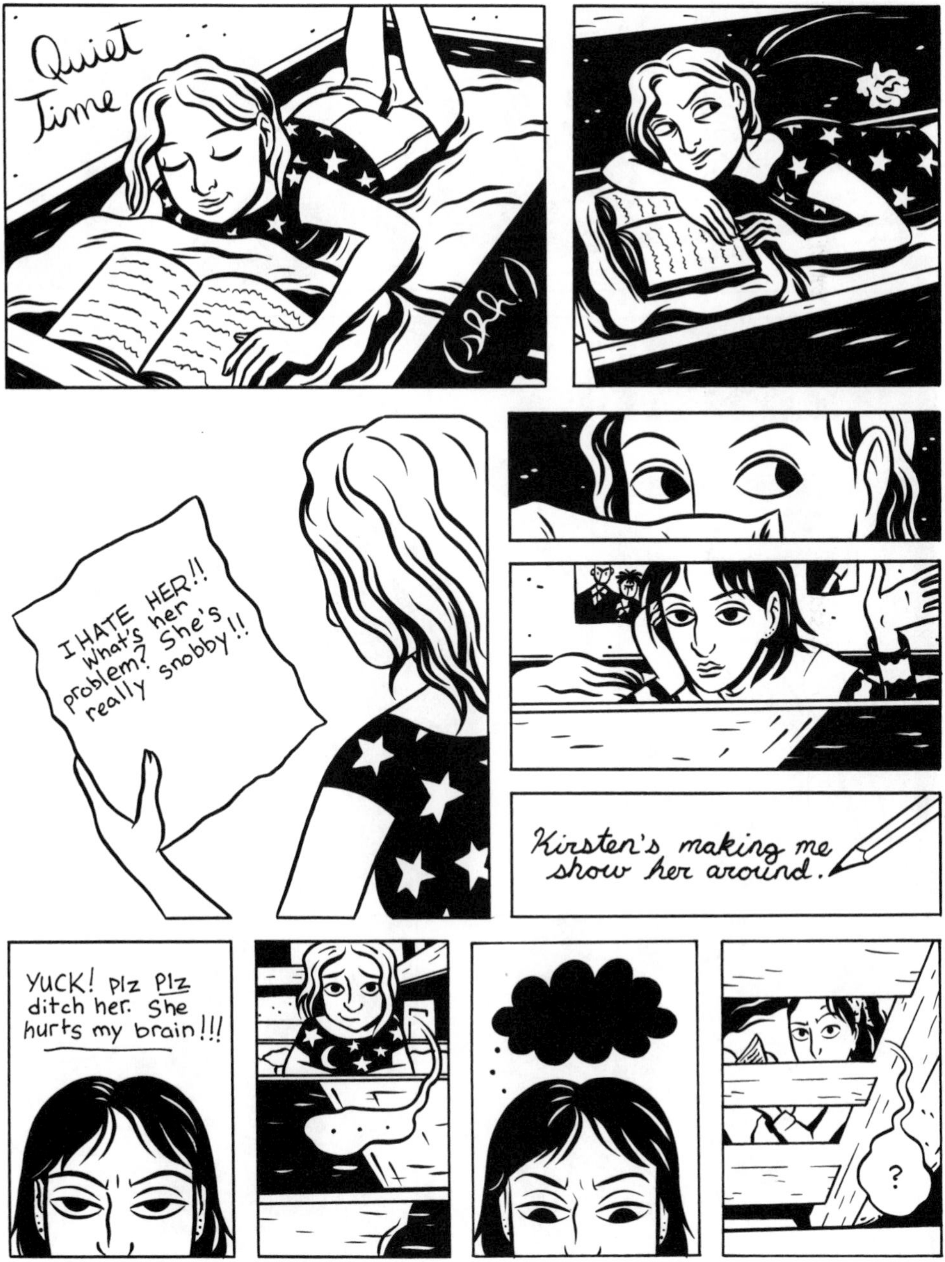
Quiet Time
I HATE HER!! What's her problem? She's really snobby!!
Kirsten's making me show her around.
YUCK! plz Plz ditch her. She hurts my brain!!!
?

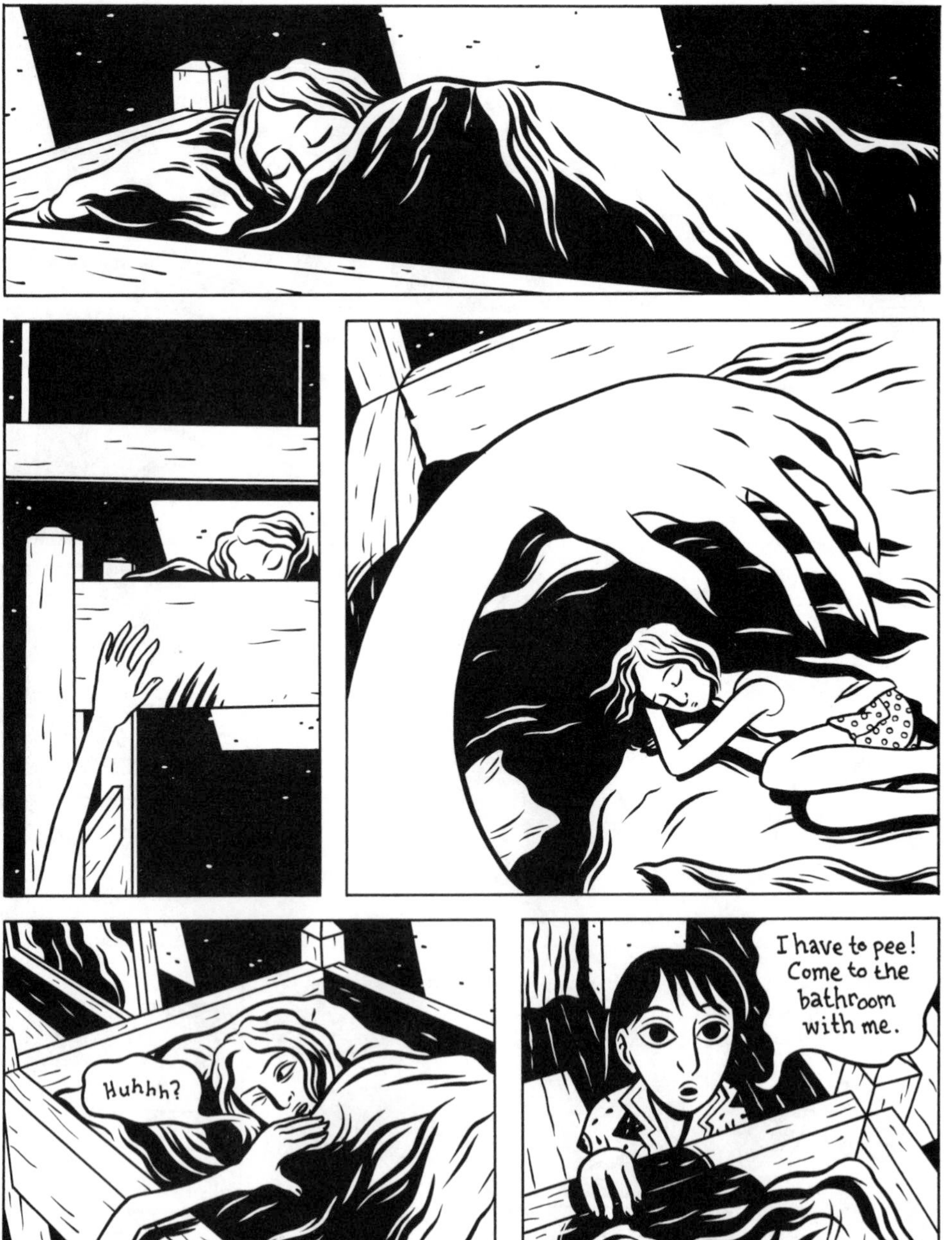
Huhhh?
I have to pee! Come to the bathroom with me.

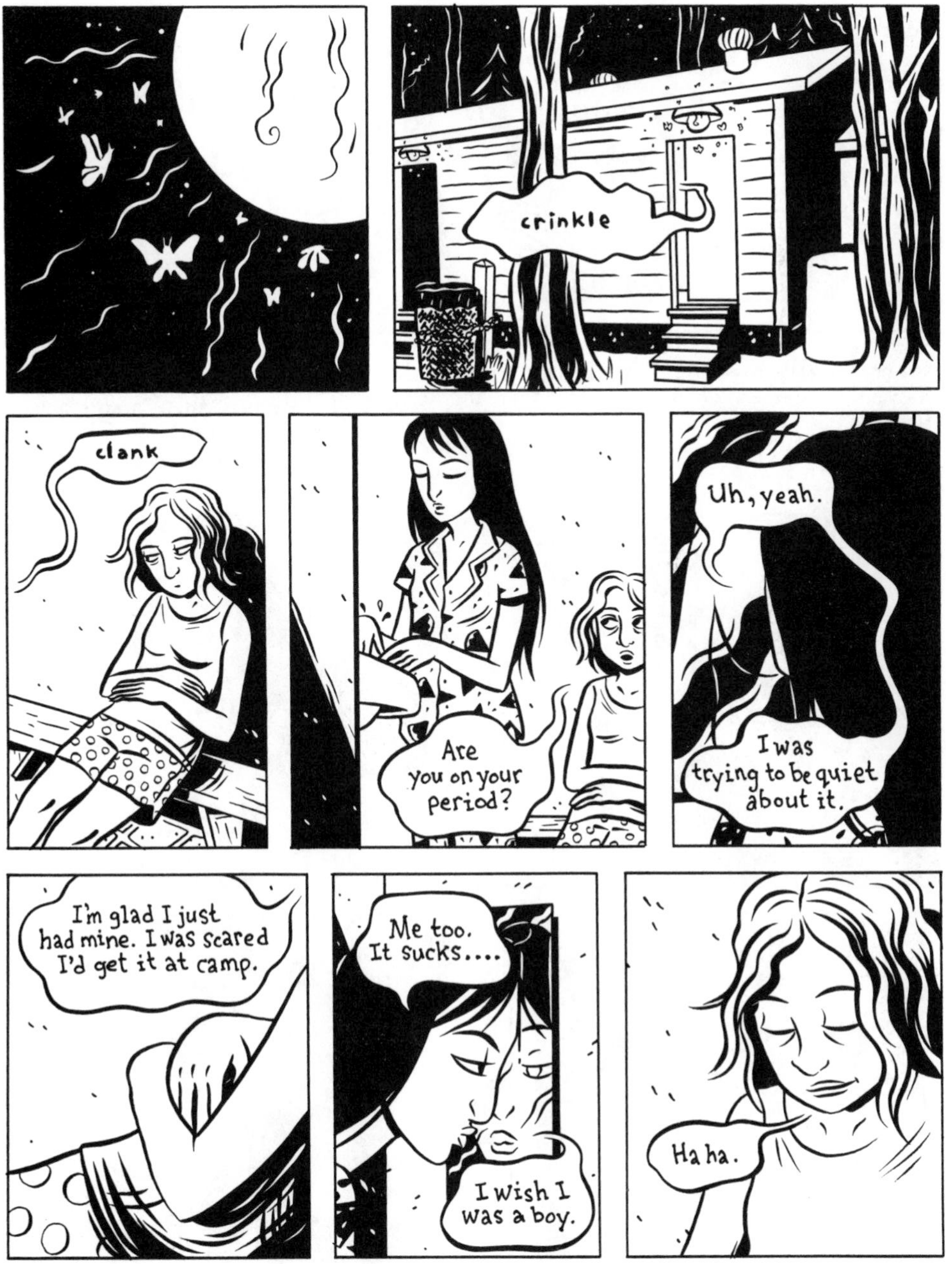
crinkle
clank
Are you on your period?
Uh, yeah.
I was trying to be quiet about it.
I'm glad I just had mine. I was scared I'd get it at camp.
Me too. It sucks....
I wish I was a boy.
Ha ha.

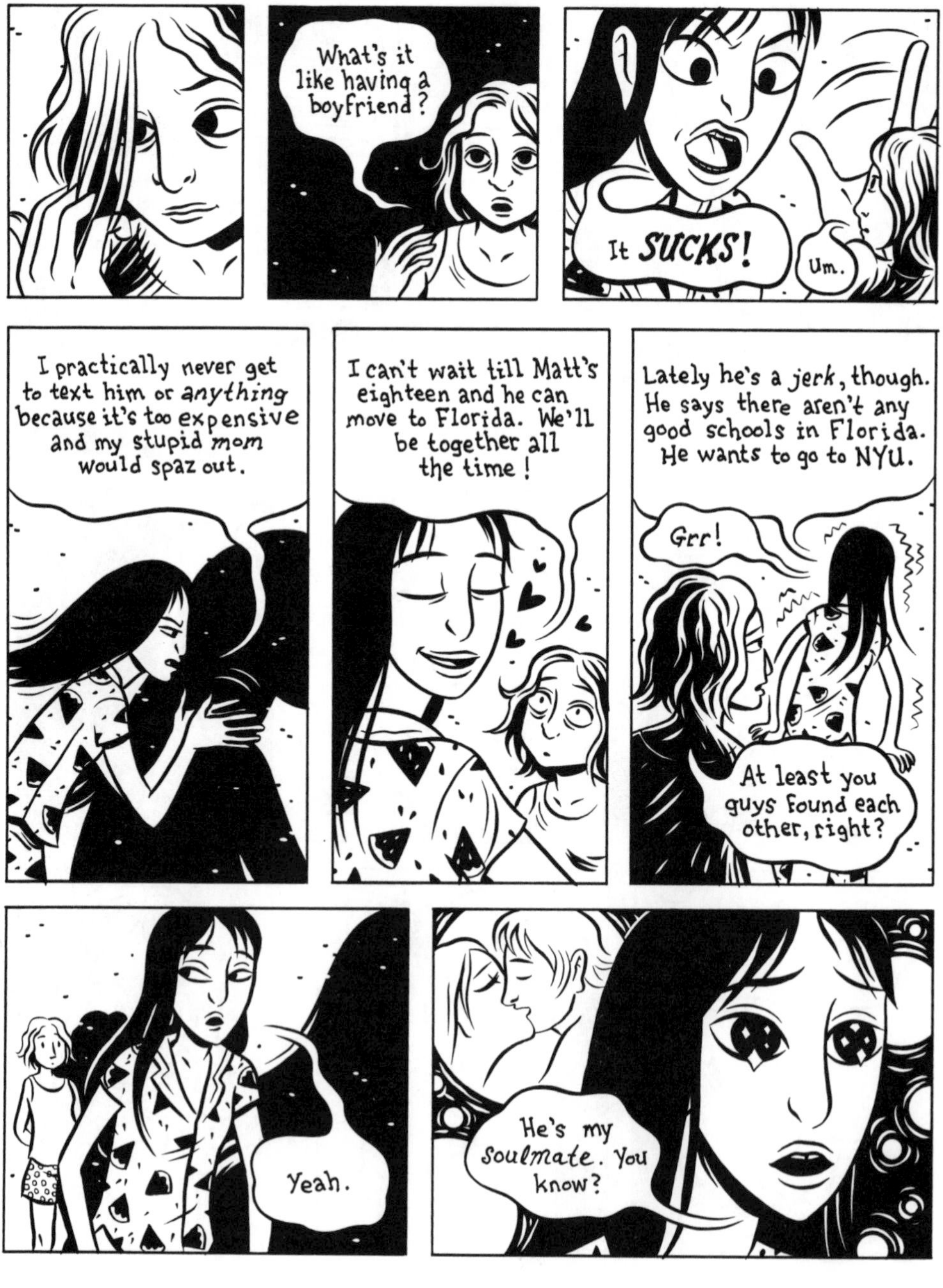
What's it like having a boyfriend?
It SUCKS!
Um.
I practically never get to text him or anything because it's too expensive and my stupid mom would spaz out.
I can't wait till Matt's eighteen and he can move to Florida. We'll be together all the time!
Lately he's a jerk, though. He says there aren't any good schools in Florida. He wants to go to NYU.
Grr!
At least you guys found each other, right?
Yeah.
He's my soulmate. You know?

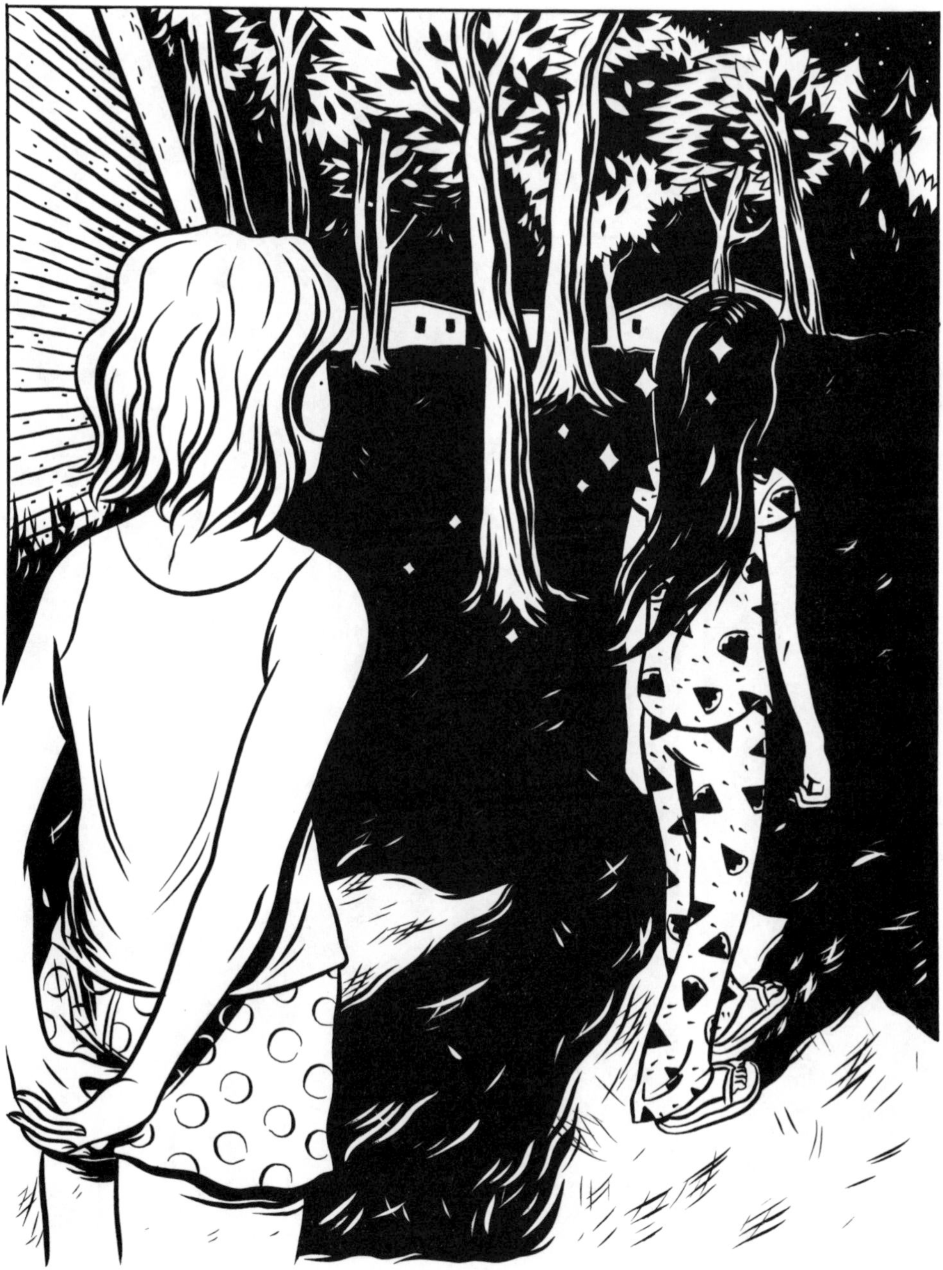

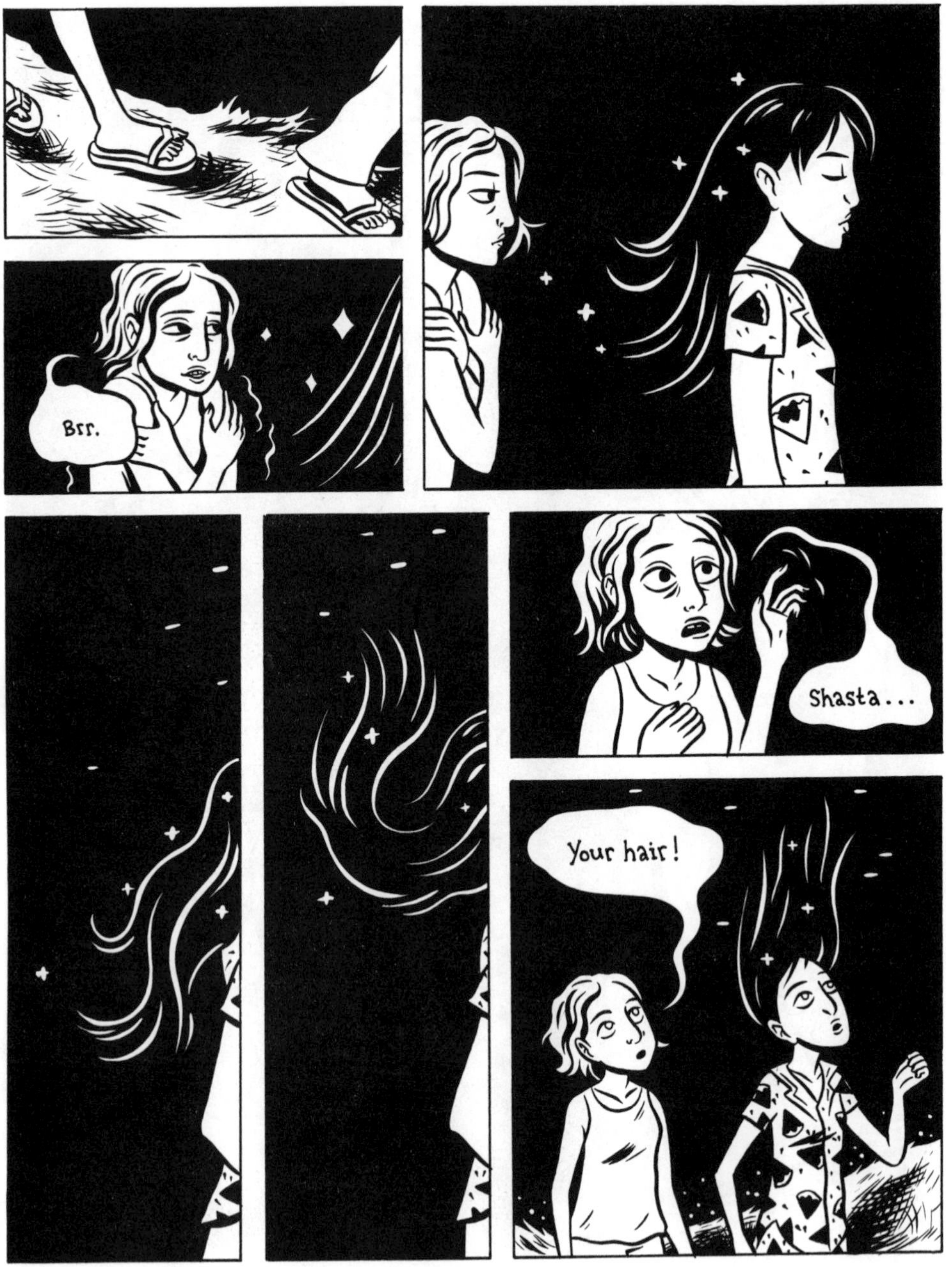
Brr.
Shasta...
Your hair!

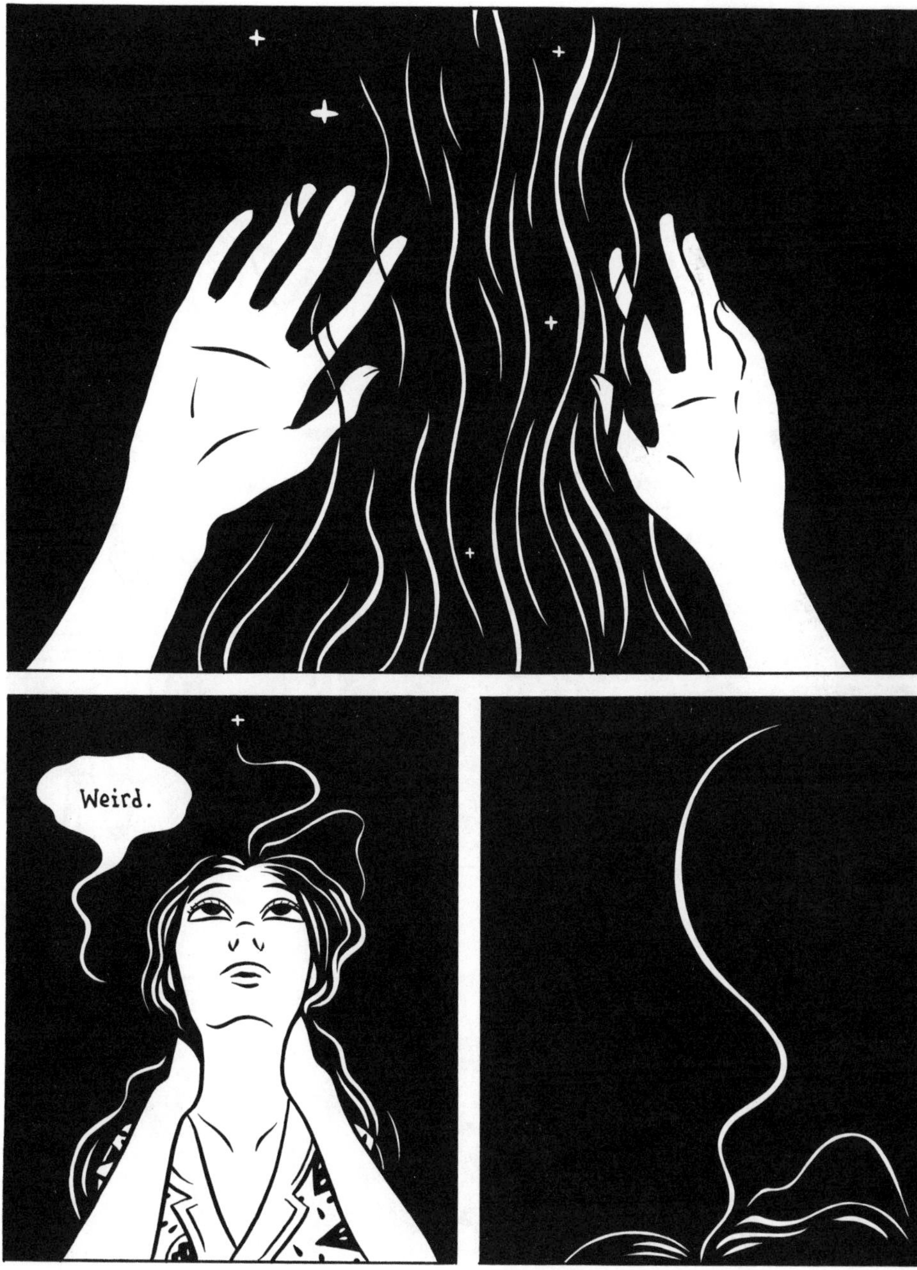
Weird.

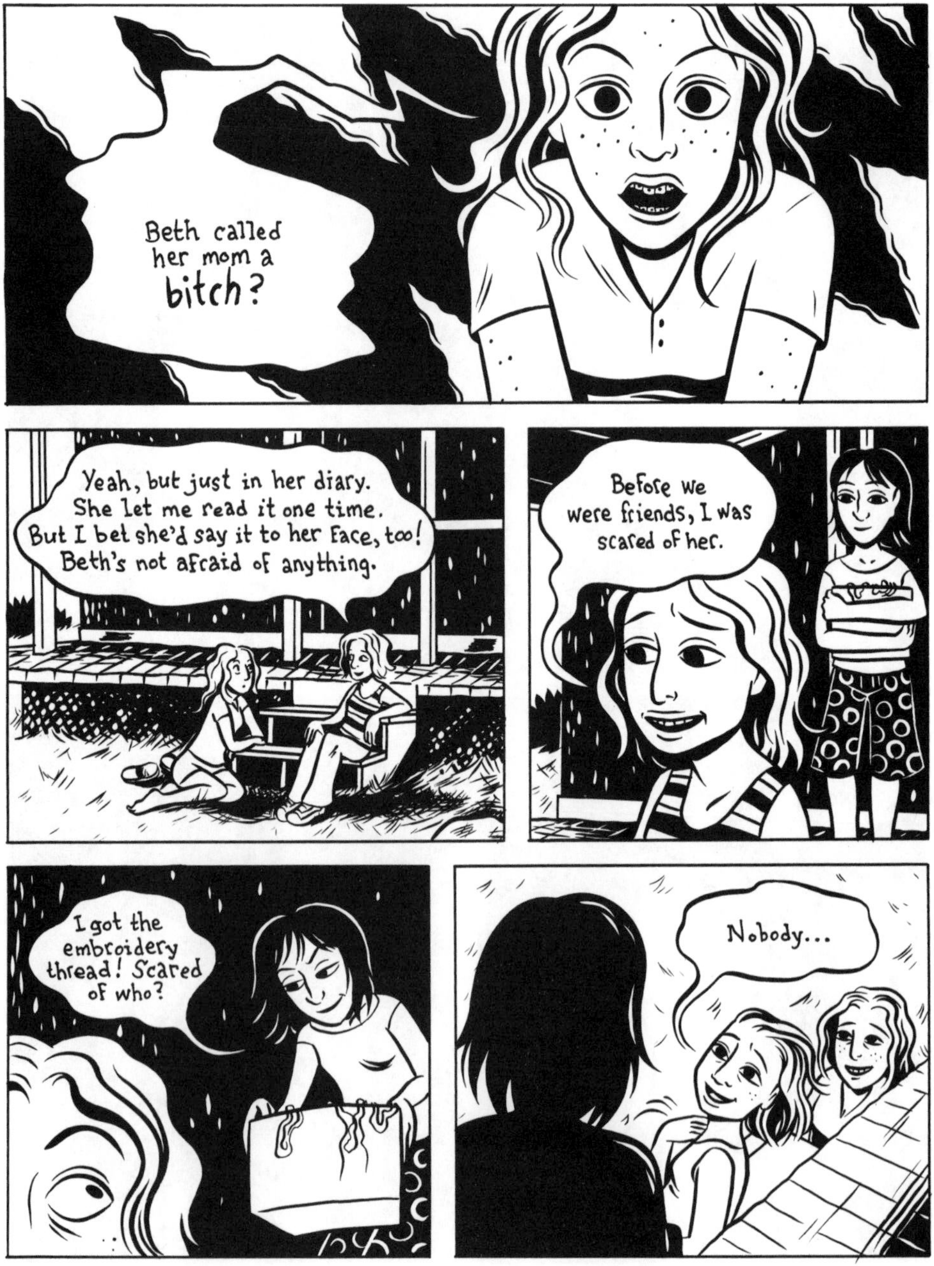

Beth called her mom a bitch?
Yeah, but just in her diary. She let me read it one time. But I bet she'd say it to her face, too! Beth's not afraid of anything.
Before we were friends, I was scared of her.
I got the embroidery thread! Scared of who?
Nobody...

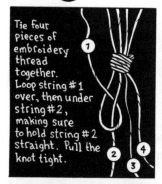

how to make a friendship bracelet

beth ♥

Tie four pieces of embroidery thread together. Loop string #1 over, then under string #2, making sure to hold string #2 straight. Pull the knot tight.

1 · 2 · 4 · 3

Repeat step one to make a double knot.

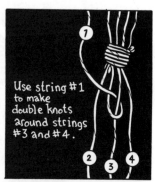

Use string #1 to make double knots around strings #3 and #4.

1 · 2 · 3 · 4

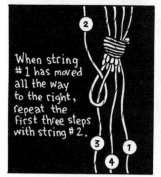

When string #1 has moved all the way to the right, repeat the first three steps with string #2.

2 · 3 · 4 · 1

Continue until you have a bracelet long enough for your wrist.

Knot the end of your bracelet. You're finished!

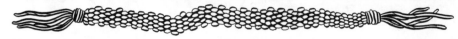

I was scared of *you* at first! I thought you'd be mean, or else really nerdy.

Oh, *thanks.*

57

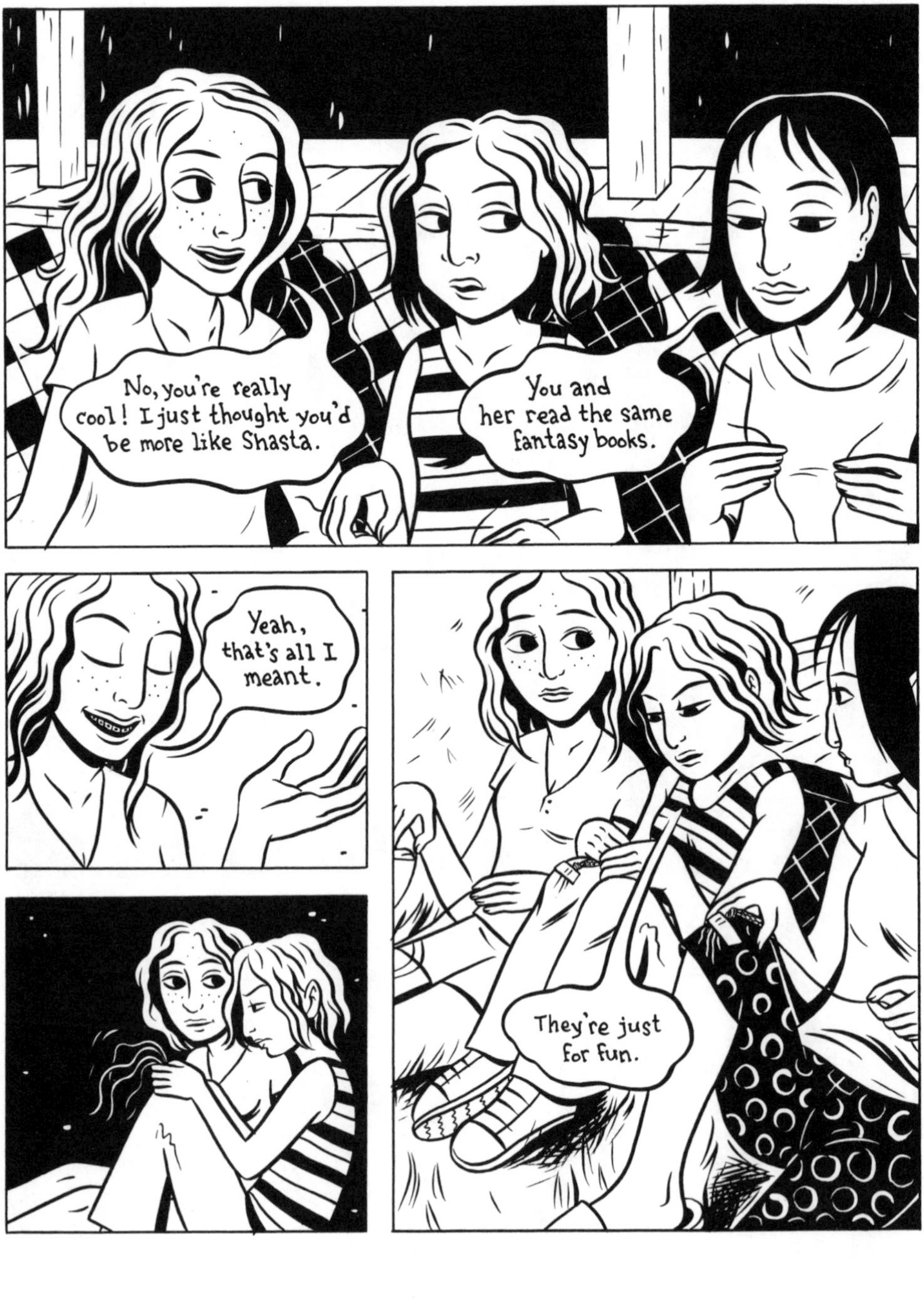
No, you're really cool! I just thought you'd be more like Shasta.
You and her read the same fantasy books.
Yeah, that's all I meant.
They're just for fun.

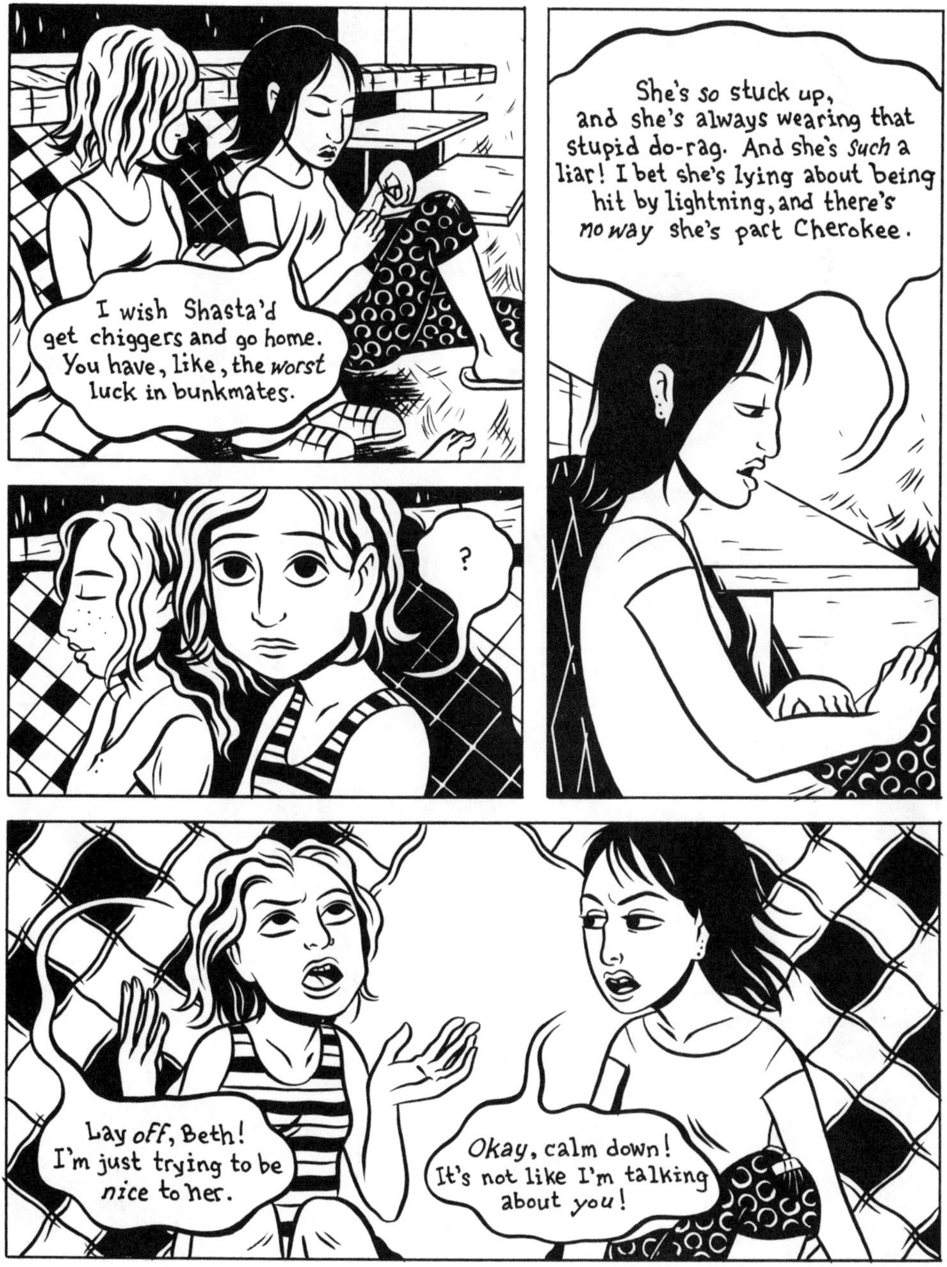
I wish Shasta'd get chiggers and go home. You have, like, the *worst* luck in bunkmates.
She's *so* stuck up, and she's always wearing that stupid do-rag. And she's *such* a liar! I bet she's lying about being hit by lightning, and there's *no way* she's part Cherokee.
?
Lay *off*, Beth! I'm just trying to be *nice* to her.
Okay, calm down! It's not like I'm talking about *you*!

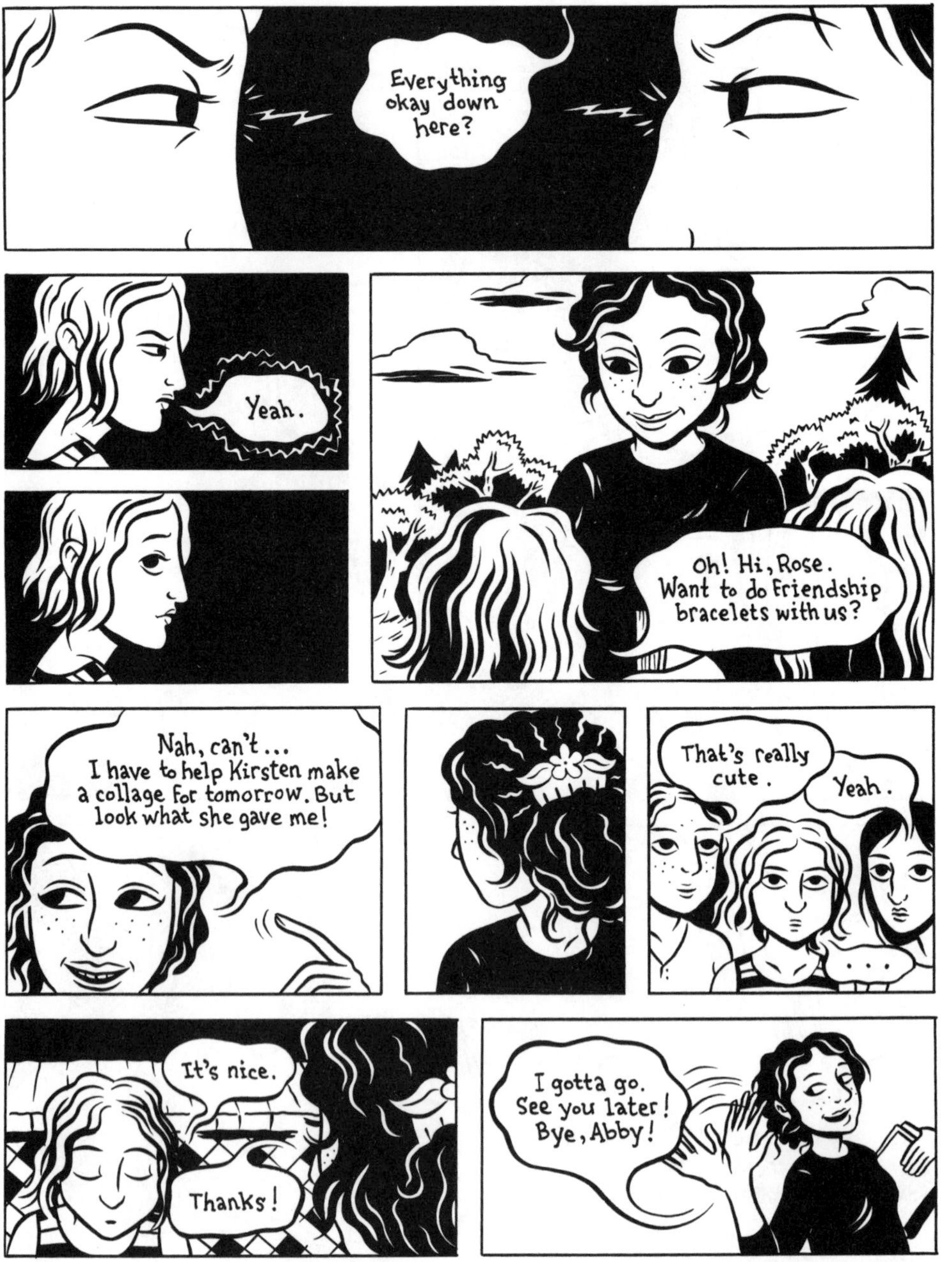
Everything okay down here?
Yeah.
Oh! Hi, Rose. Want to do friendship bracelets with us?
Nah, can't... I have to help Kirsten make a collage for tomorrow. But look what she gave me!
That's really cute.
Yeah.
...
It's nice.
Thanks!
I gotta go. See you later! Bye, Abby!

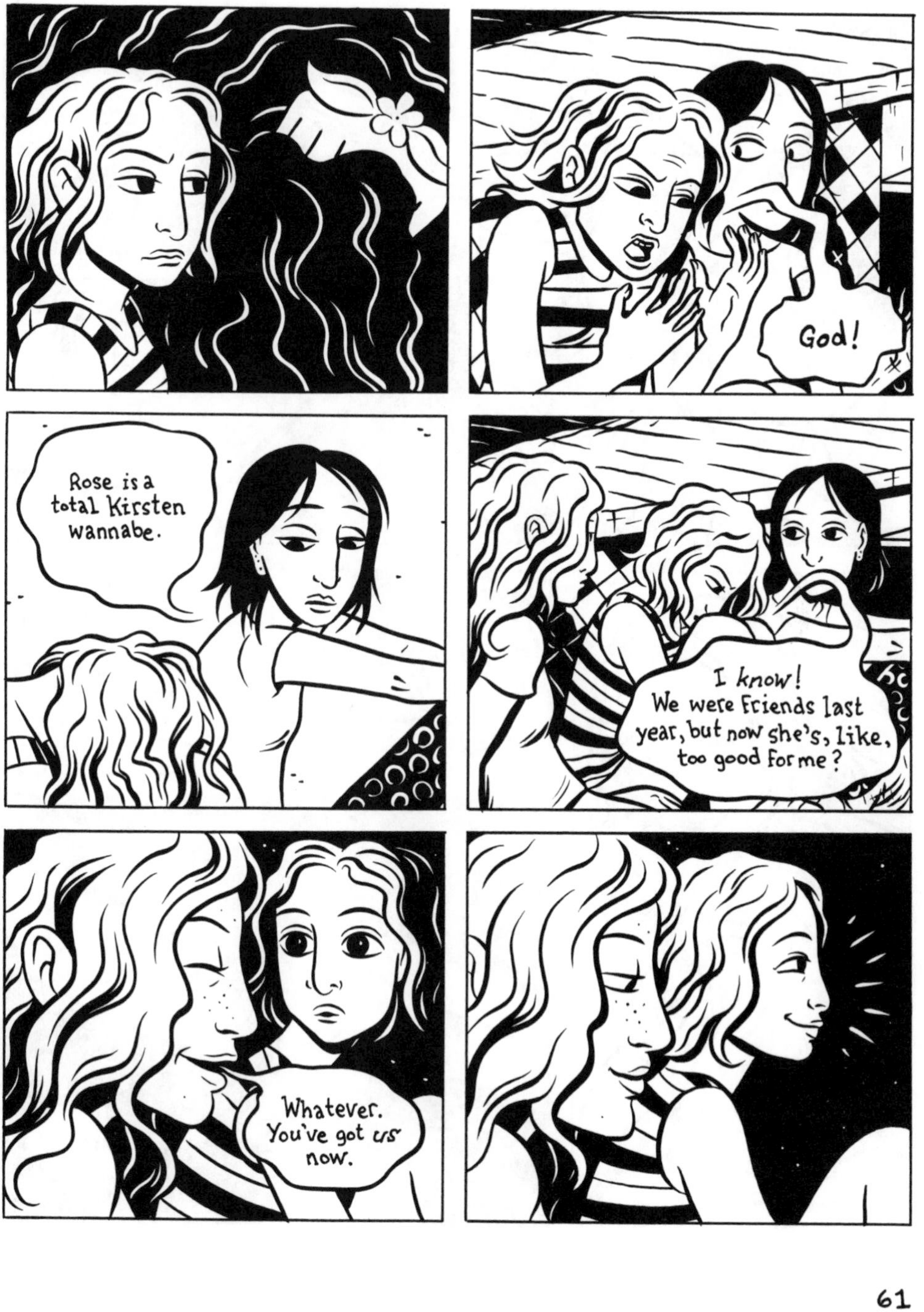
God!
Rose is a total Kirsten wannabe.
I know! We were friends last year, but now she's, like, too good for me?
Whatever. You've got us now.

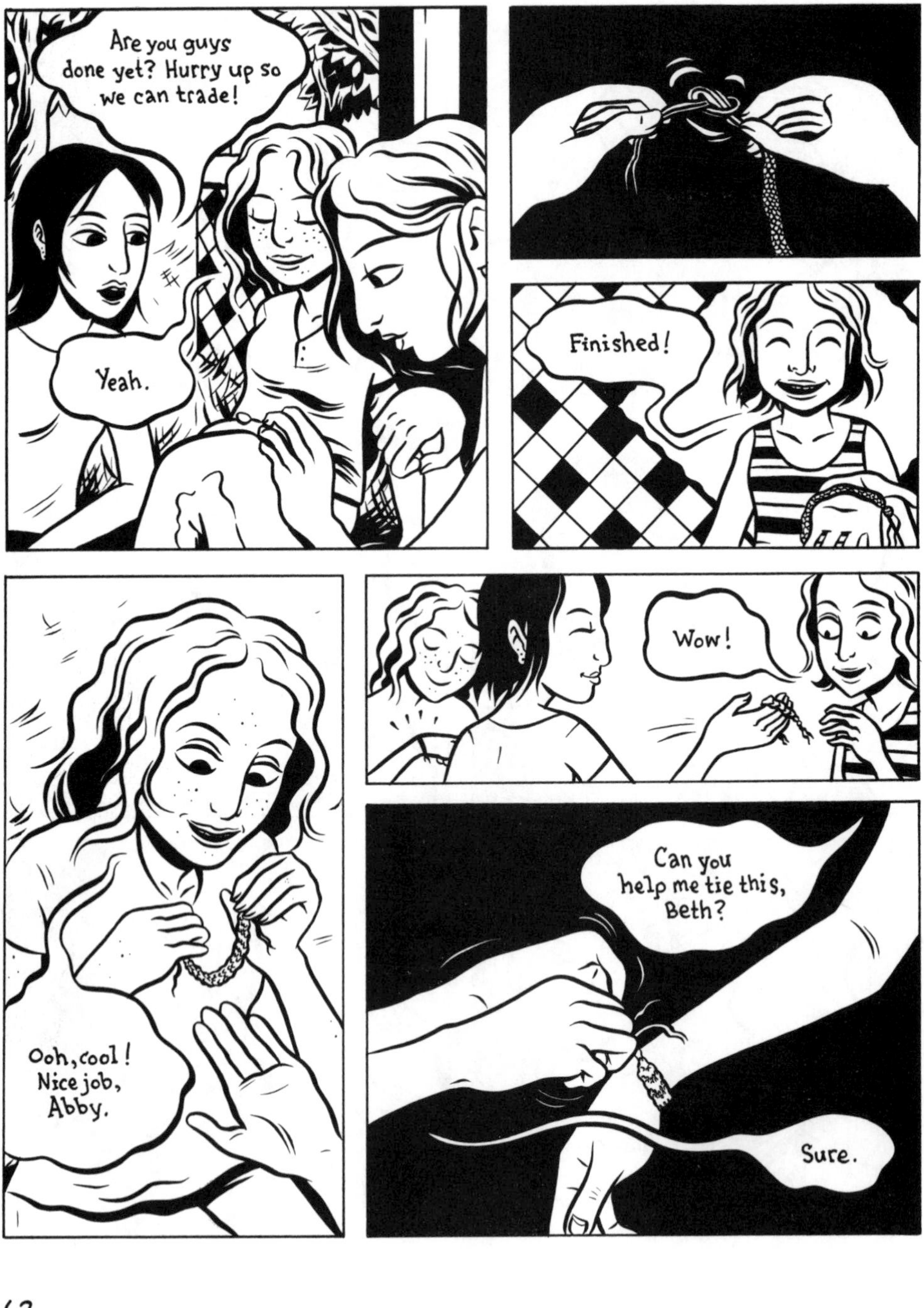
Are you guys done yet? Hurry up so we can trade!
Yeah.
Finished!
Ooh, cool! Nice job, Abby.
Wow!
Can you help me tie this, Beth?
Sure.

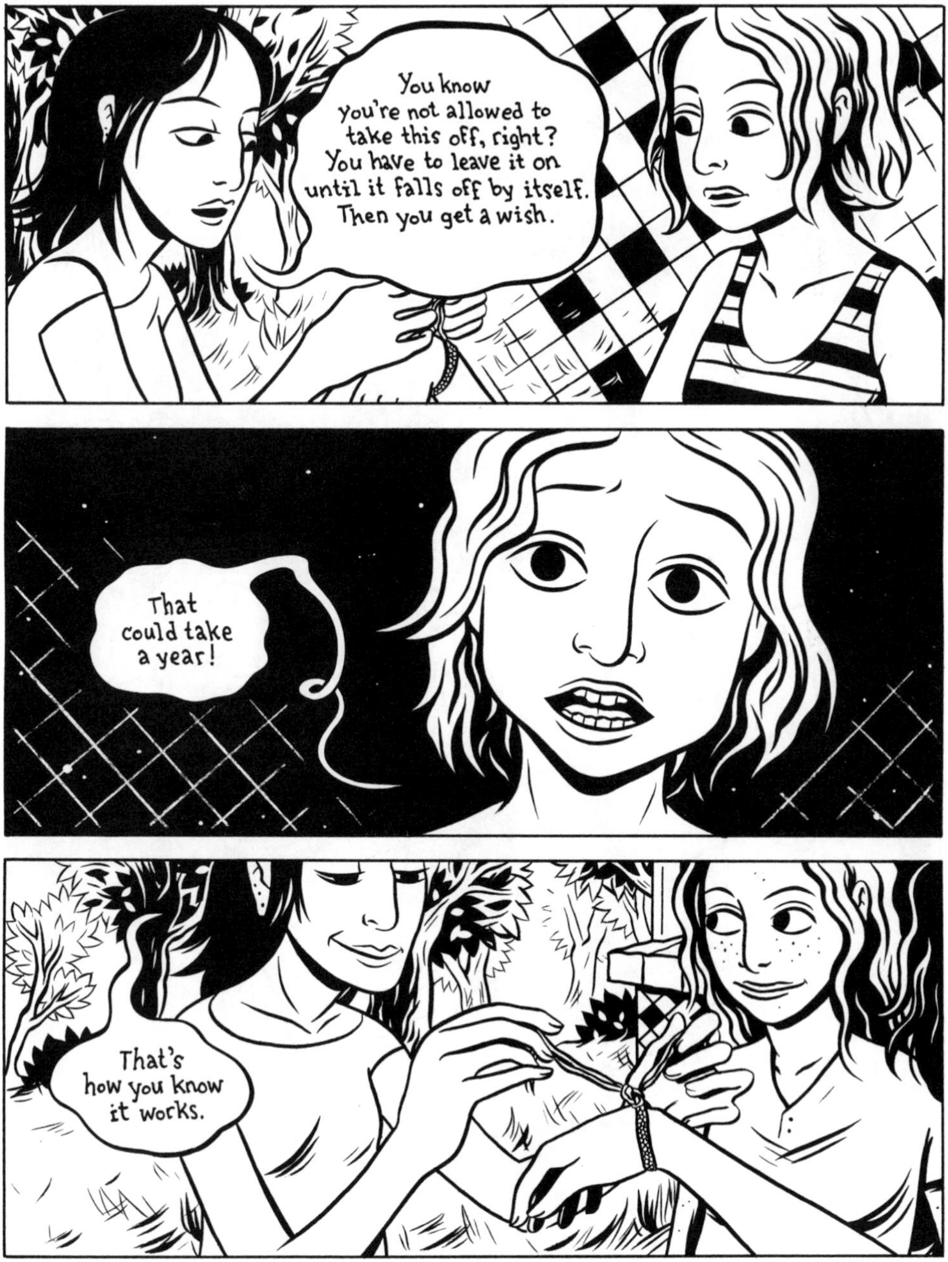
You know you're not allowed to take this off, right? You have to leave it on until it falls off by itself. Then you get a wish.
That could take a year!
That's how you know it works.

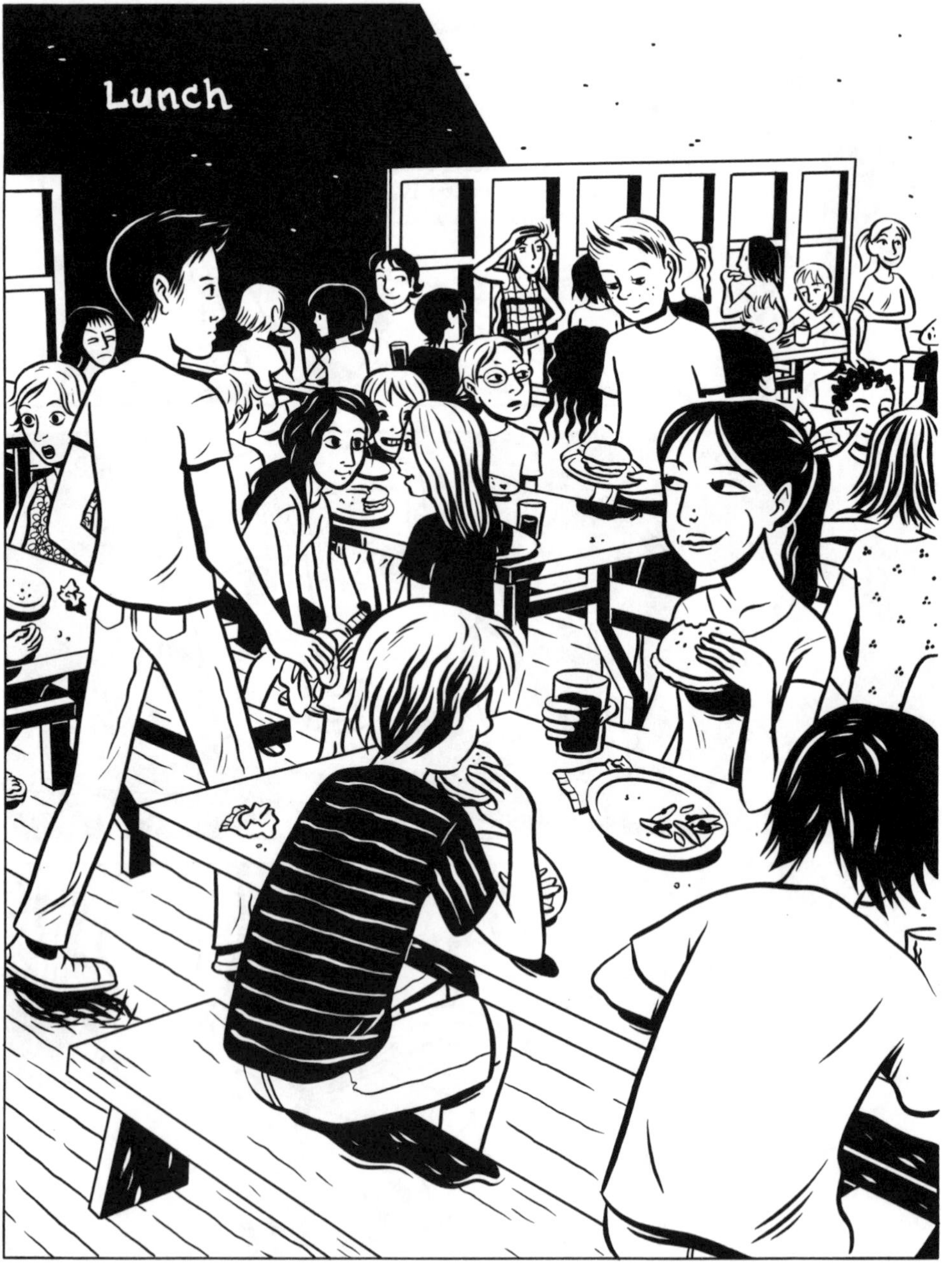
Lunch

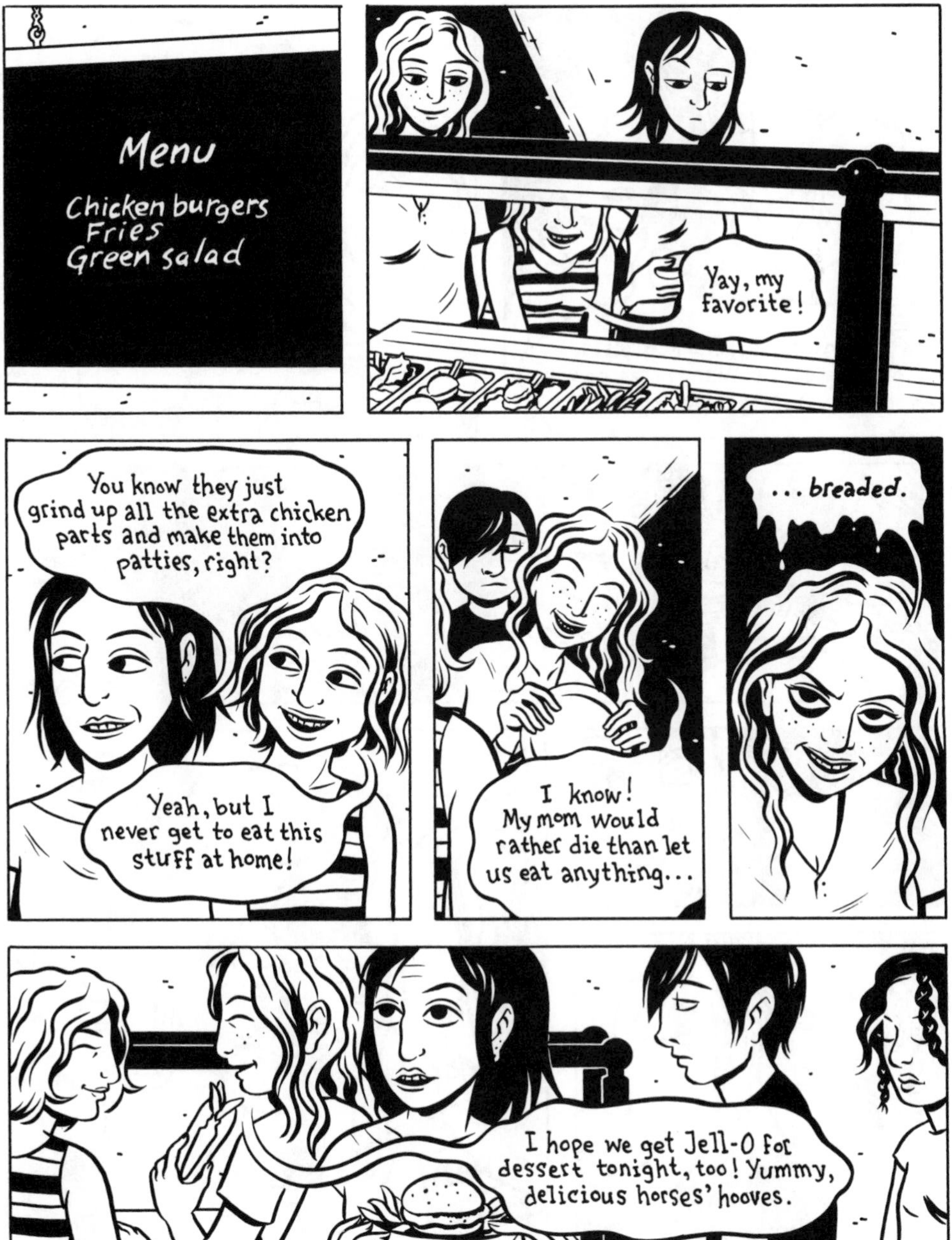
Menu
Chicken burgers
Fries
Green salad
Yay, my favorite!
You know they just grind up all the extra chicken parts and make them into patties, right?
Yeah, but I never get to eat this stuff at home!
I know! My mom would rather die than let us eat anything...
...breaded.
I hope we get Jell-O for dessert tonight, too! Yummy, delicious horses' hooves.

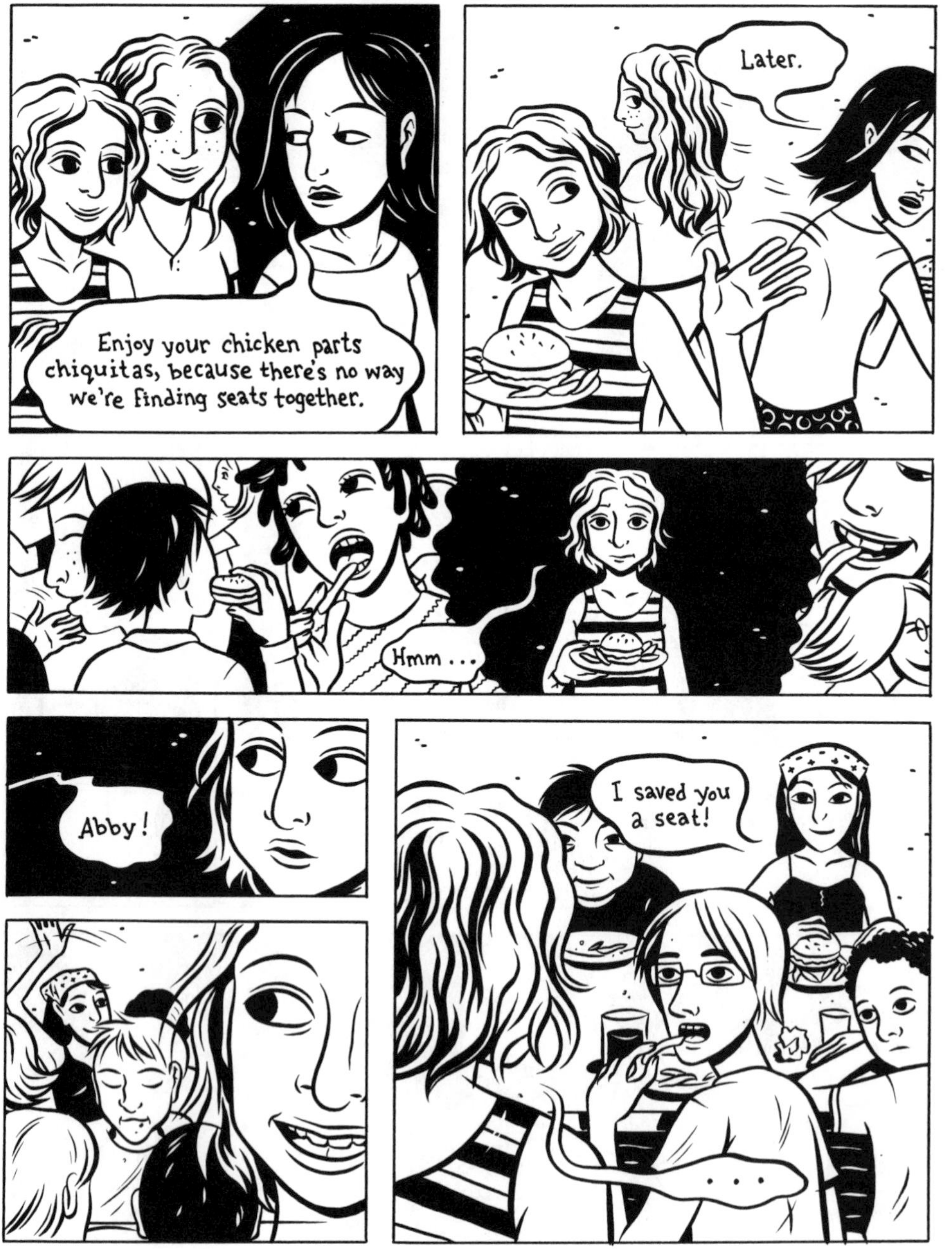
Enjoy your chicken parts chiquitas, because there's no way we're finding seats together.
Later.
Hmm . . .
Abby!
I saved you a seat!
. . .

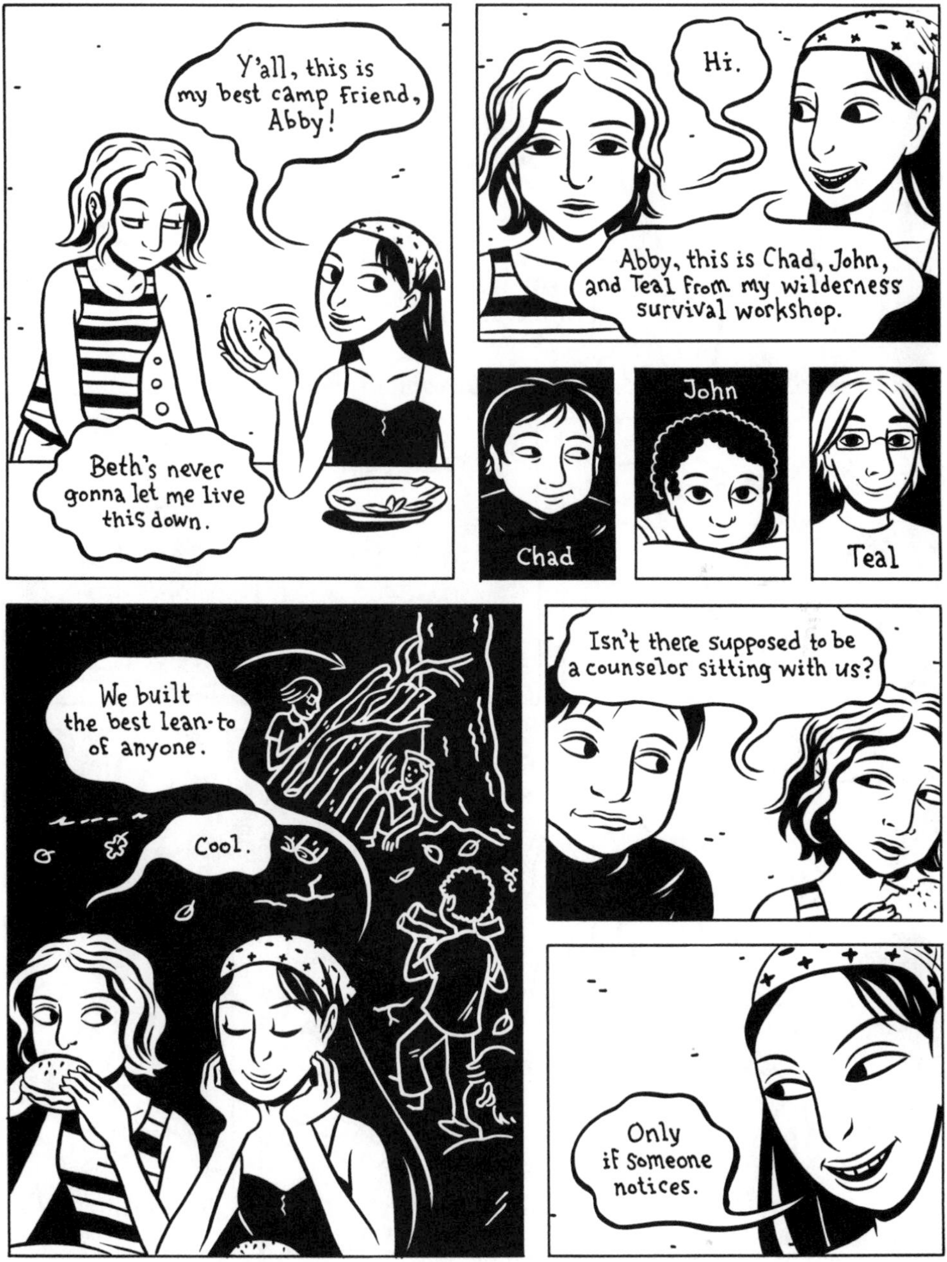

Y'all, this is my best camp friend, Abby!
Beth's never gonna let me live this down.
Hi.
Abby, this is Chad, John, and Teal from my wilderness survival workshop.
Chad
John
Teal
We built the best lean-to of anyone.
Cool.
Isn't there supposed to be a counselor sitting with us?
Only if someone notices.

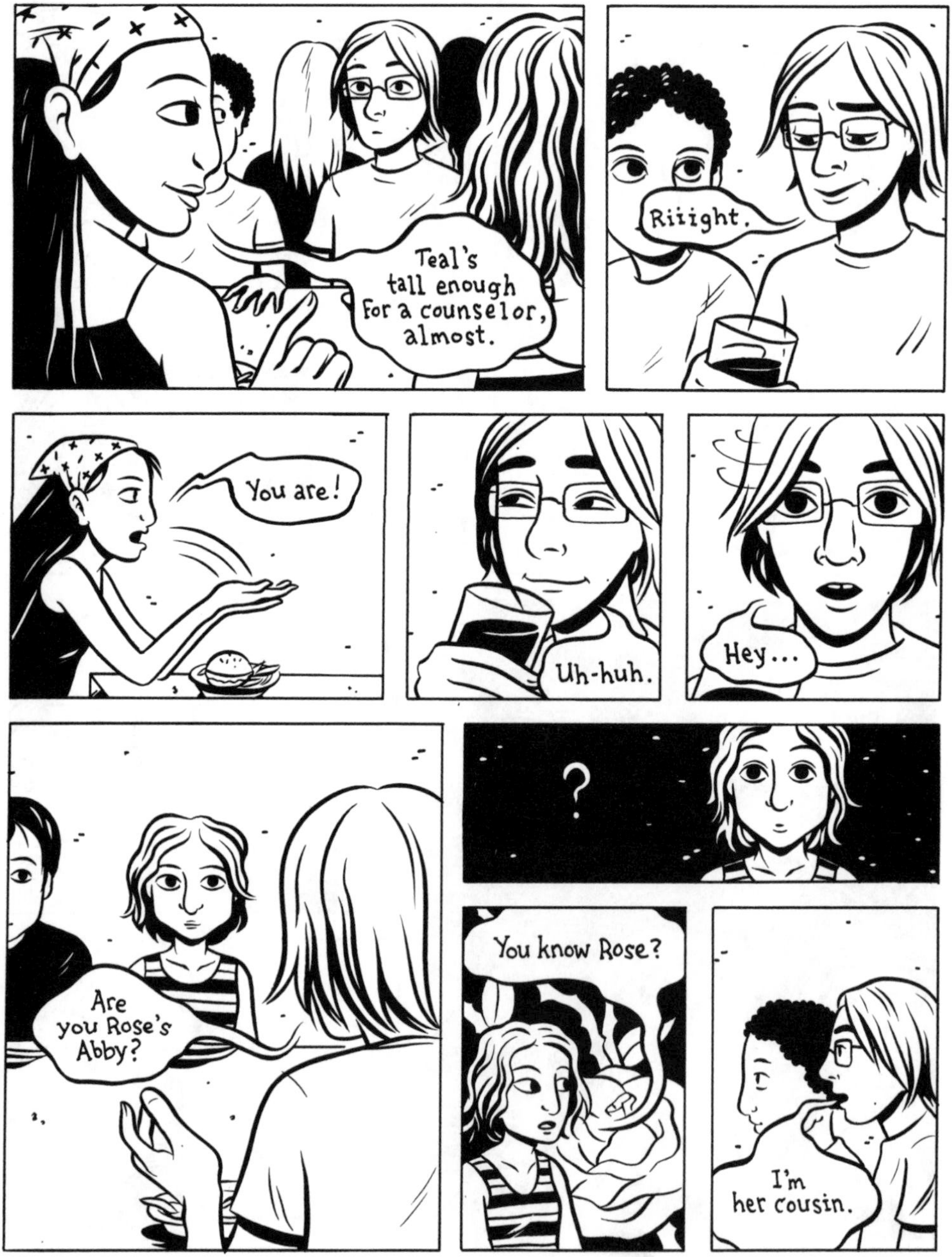
Teal's tall enough for a counselor, almost.
Riiight.
You are!
Uh-huh.
Hey...
?
Are you Rose's Abby?
You know Rose?
I'm her cousin.

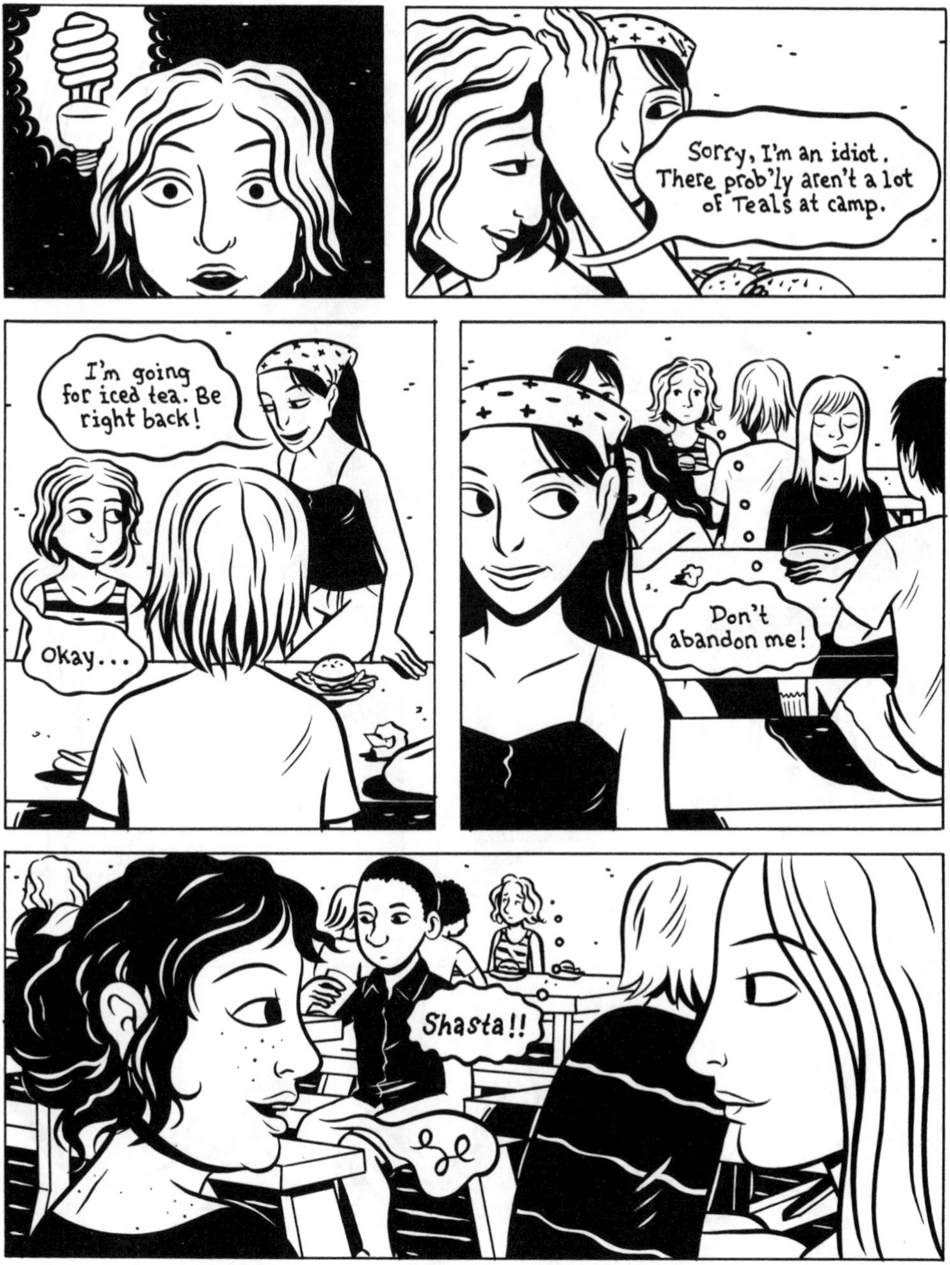
Sorry, I'm an idiot. There prob'ly aren't a lot of Teals at camp.
I'm going for iced tea. Be right back!
Okay...
Don't abandon me!
Shasta!!

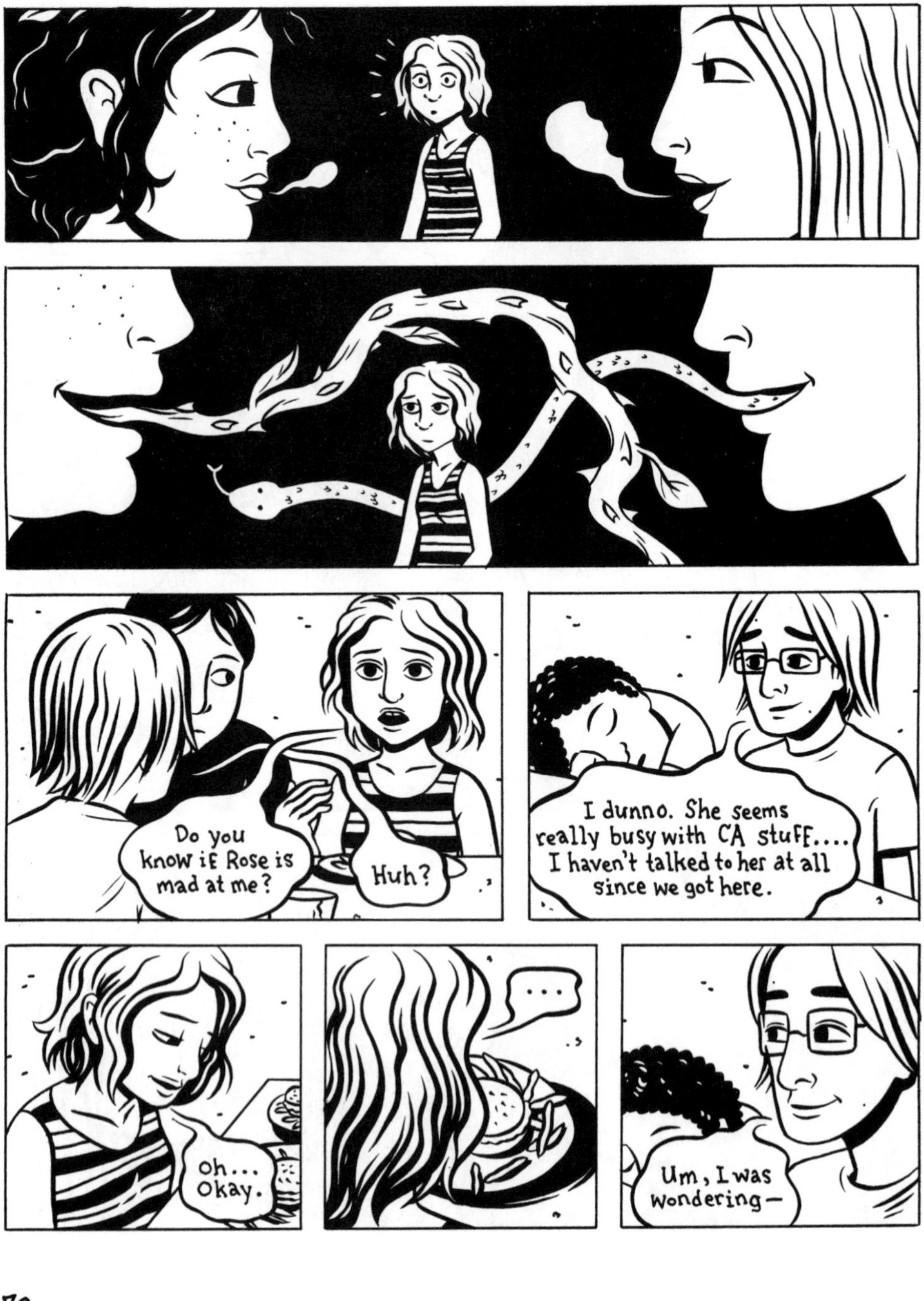
Do you know if Rose is mad at me?
Huh?
I dunno. She seems really busy with CA stuff.... I haven't talked to her at all since we got here.
Oh... Okay.
...
Um, I was wondering—

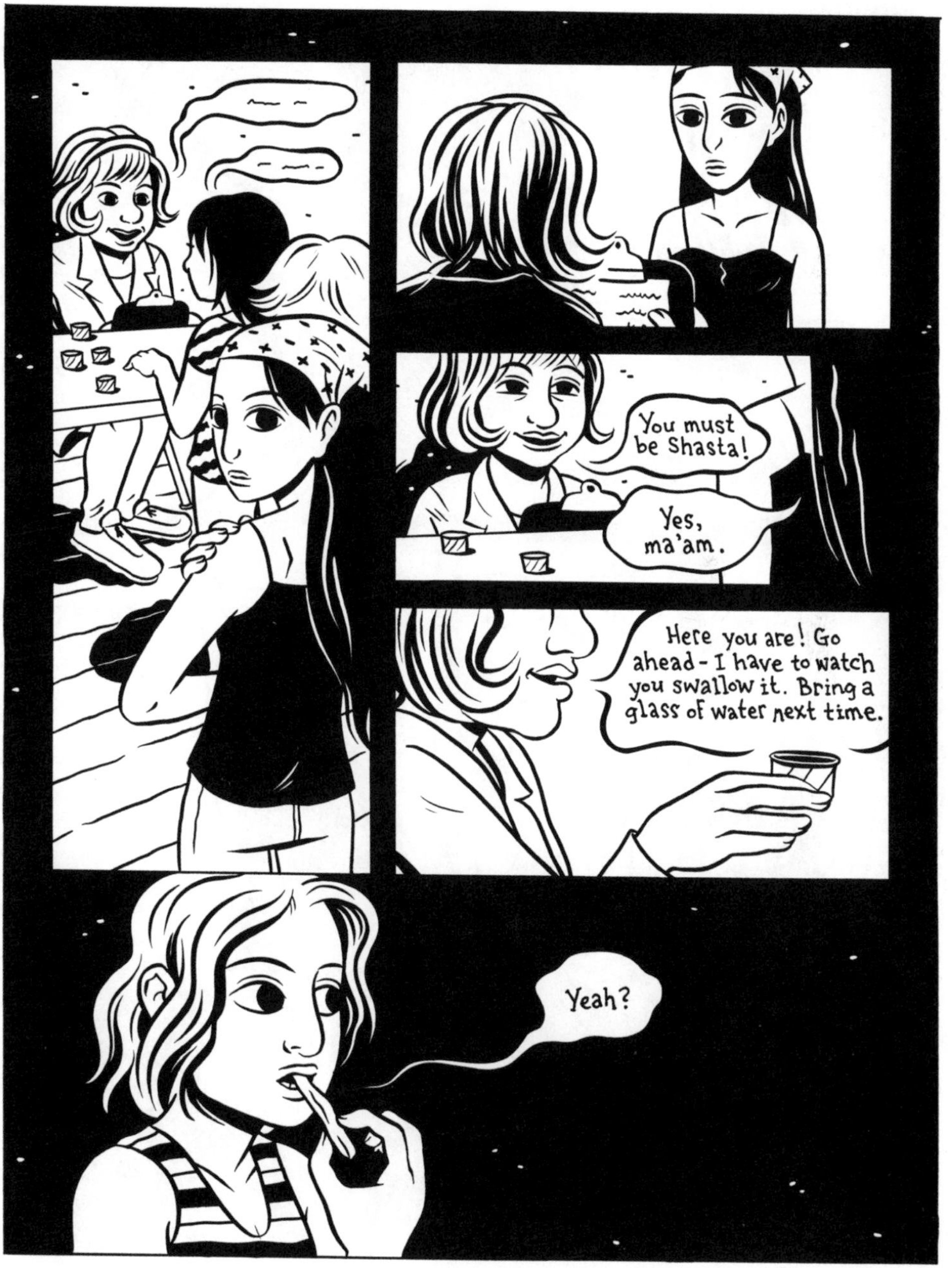
You must be Shasta!
Yes, ma'am.
Here you are! Go ahead - I have to watch you swallow it. Bring a glass of water next time.
Yeah?

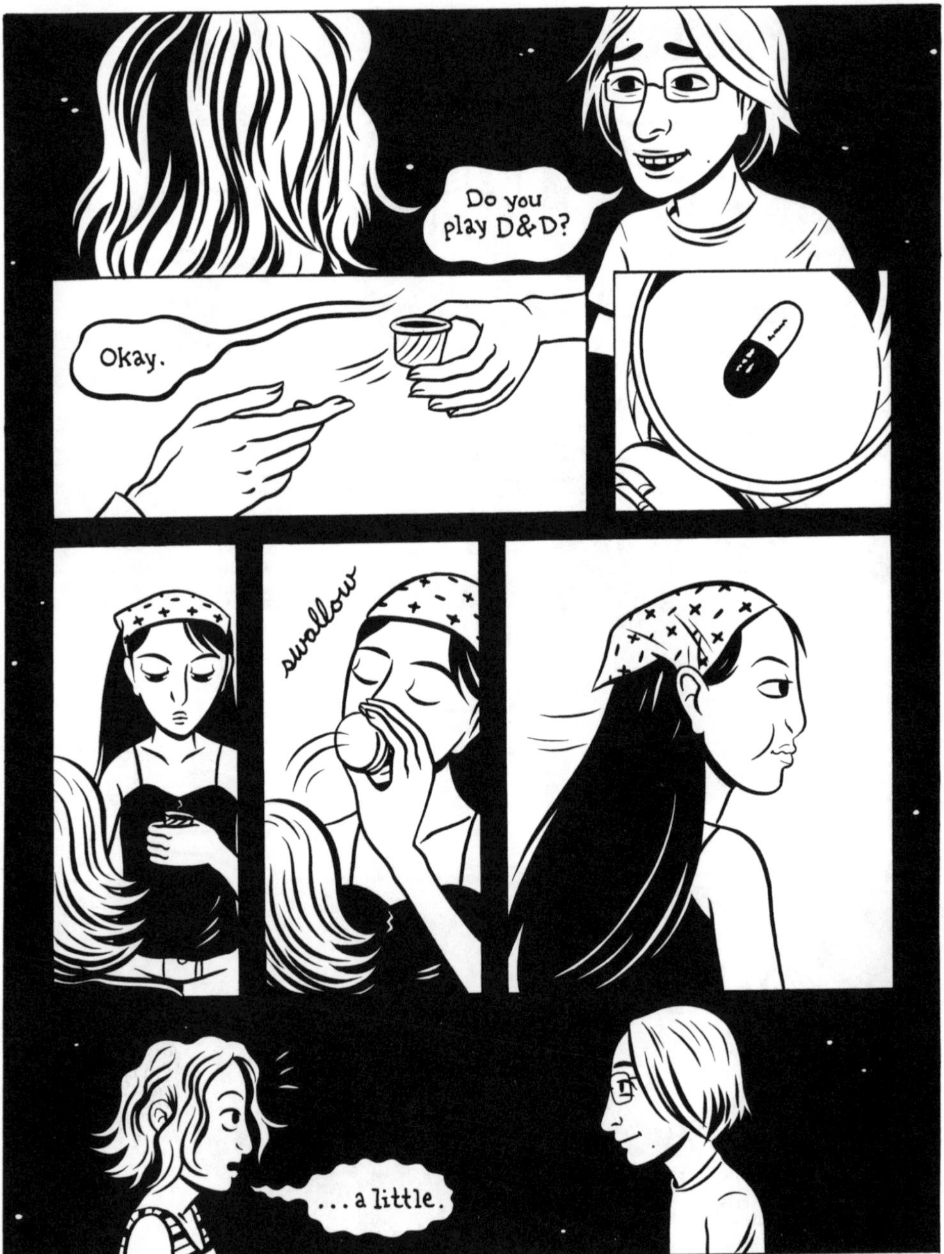
Do you play D&D?
Okay.
swallow
...a little.

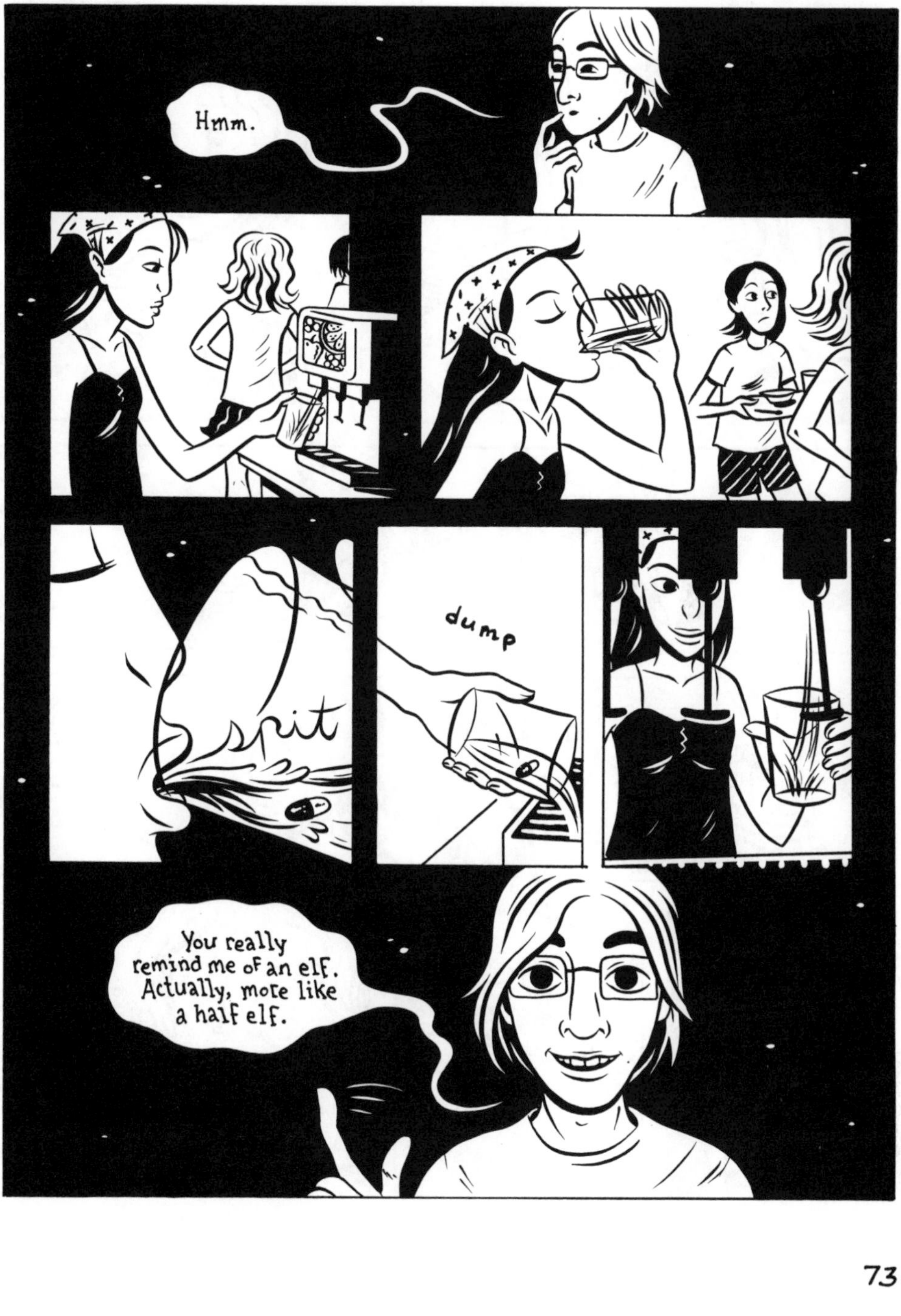
Hmm.
spit
dump
You really remind me of an elf. Actually, more like a half elf.

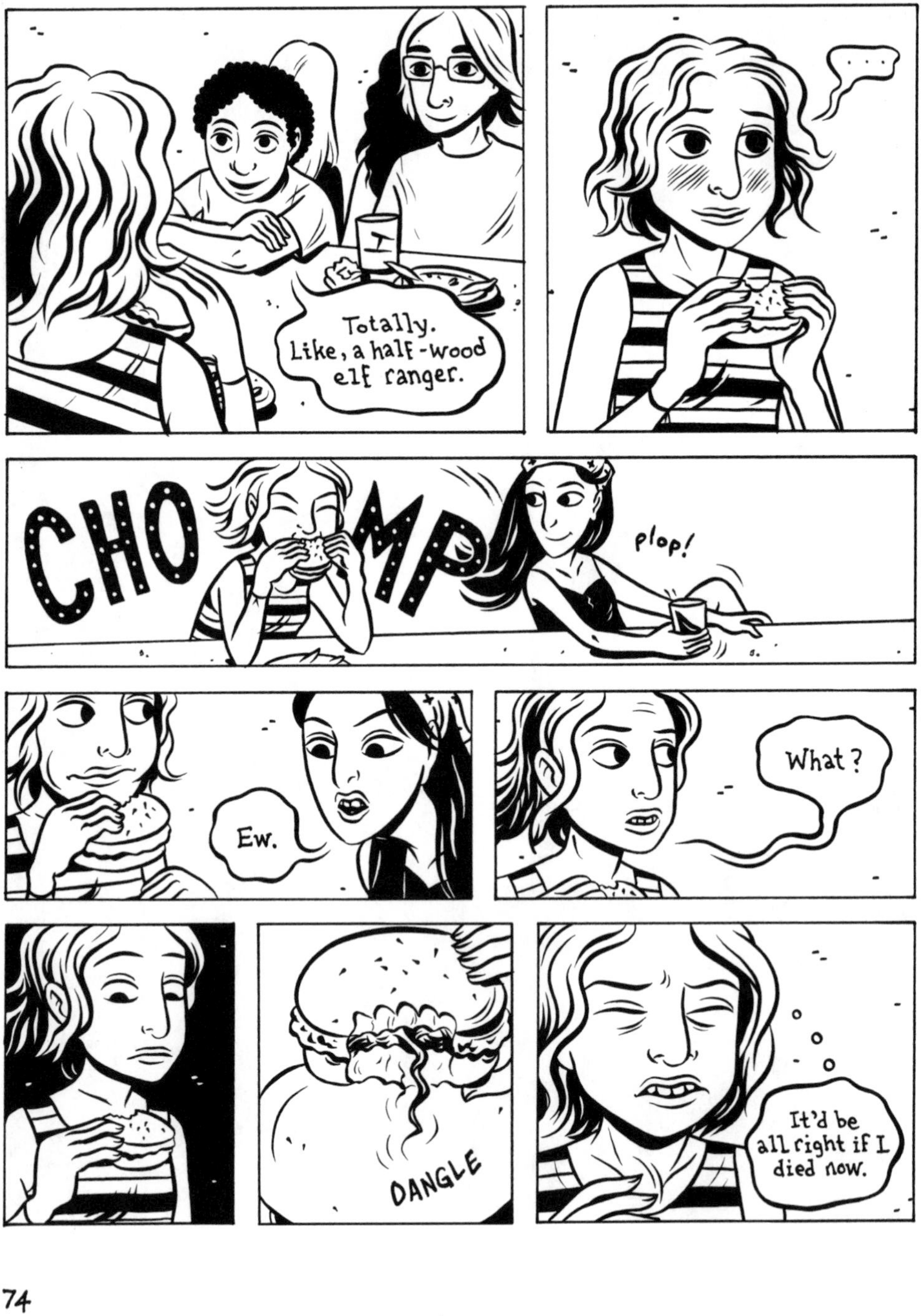
Totally. Like, a half-wood elf ranger.
. . .
CHOMP
plop!
Ew.
What?
DANGLE
It'd be all right if I died now.

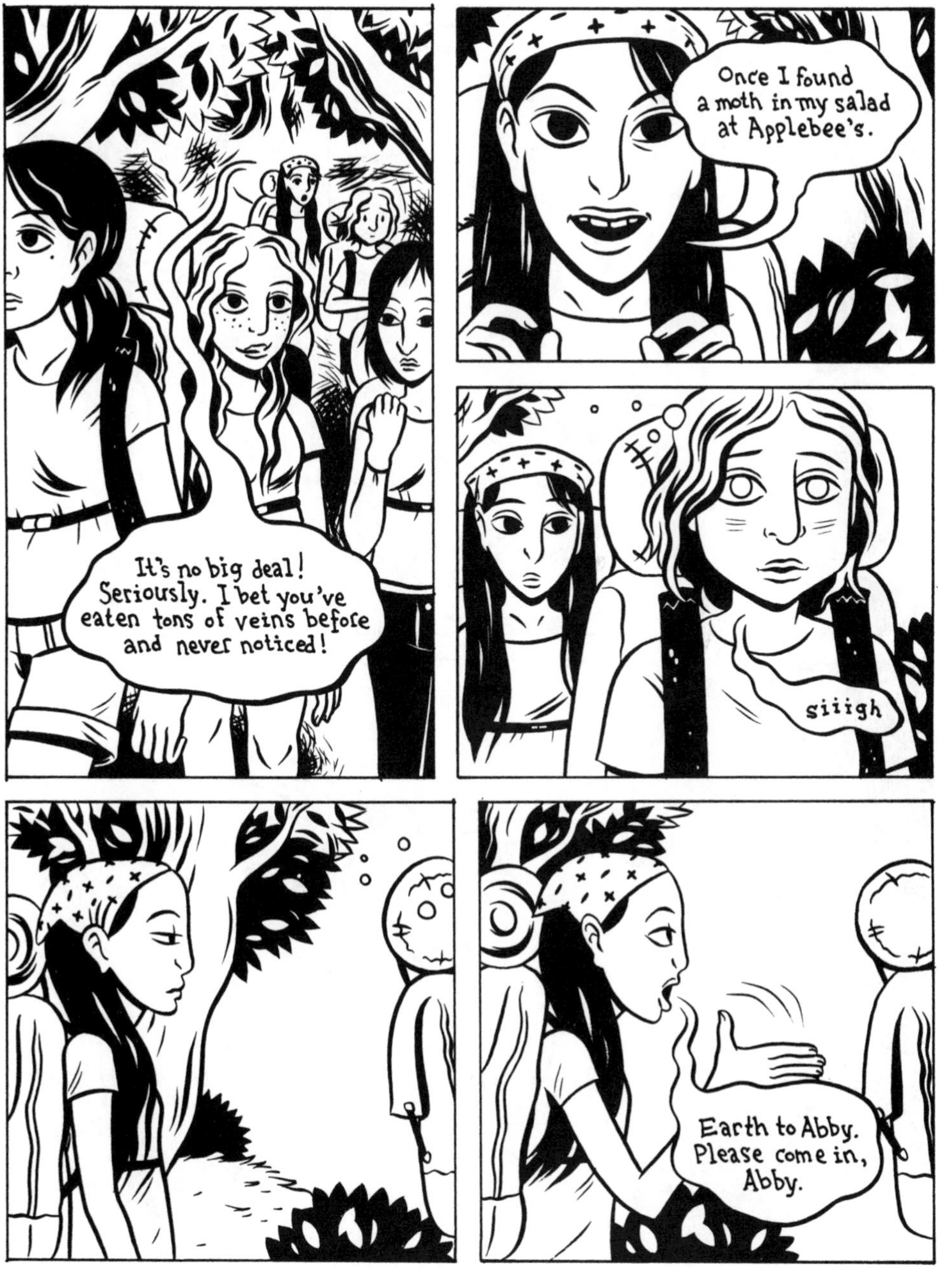
It's no big deal! Seriously. I bet you've eaten tons of veins before and never noticed!
Once I found a moth in my salad at Applebee's.
siiigh
Earth to Abby. Please come in, Abby.

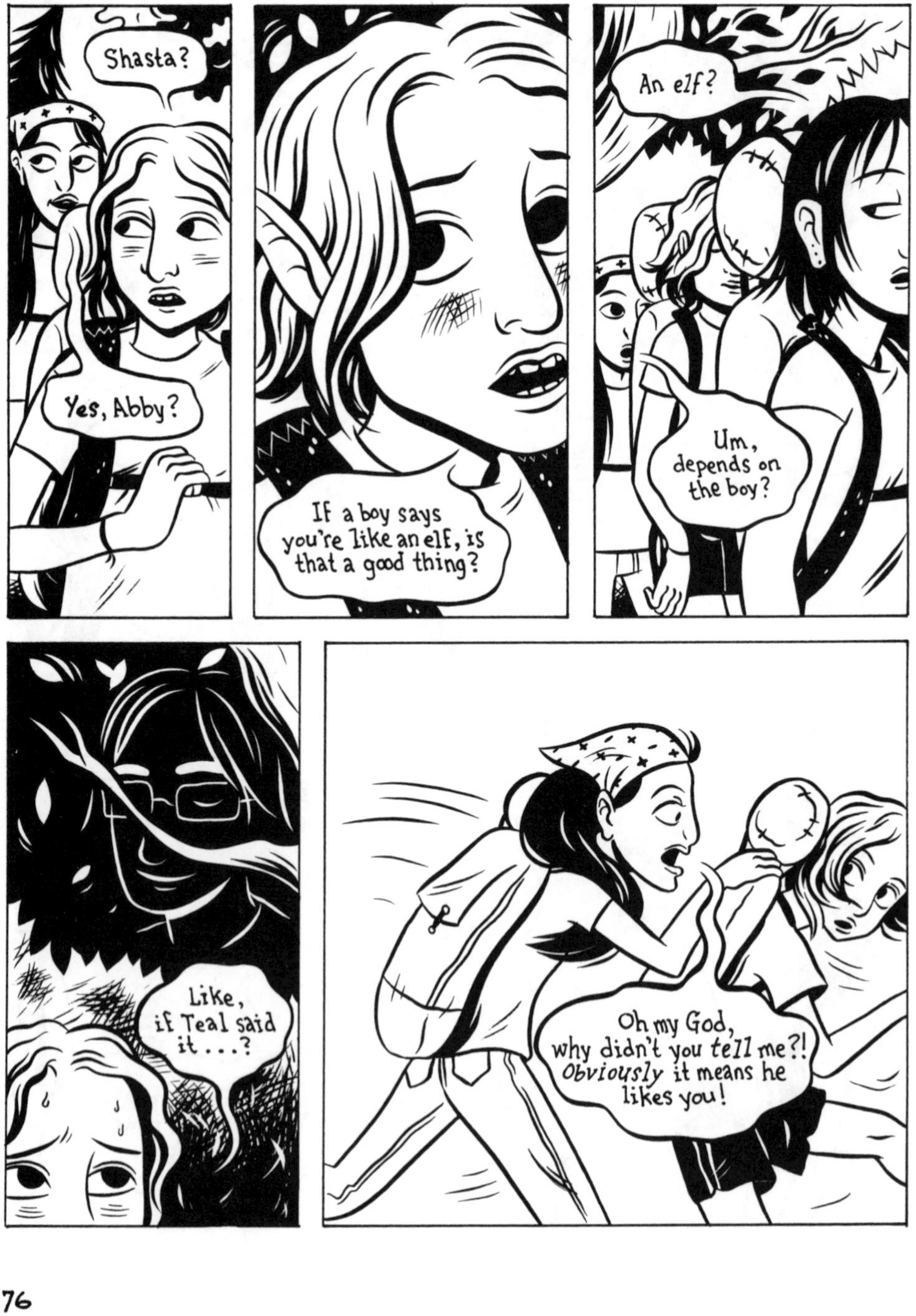
Shasta?
Yes, Abby?
If a boy says you're like an elf, is that a good thing?
An elf?
Um, depends on the boy?
Like, if Teal said it . . .?
Oh my God, why didn't you *tell* me?! *Obviously* it means he likes you!

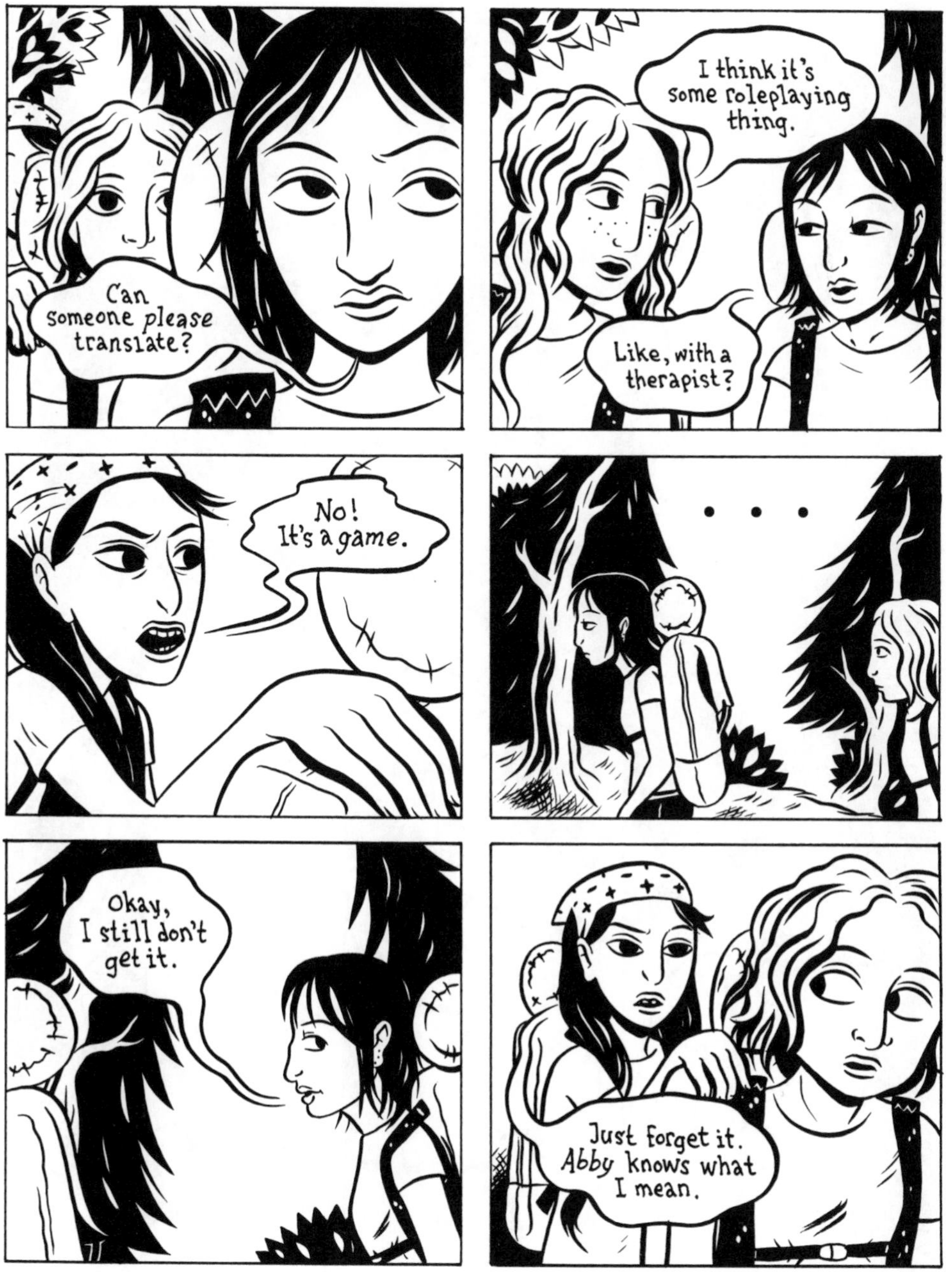

Can someone *please* translate?
I think it's some roleplaying thing.
Like, with a therapist?
No! It's a *game*.
• • •
Okay, I still don't get it.
Just forget it. Abby knows what I mean.

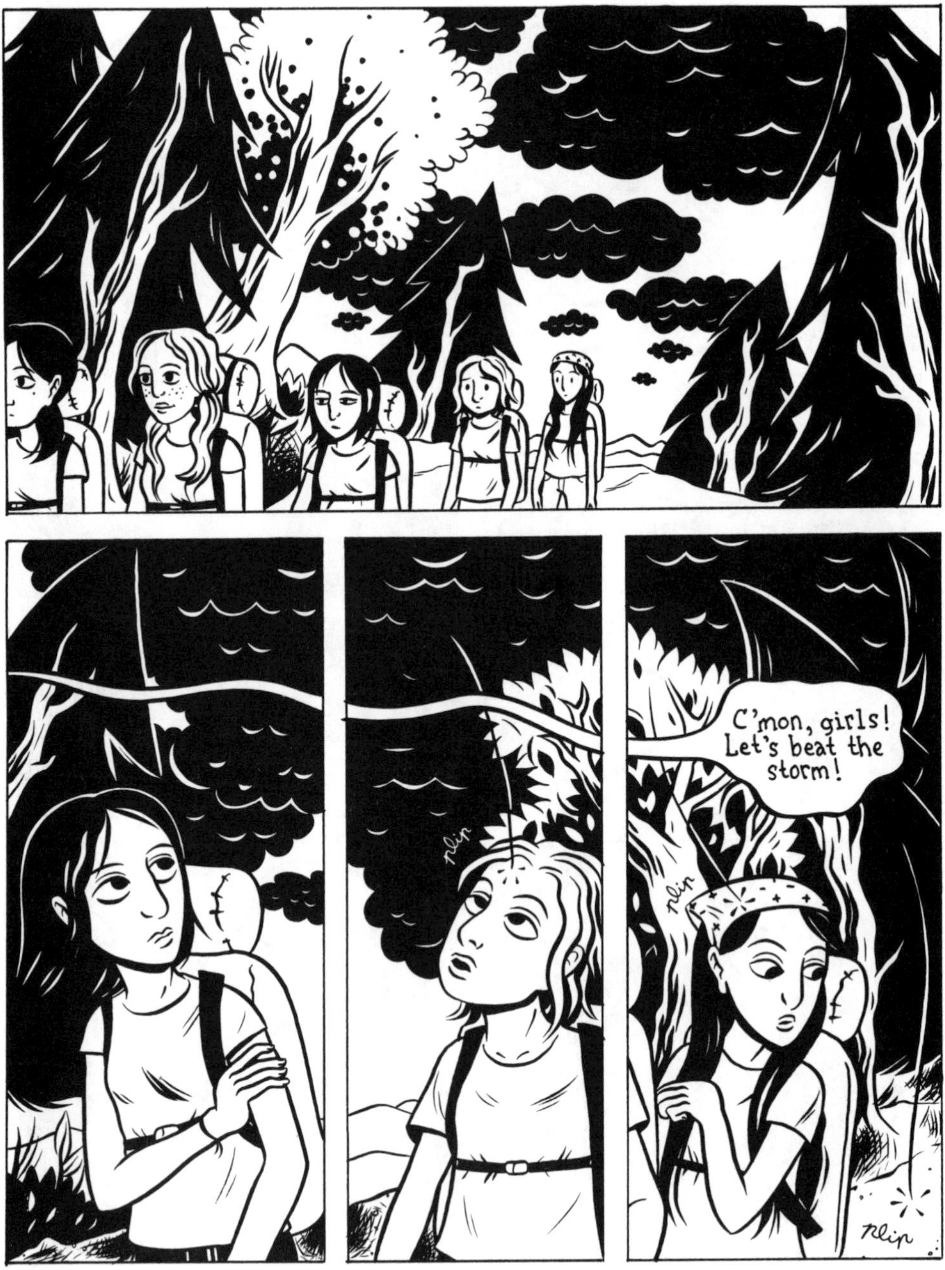
plip
C'mon, girls! Let's beat the storm!
plip
plip

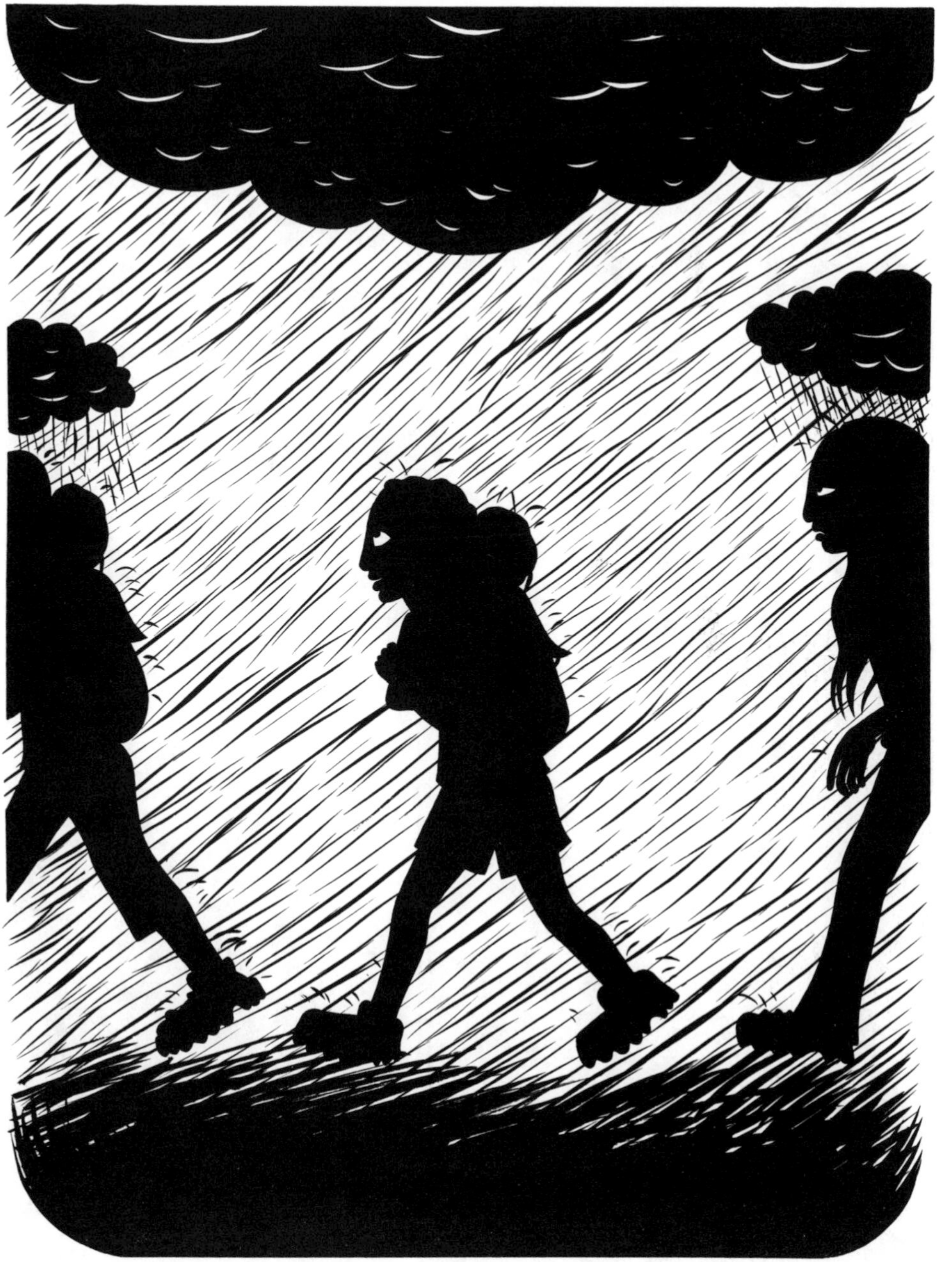

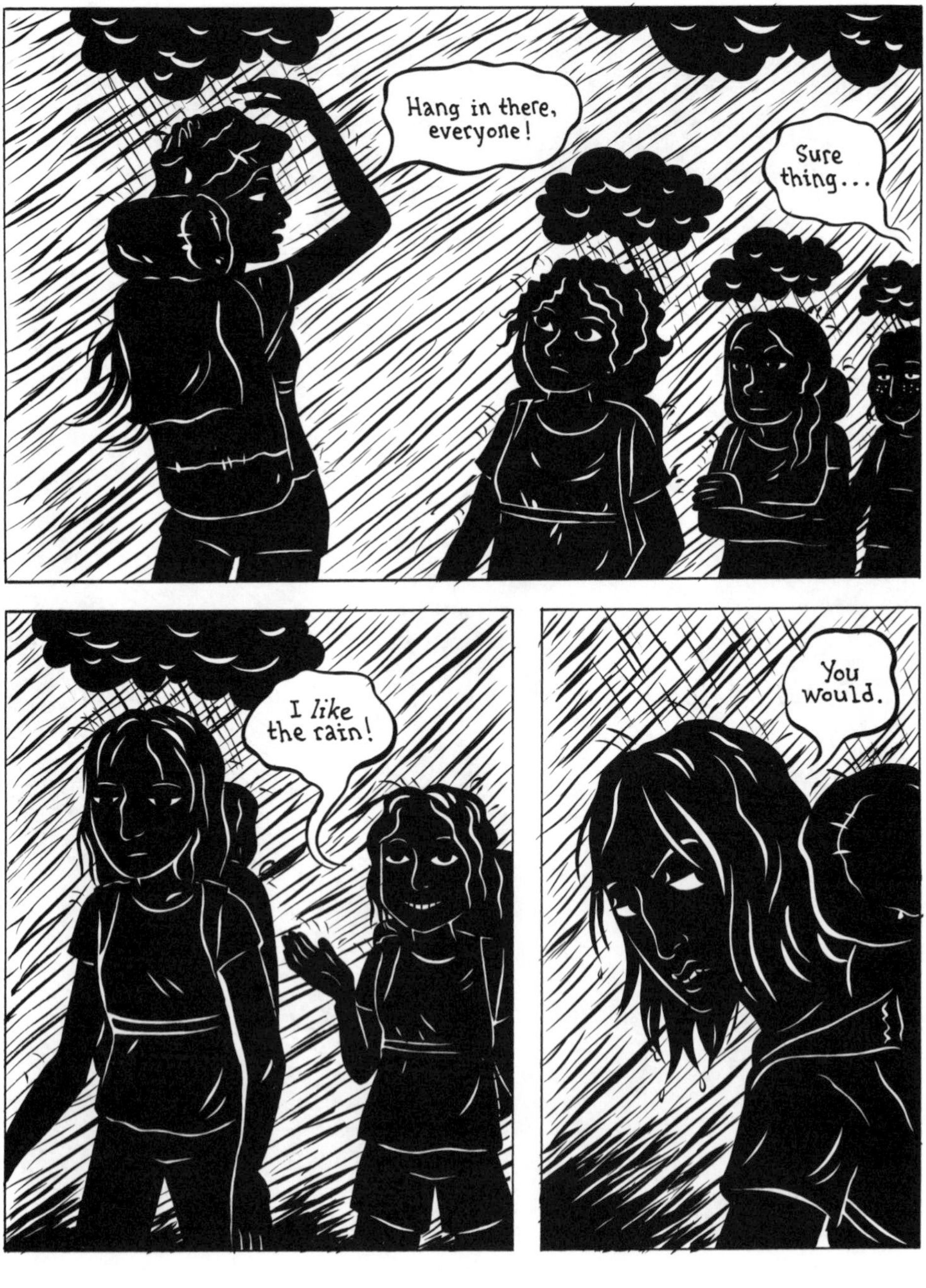
Hang in there, everyone!
Sure thing...
I *like* the rain!
You would.

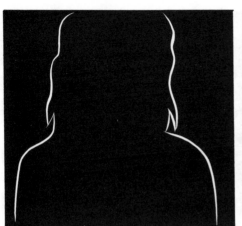

In olden times, during the Civil War, there was a boy named Timothy Blake, who was a scout for the Union. One night he was in the mountains-not far from here-spying on a Confederate regiment, when he was caught and taken prisoner.

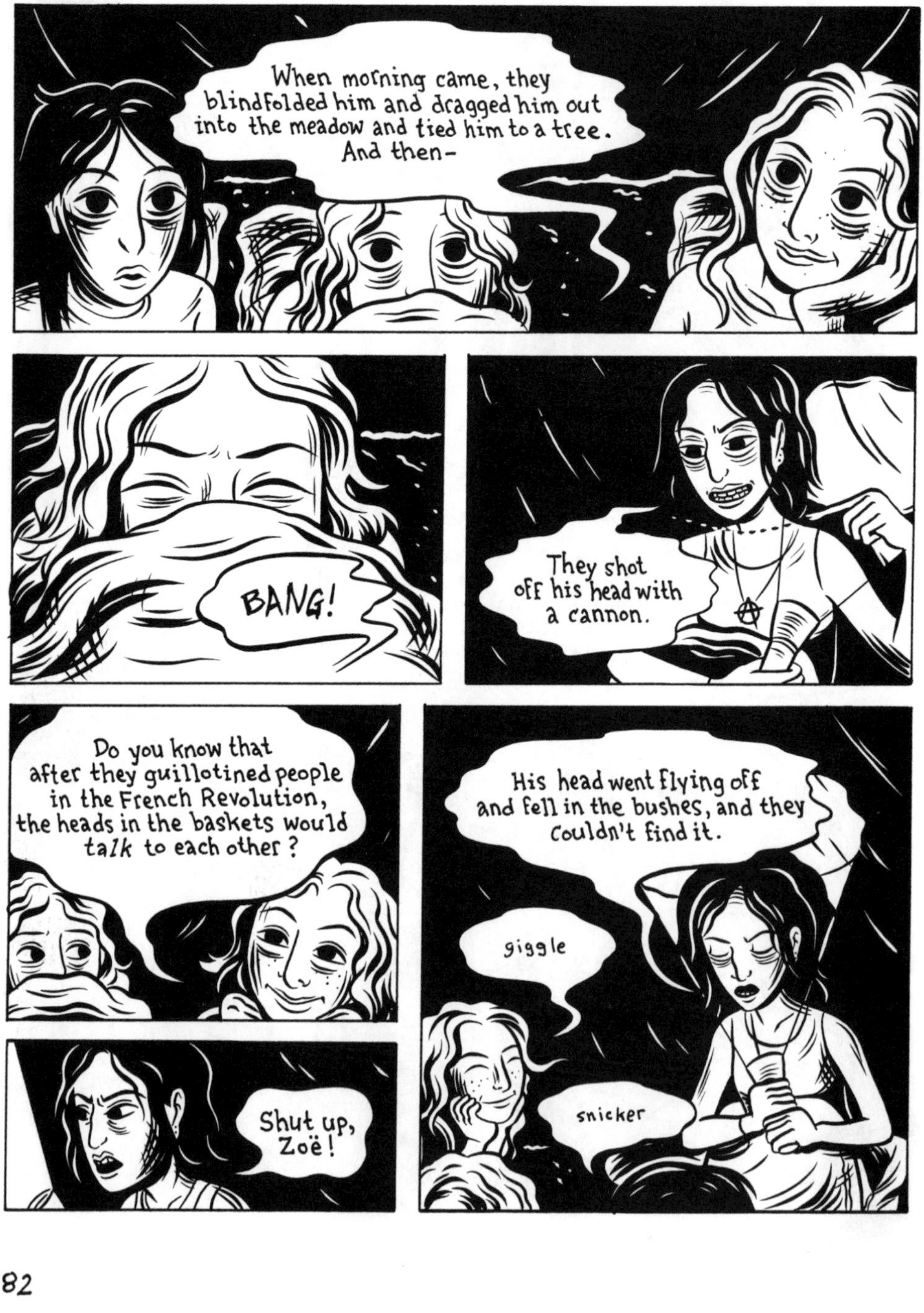
When morning came, they blindfolded him and dragged him out into the meadow and tied him to a tree. And then-
BANG!
They shot off his head with a cannon.
Do you know that after they guillotined people in the French Revolution, the heads in the baskets would *talk* to each other?
His head went flying off and fell in the bushes, and they couldn't find it.
giggle
snicker
Shut up, Zoë!

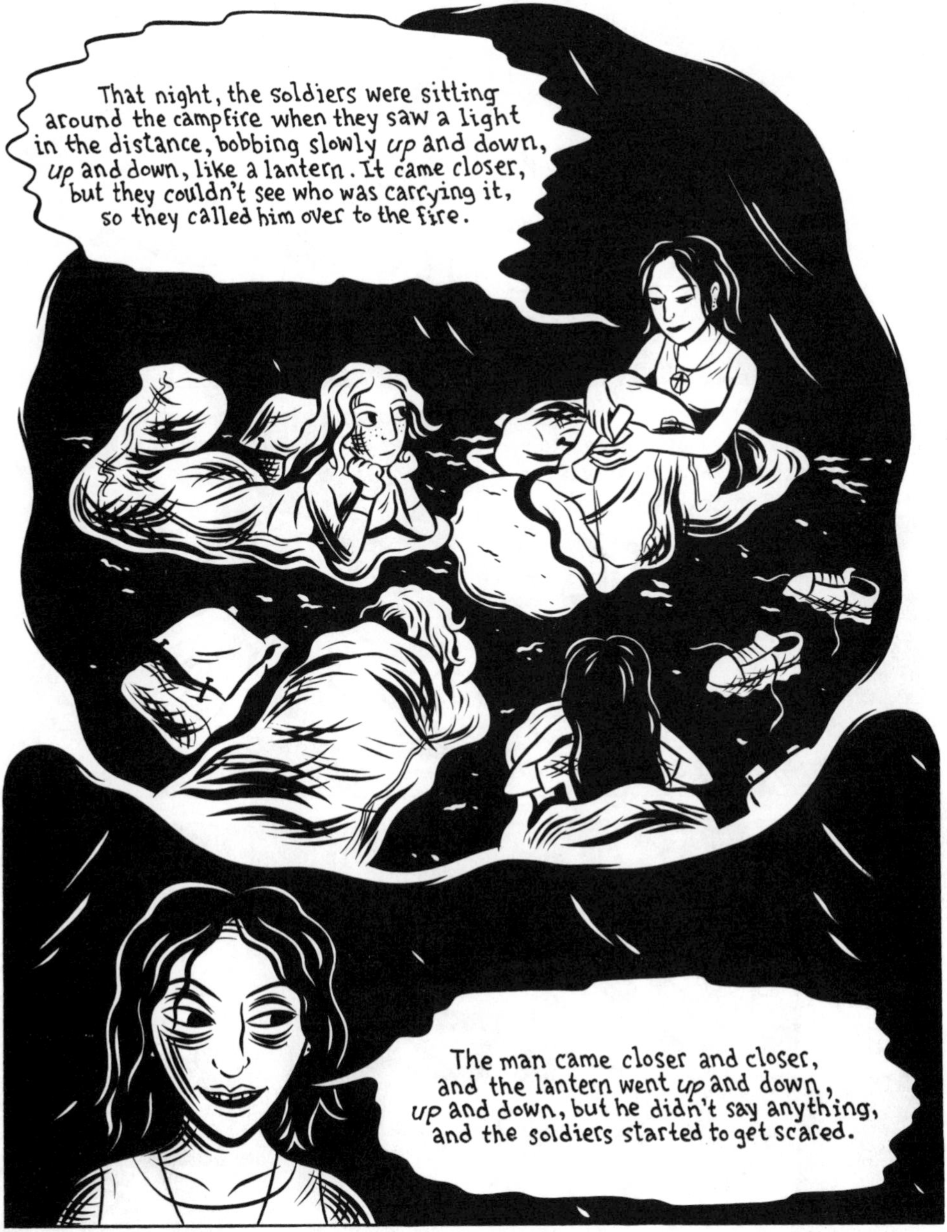
That night, the soldiers were sitting around the campfire when they saw a light in the distance, bobbing slowly *up* and down, *up* and down, like a lantern. It came closer, but they couldn't see who was carrying it, so they called him over to the fire.
The man came closer and closer, and the lantern went *up* and down, *up* and down, but he didn't say anything, and the soldiers started to get scared.

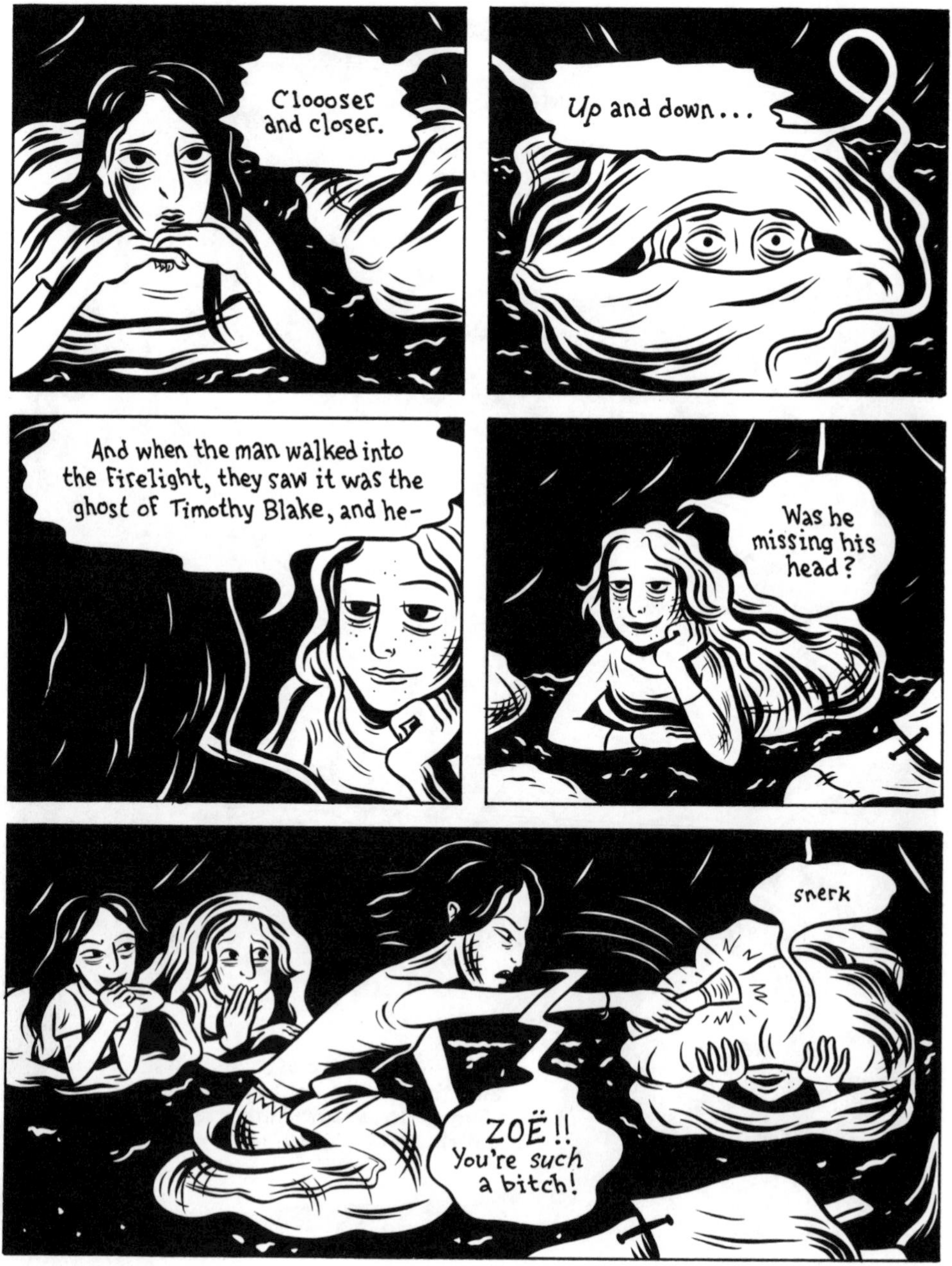

Cloooser and closer.
Up and down...
And when the man walked into the Firelight, they saw it was the ghost of Timothy Blake, and he-
Was he missing his head?
snerk
ZOË!! You're *such* a bitch!

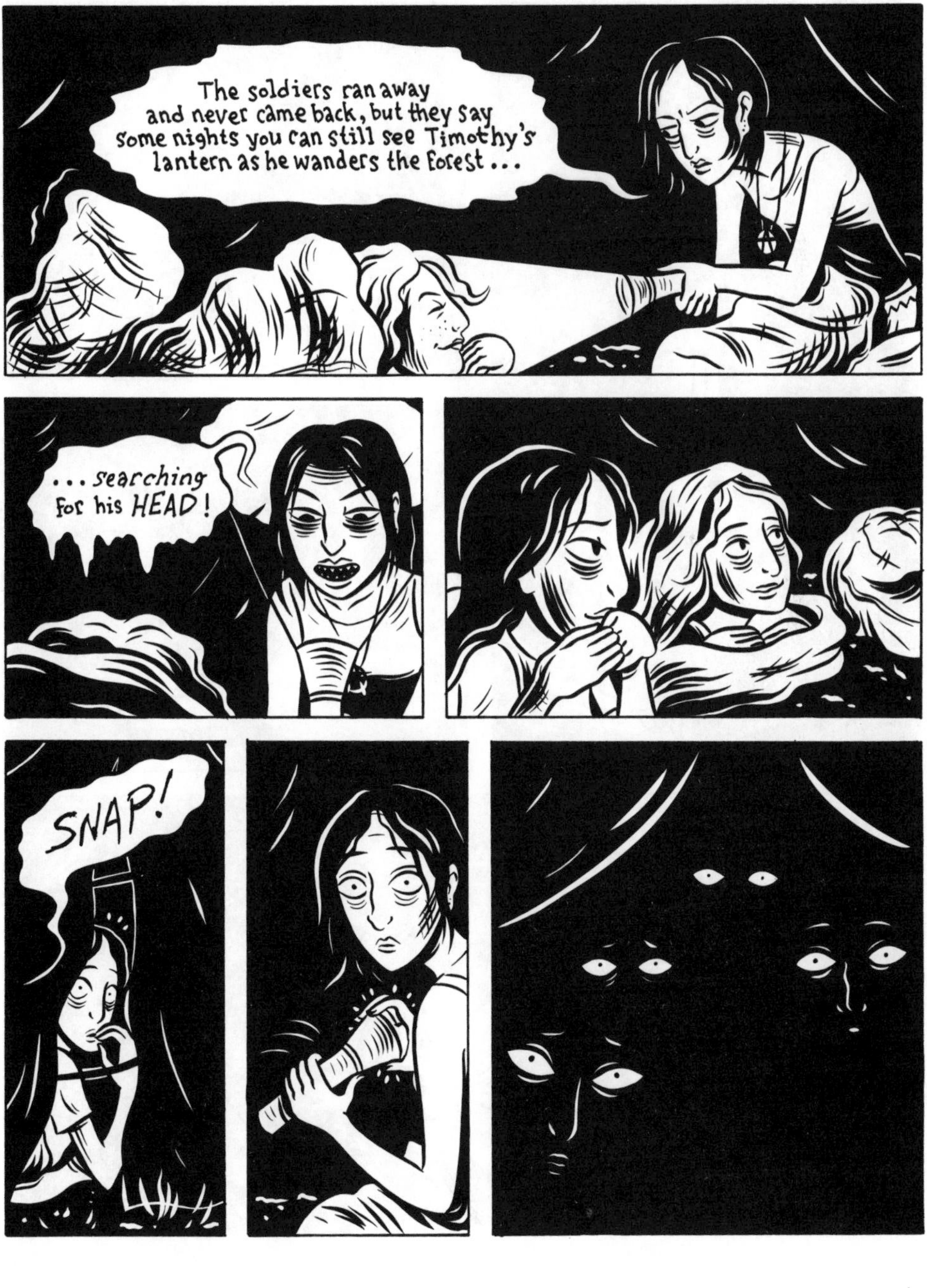
The soldiers ran away and never came back, but they say some nights you can still see Timothy's lantern as he wanders the forest...
...searching for his HEAD!
SNAP!

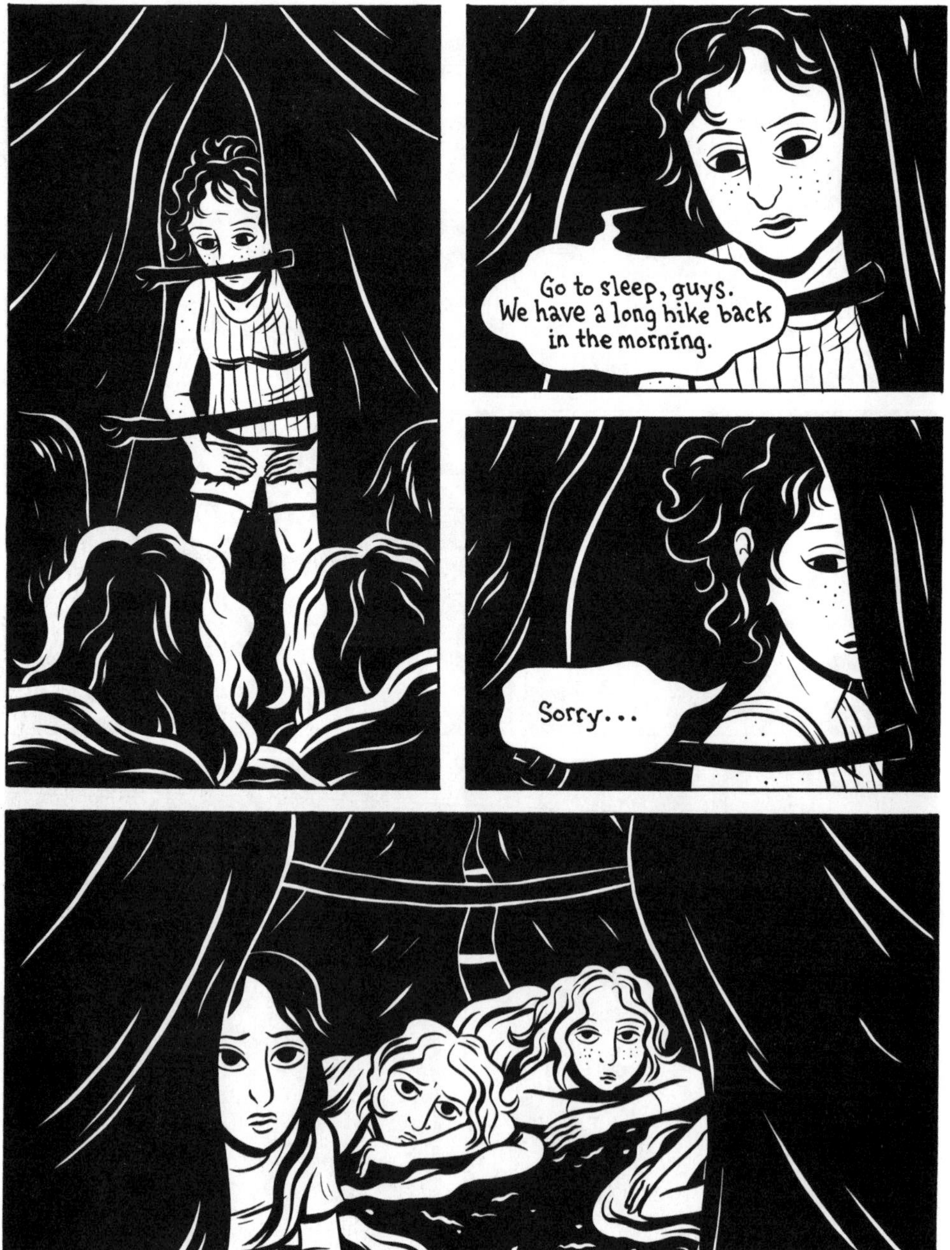
Go to sleep, guys. We have a long hike back in the morning.
Sorry...

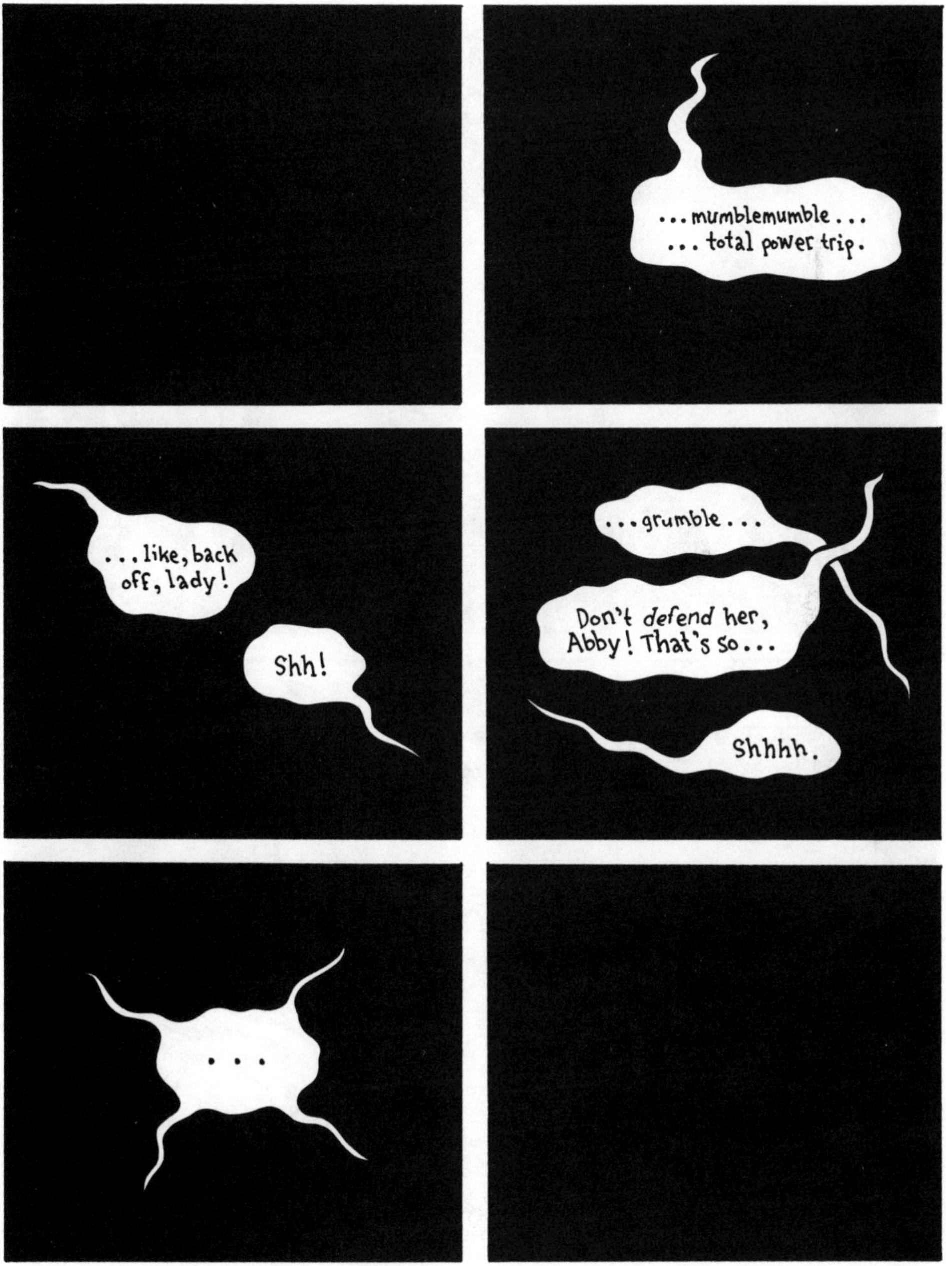
...mumblemumble...
...total power trip.
...like, back off, lady!
Shh!
...grumble...
Don't *defend* her, Abby! That's so...
Shhhh.
...

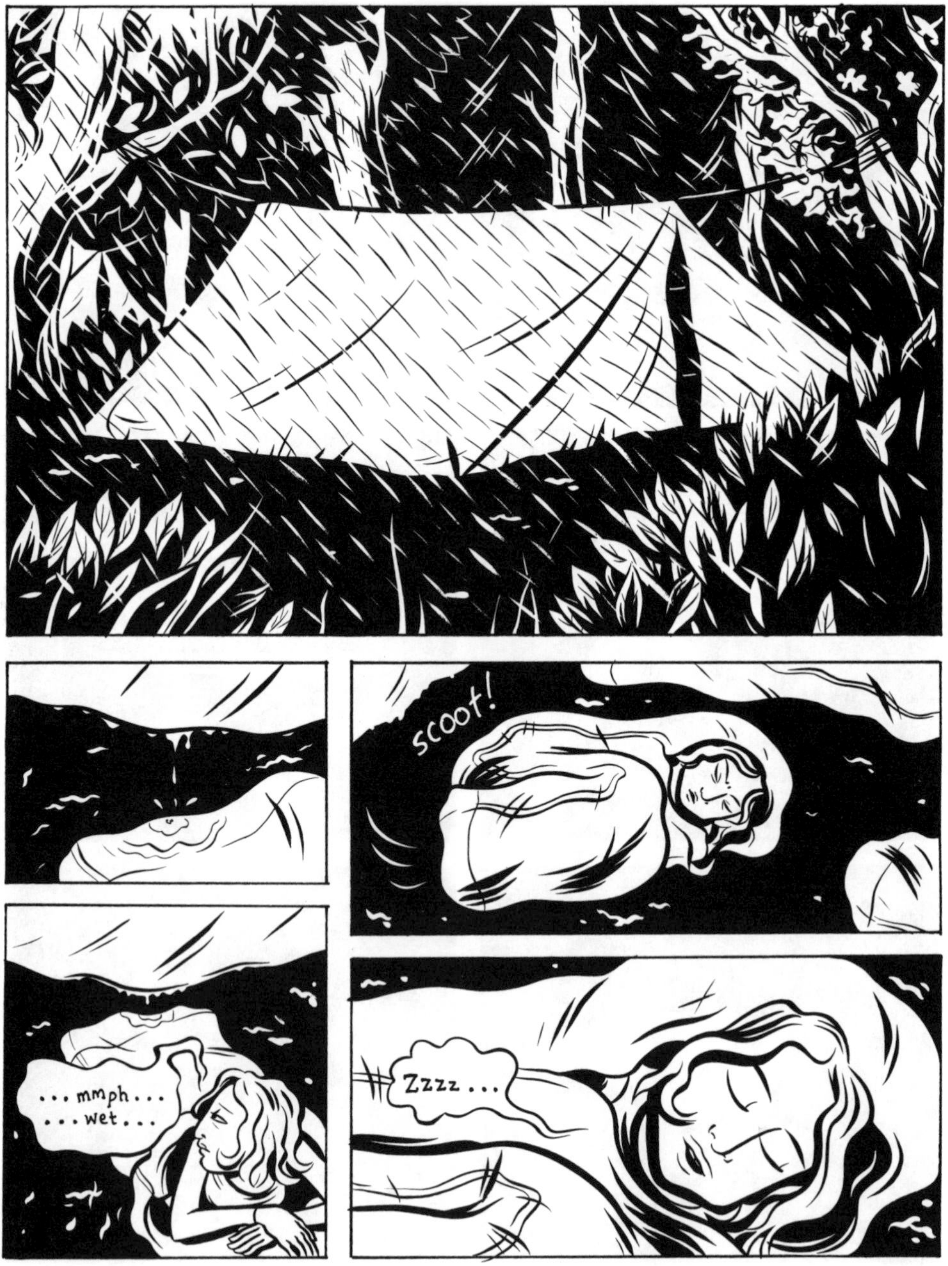
scoot!
...mmph...
...wet...
Zzzz...

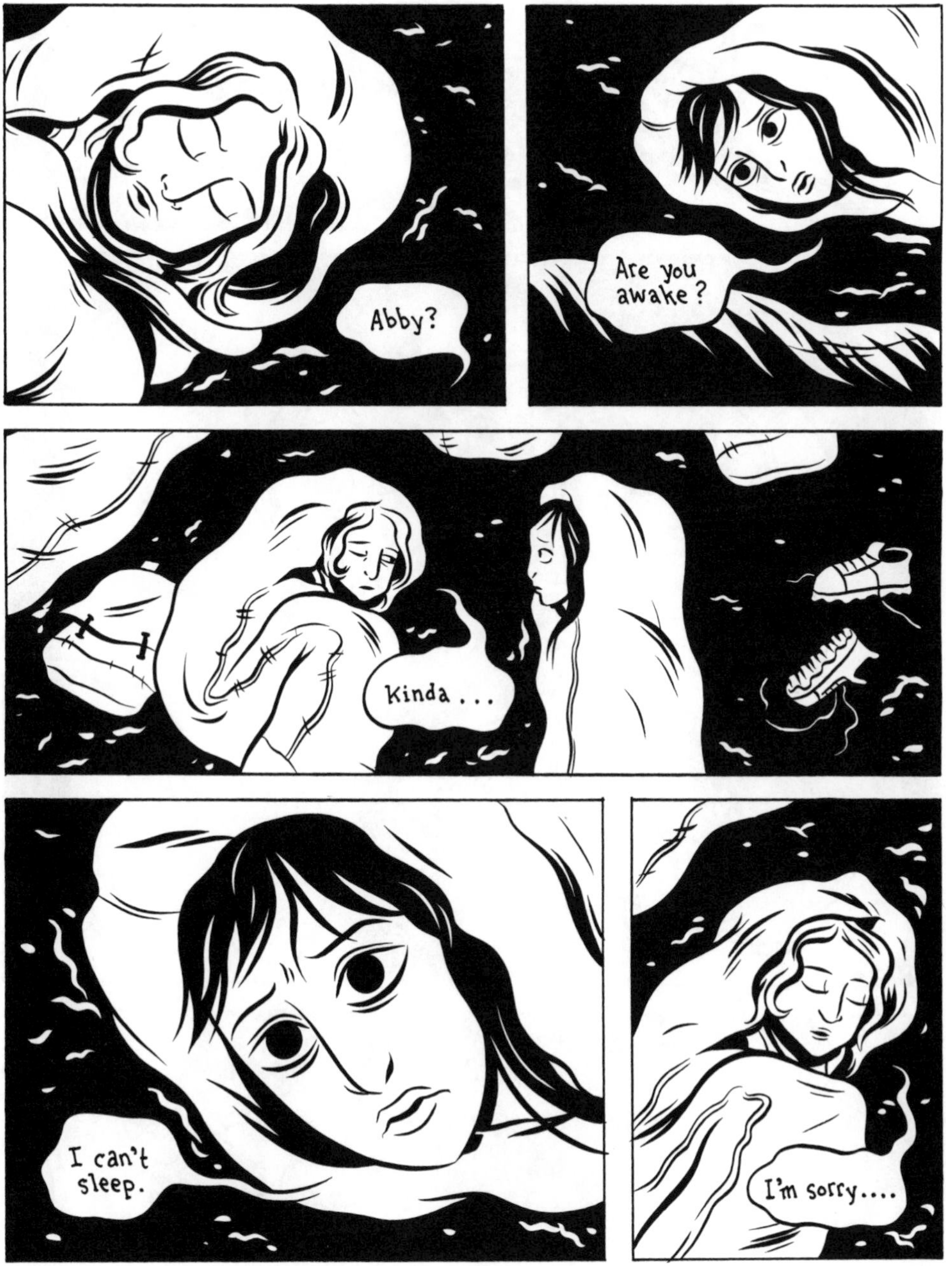
Abby?
Are you awake?
Kinda . . .
I can't sleep.
I'm sorry....

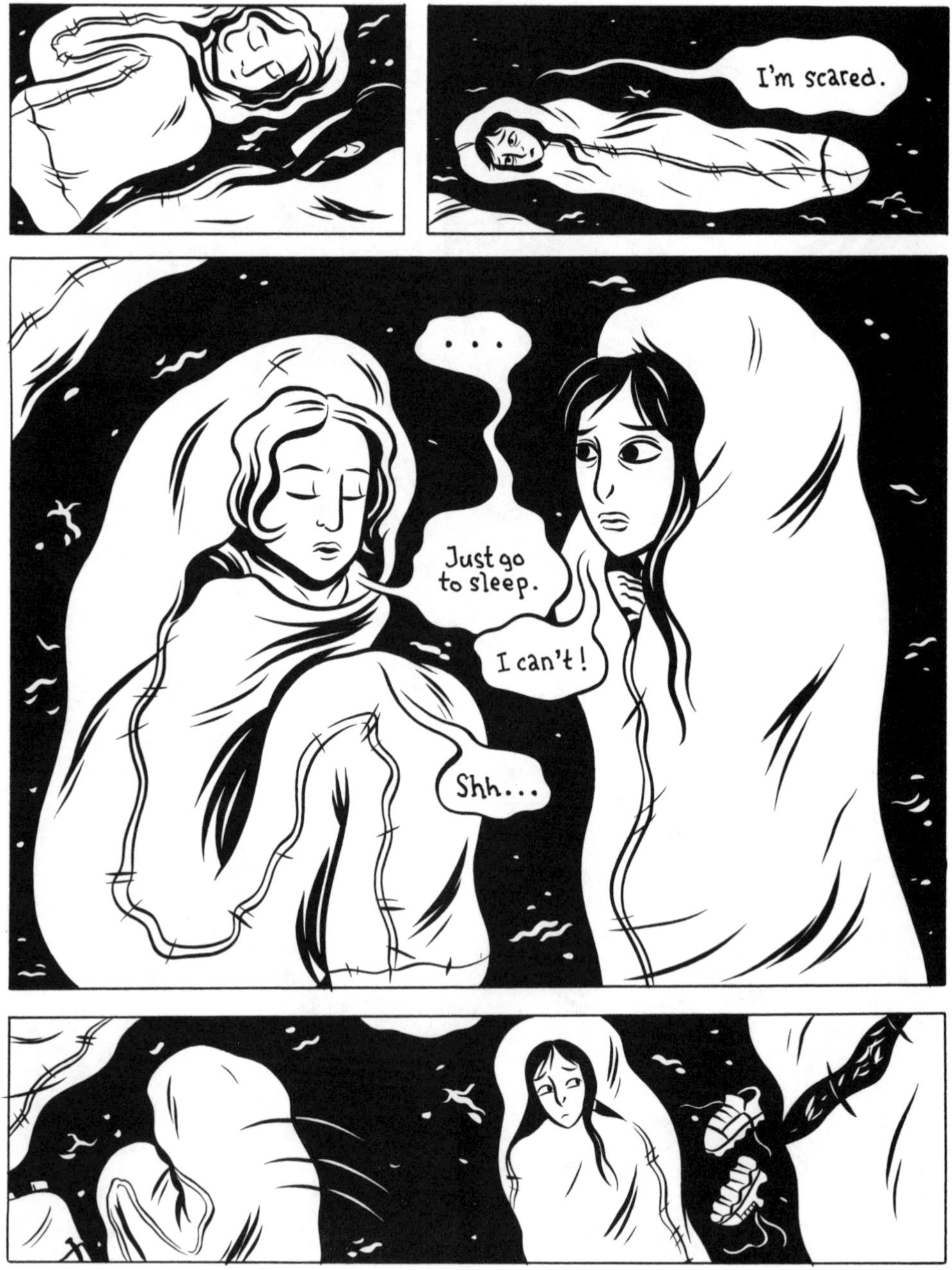
I'm scared.
. . .
Just go to sleep.
I can't!
Shh...

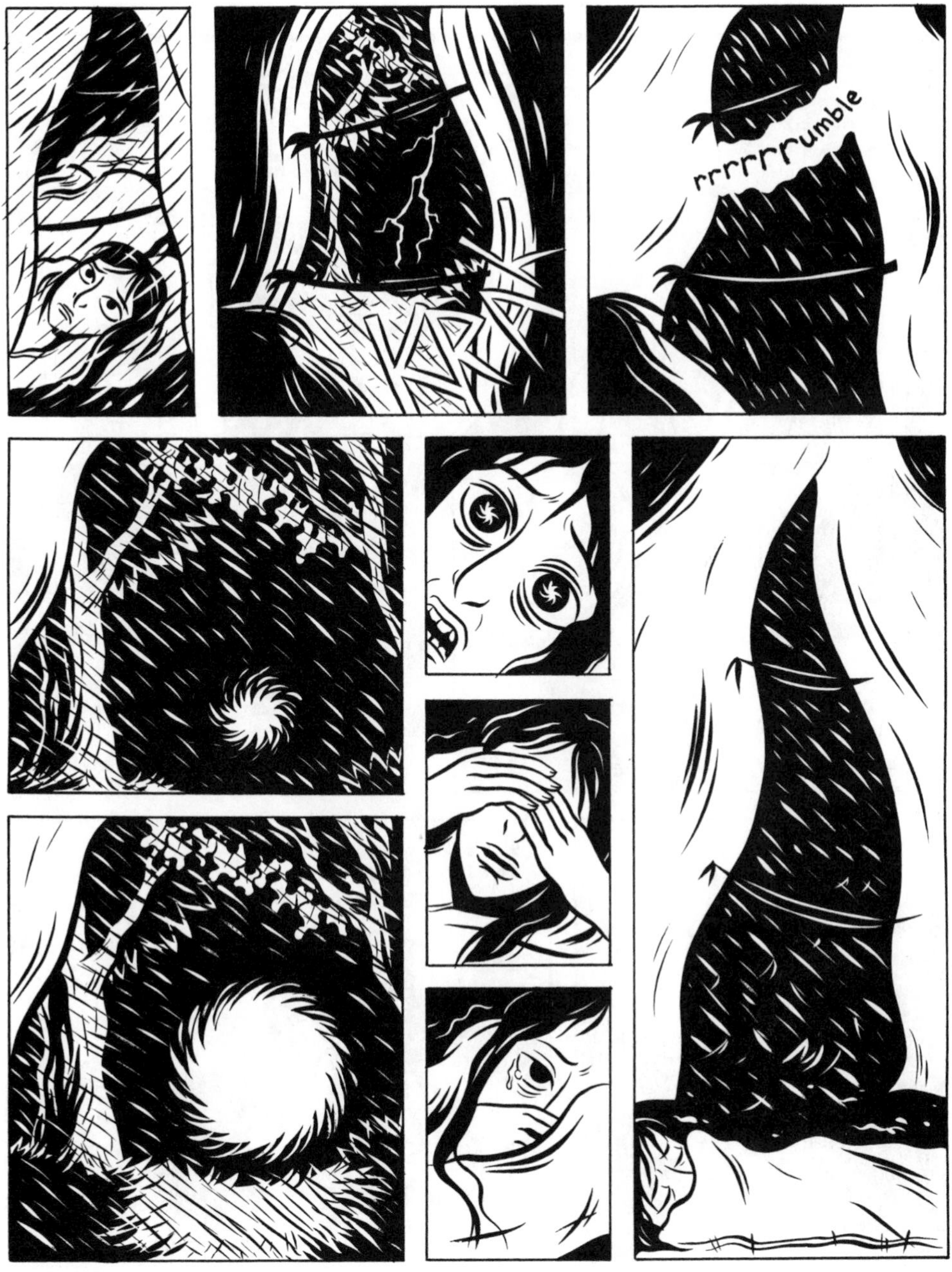
rrrrrrumble

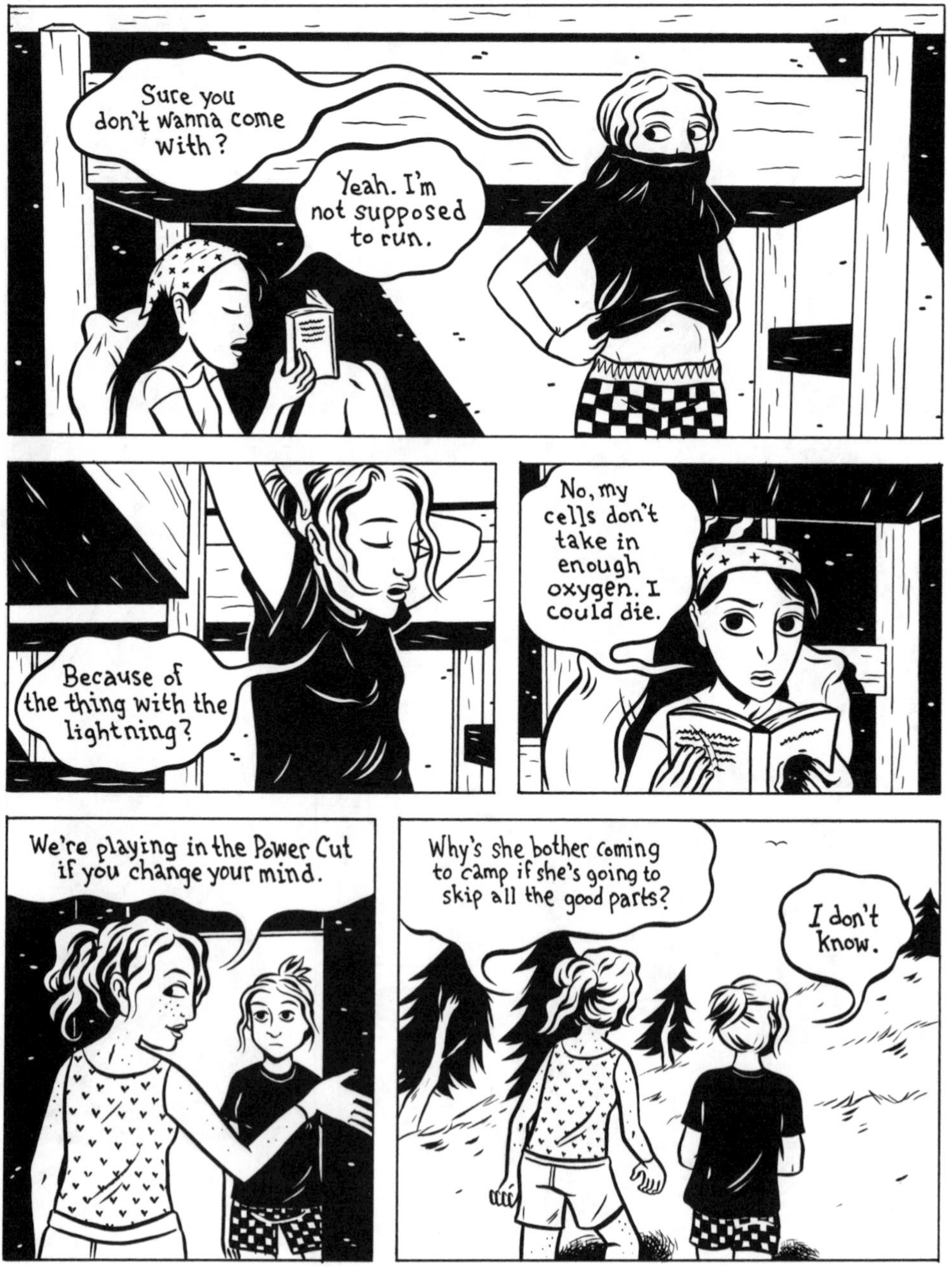
Sure you don't wanna come with?
Yeah. I'm not supposed to run.
Because of the thing with the lightning?
No, my cells don't take in enough oxygen. I could die.
We're playing in the Power Cut if you change your mind.
Why's she bother coming to camp if she's going to skip all the good parts?
I don't know.

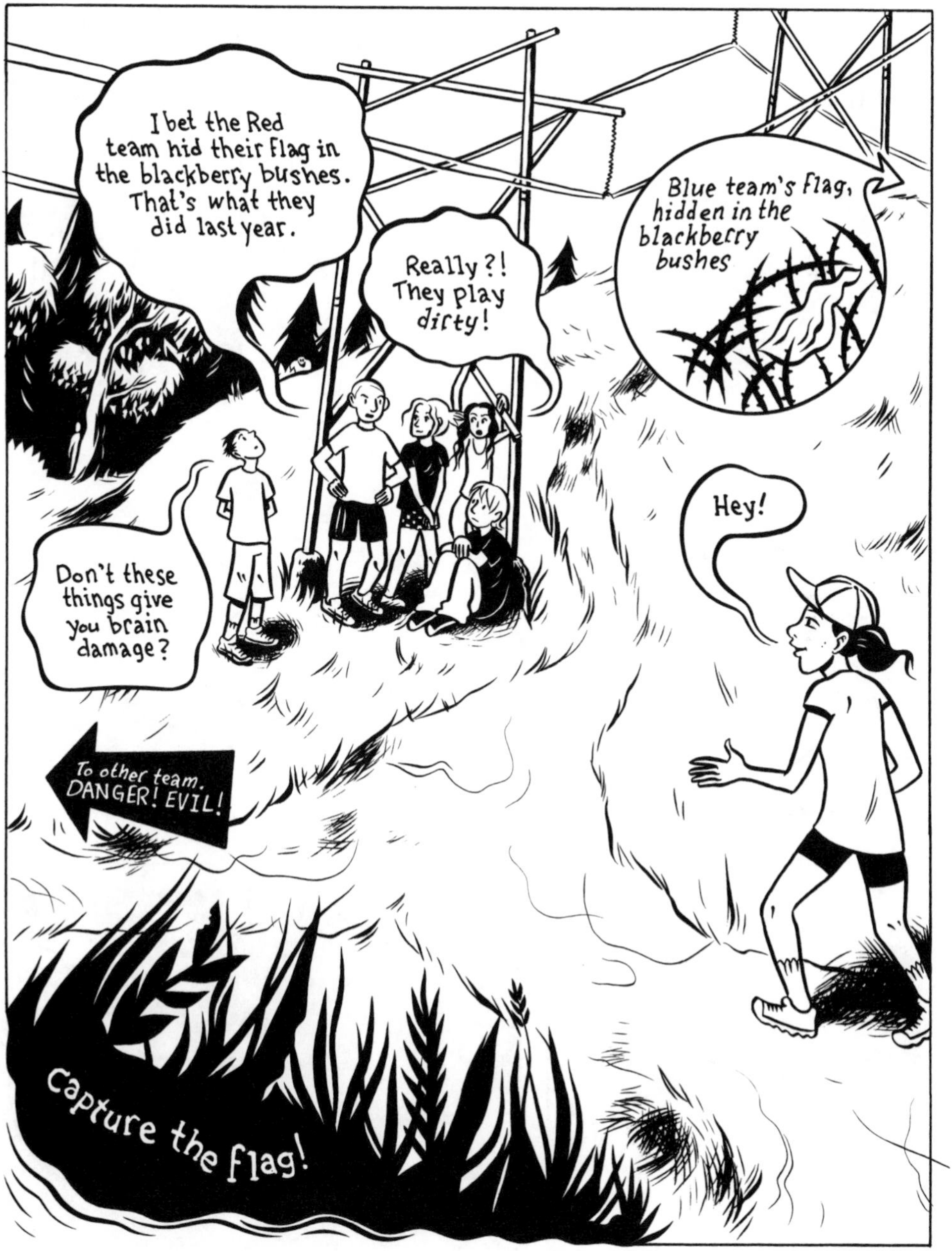
I bet the Red team hid their flag in the blackberry bushes. That's what they did last year.
Really?! They play dirty!
Blue team's flag, hidden in the blackberry bushes
Don't these things give you brain damage?
Hey!
To other team. DANGER! EVIL!
Capture the flag!

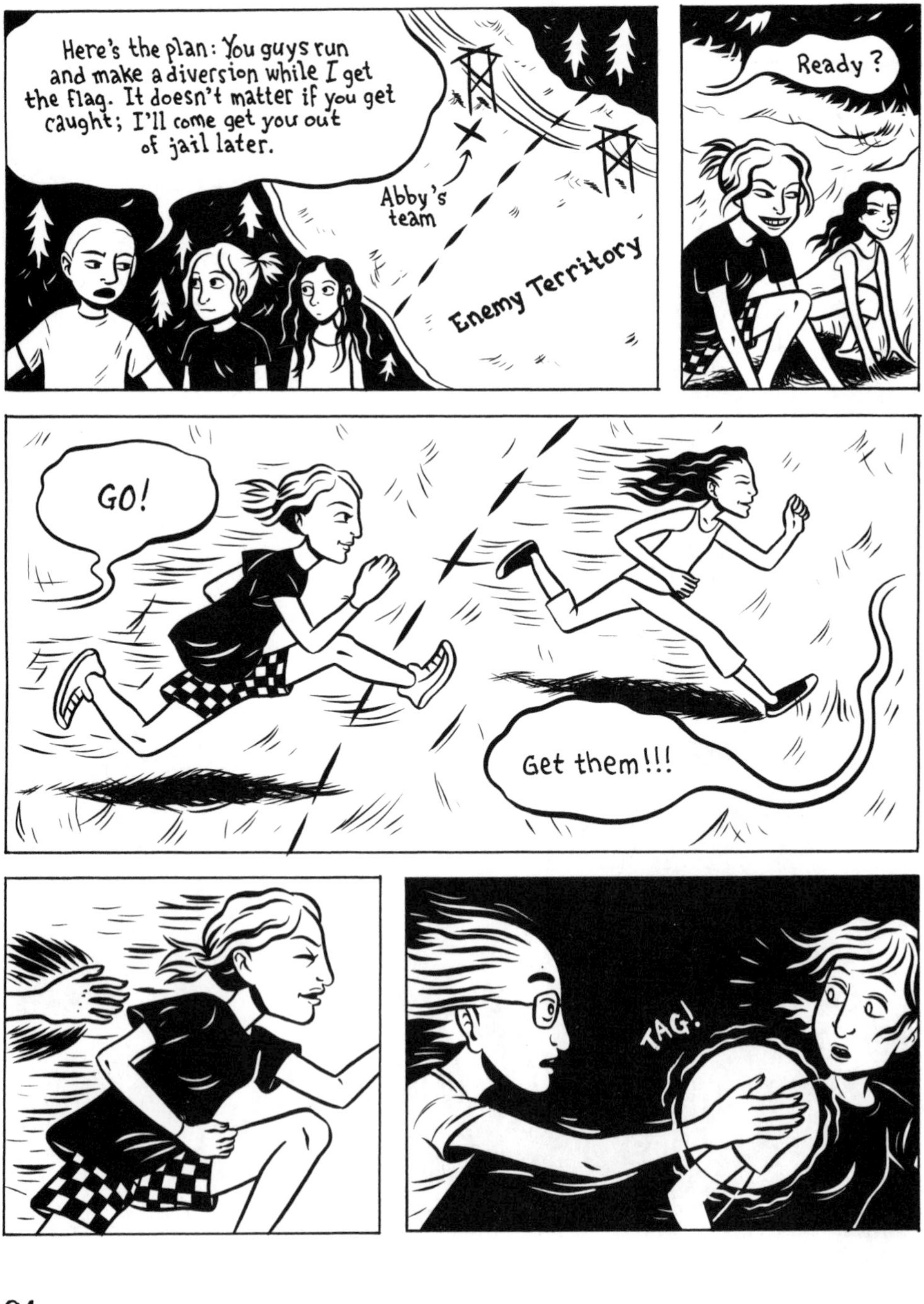
Here's the plan: You guys run and make a diversion while I get the flag. It doesn't matter if you get caught; I'll come get you out of jail later.
Abby's team
Enemy Territory
Ready?
GO!
Get them!!!
TAG!

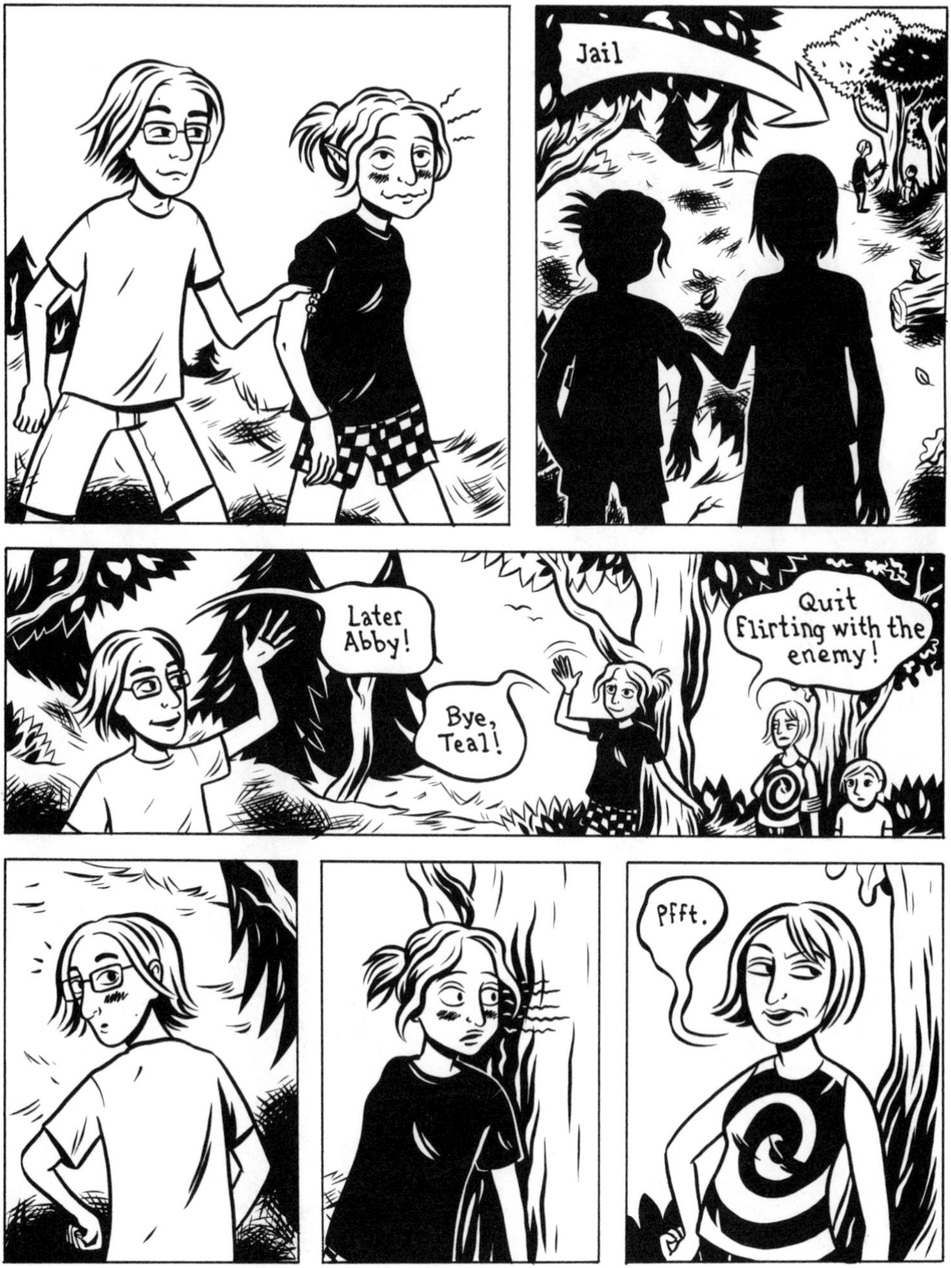
Jail
Later Abby!
Bye, Teal!
Quit Flirting with the enemy!
pfft.

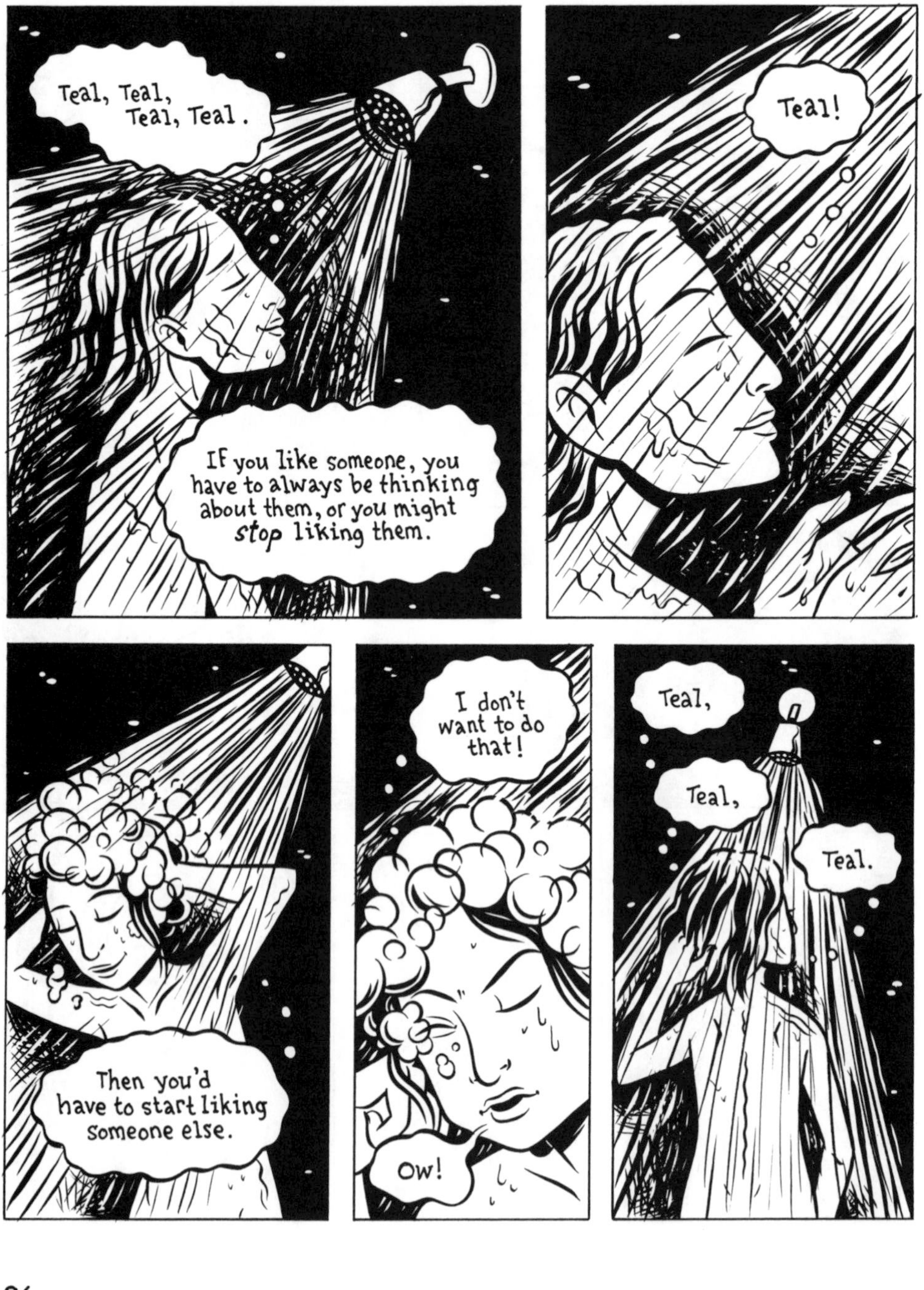
Teal, Teal,
Teal, Teal.
If you like someone, you have to always be thinking about them, or you might *stop* liking them.
Teal!
Then you'd have to start liking someone else.
I don't want to do that!
Ow!
Teal,
Teal,
Teal.

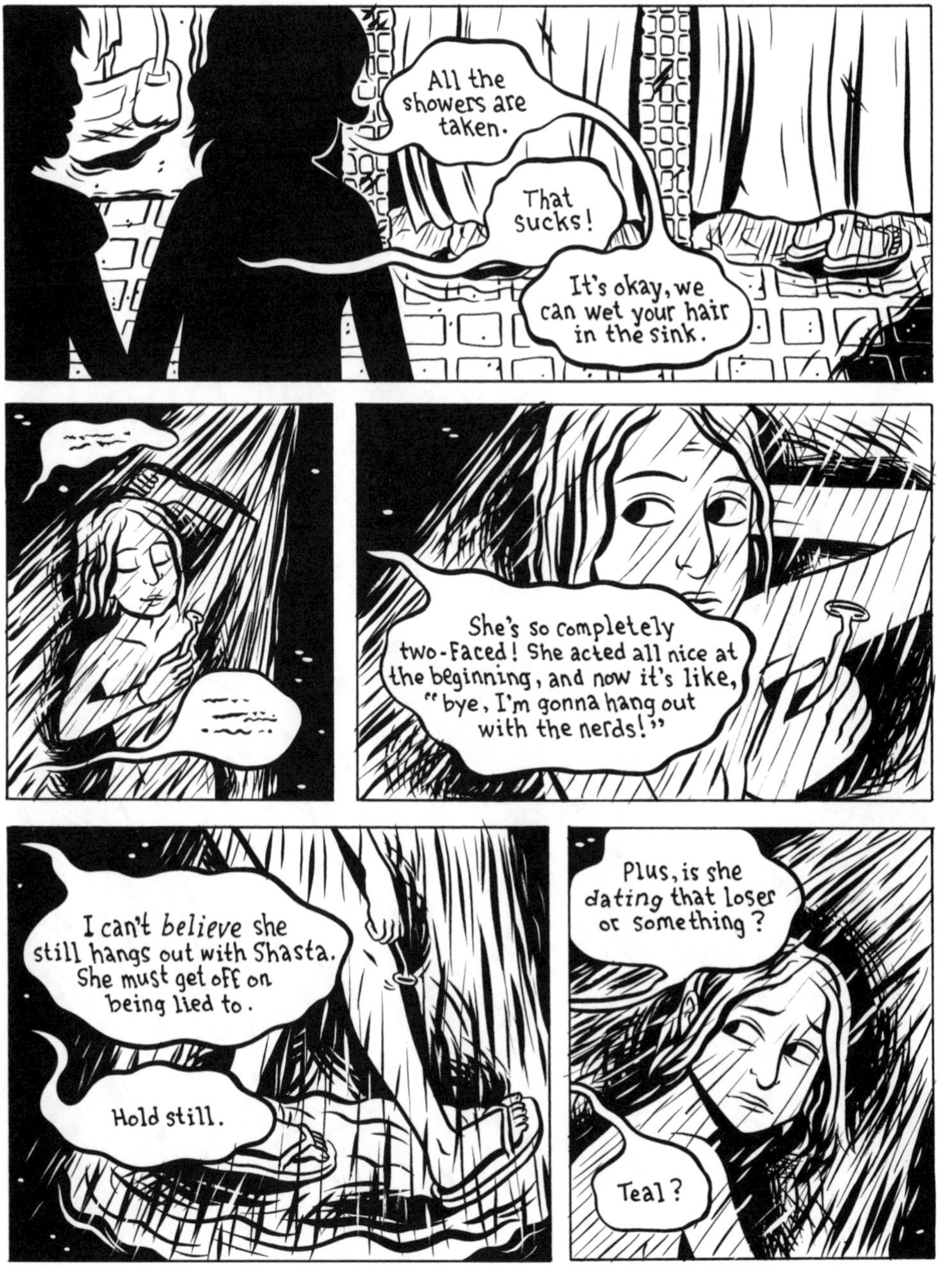
All the showers are taken.
That sucks!
It's okay, we can wet your hair in the sink.
She's so completely two-faced! She acted all nice at the beginning, and now it's like, "bye, I'm gonna hang out with the nerds!"
I can't *believe* she still hangs out with Shasta. She must get off on being lied to.
Hold still.
Plus, is she *dating* that loser or something?
Teal?

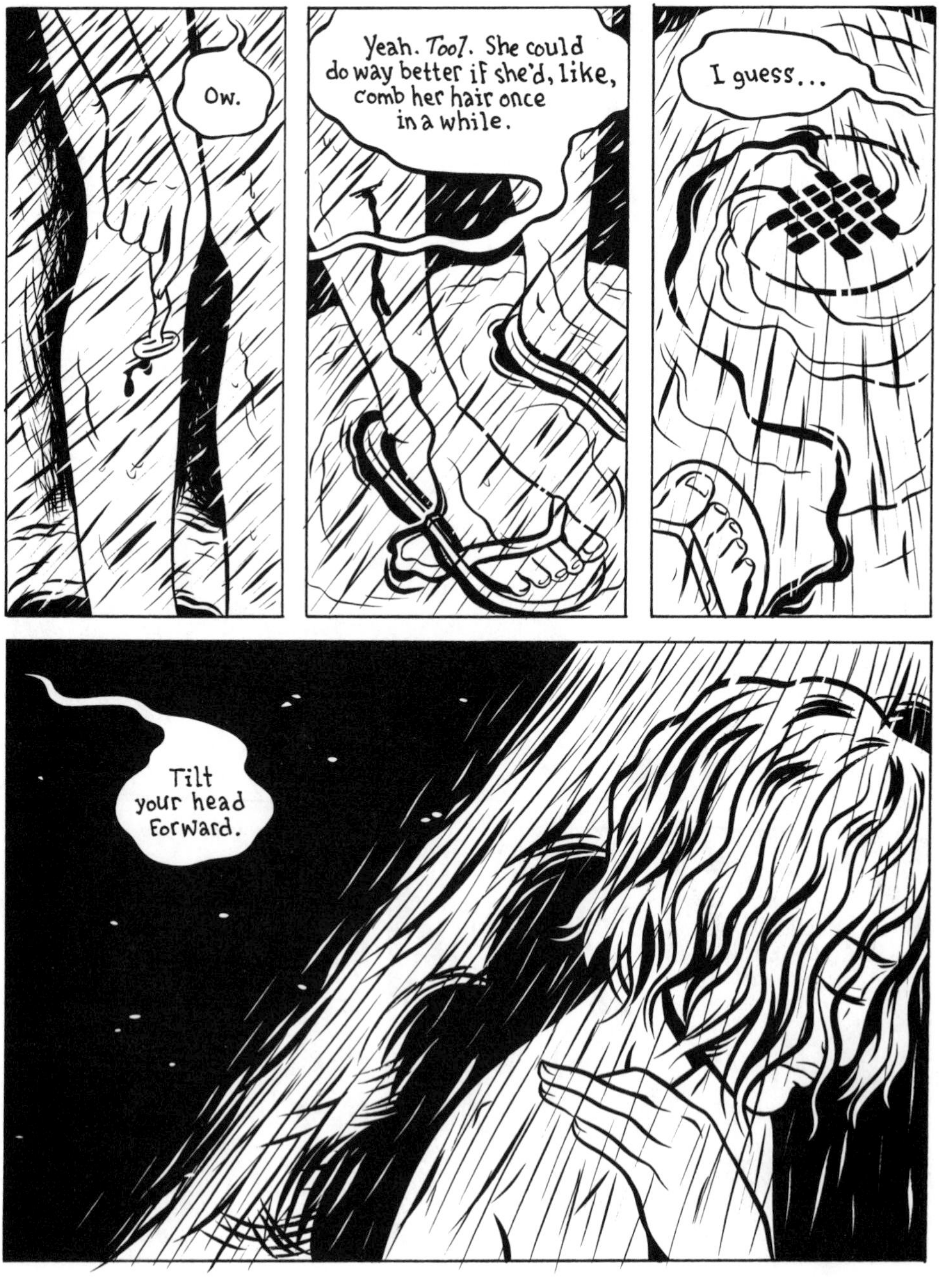
Ow.
Yeah. *Tool*. She could do way better if she'd, like, comb her hair once in a while.
I guess...
Tilt your head forward.

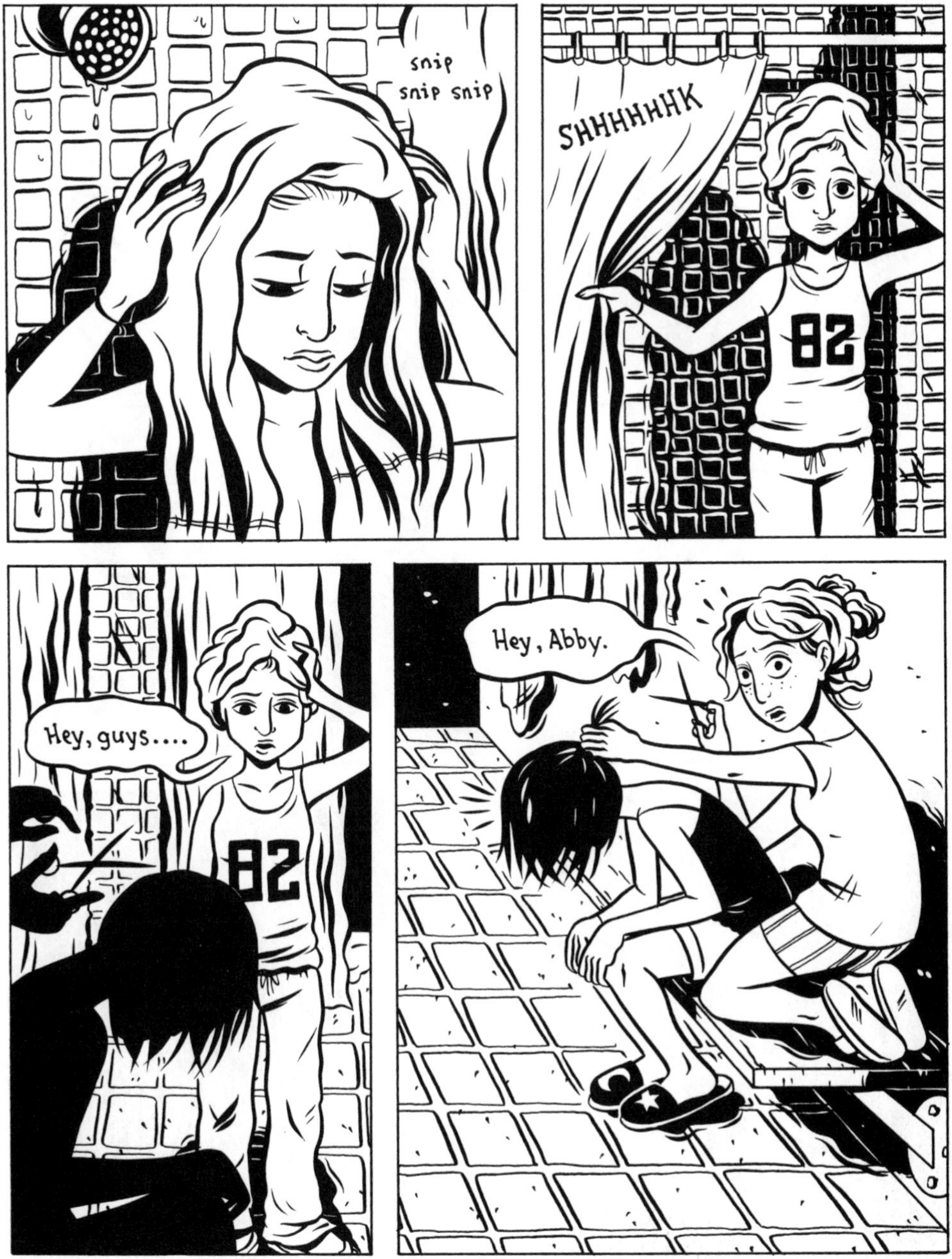
snip
snip snip
SHHHHHHK
Hey, guys....
Hey, Abby.

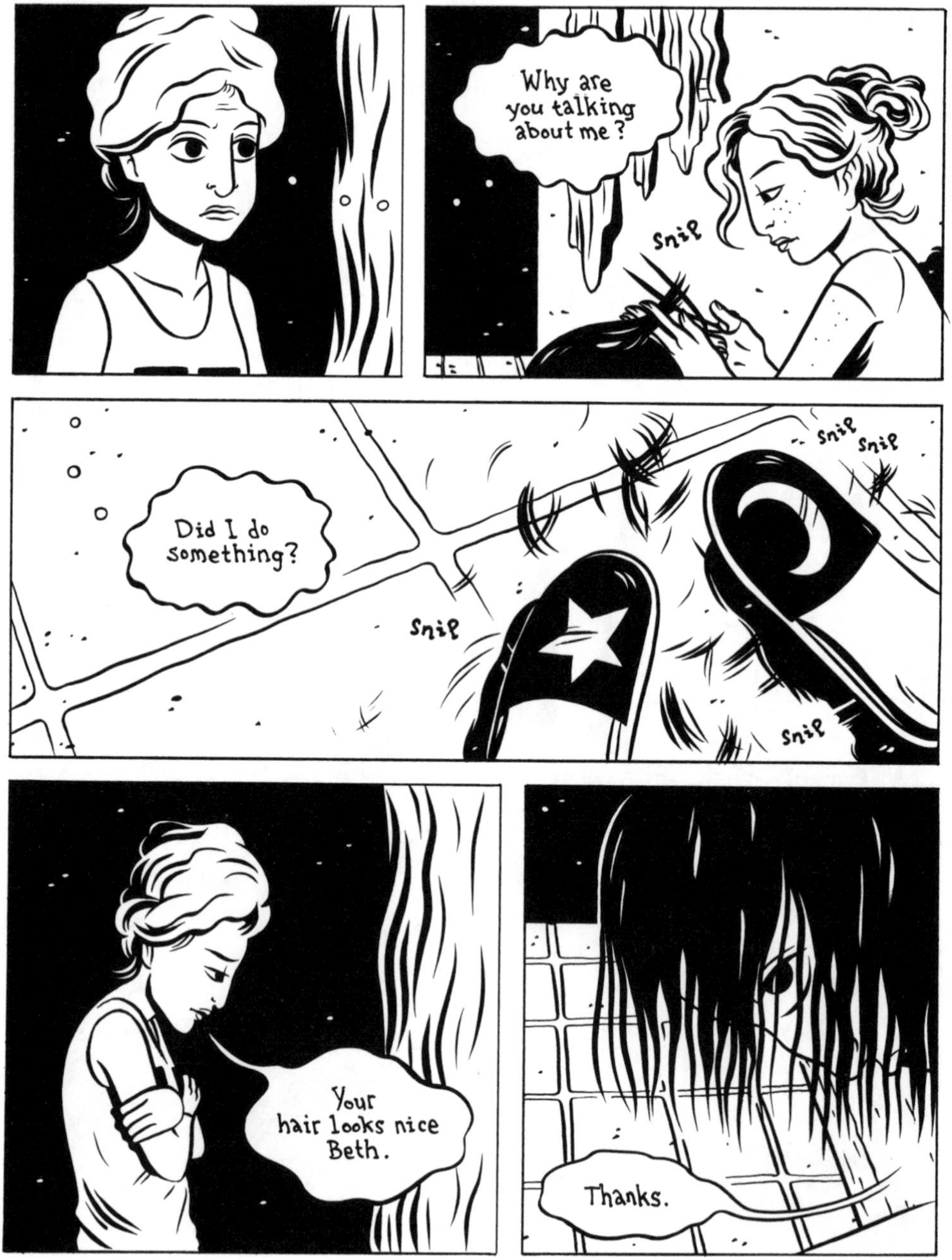
Why are you talking about me?
Snip
Did I do something?
Snip
Snip
Snip
Snip
Your hair looks nice Beth.
Thanks.

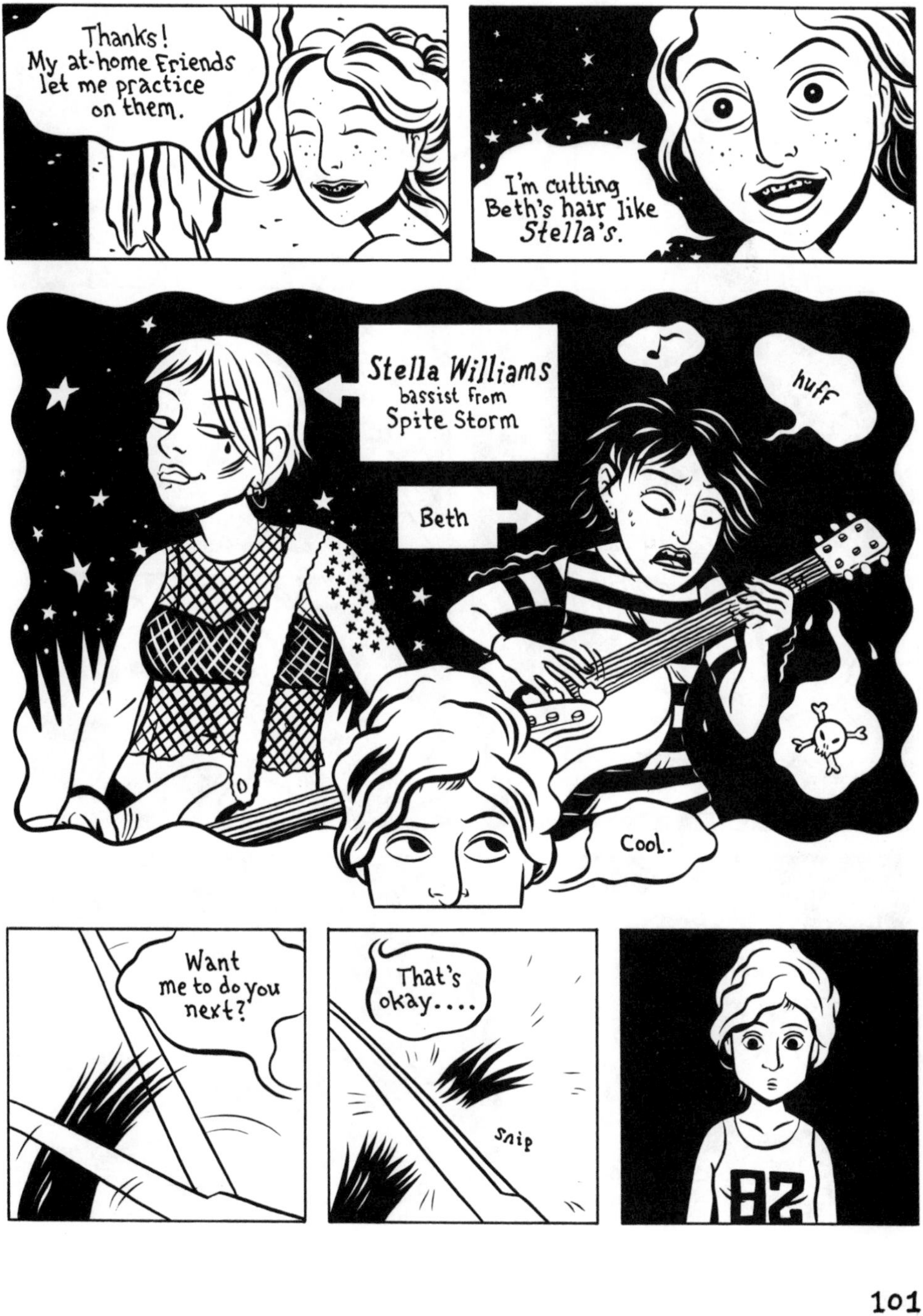

Thanks! My at-home friends let me practice on them.
I'm cutting Beth's hair like Stella's.
Stella Williams bassist from Spite Storm
huff
Beth
Cool.
Want me to do you next?
That's okay....
snip

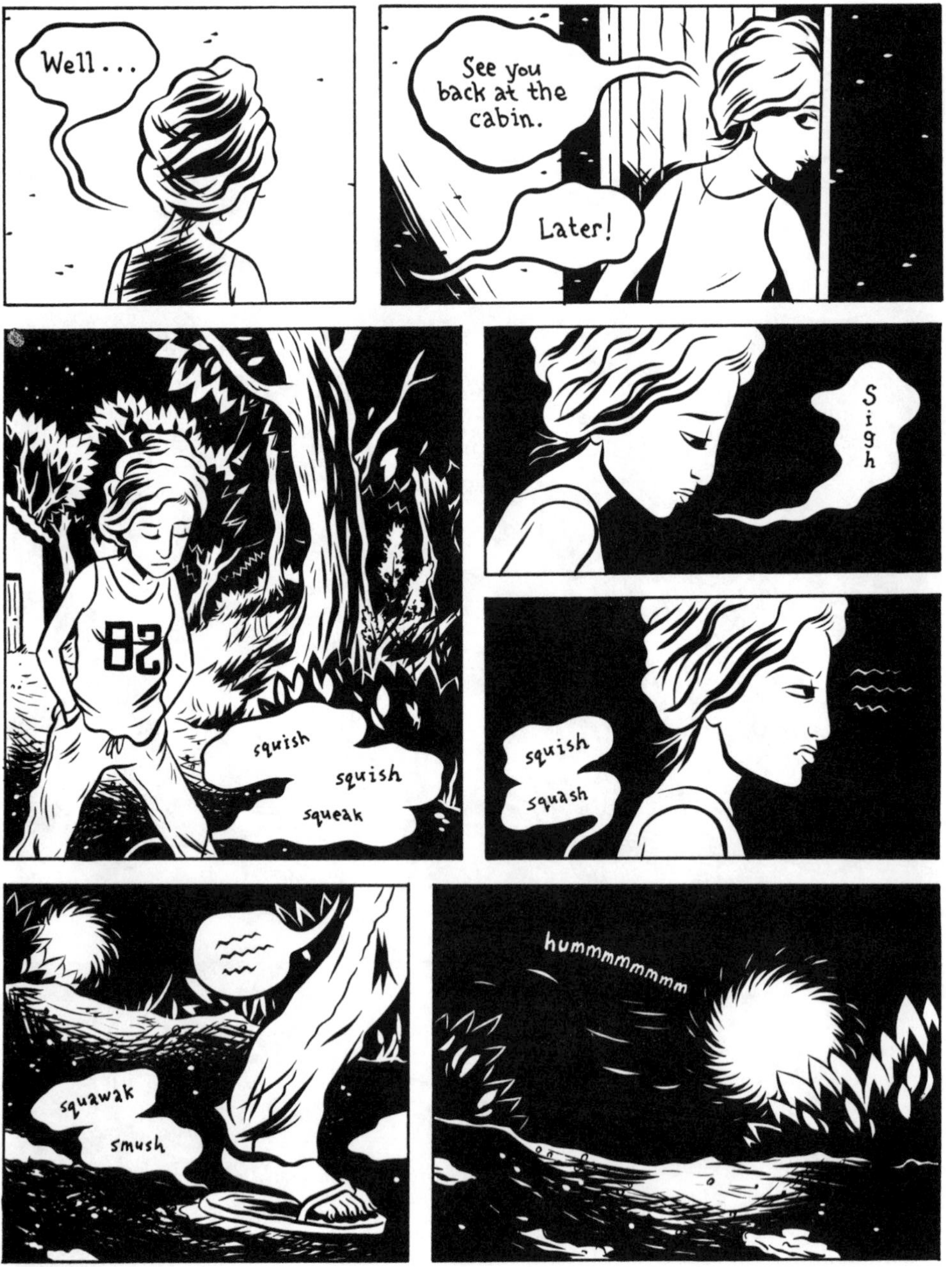
Well...
See you back at the cabin.
Later!
Sigh
squish
squish
squeak
squish
squash
squawak
smush
hummmmmmmm

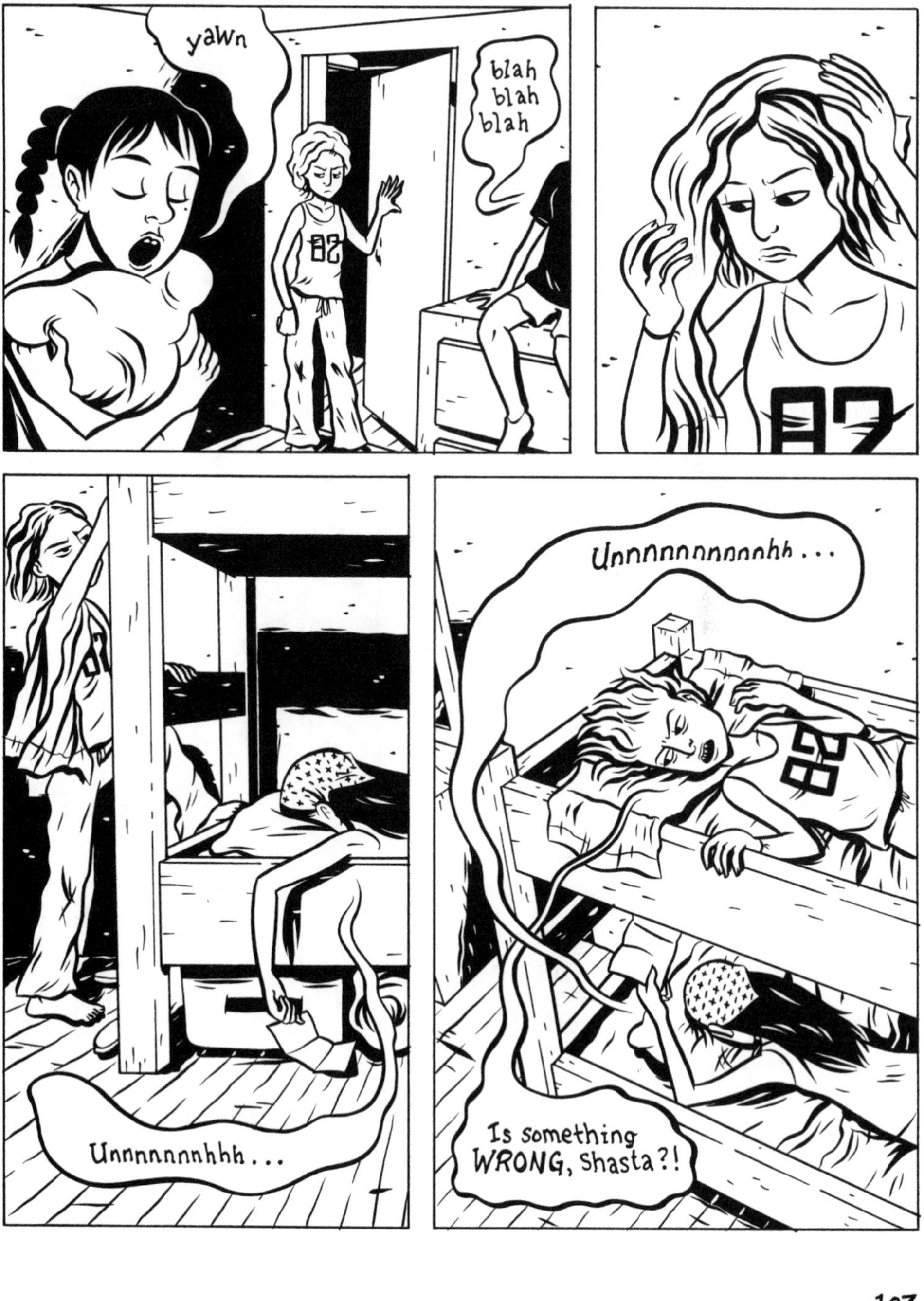
yawn
blah blah blah
Unnnnnnnhhh...
Unnnnnnnnnnhh...
Is something WRONG, Shasta?!

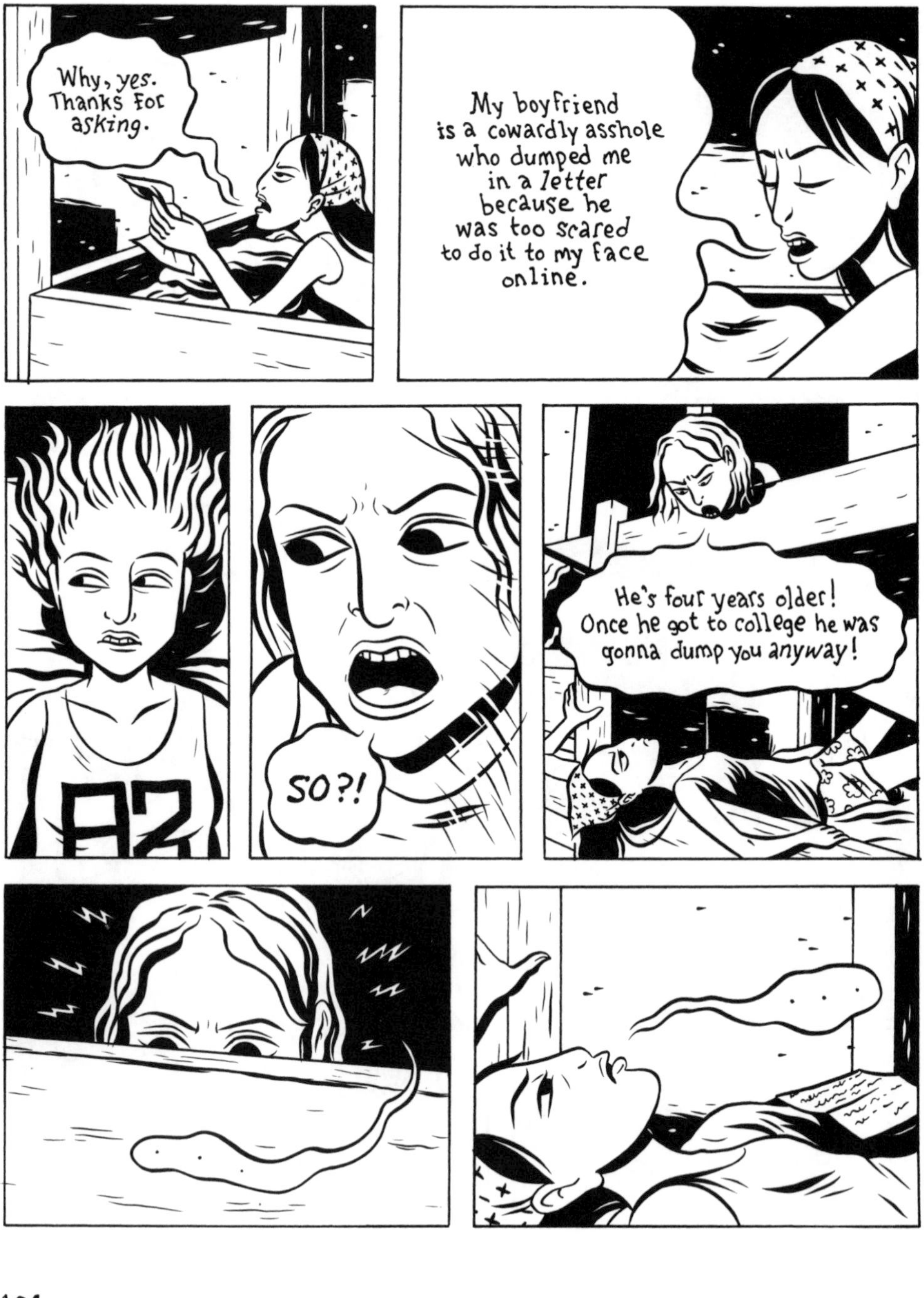
Why, yes. Thanks for asking.
My boyfriend is a cowardly asshole who dumped me in a letter because he was too scared to do it to my face online.
SO?!
He's four years older! Once he got to college he was gonna dump you anyway!
AZ

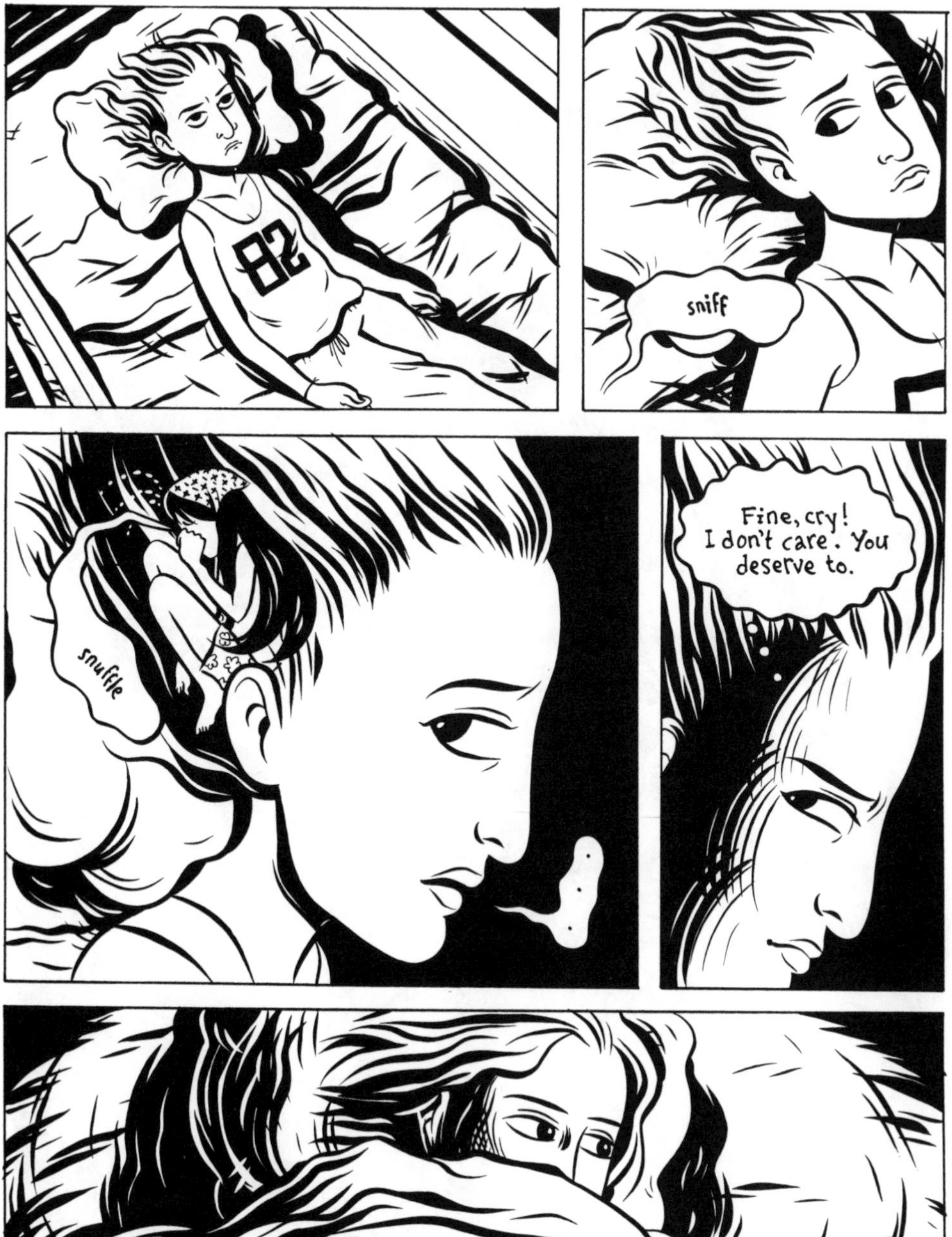
sniff
snufle
Fine, cry! I don't care. You deserve to.

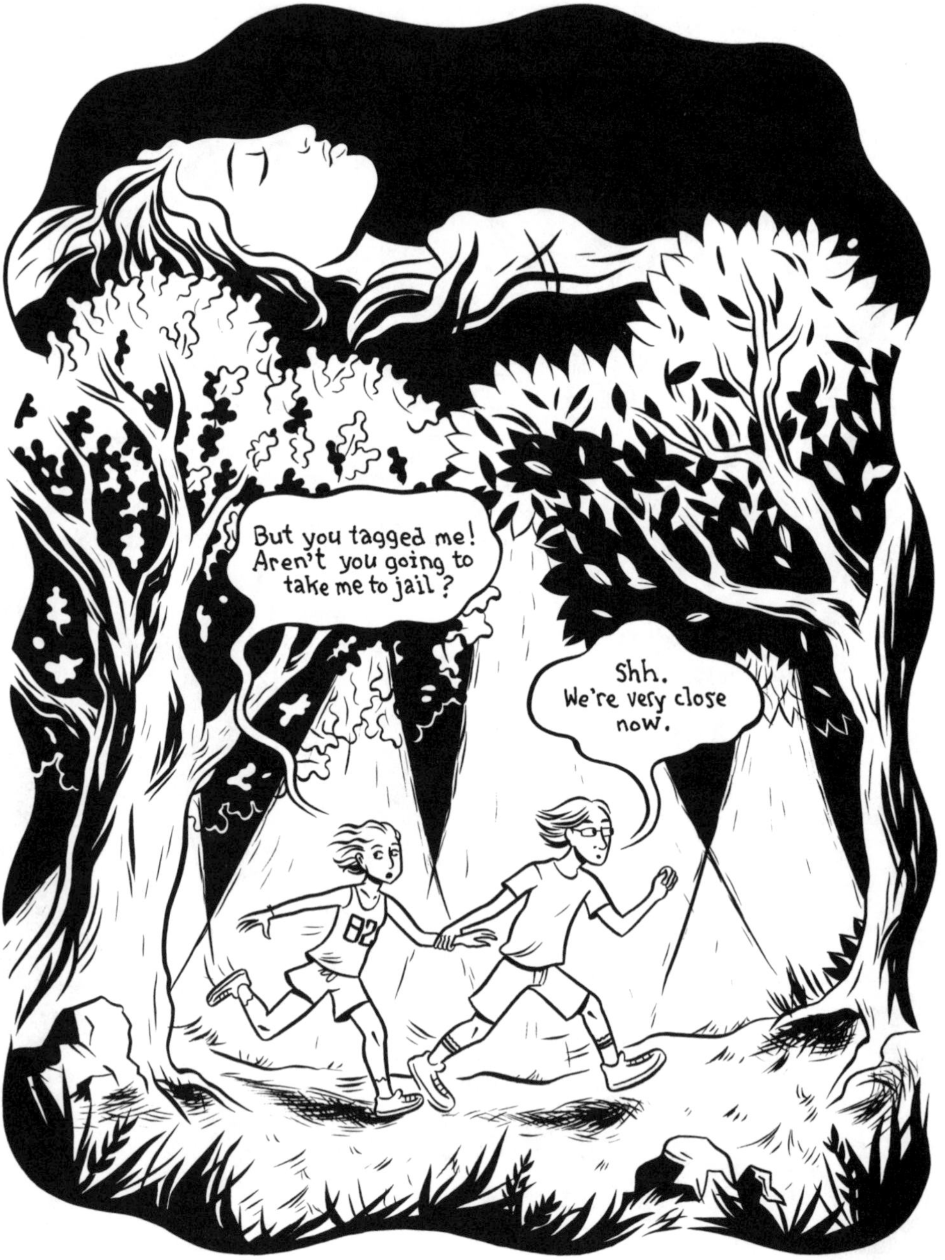
But you tagged me! Aren't you going to take me to jail?
Shh. We're very close now.

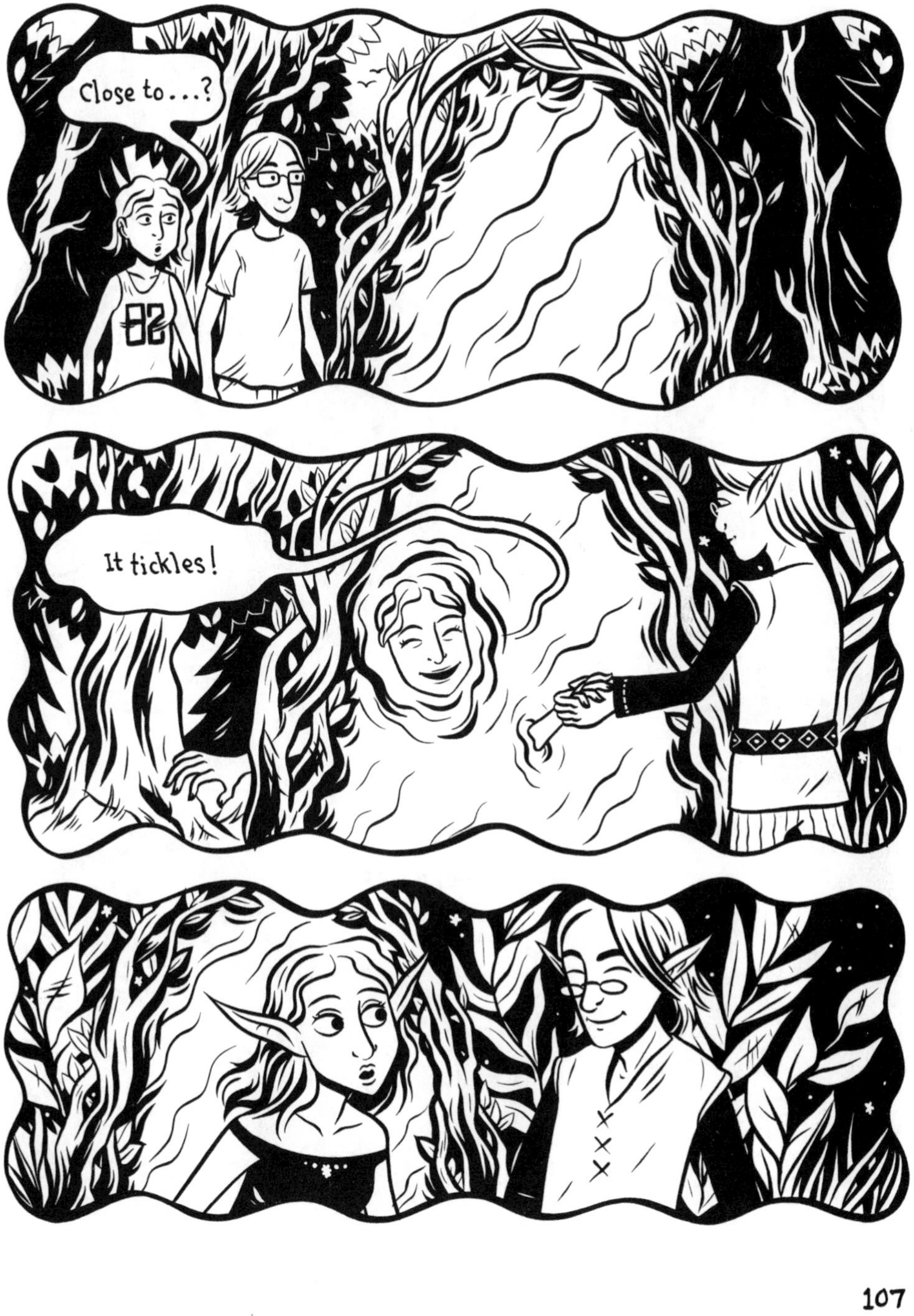
Close to...?
It tickles!

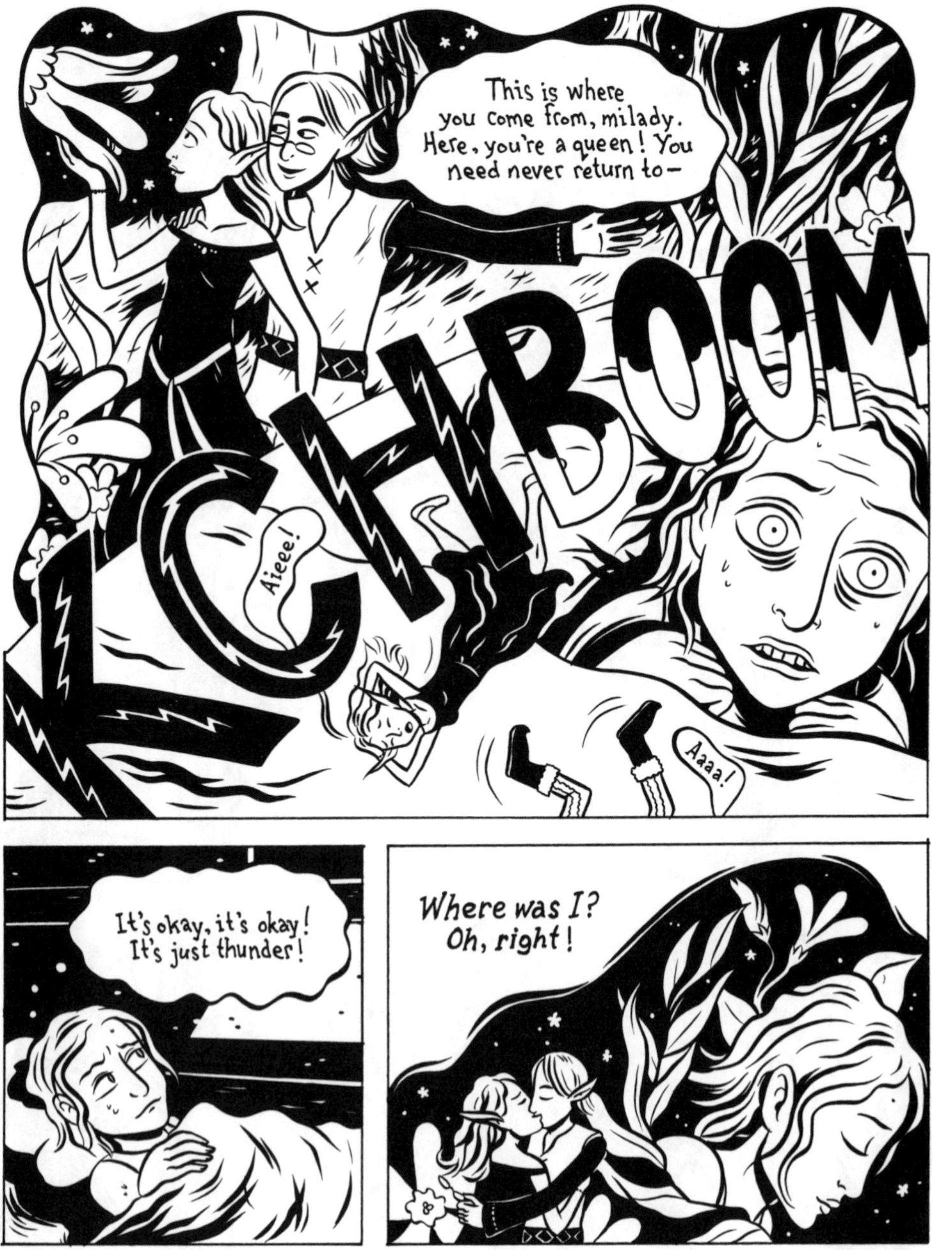
This is where you come from, milady. Here, you're a queen! You need never return to—
KCHBOOM
Aieeee!
Aaaa!
It's okay, it's okay! It's just thunder!
Where was I? Oh, right!

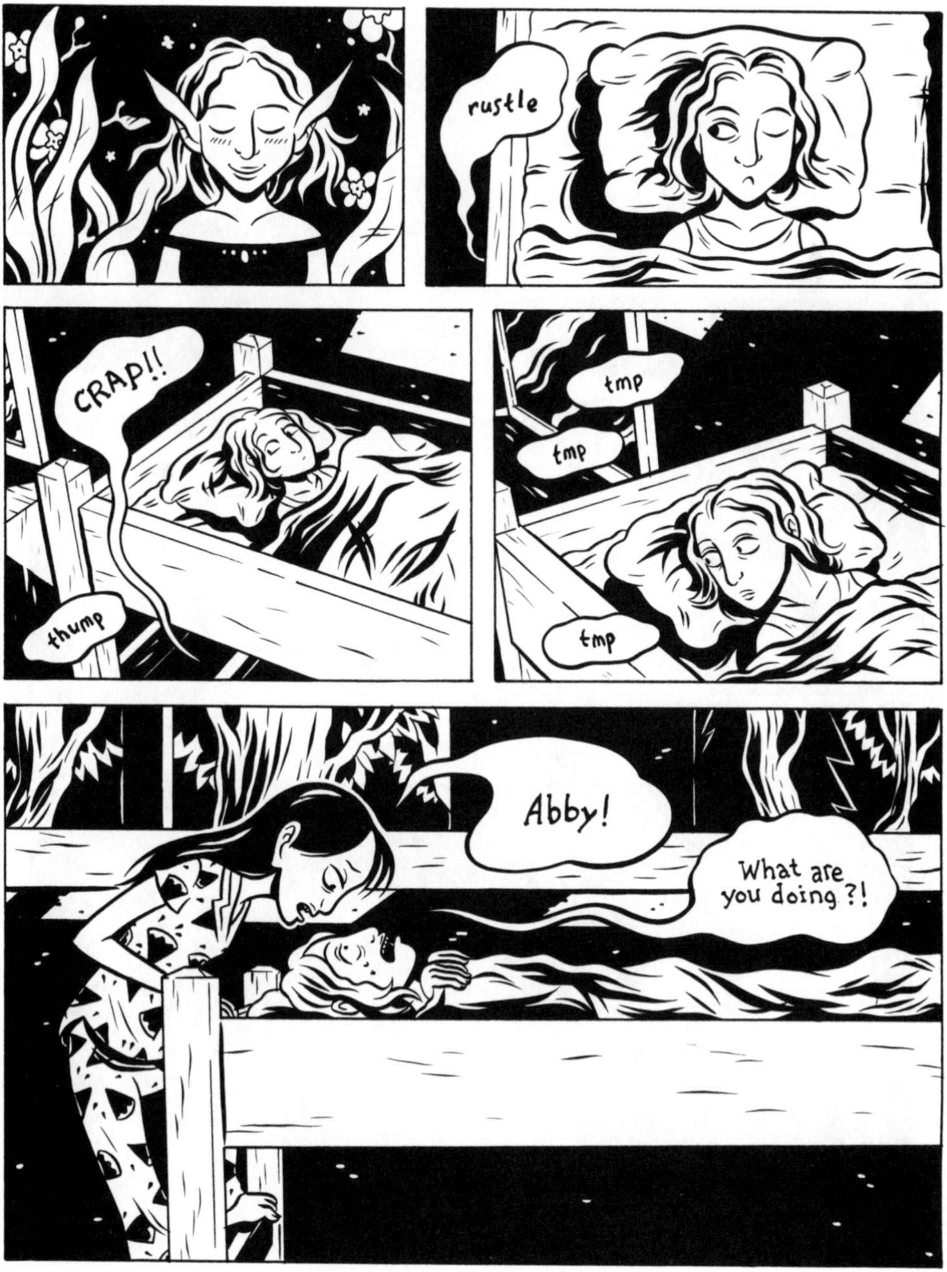
rustle
CRAP!!
thump
tmp
tmp
tmp
Abby!
What are you doing ?!

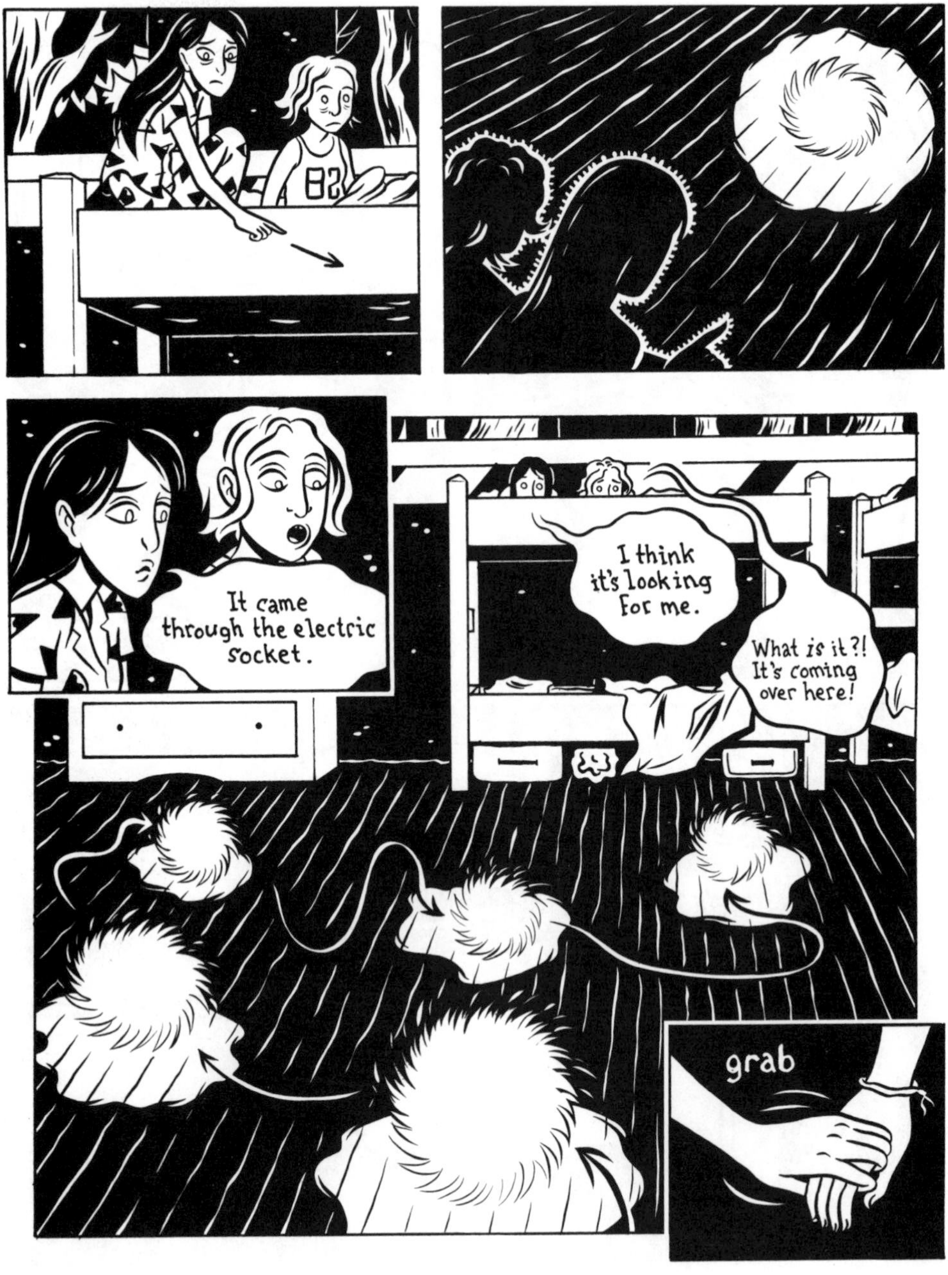
82
It came through the electric socket.
I think it's looking for me.
What is it?! It's coming over here!
grab

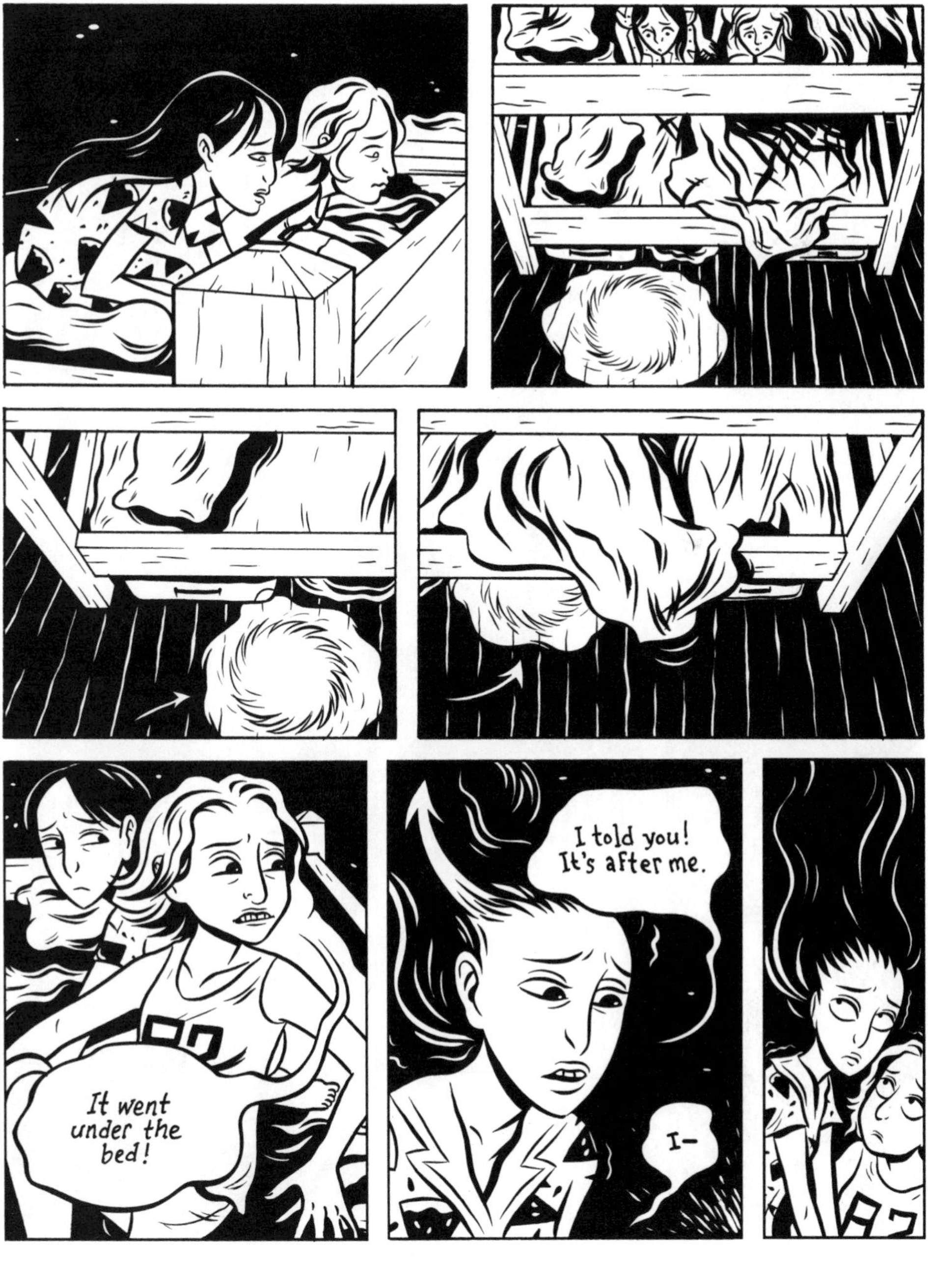
It went under the bed!
I told you! It's after me.
I-

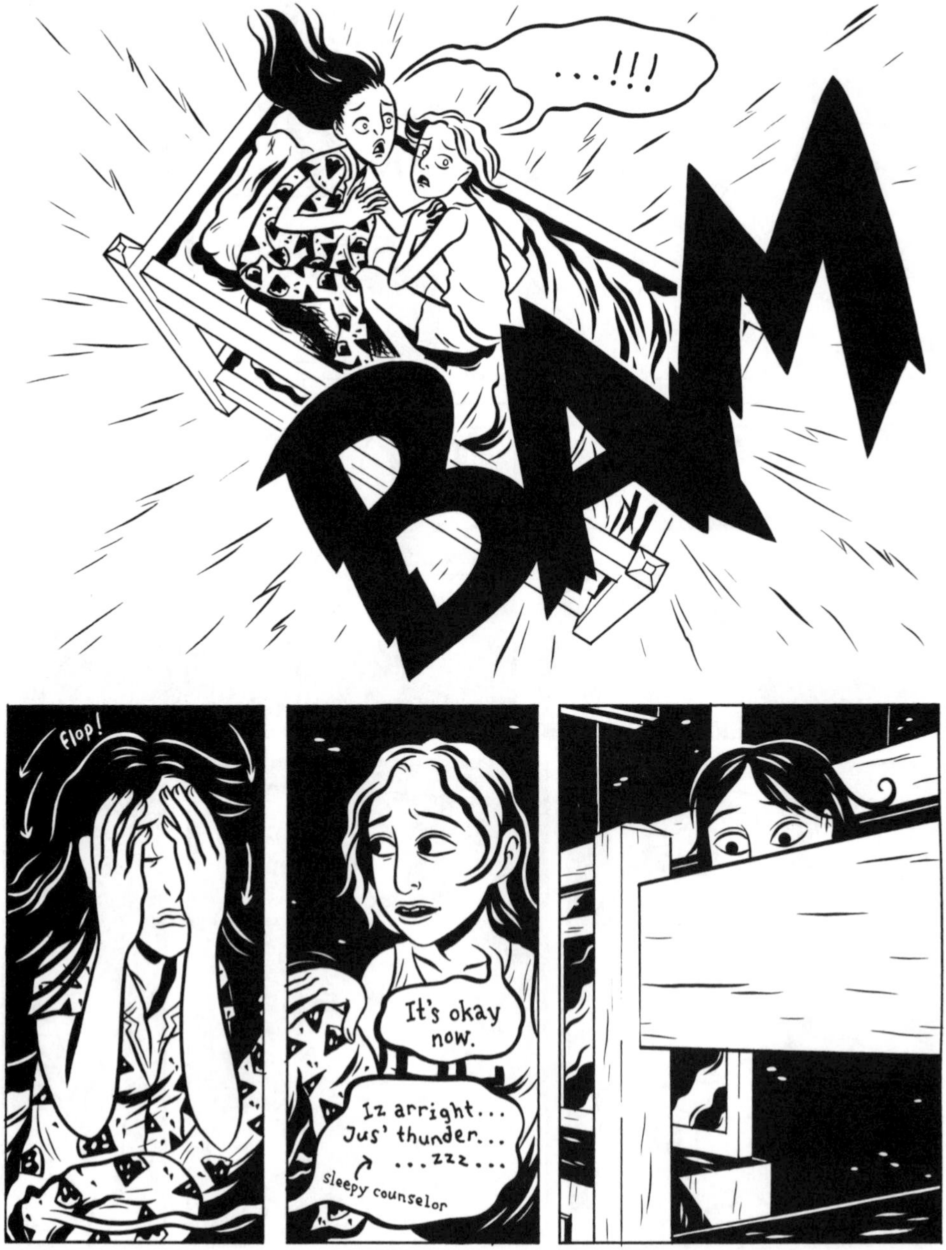

...!!!
BAM
Flop!
It's okay now.
Iz arright...
Jus' thunder...
...zzz...
sleepy counselor

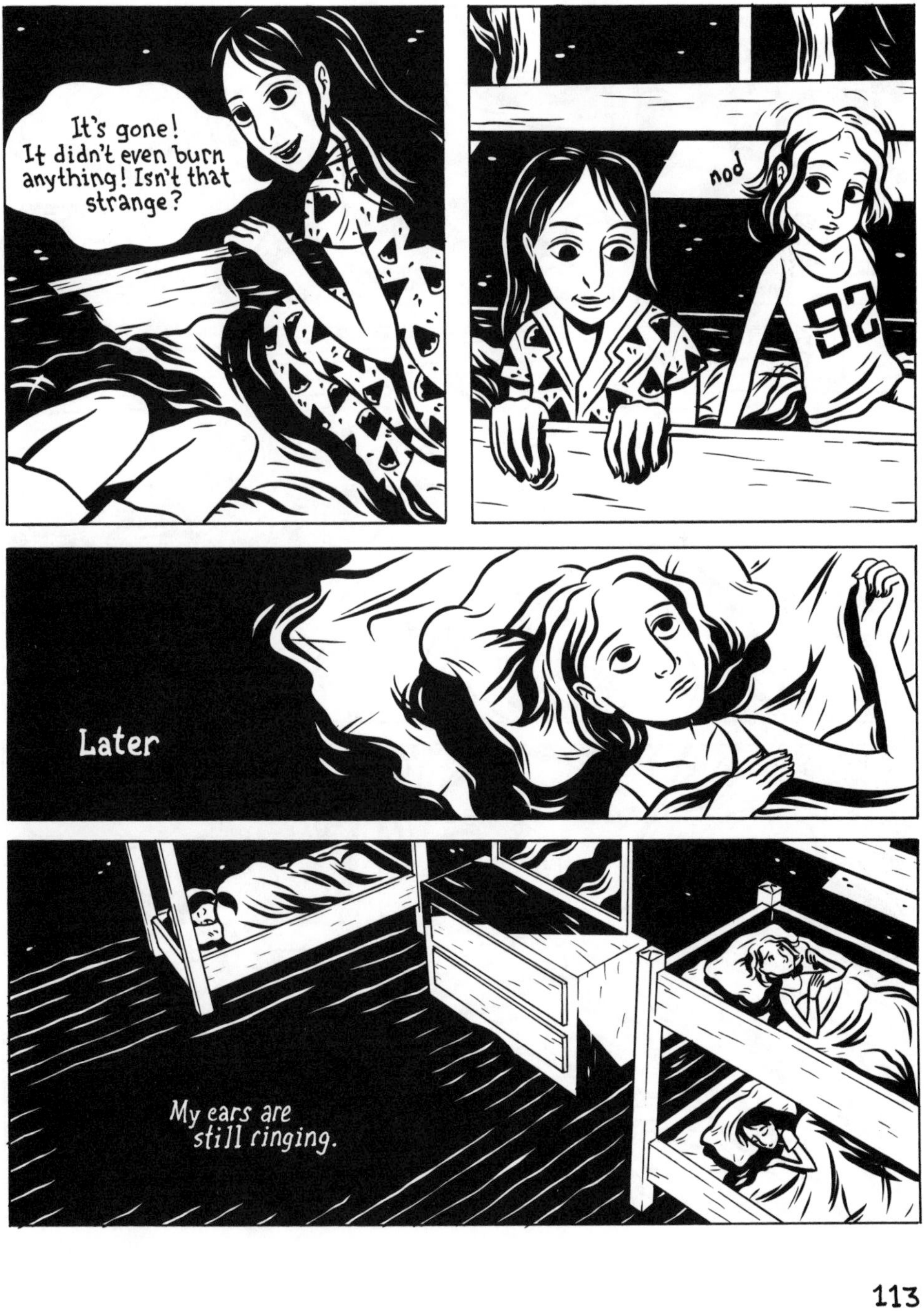
It's gone!
It didn't even burn anything! Isn't that strange?
nod
Later
My ears are still ringing.

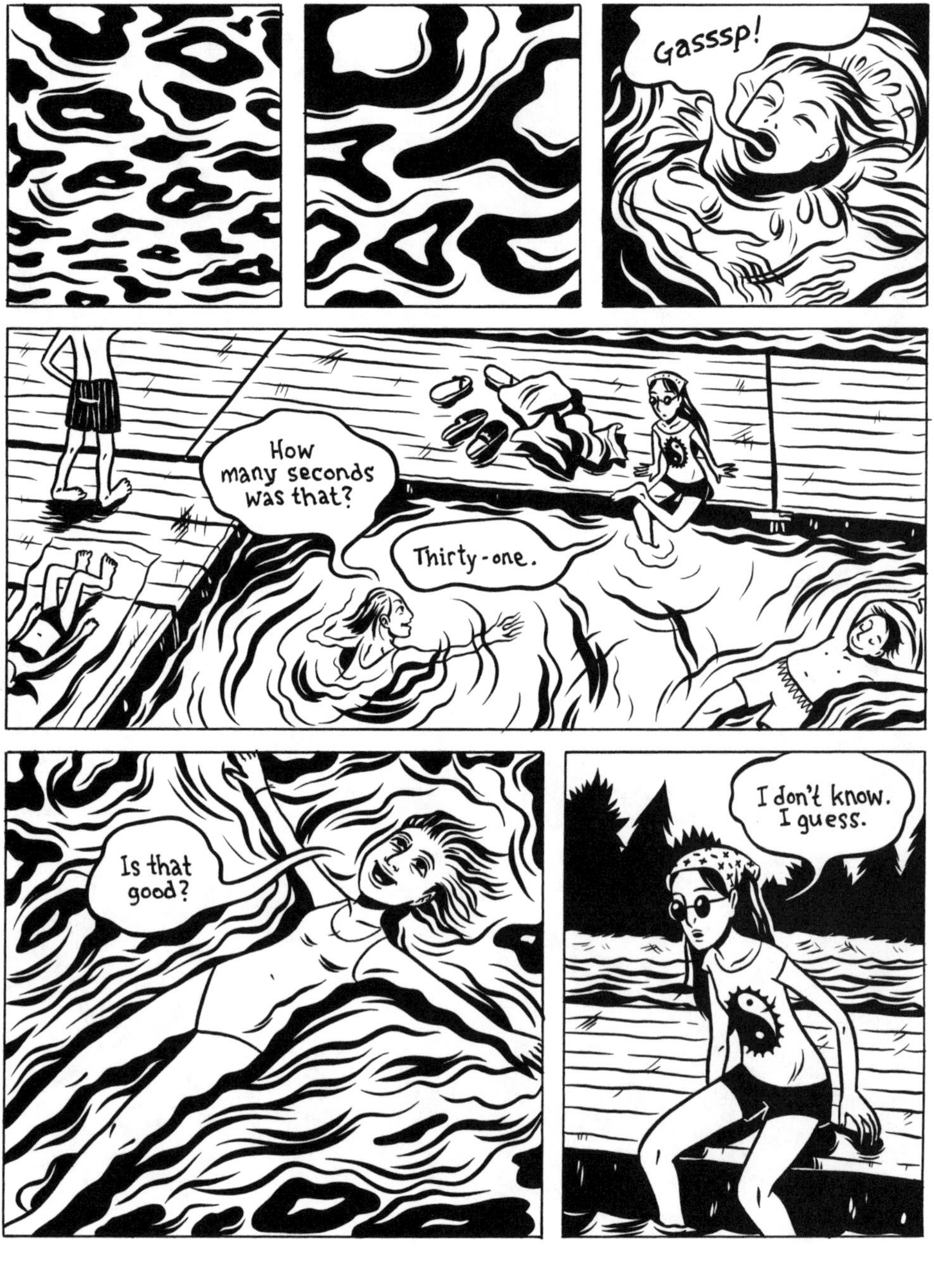

Gasssp!
How many seconds was that?
Thirty-one.
Is that good?
I don't know. I guess.

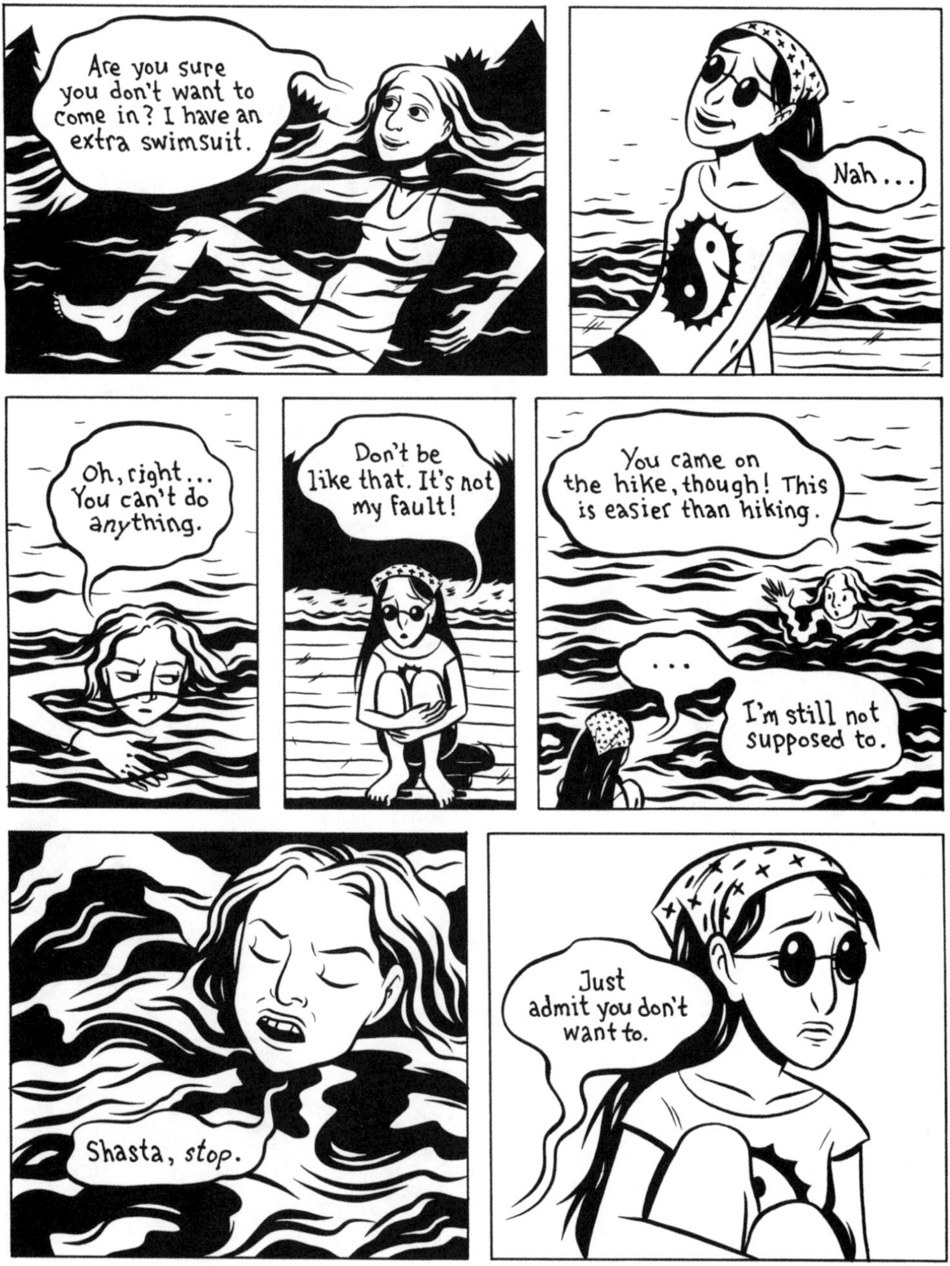
Are you sure you don't want to come in? I have an extra swimsuit.
Nah...
Oh, right... You can't do *any*thing.
Don't be like that. It's not my fault!
You came on the hike, though! This is easier than hiking.
...
I'm still not supposed to.
Shasta, *stop*.
Just admit you don't want to.

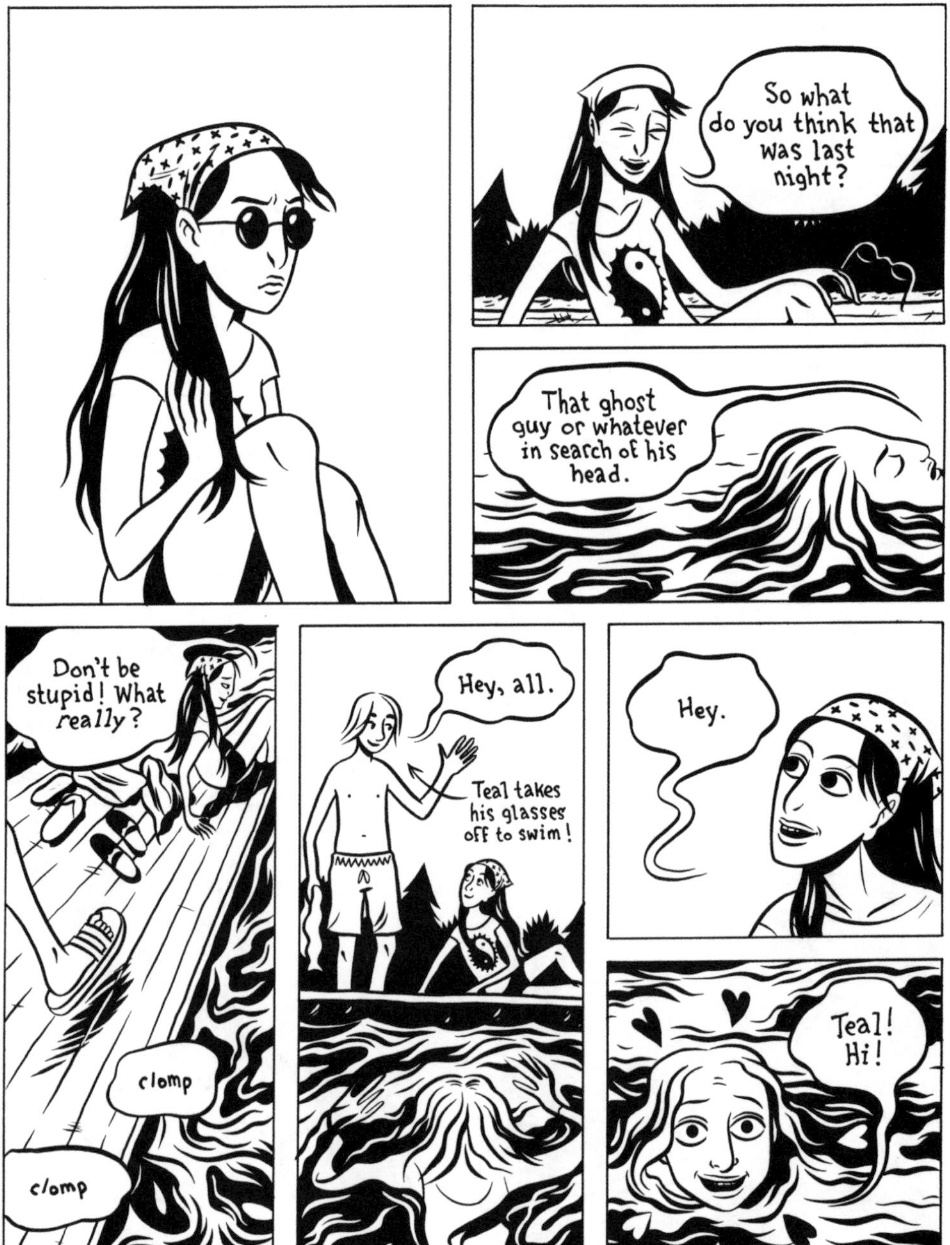
So what do you think that was last night?
That ghost guy or whatever in search of his head.
Don't be stupid! What *really*?
clomp
clomp
Hey, all.
Teal takes his glasses off to swim!
Hey.
Teal! Hi!

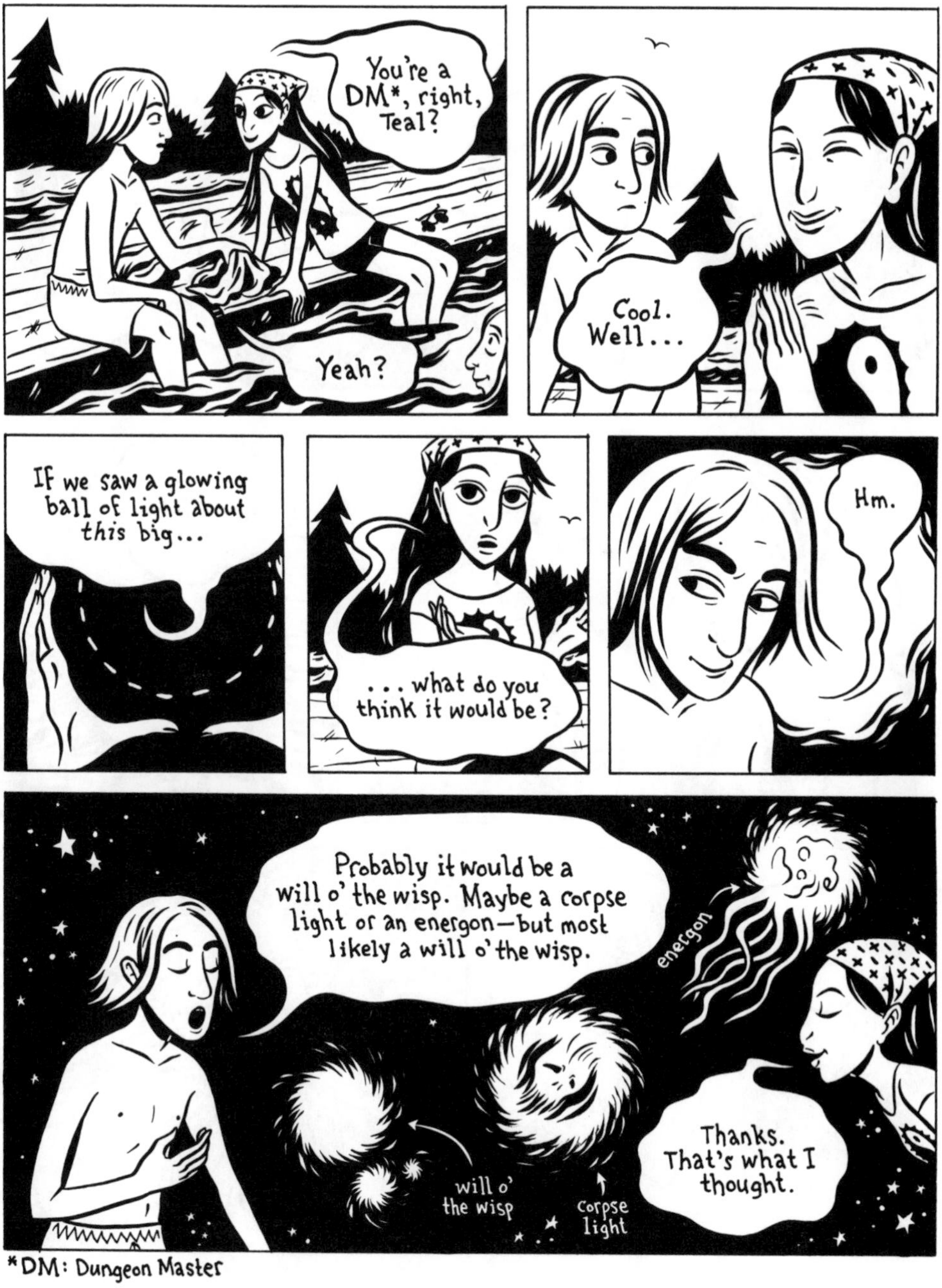
You're a DM*, right, Teal?
Yeah?
Cool. Well...
If we saw a glowing ball of light about *this* big...
...what do you think it would be?
Hm.
Probably it would be a will o' the wisp. Maybe a corpse light or an energon—but most likely a will o' the wisp.
energon
will o' the wisp
corpse light
Thanks. That's what I thought.

*DM: Dungeon Master

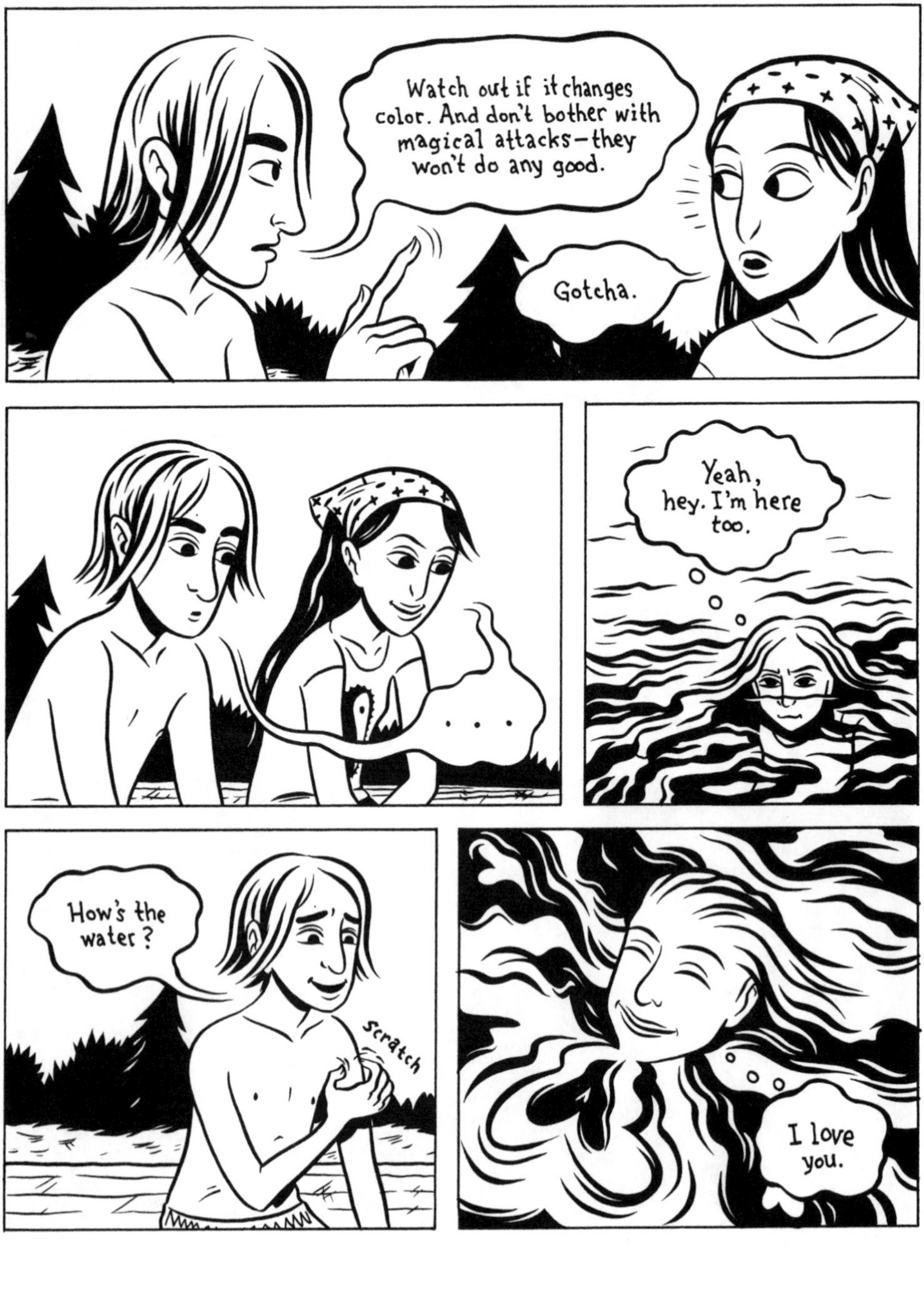
Watch out if it changes color. And don't bother with magical attacks—they won't do any good.
Gotcha.
. . .
Yeah, hey. I'm here too.
How's the water?
Scratch
I love you.

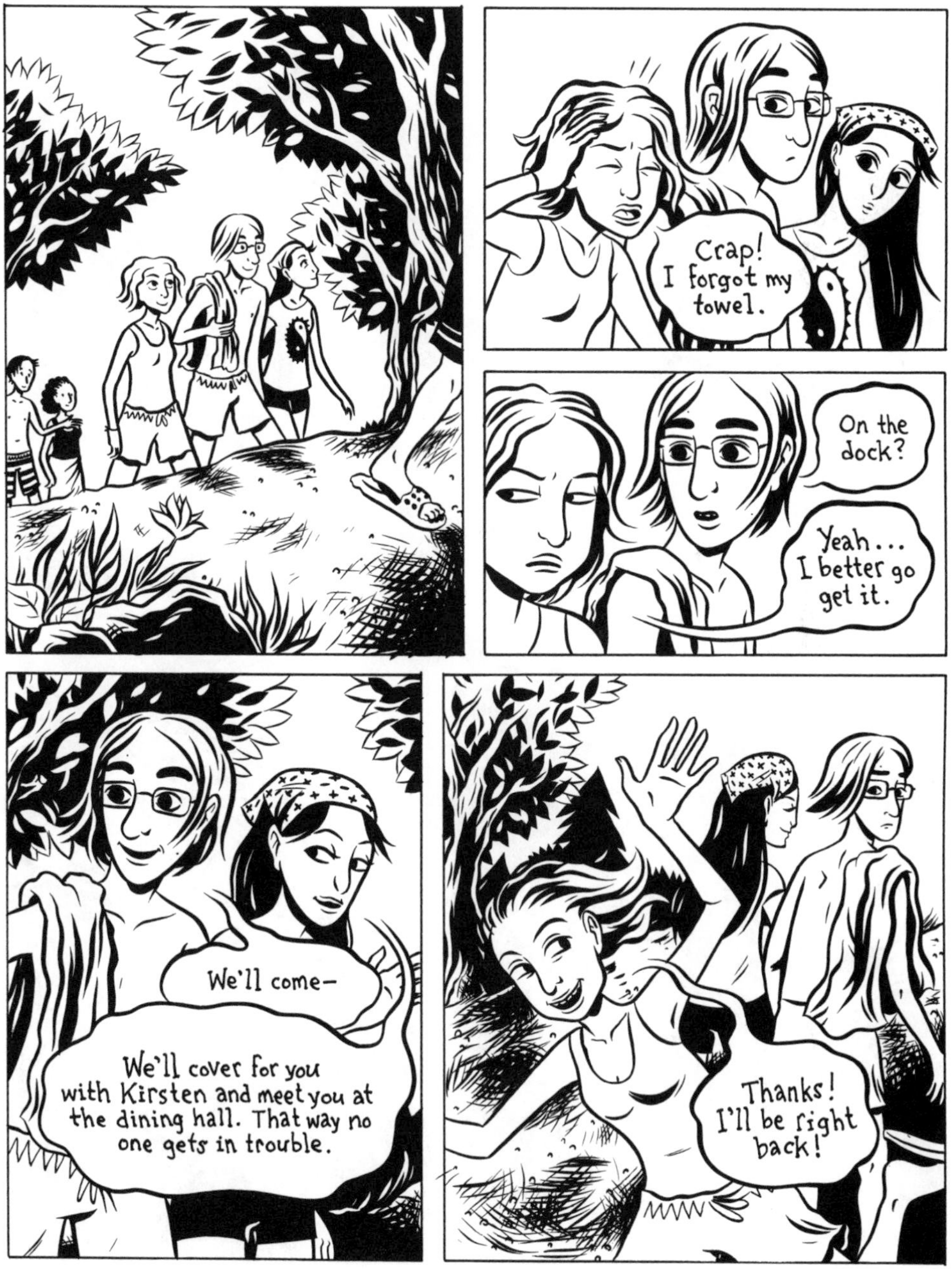

Crap! I forgot my towel.
On the dock?
Yeah... I better go get it.
We'll come–
We'll cover for you with Kirsten and meet you at the dining hall. That way no one gets in trouble.
Thanks! I'll be right back!

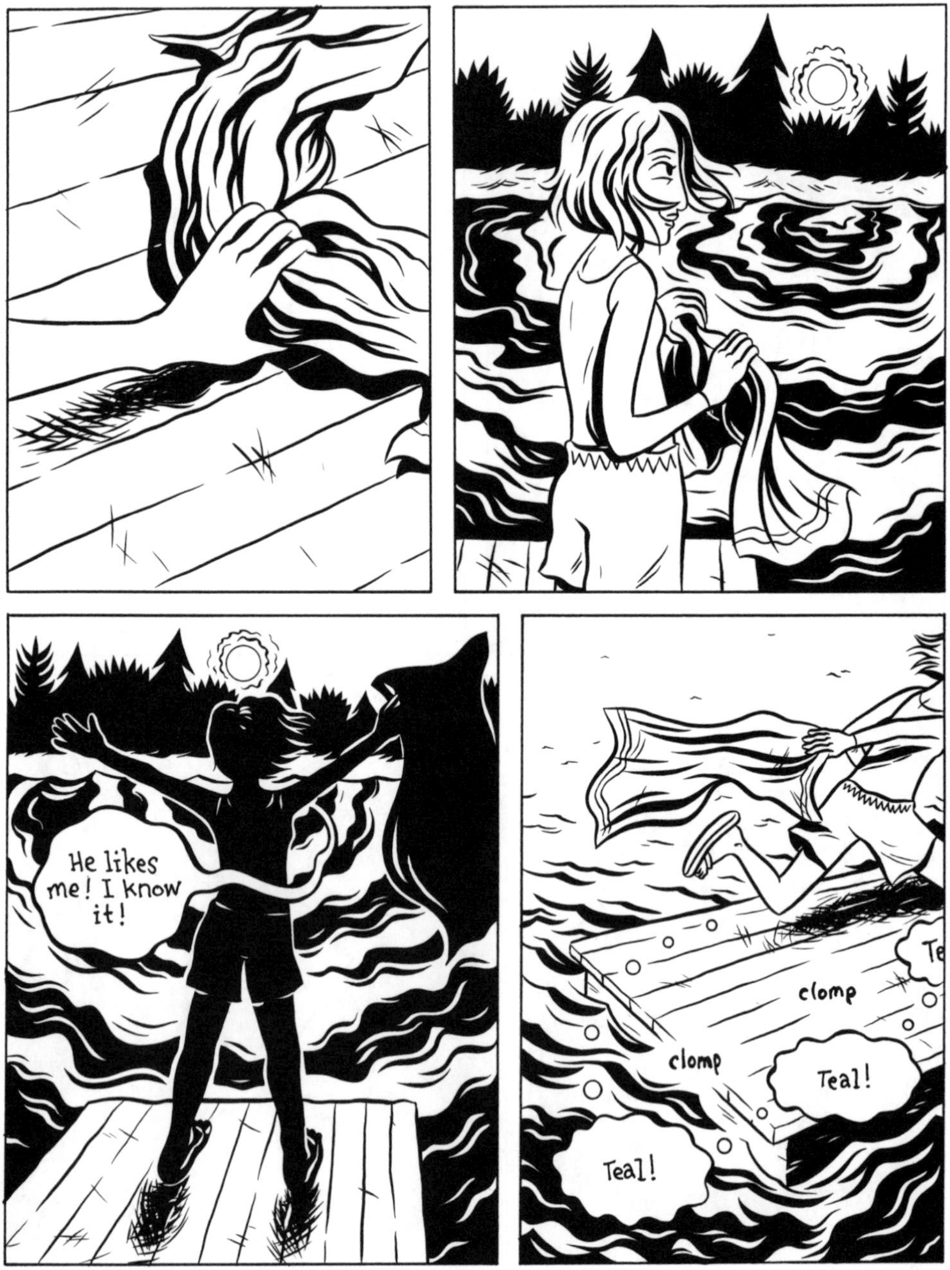
He likes me! I know it!
clomp
clomp
Teal!
Teal!

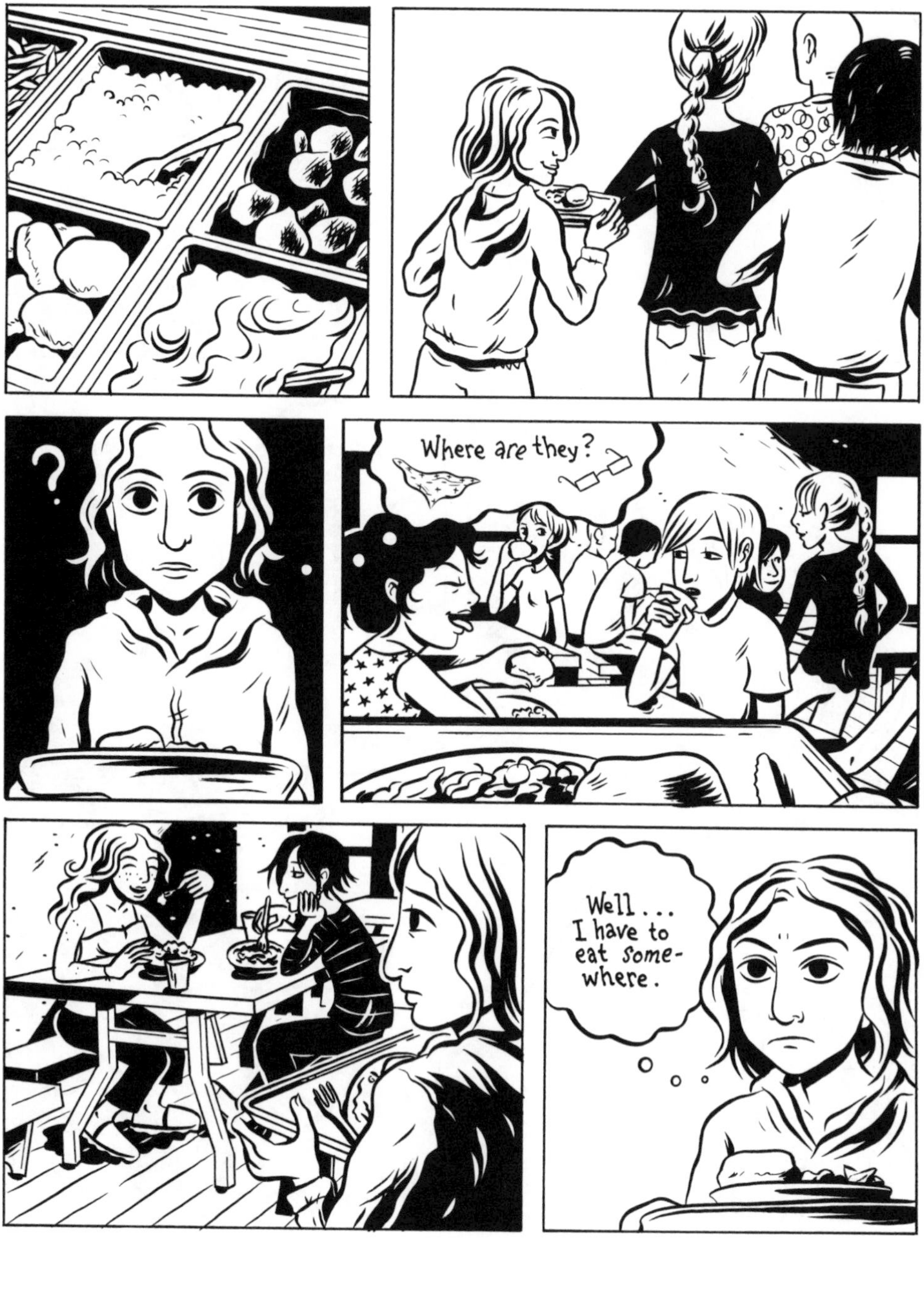
Where are they?
Well... I have to eat some-where.

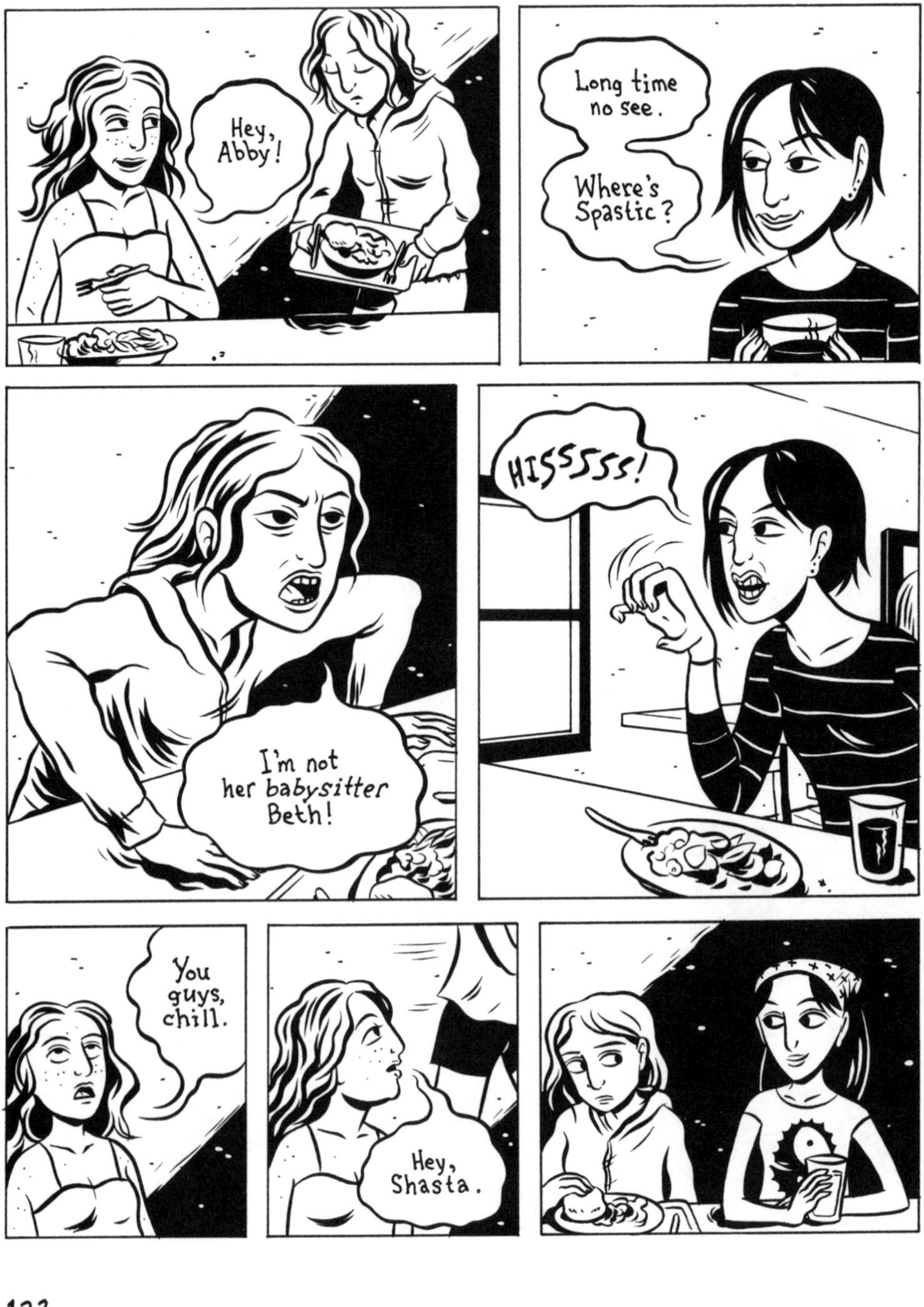

Hey, Abby!
Long time no see.
Where's Spastic?
I'm not her *babysitter* Beth!
HISSSSSS!
You guys, chill.
Hey, Shasta.

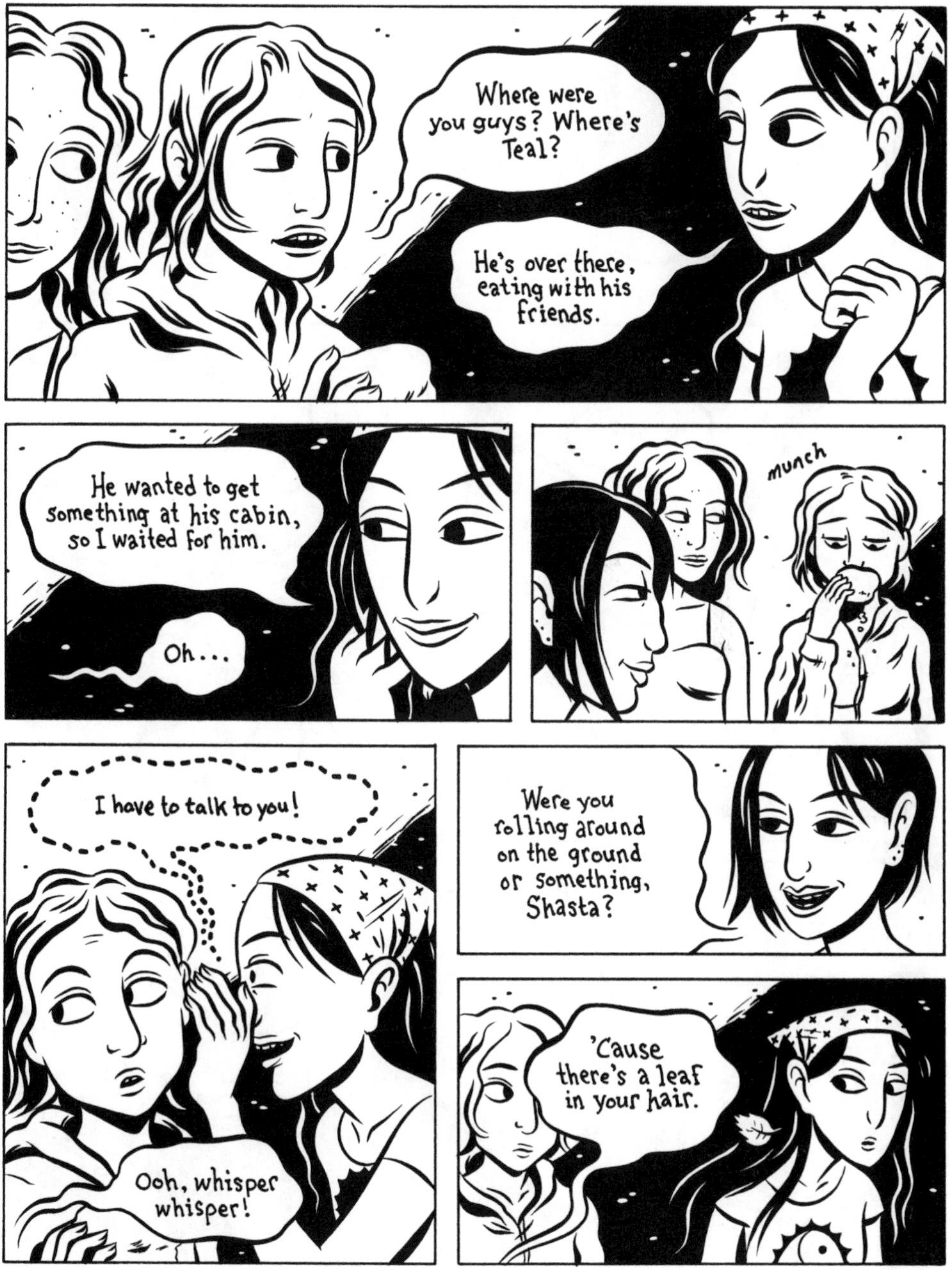
Where were you guys? Where's Teal?
He's over there, eating with his friends.
He wanted to get something at his cabin, so I waited for him.
Oh...
munch
I have to talk to you!
Ooh, whisper whisper!
Were you rolling around on the ground or something, Shasta?
'Cause there's a leaf in your hair.

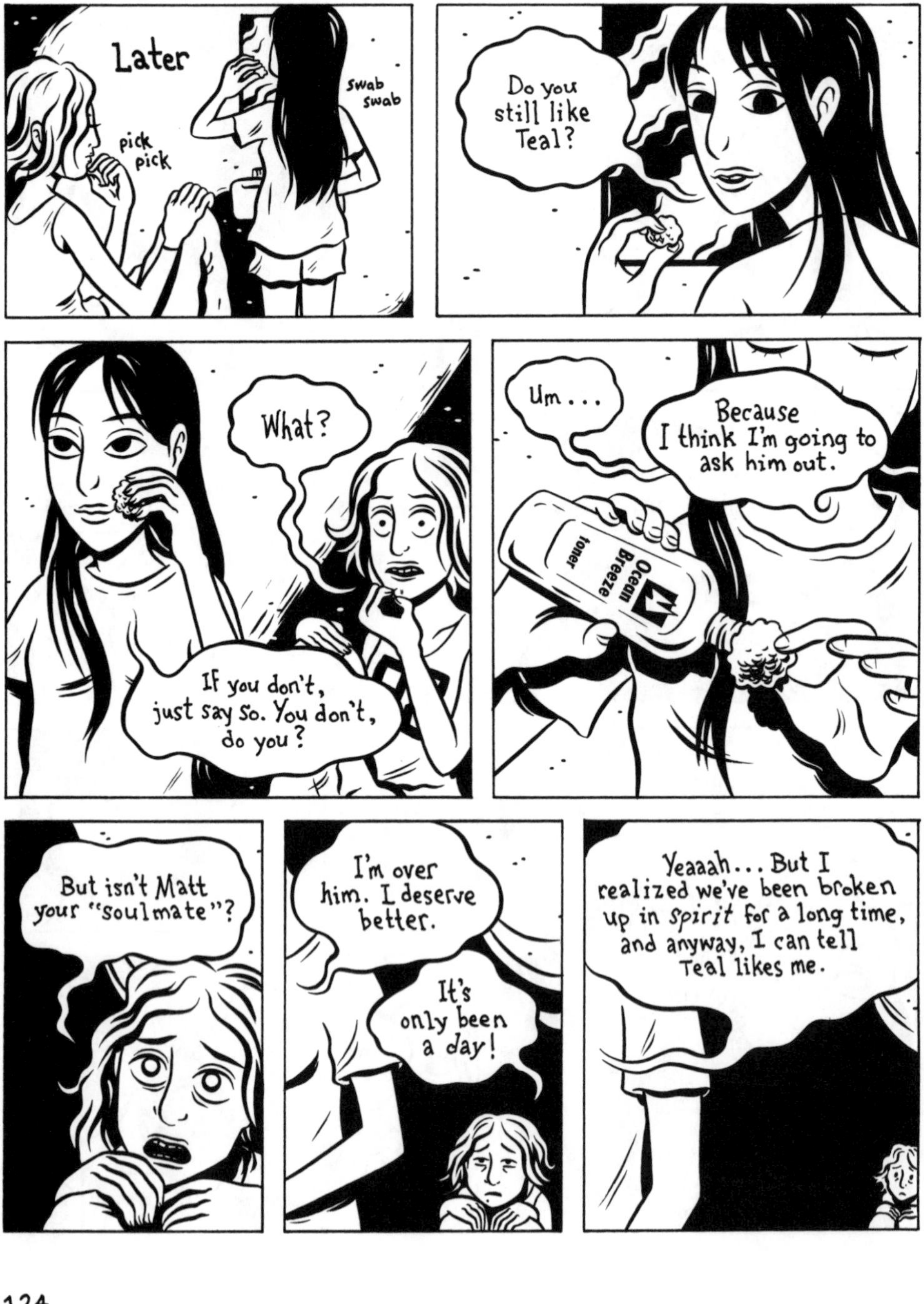
Later
swab swab
pick pick
Do you still like Teal?
What?
If you don't, just say so. You don't, do you?
Um . . .
Because I think I'm going to ask him out.
Ocean Breeze toner
But isn't Matt your "soulmate"?
I'm over him. I deserve better.
It's only been a day!
Yeaaah . . . But I realized we've been broken up in *spirit* for a long time, and anyway, I can tell Teal likes me.

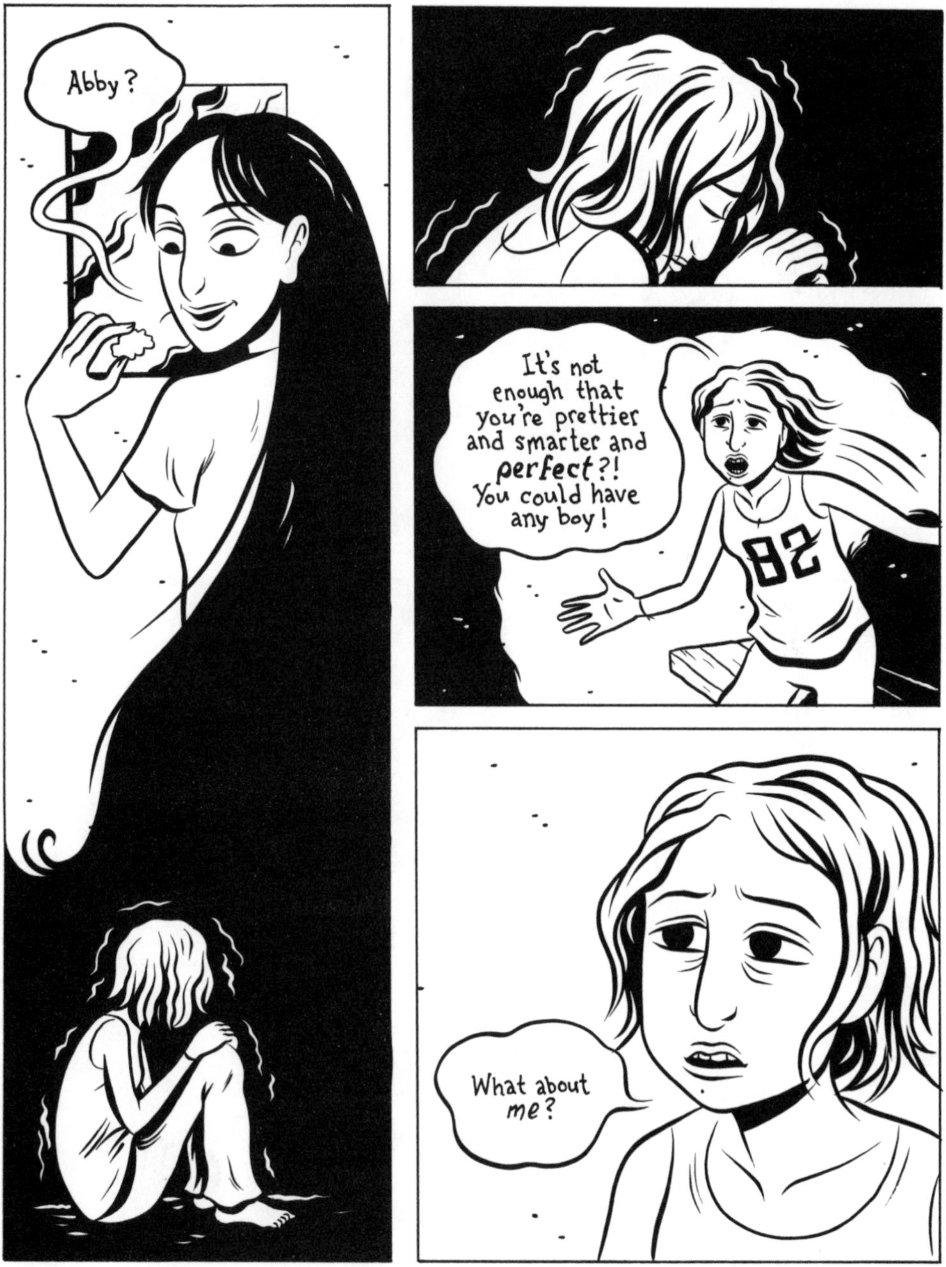
Abby?
It's not enough that you're prettier and smarter and perfect?! You could have any boy!
82
What about me?

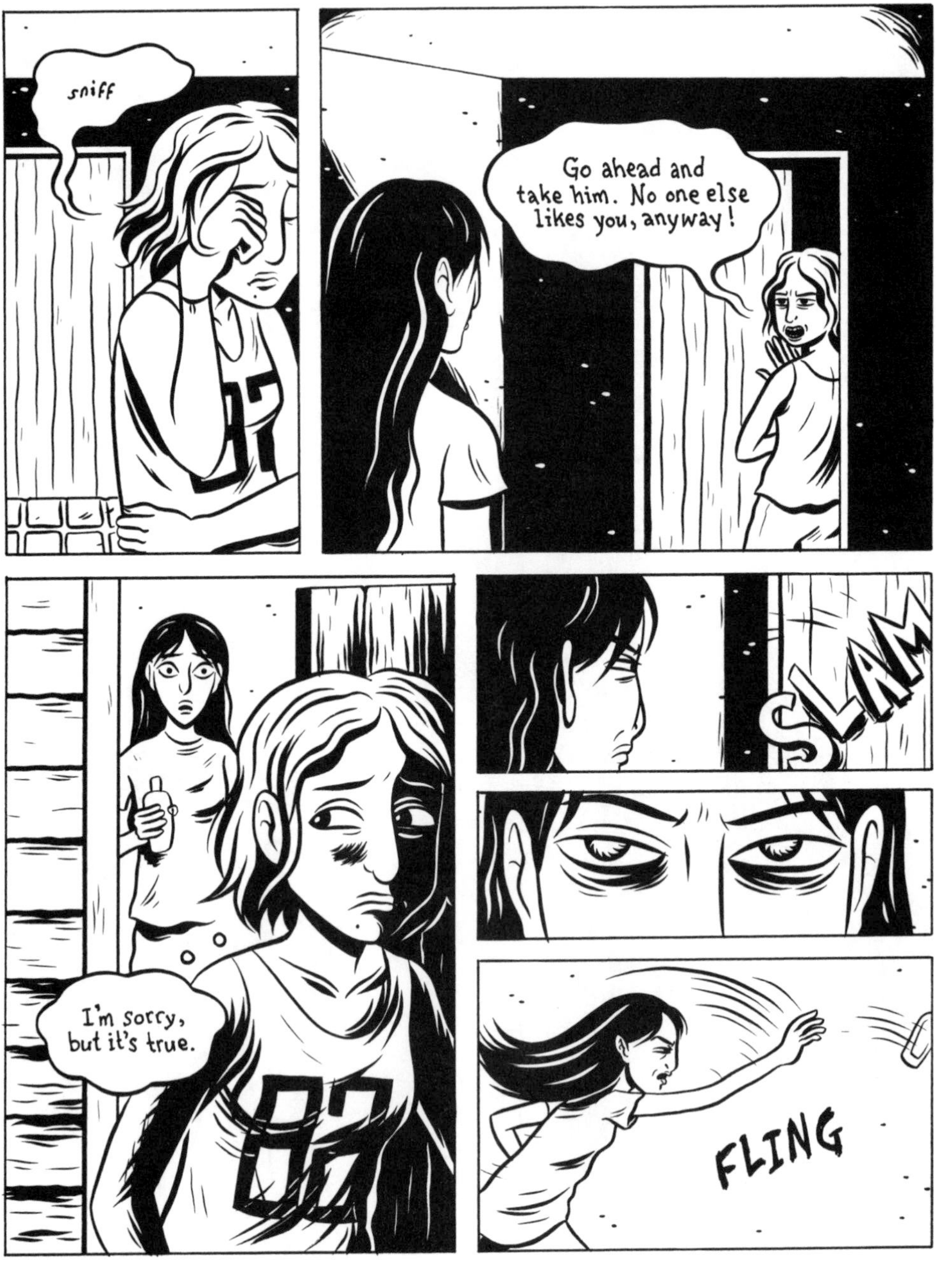
sniff
Go ahead and take him. No one else likes you, anyway!
SLAM
I'm sorry, but it's true.
FLING

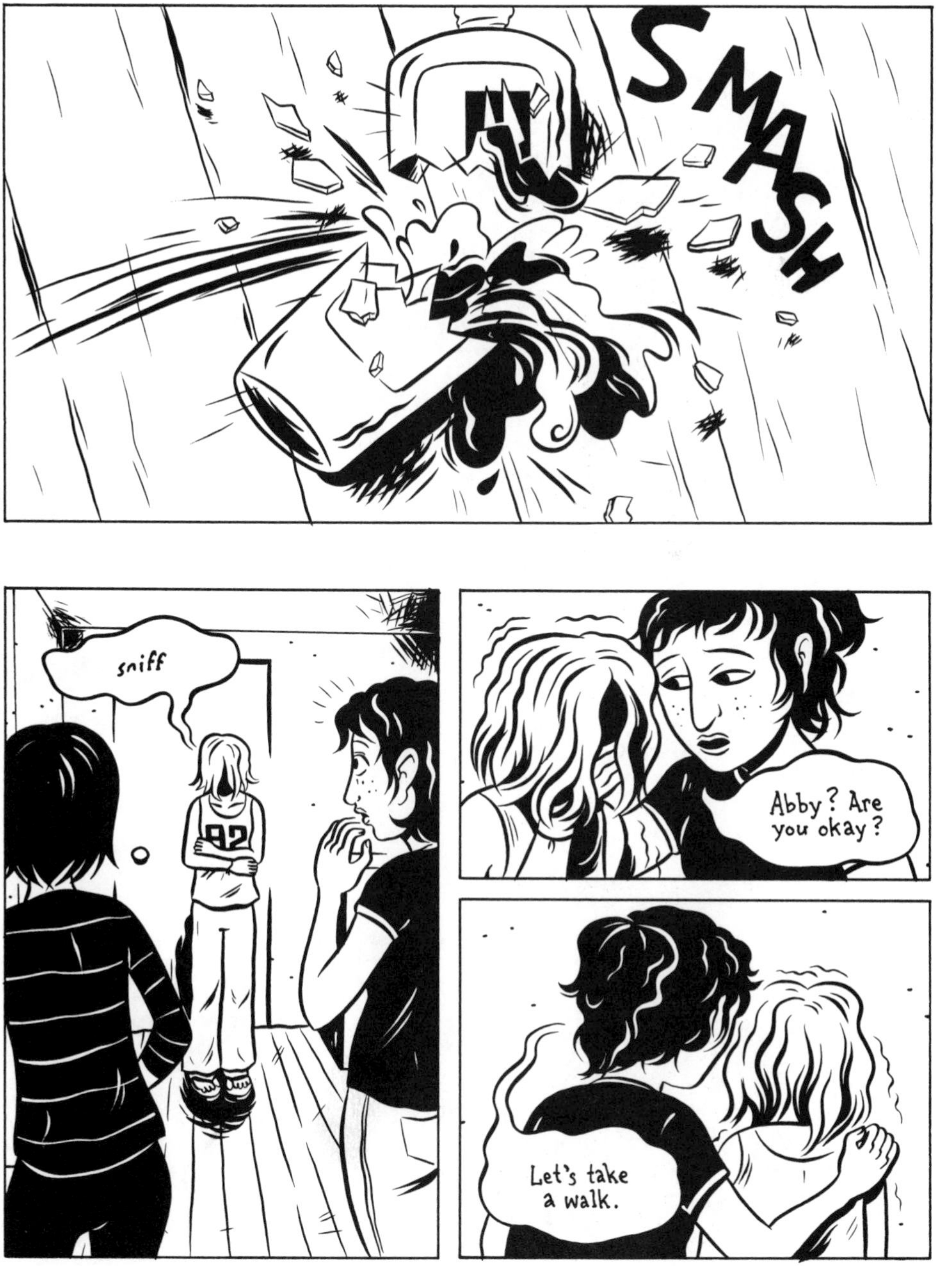
SMASH
sniff
Abby? Are you okay?
Let's take a walk.

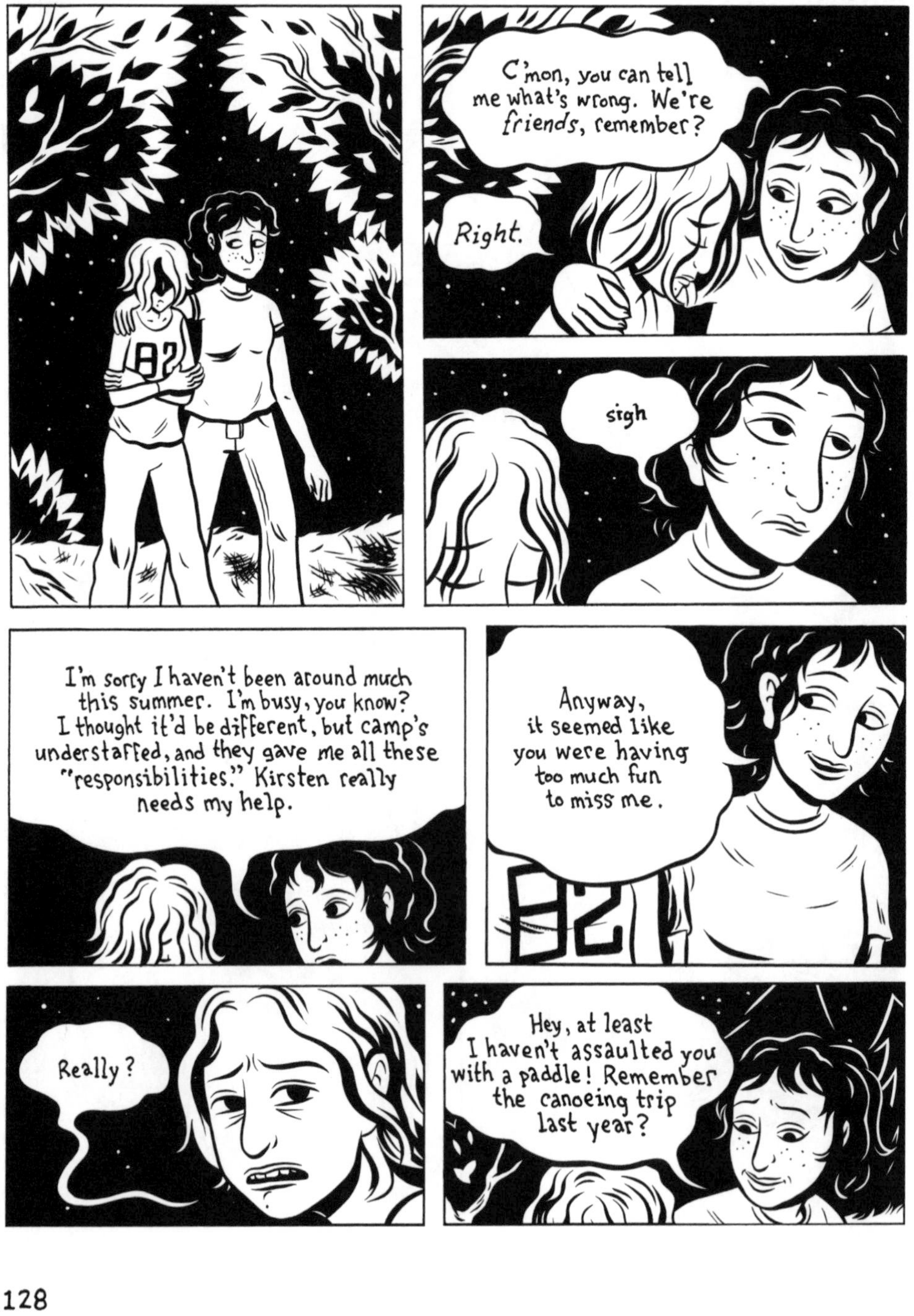
C'mon, you can tell me what's wrong. We're *friends*, remember?
Right.
sigh
I'm sorry I haven't been around much this summer. I'm busy, you know? I thought it'd be different, but camp's understaffed, and they gave me all these "responsibilities." Kirsten really needs my help.
Anyway, it seemed like you were having too much fun to miss me.
Really?
Hey, at least I haven't assaulted you with a paddle! Remember the canoeing trip last year?

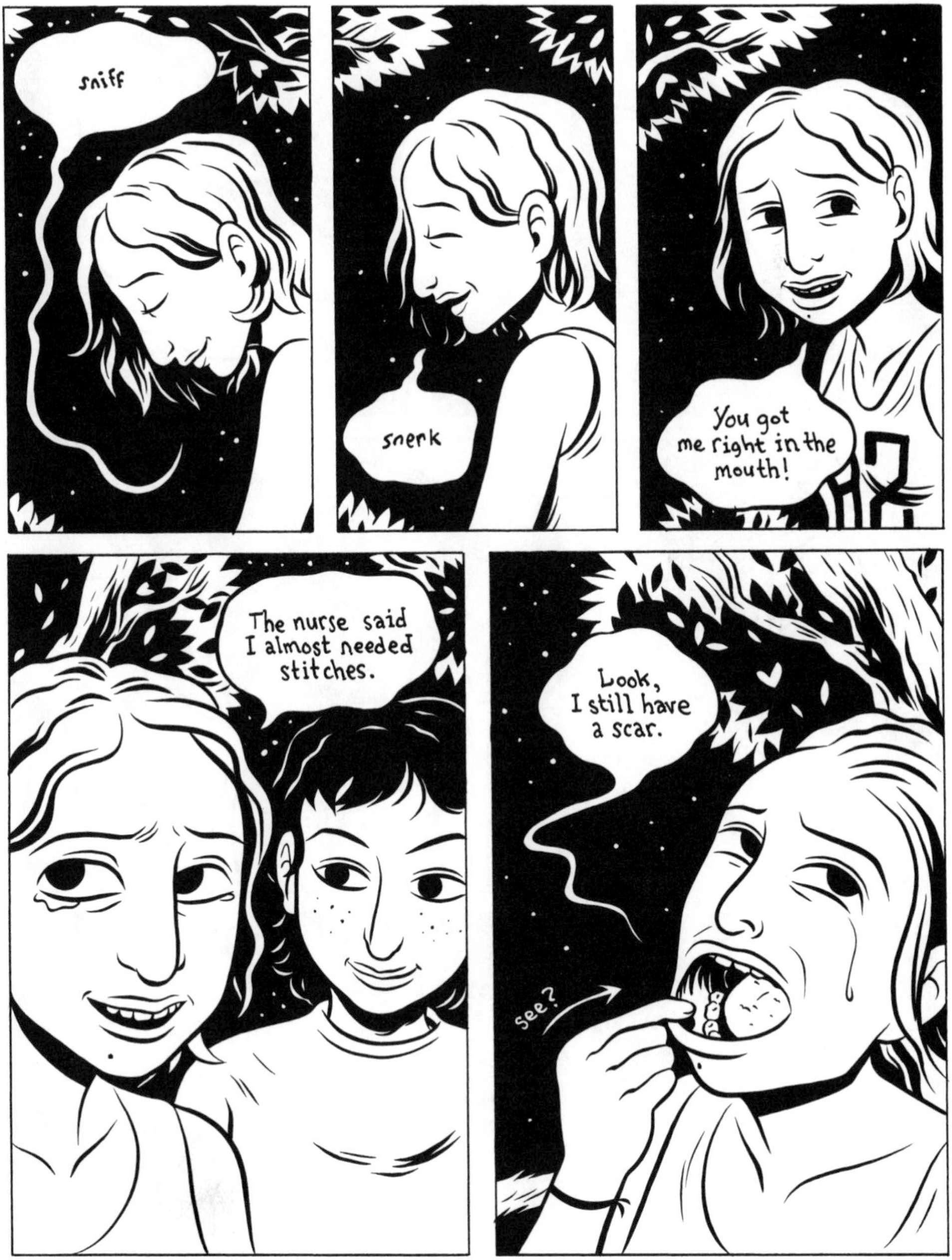
sniff
snerk
You got me right in the mouth!
The nurse said I almost needed stitches.
Look, I still have a scar.
see?

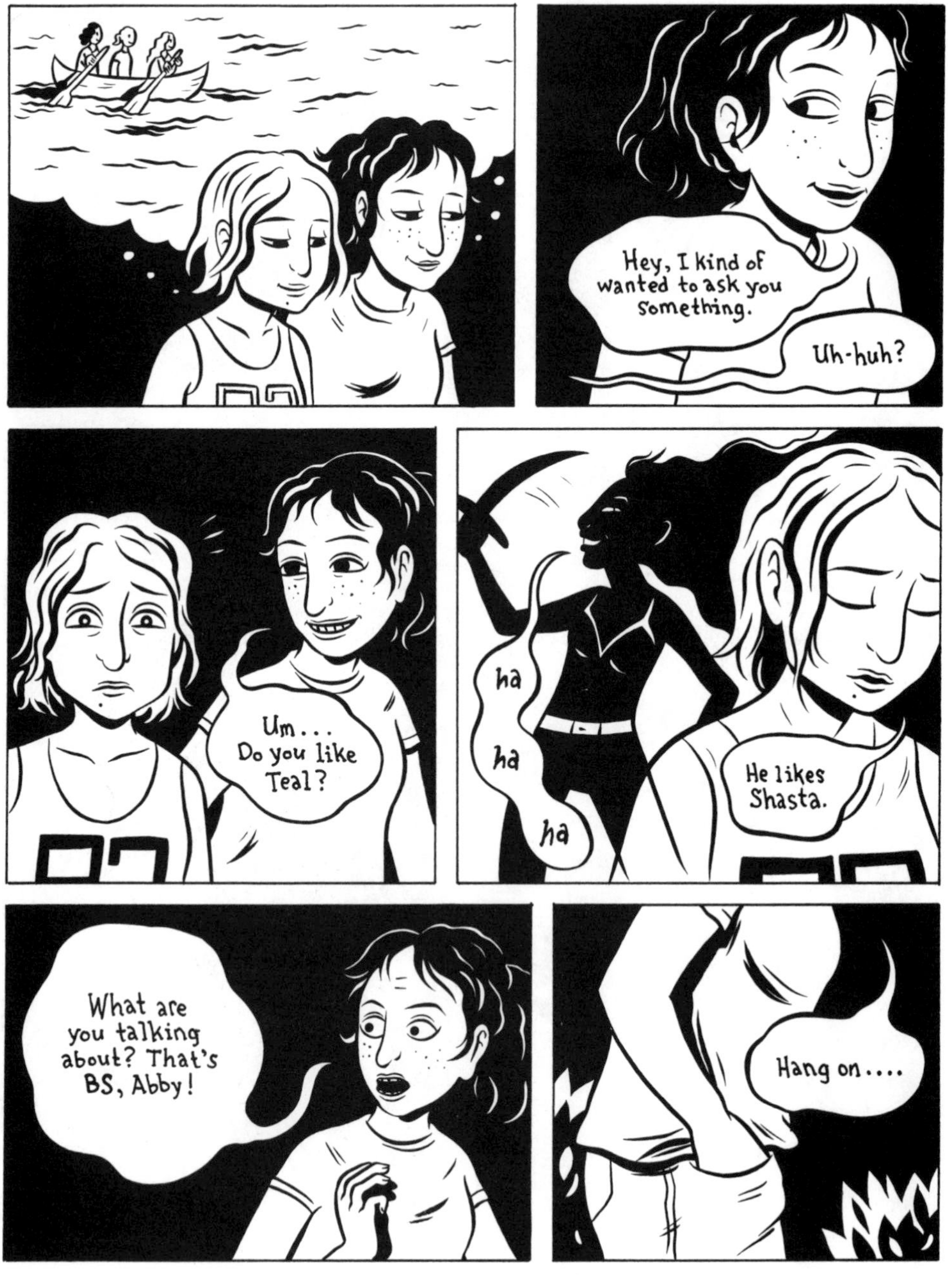
Hey, I kind of wanted to ask you something.
Uh-huh?
Um... Do you like Teal?
ha
ha
ha
He likes Shasta.
What are you talking about? That's BS, Abby!
Hang on....

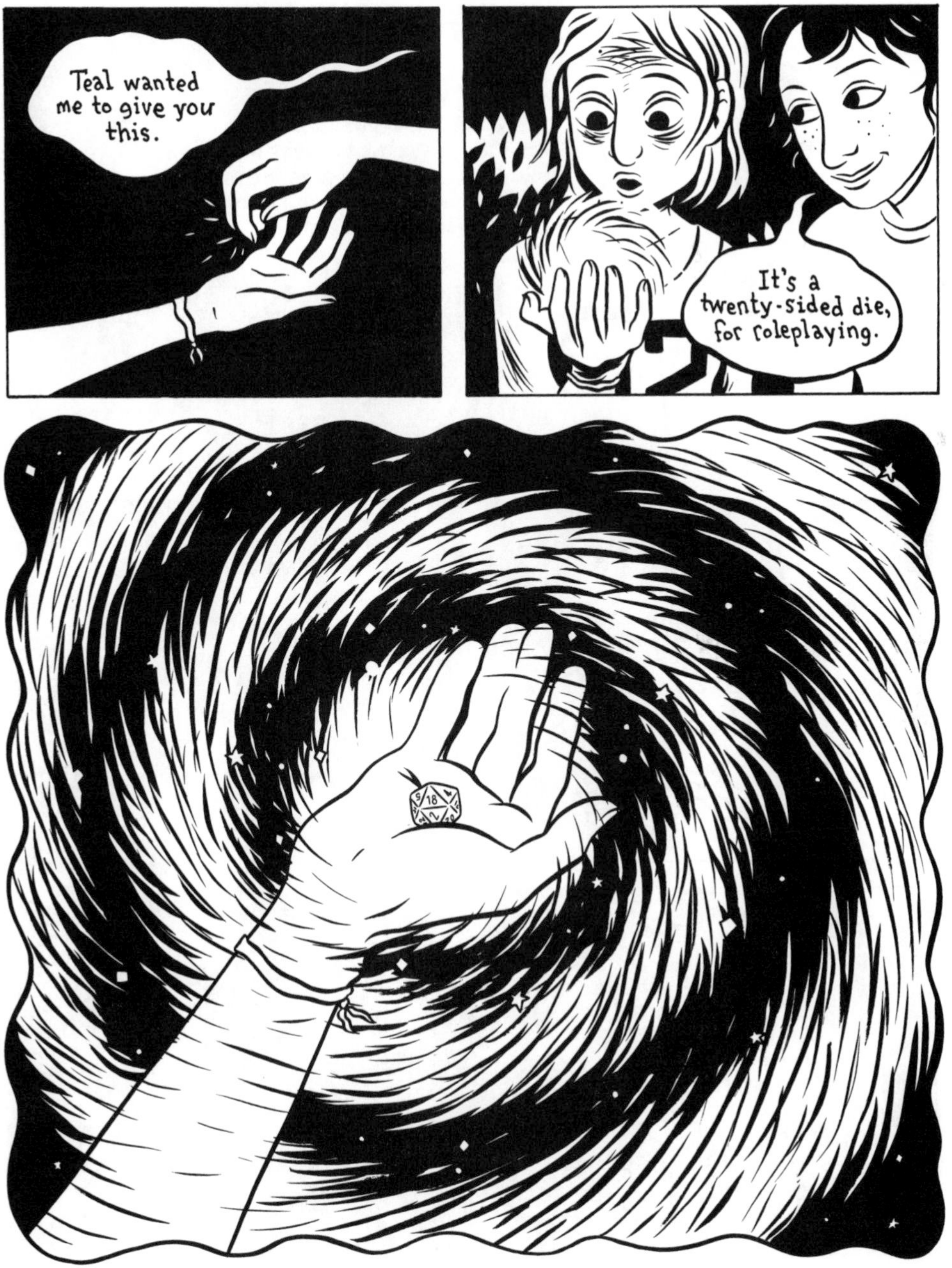
Teal wanted me to give you this.
It's a twenty-sided die, for roleplaying.

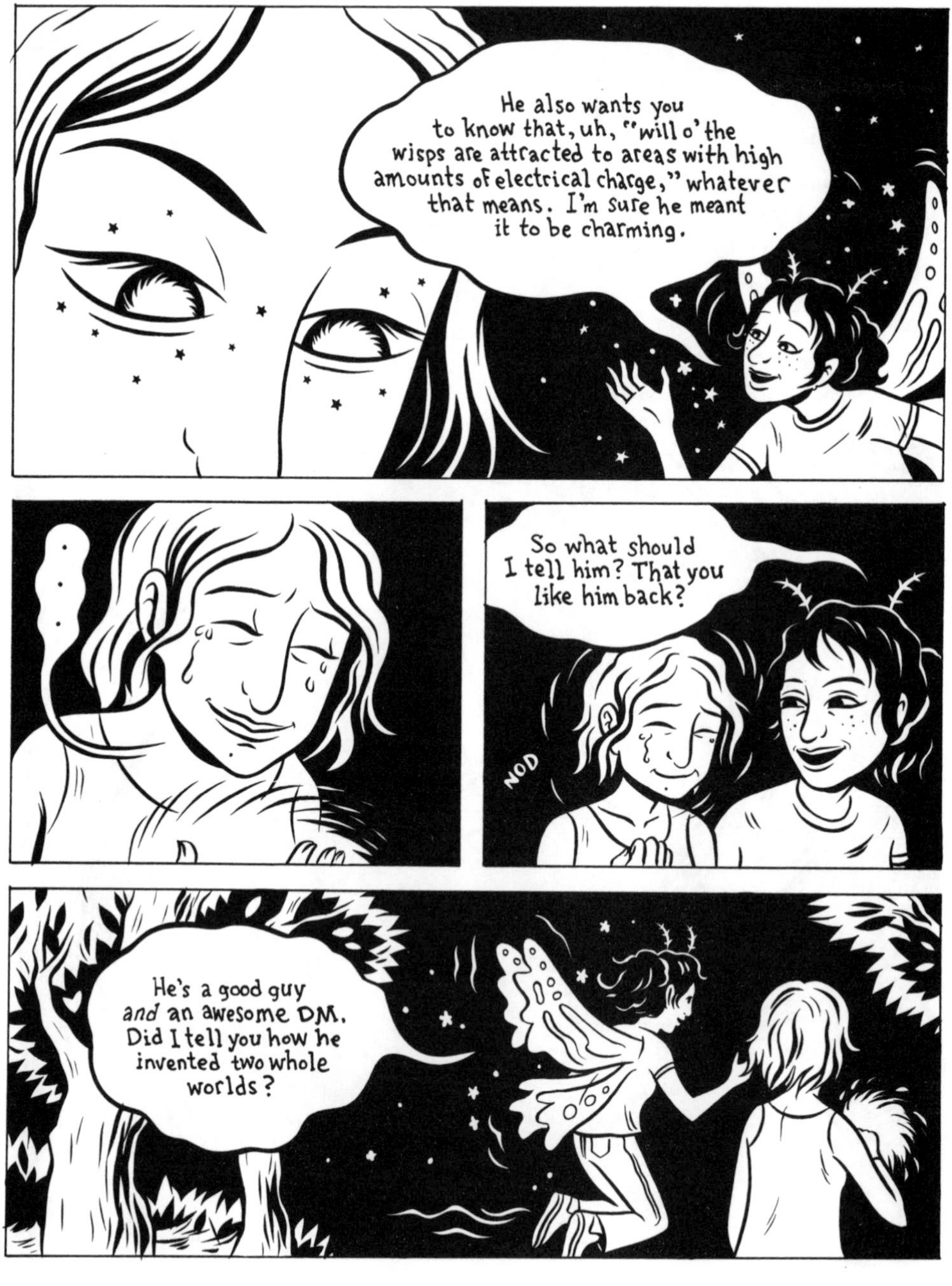
He also wants you to know that, uh, "will o' the wisps are attracted to areas with high amounts of electrical charge," whatever that means. I'm sure he meant it to be charming.
So what should I tell him? That you like him back?
NOD
He's a good guy *and* an awesome DM. Did I tell you how he invented two whole worlds?

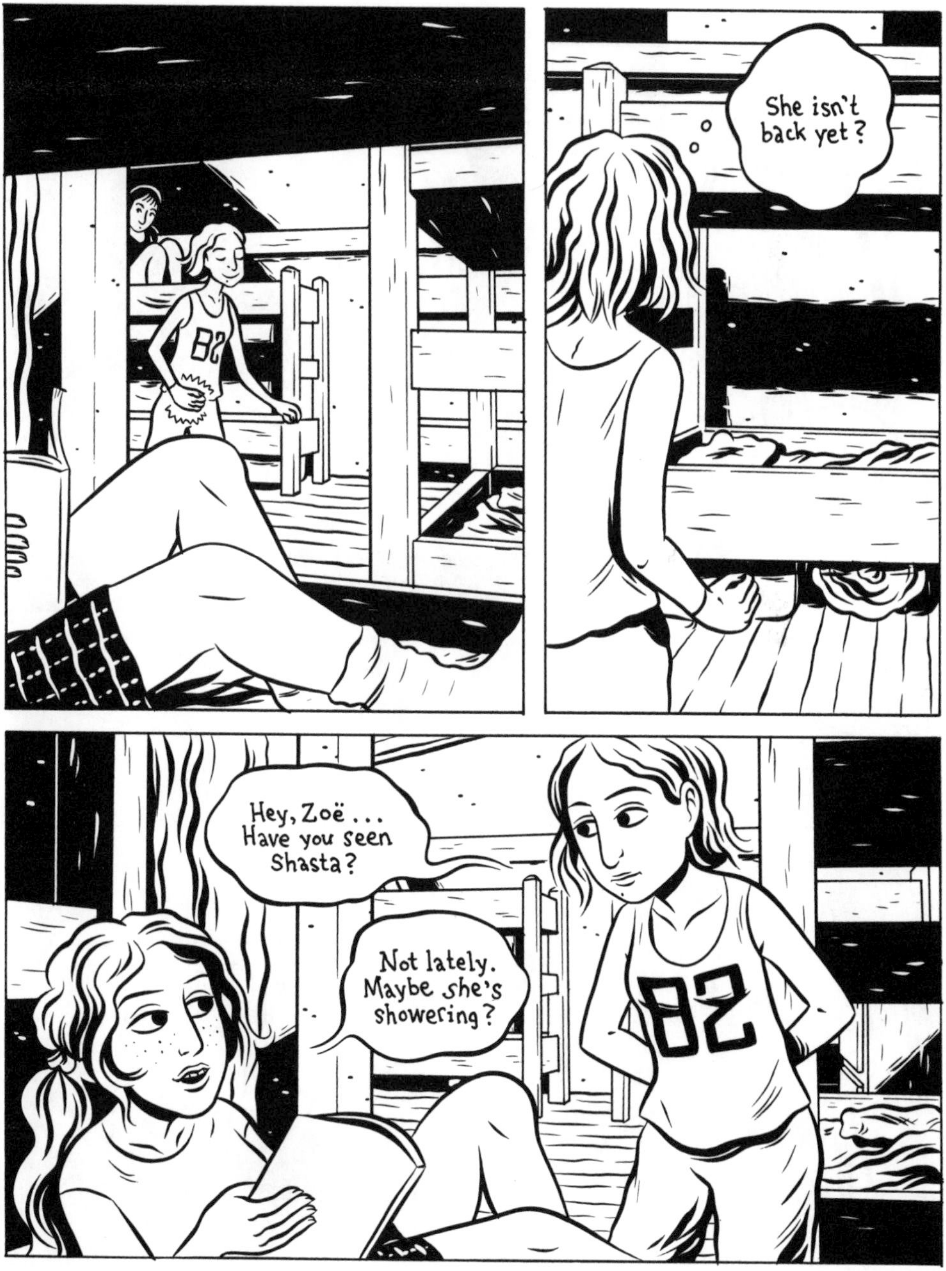
She isn't back yet?
Hey, Zoë . . . Have you seen Shasta?
Not lately. Maybe she's showering?

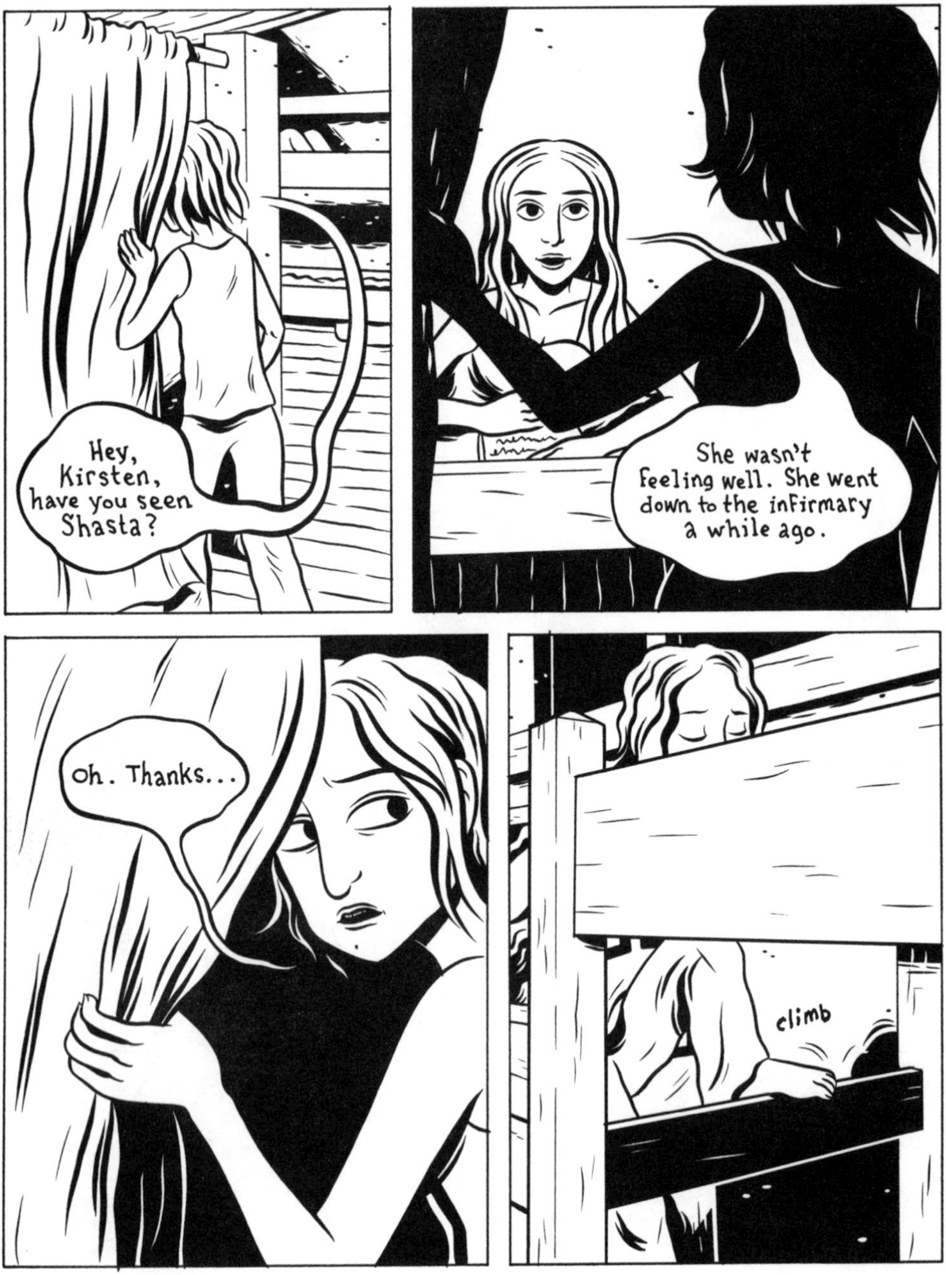
Hey, Kirsten, have you seen Shasta?
She wasn't feeling well. She went down to the infirmary a while ago.
Oh. Thanks...
climb

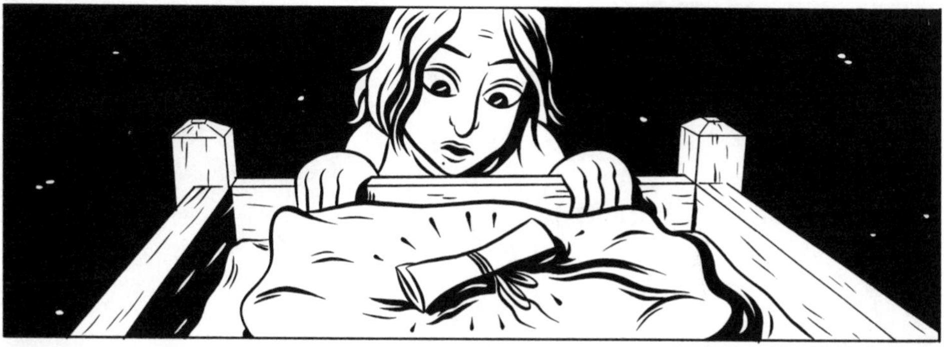

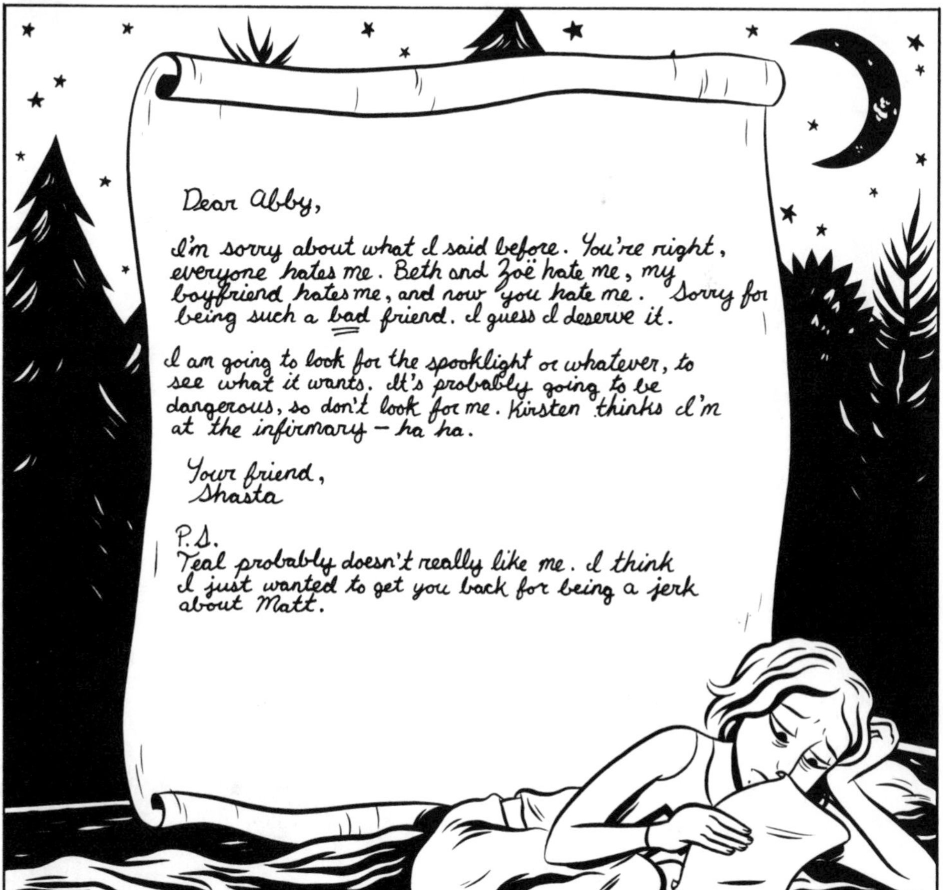
Dear Abby,
I'm sorry about what I said before. You're right, everyone hates me. Beth and Zoë hate me, my boyfriend hates me, and now you hate me. Sorry for being such a bad friend. I guess I deserve it.
I am going to look for the spooklight or whatever, to see what it wants. It's probably going to be dangerous, so don't look for me. Kirsten thinks I'm at the infirmary - ha ha.
Your friend,
Shasta
P.S.
Teal probably doesn't really like me. I think I just wanted to get you back for being a jerk about Matt.

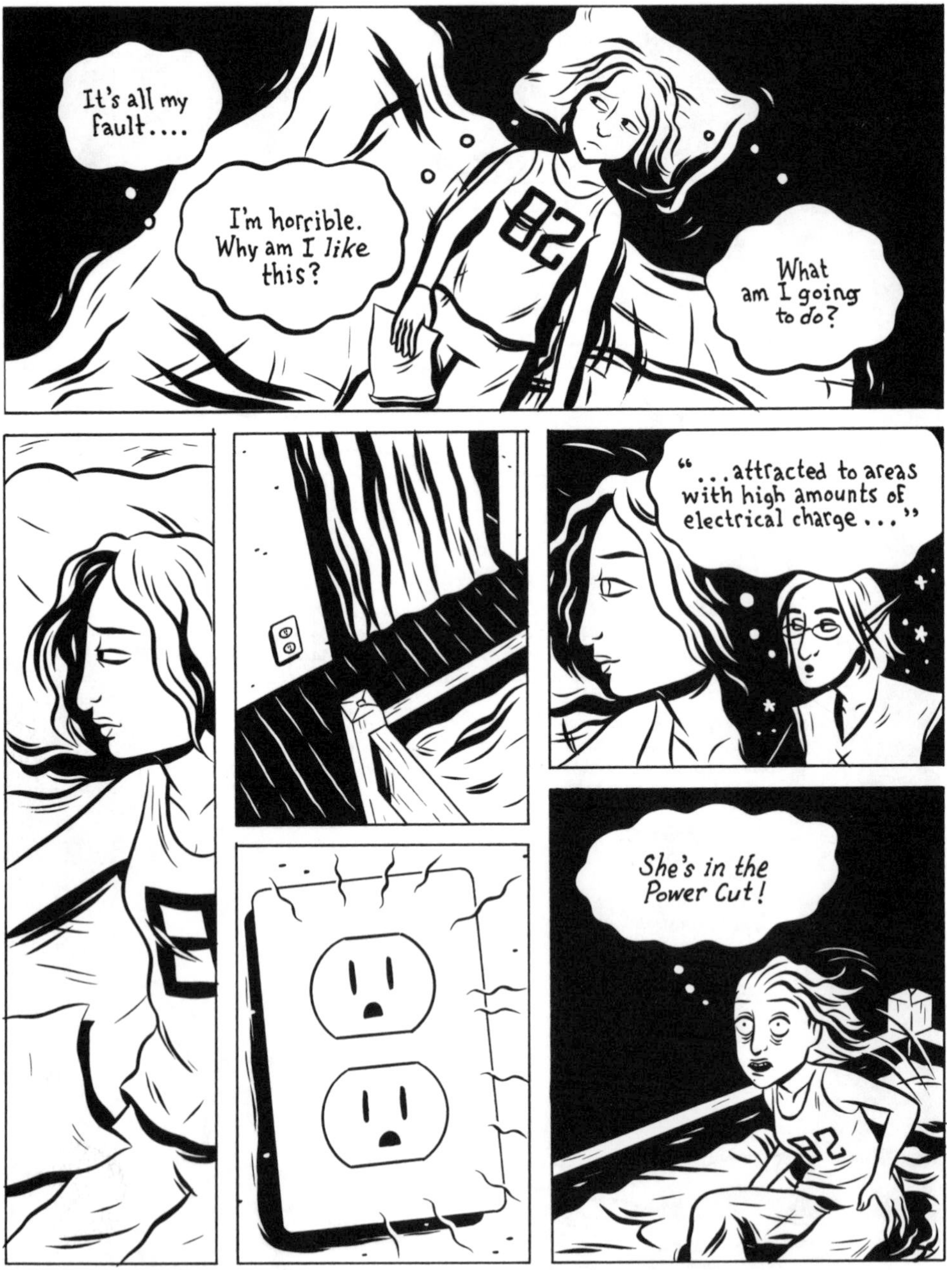
It's all my fault....
I'm horrible. Why am I like this?
What am I going to do?
"...attracted to areas with high amounts of electrical charge..."
She's in the Power Cut!

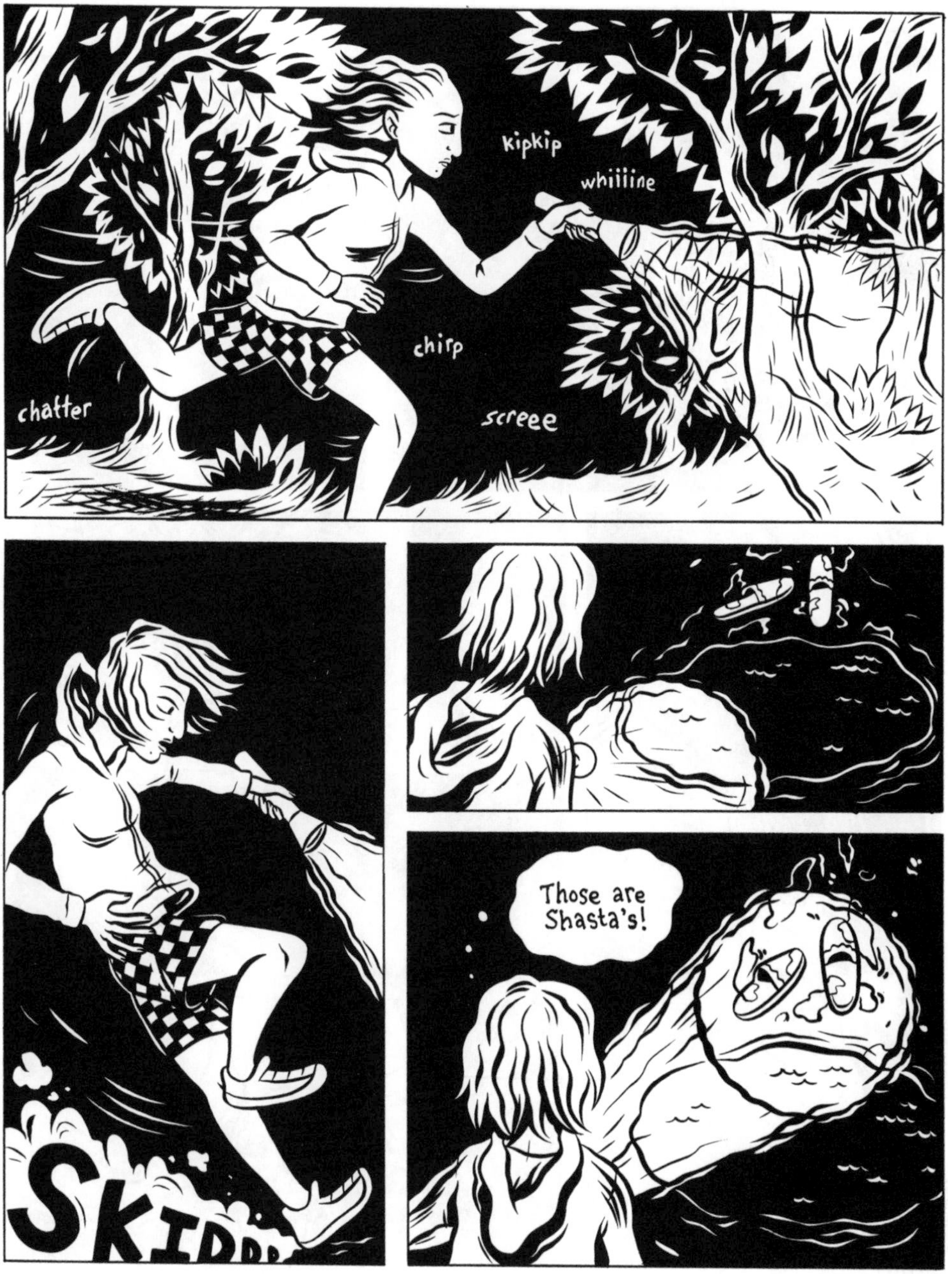
kipkip
whiiiine
chirp
chatter
screee
Those are Shasta's!

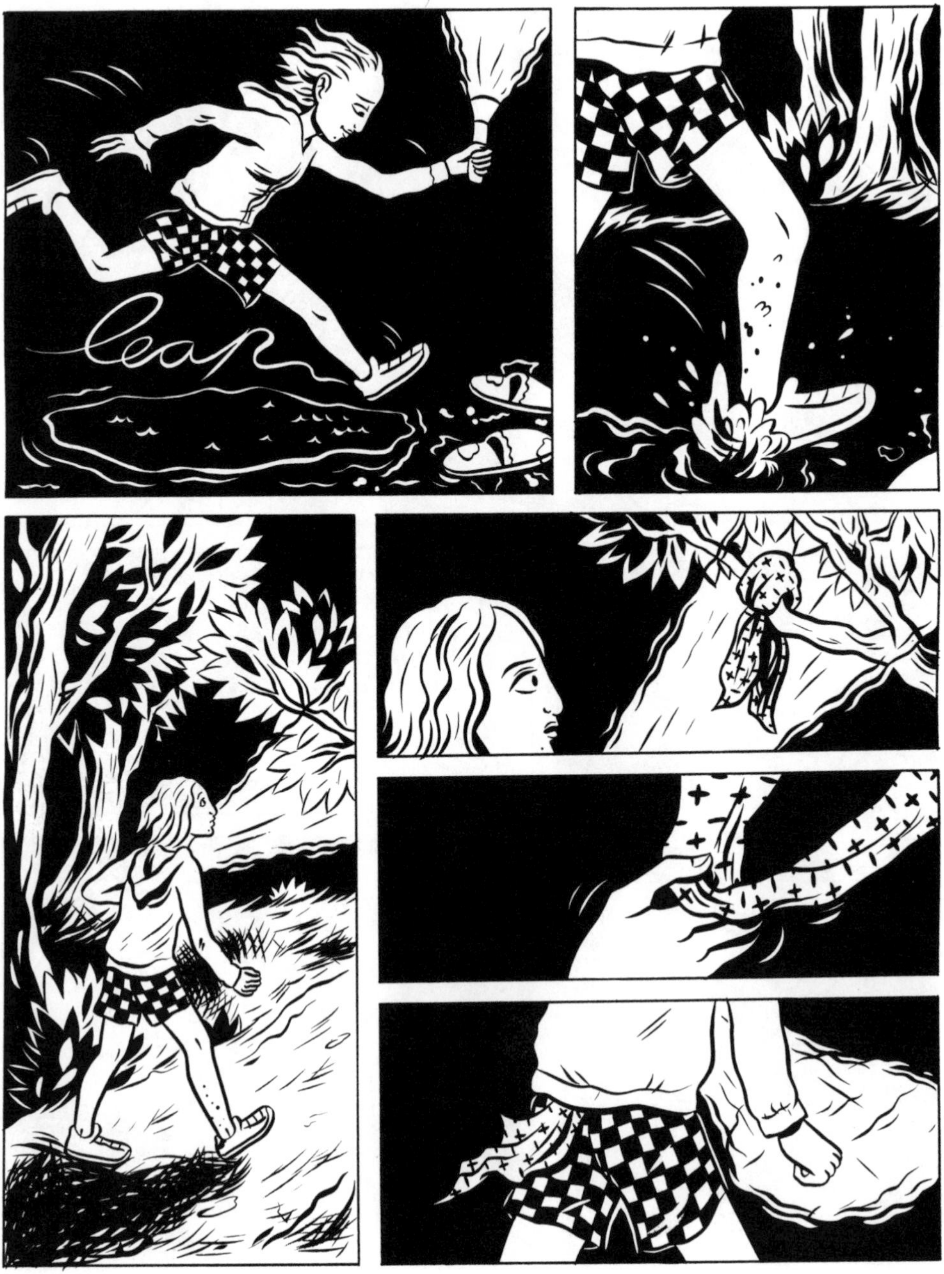
leap

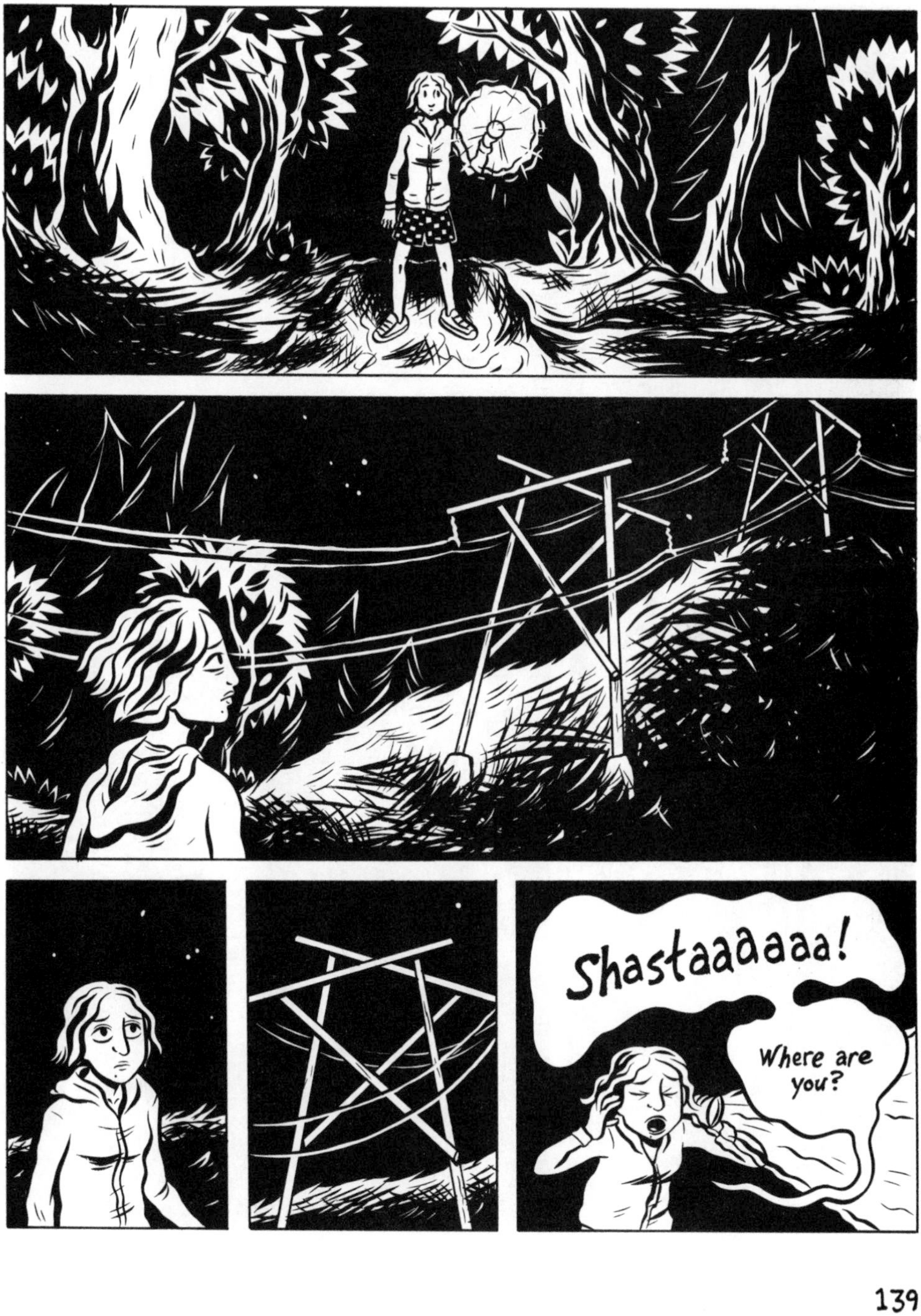
Shastaaaaaa!
Where are you?

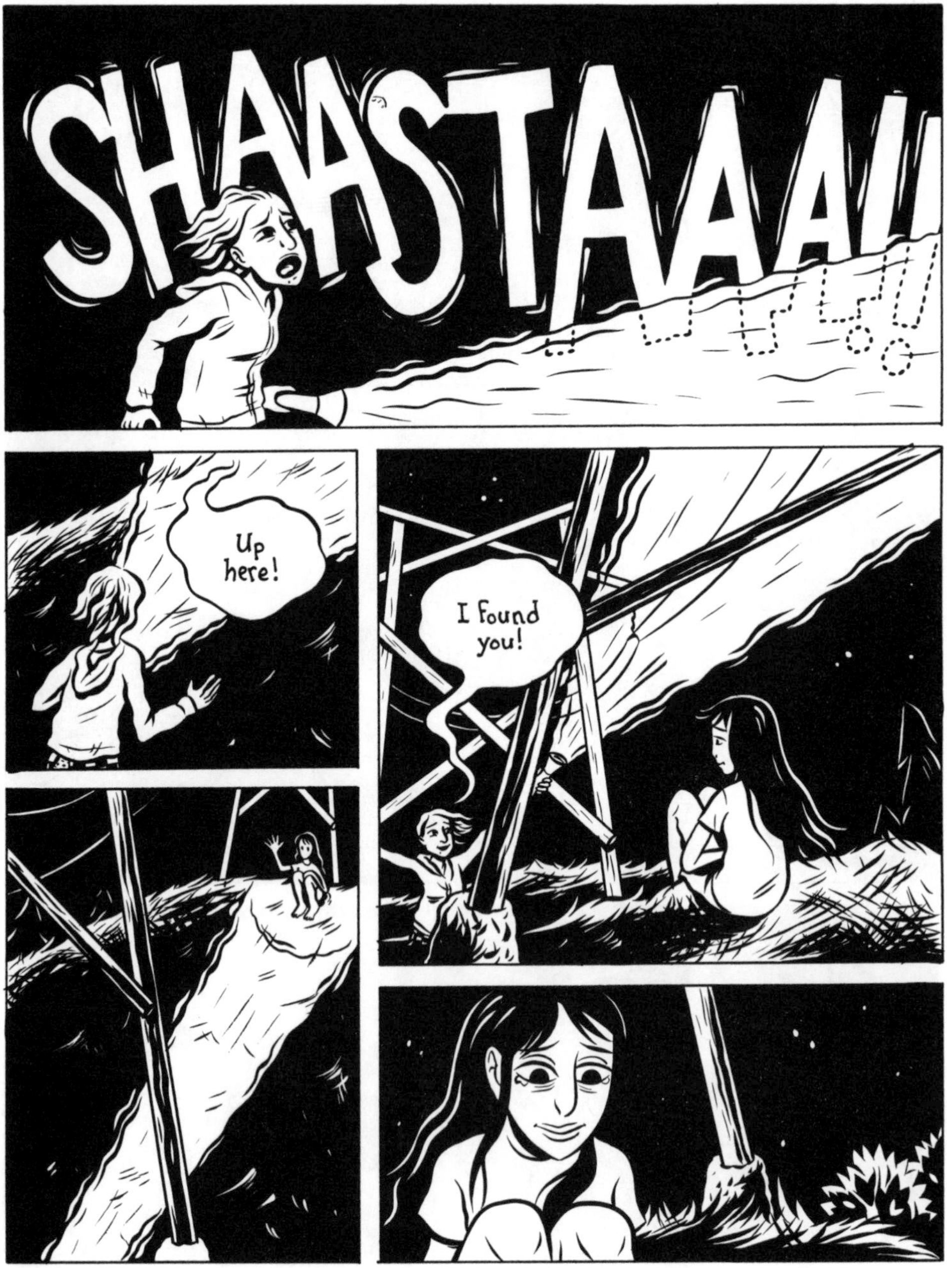
SHAASTAAA!!!!
Up here!
I found you!

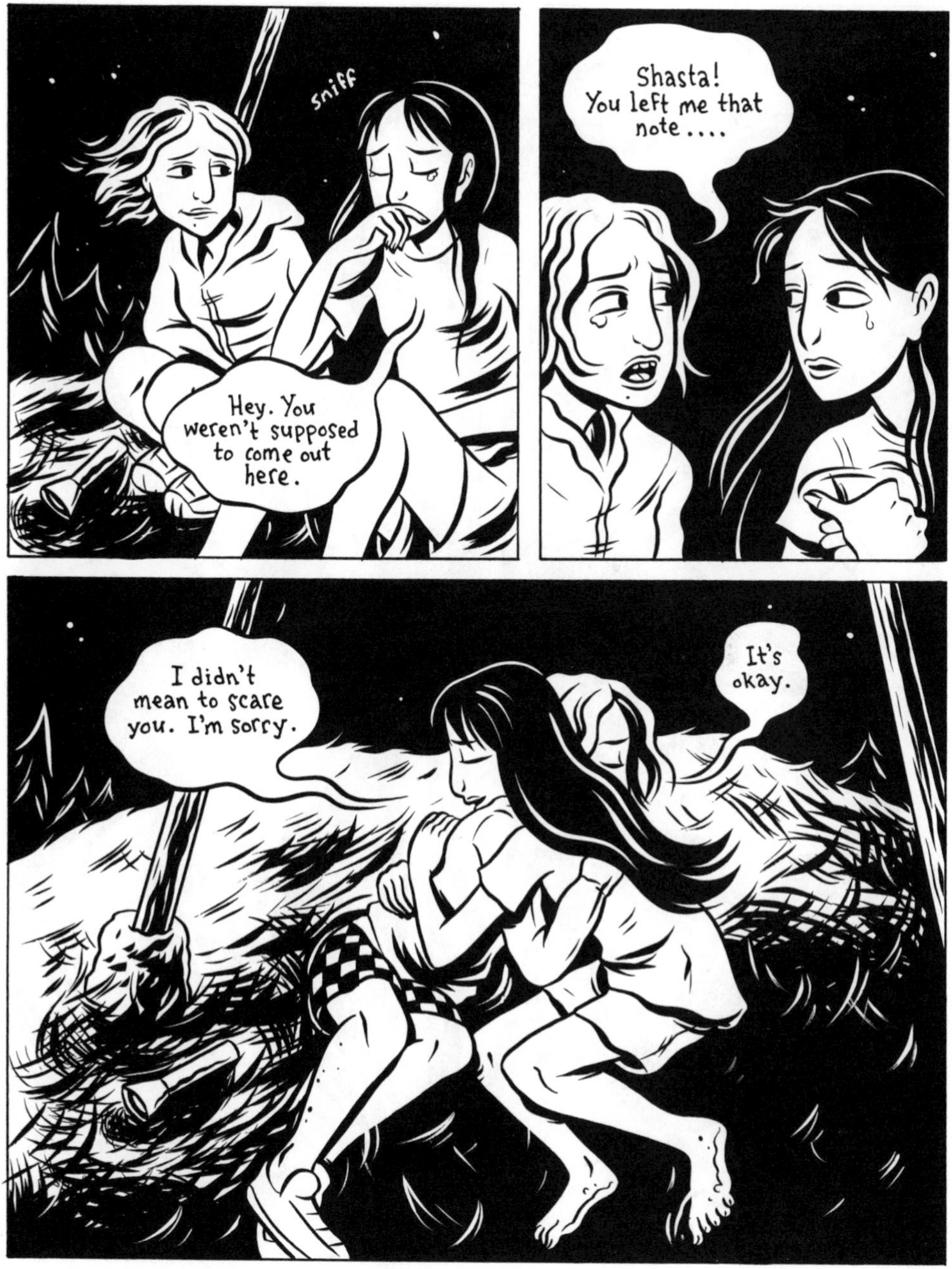
sniff
Hey. You weren't supposed to come out here.
Shasta! You left me that note....
I didn't mean to scare you. I'm sorry.
It's okay.

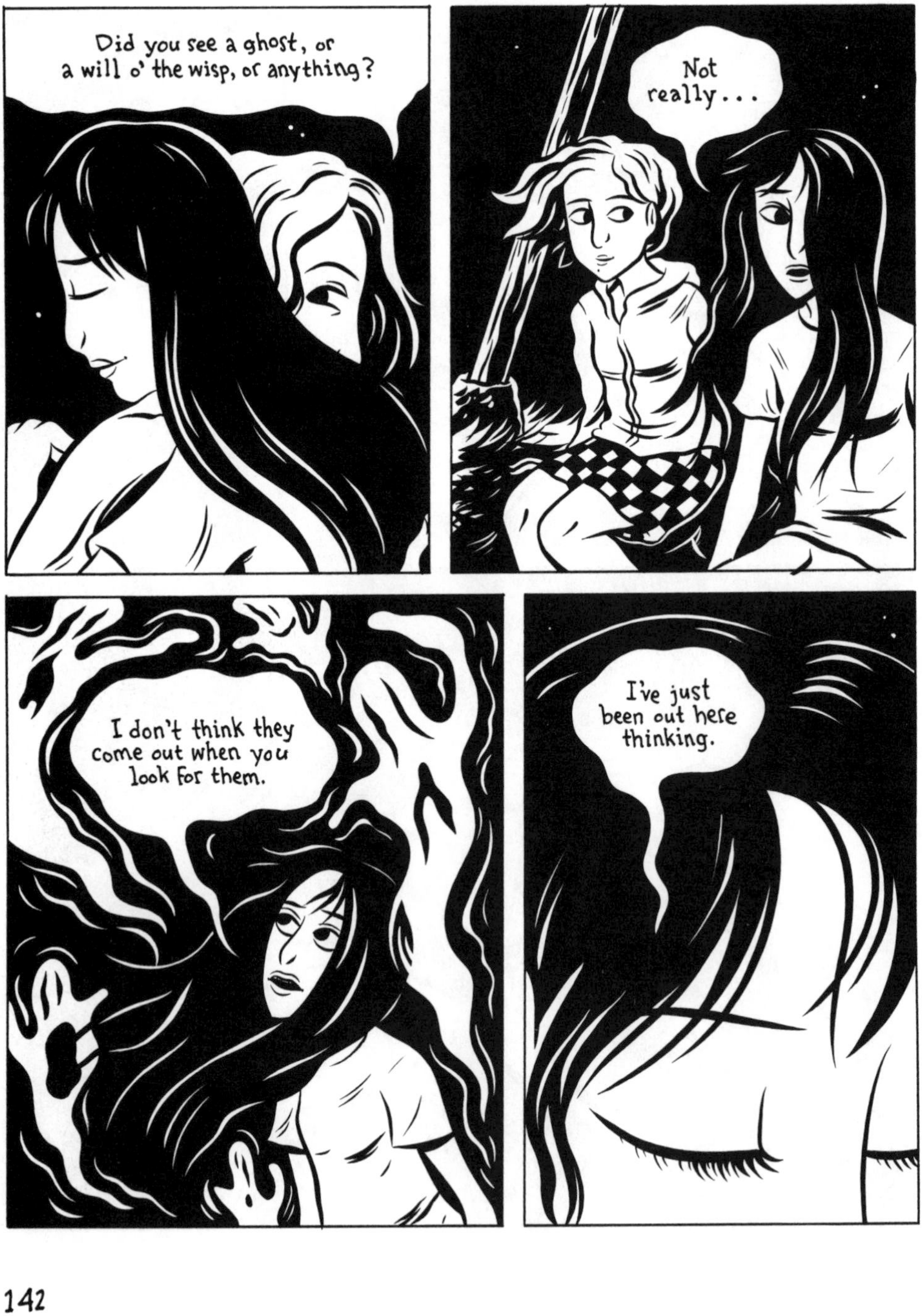
Did you see a ghost, or a will o' the wisp, or anything?
Not really...
I don't think they come out when you look for them.
I've just been out here thinking.

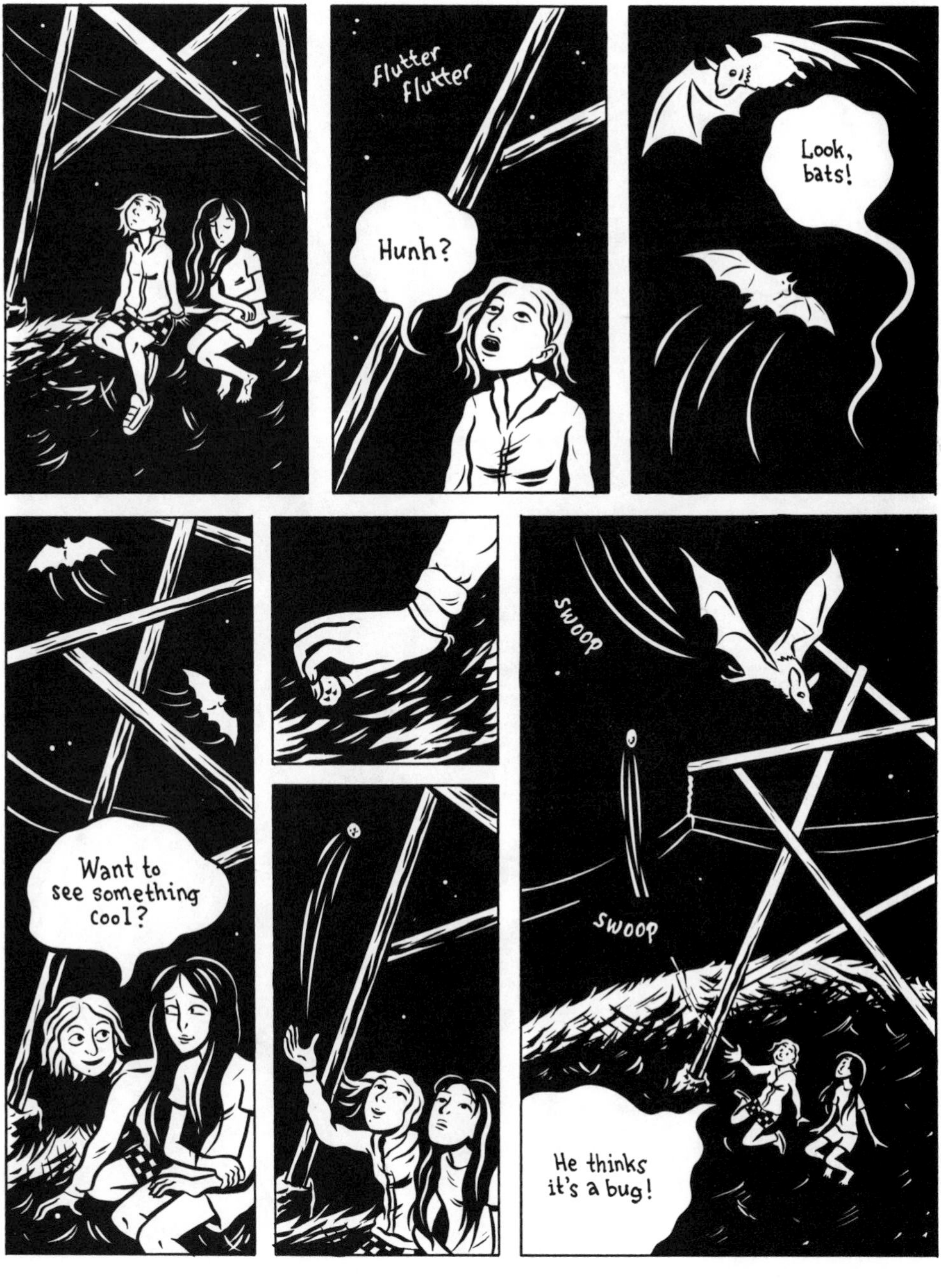

Flutter flutter
Hunh?
Look, bats!
Want to see something cool?
swoop
swoop
He thinks it's a bug!

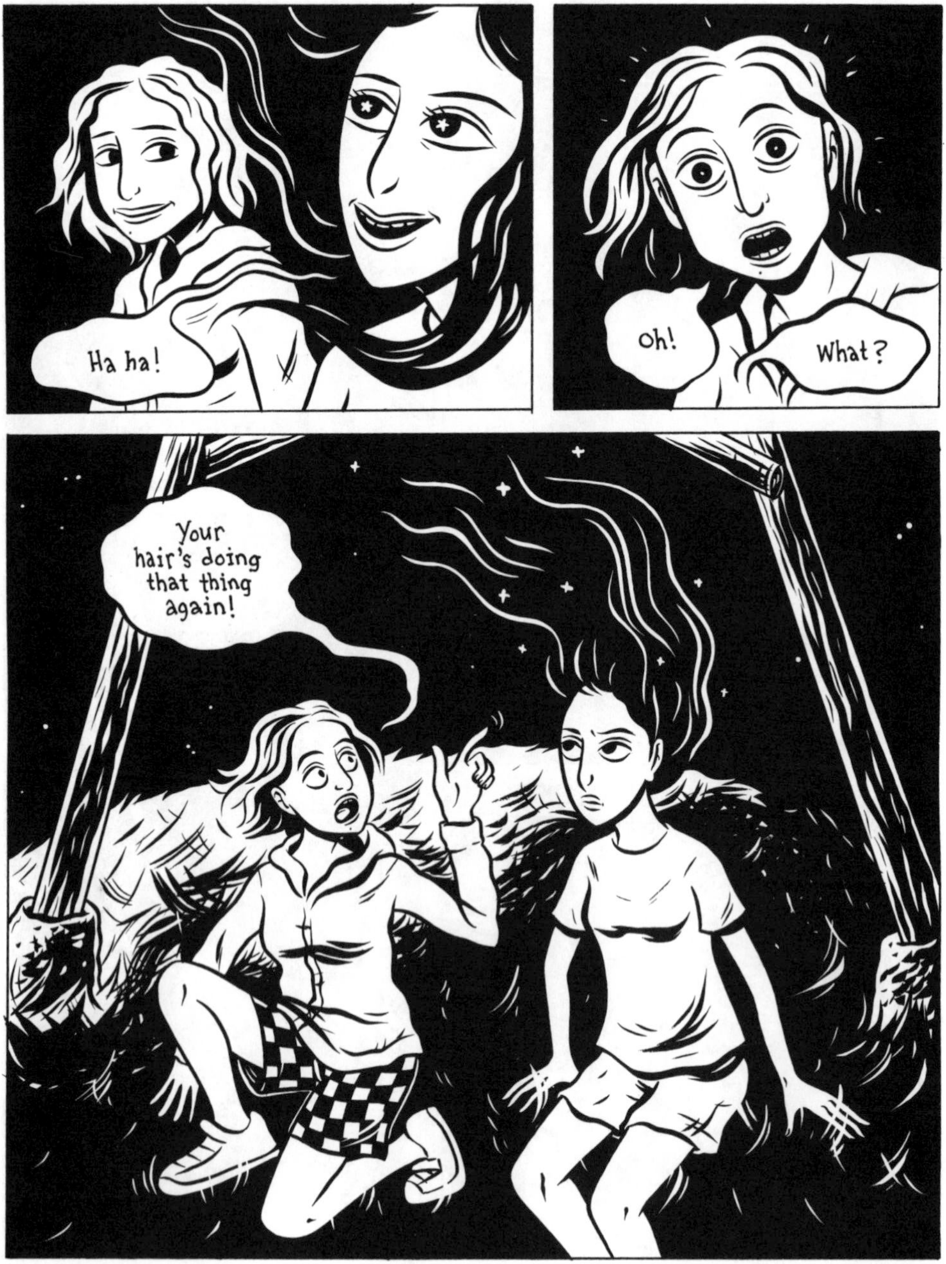
Ha ha!
Oh!
What?
Your hair's doing that thing again!

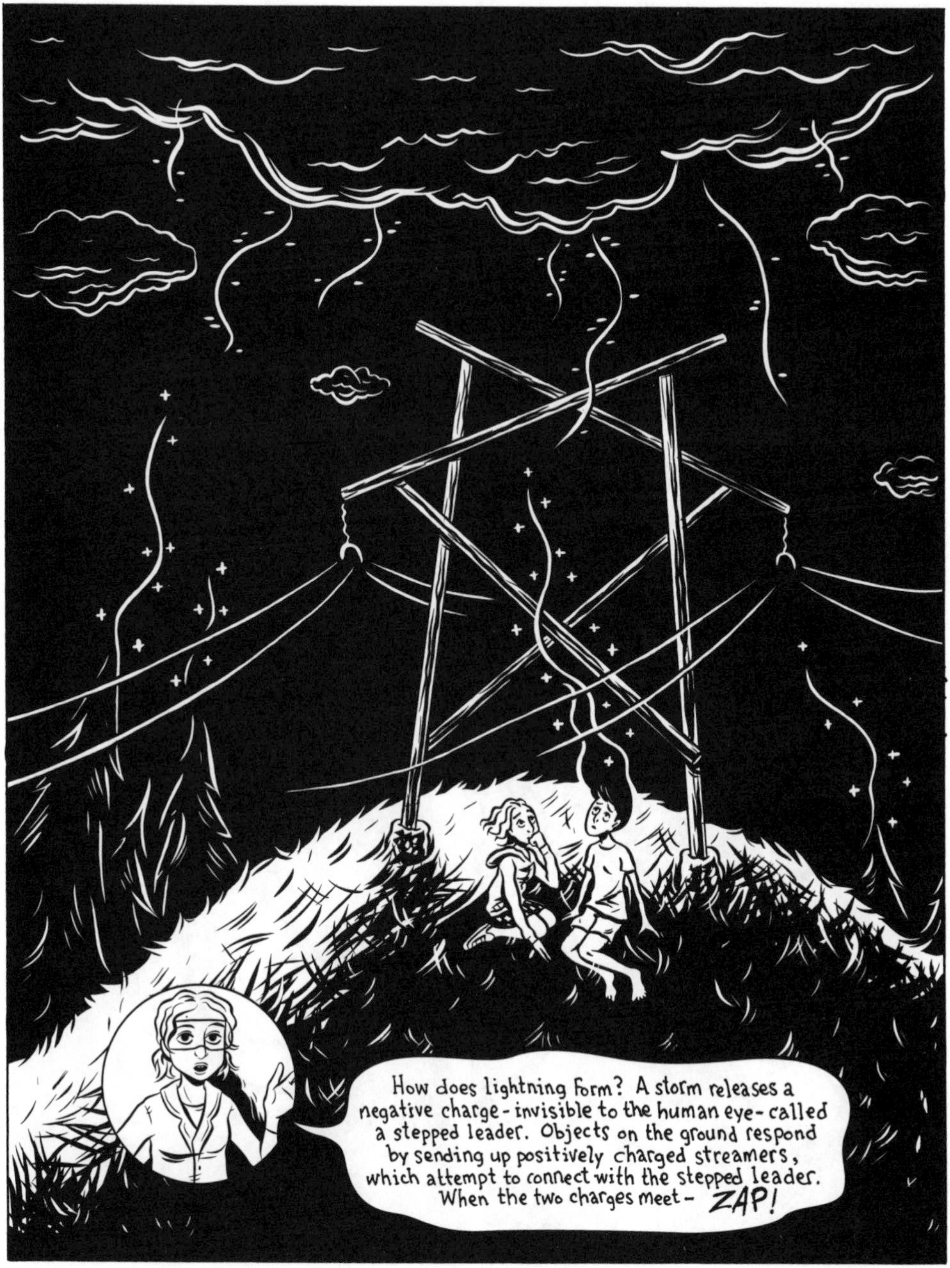
How does lightning form? A storm releases a negative charge - invisible to the human eye - called a stepped leader. Objects on the ground respond by sending up positively charged streamers, which attempt to connect with the stepped leader. When the two charges meet - ZAP!

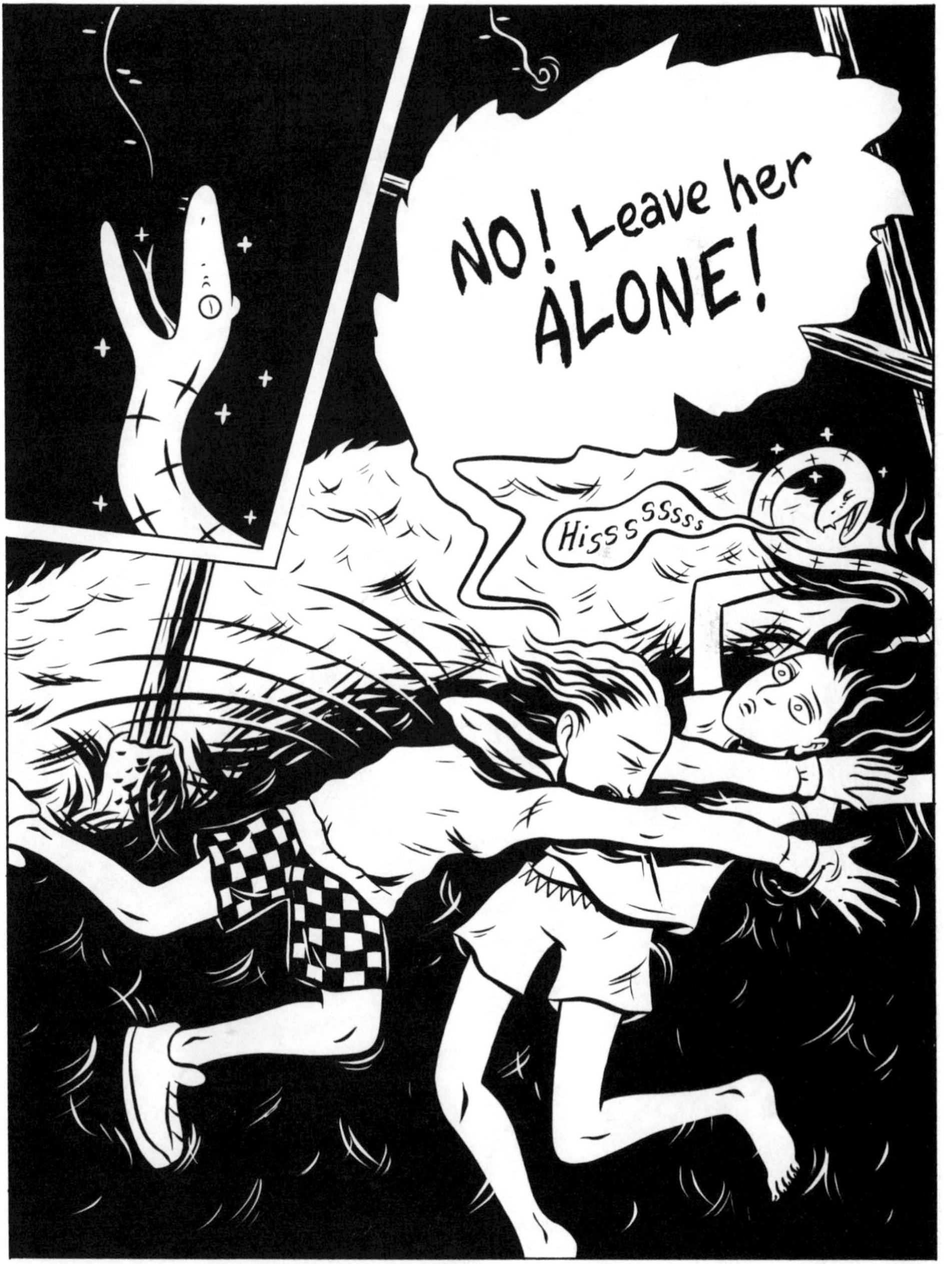
NO! Leave her ALONE!
Hisssssssss

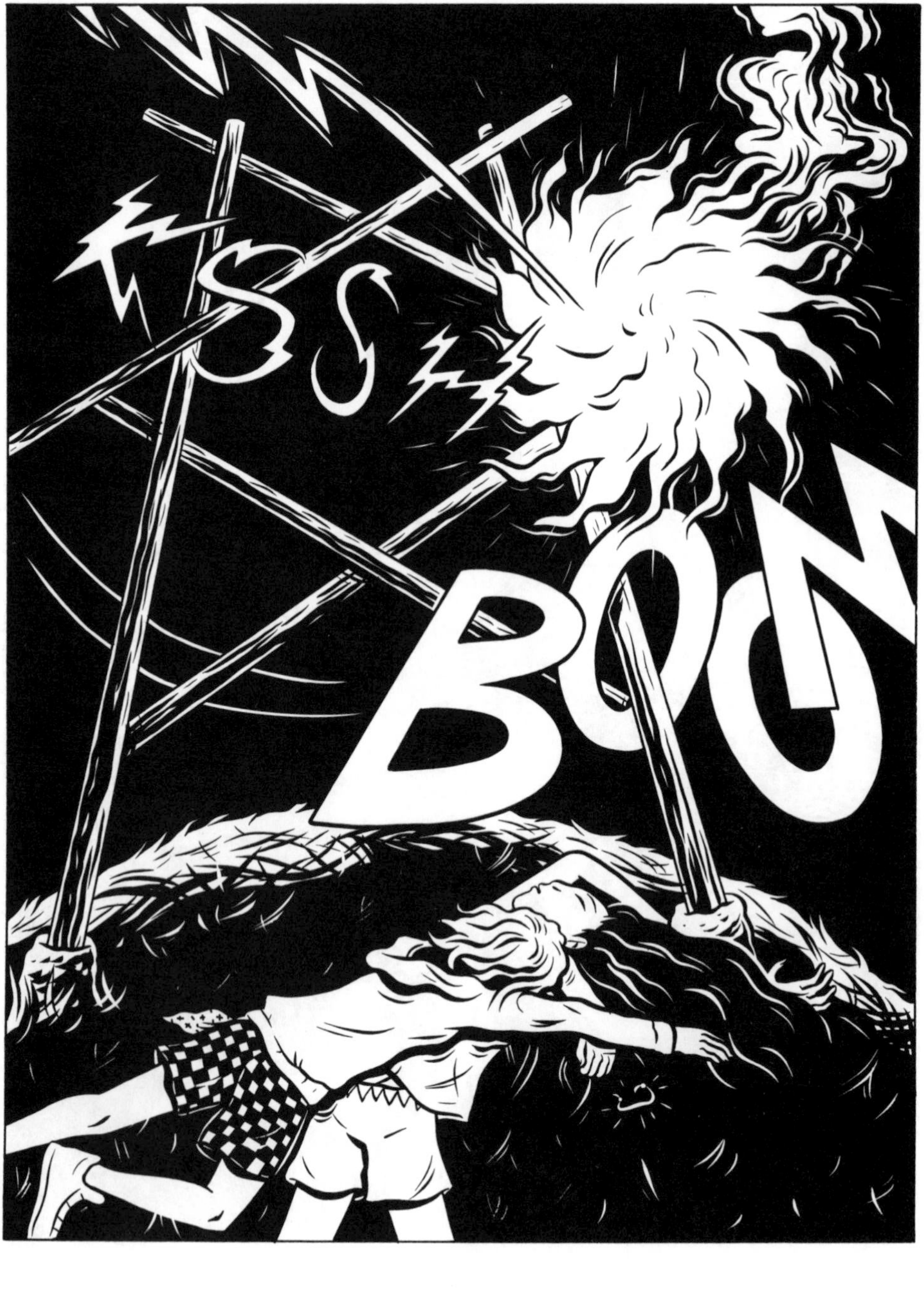

FSSH
BOOM

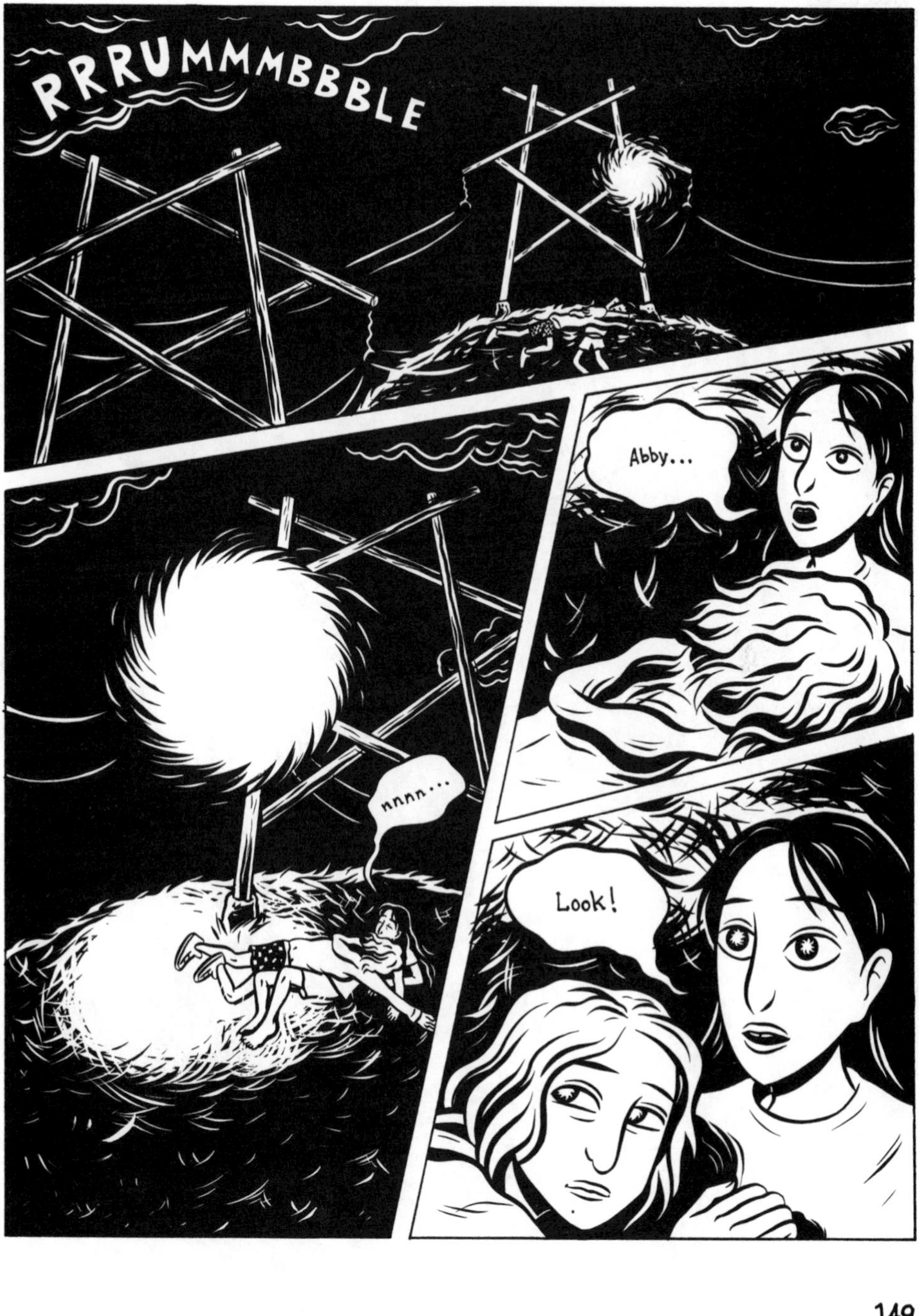
RRRUMMMBBBLE
nnnn...
Abby...
Look!

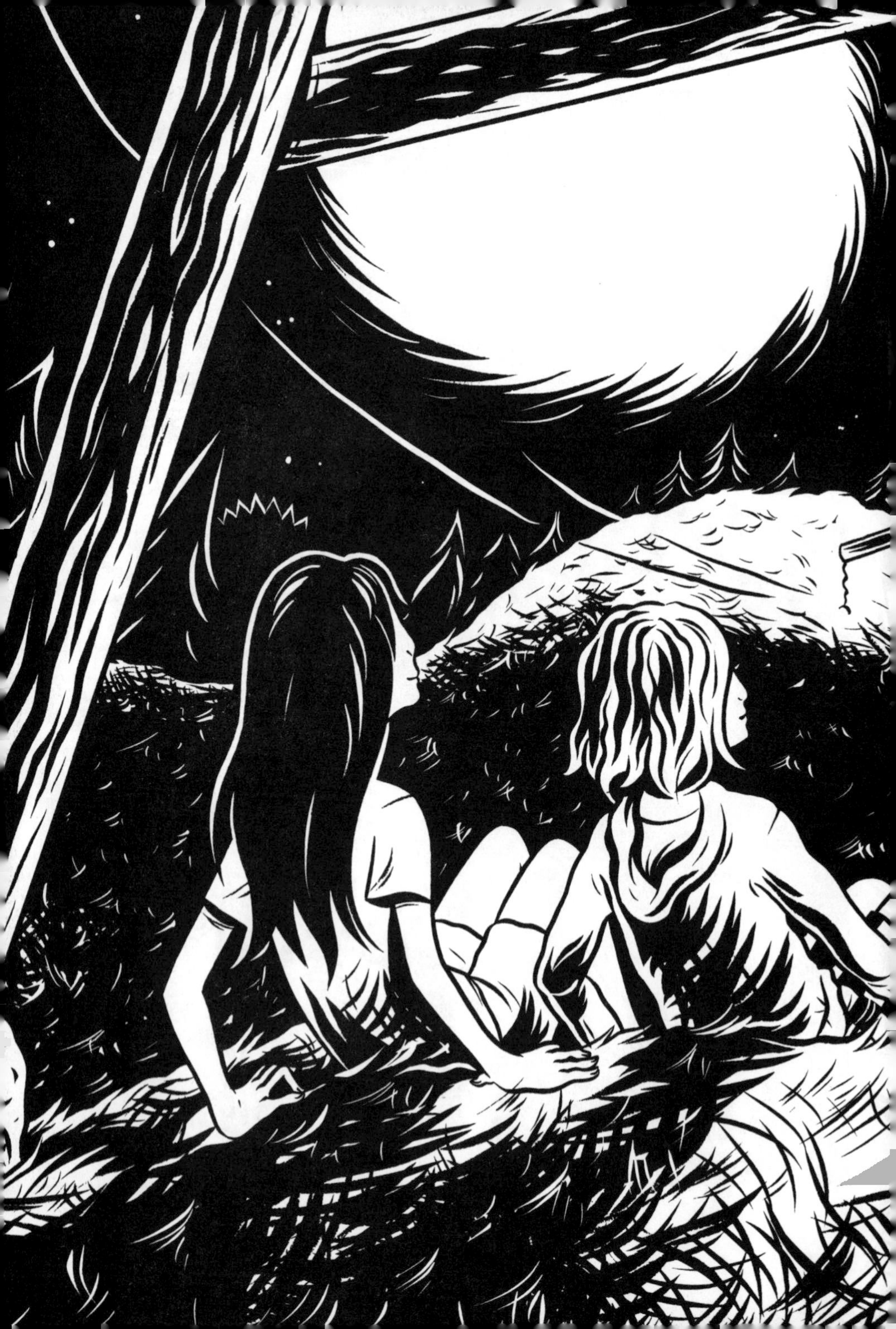

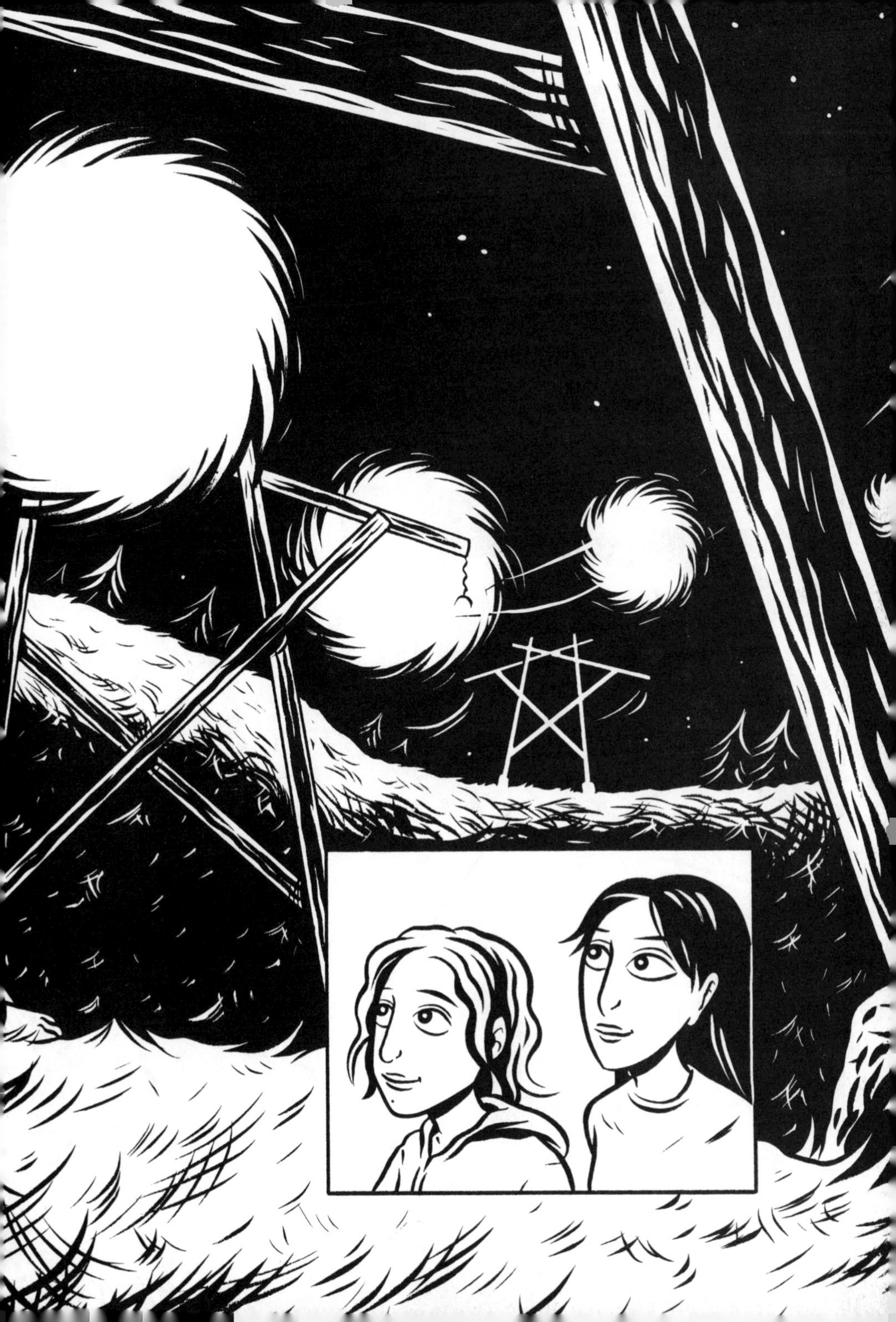

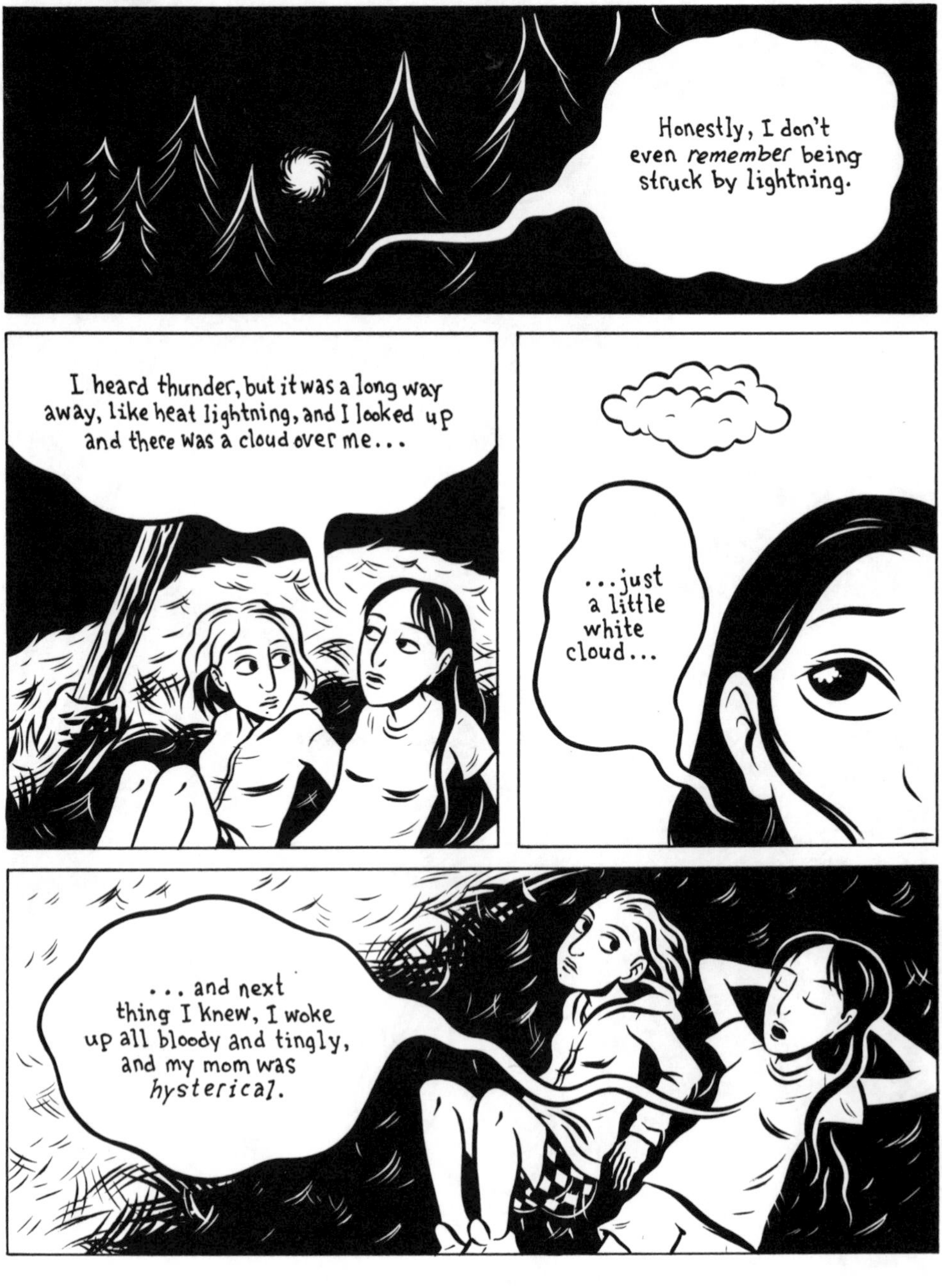
Honestly, I don't even *remember* being struck by lightning.
I heard thunder, but it was a long way away, like heat lightning, and I looked up and there was a cloud over me...
...just a little white cloud...
...and next thing I knew, I woke up all bloody and tingly, and my mom was *hysterical*.

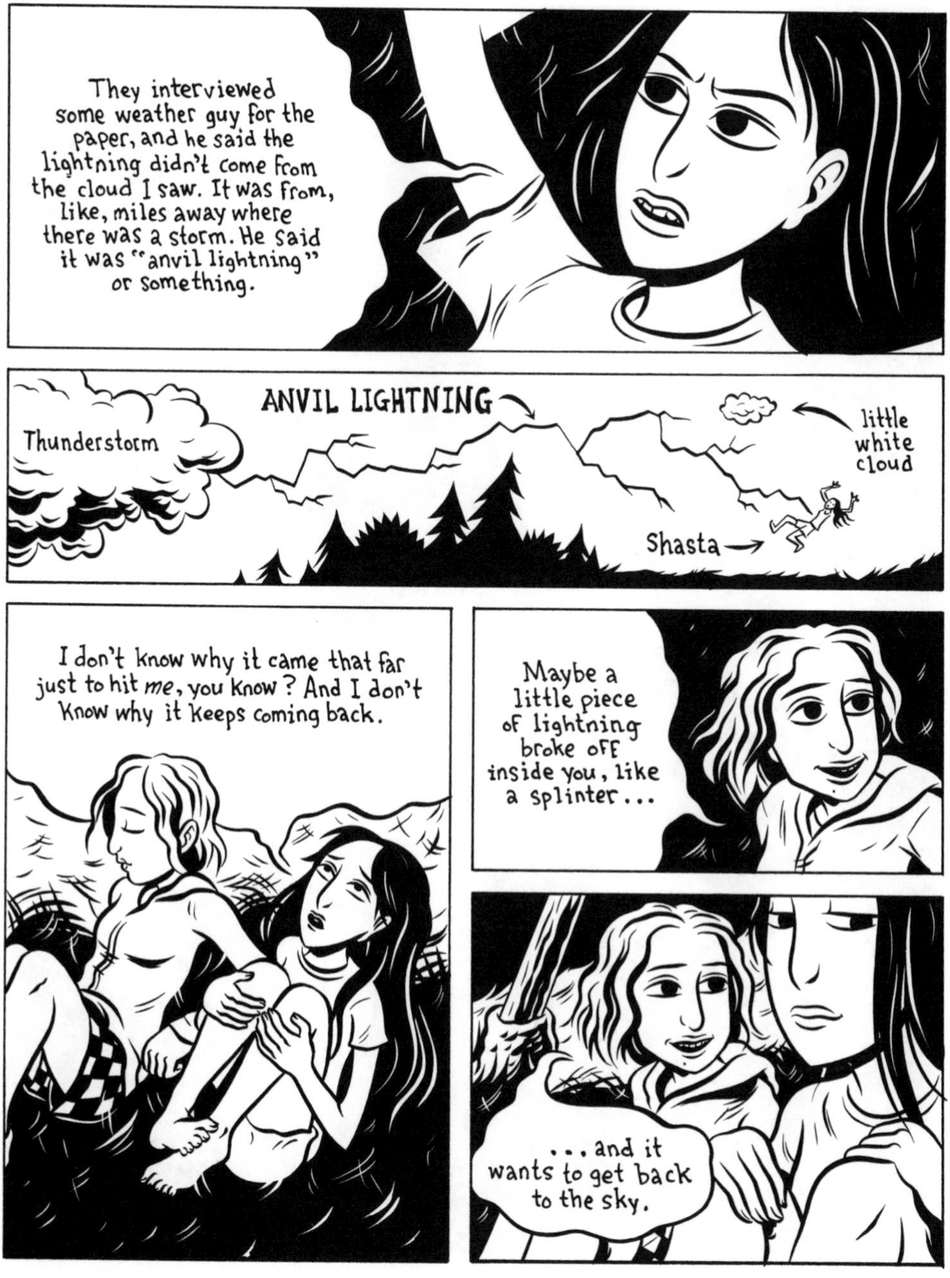
They interviewed some weather guy for the paper, and he said the lightning didn't come from the cloud I saw. It was from, like, miles away where there was a storm. He said it was "anvil lightning" or something.
ANVIL LIGHTNING
Thunderstorm
little white cloud
Shasta
I don't know why it came that far just to hit *me*, you know? And I don't know why it keeps coming back.
Maybe a little piece of lightning broke off inside you, like a splinter...
...and it wants to get back to the sky.

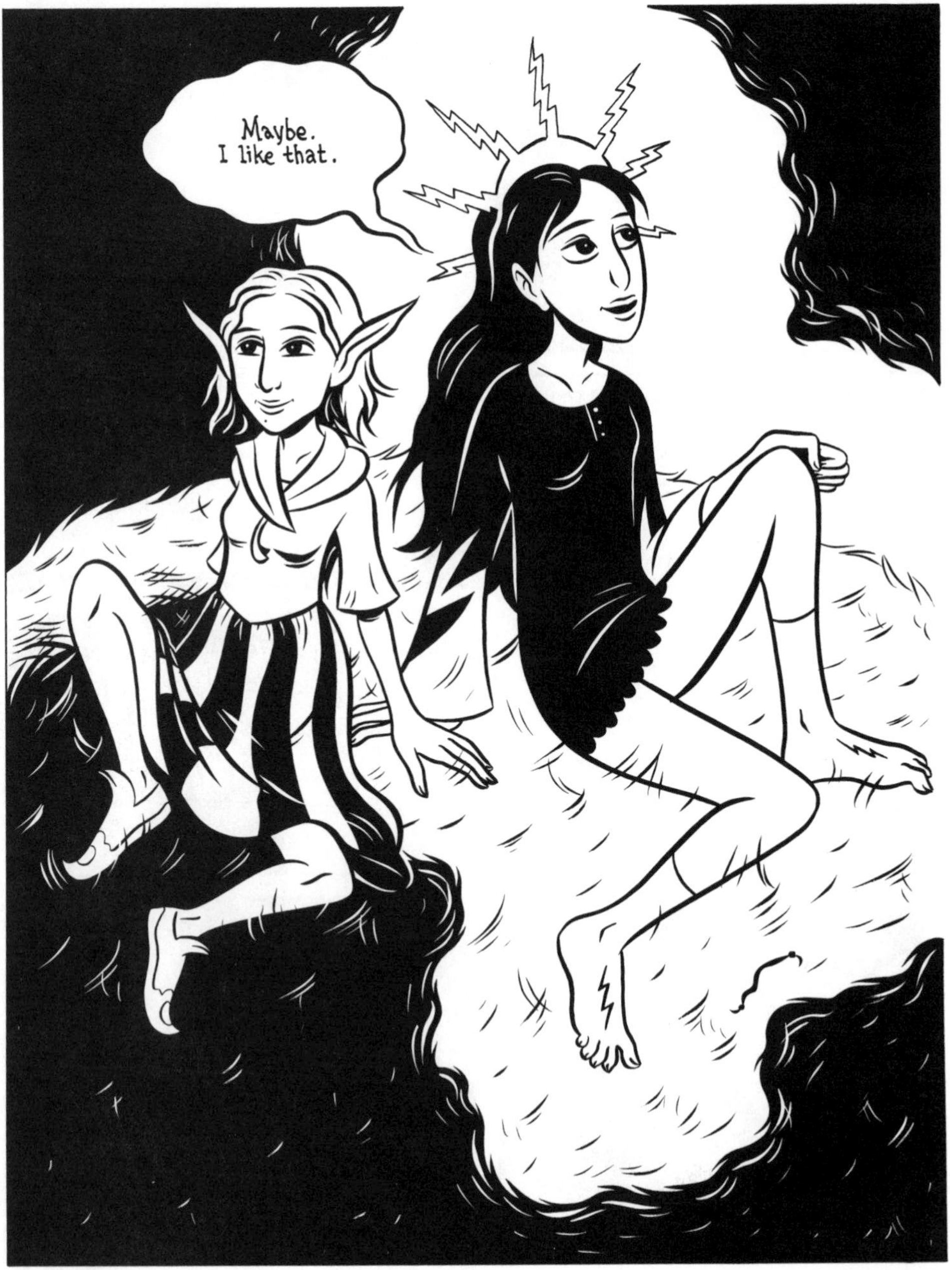
Maybe.
I like that.

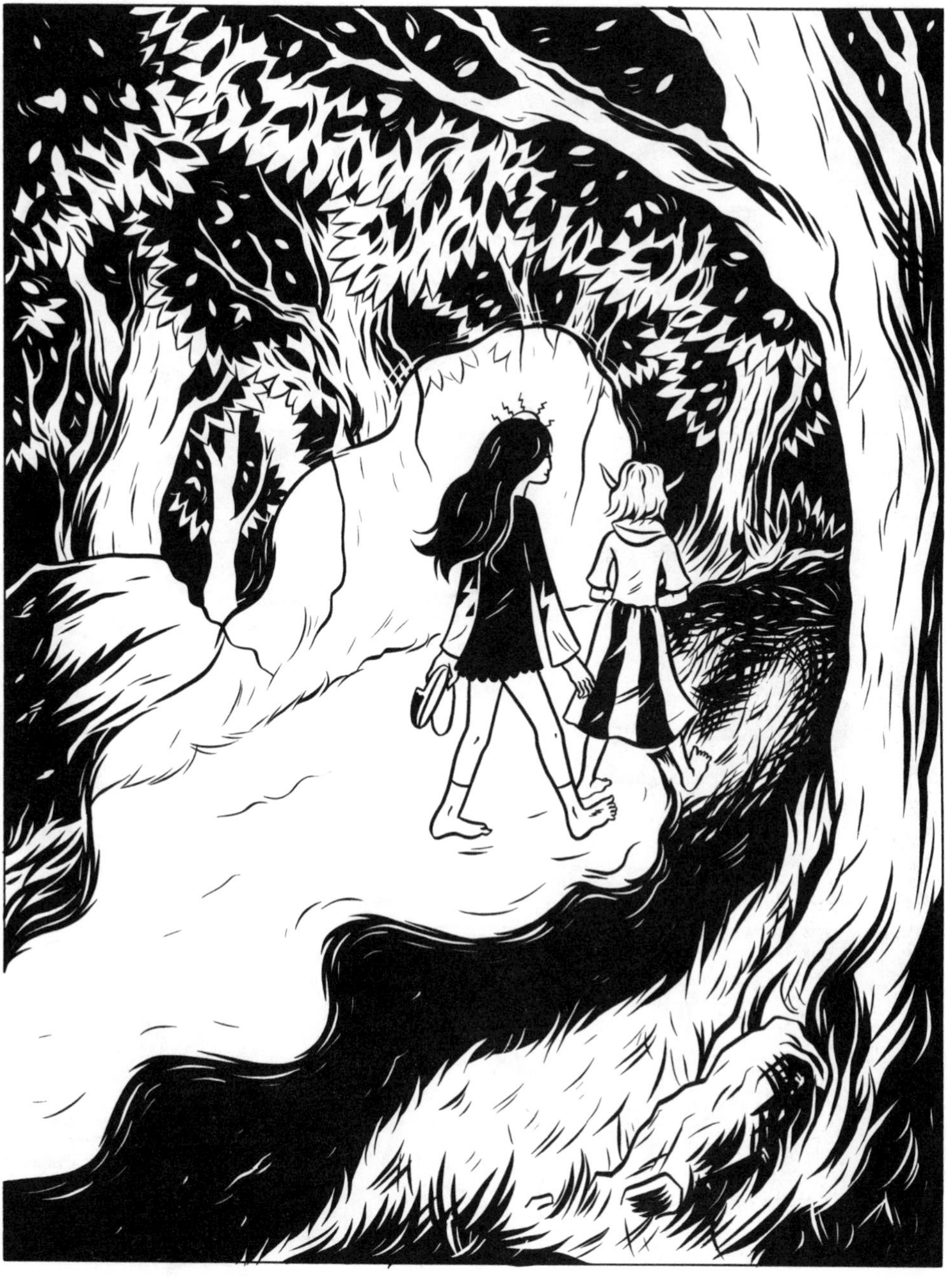

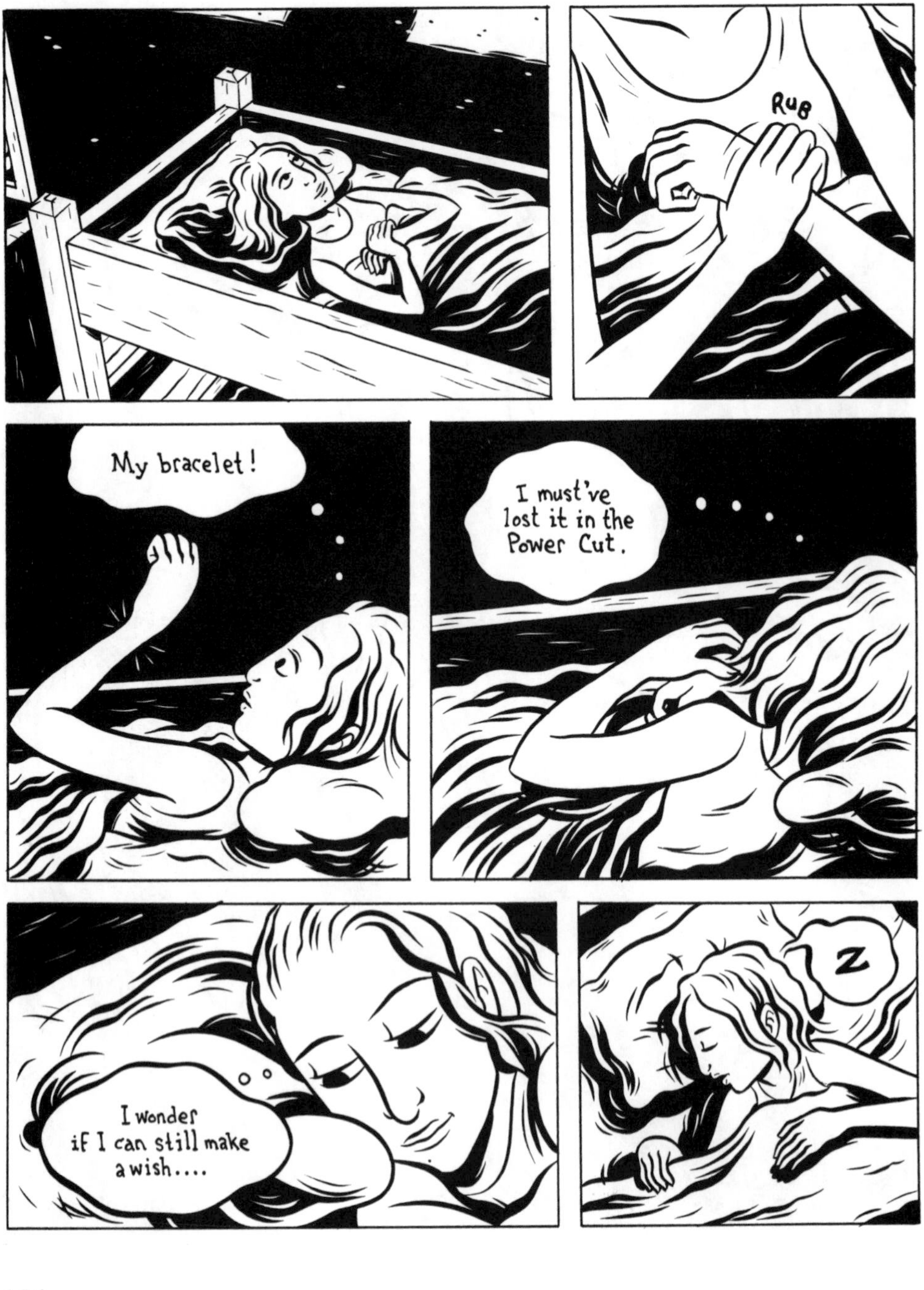
RUB
My bracelet!
I must've lost it in the Power Cut.
I wonder if I can still make a wish....
Z

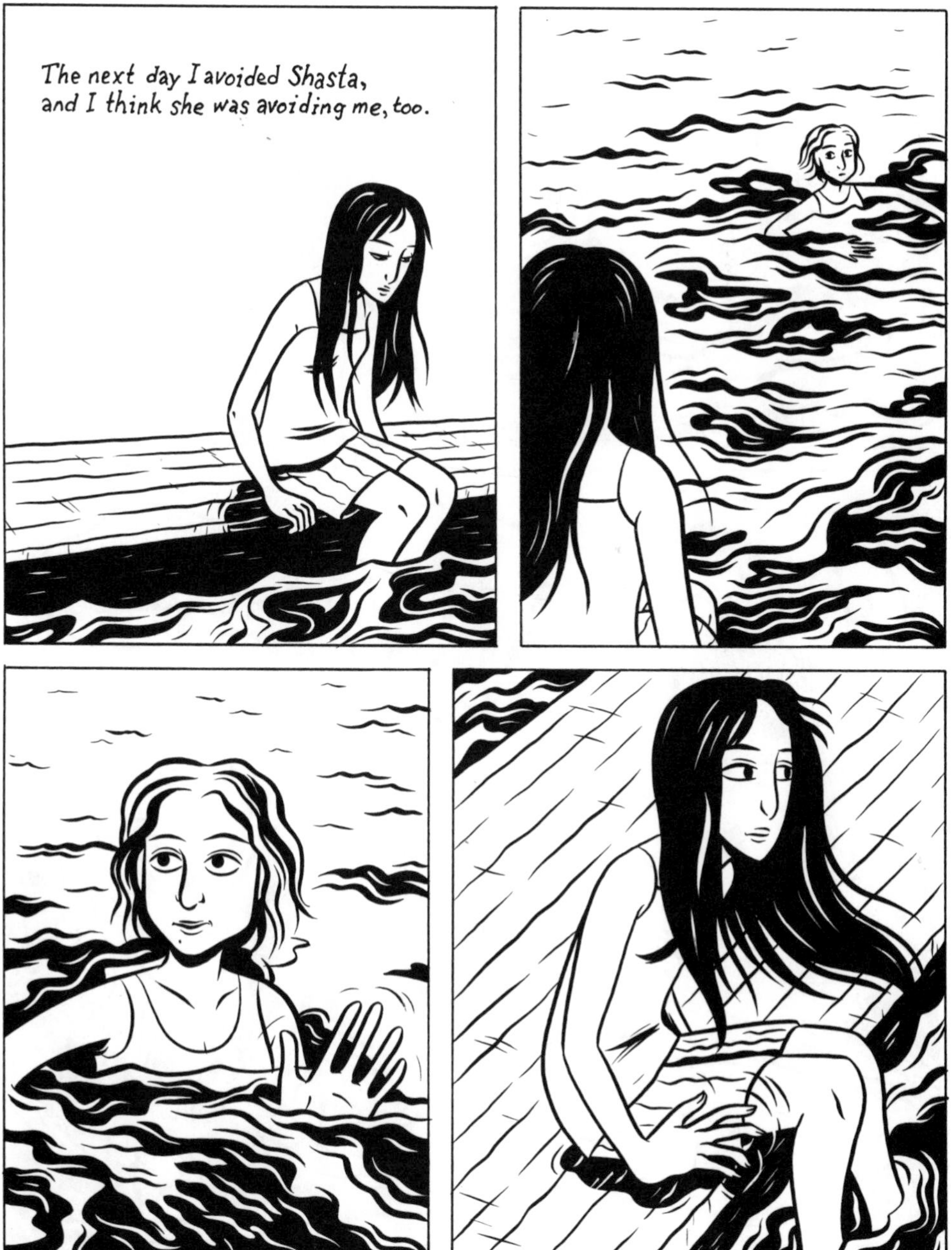
The next day I avoided Shasta,
and I think she was avoiding me, too.

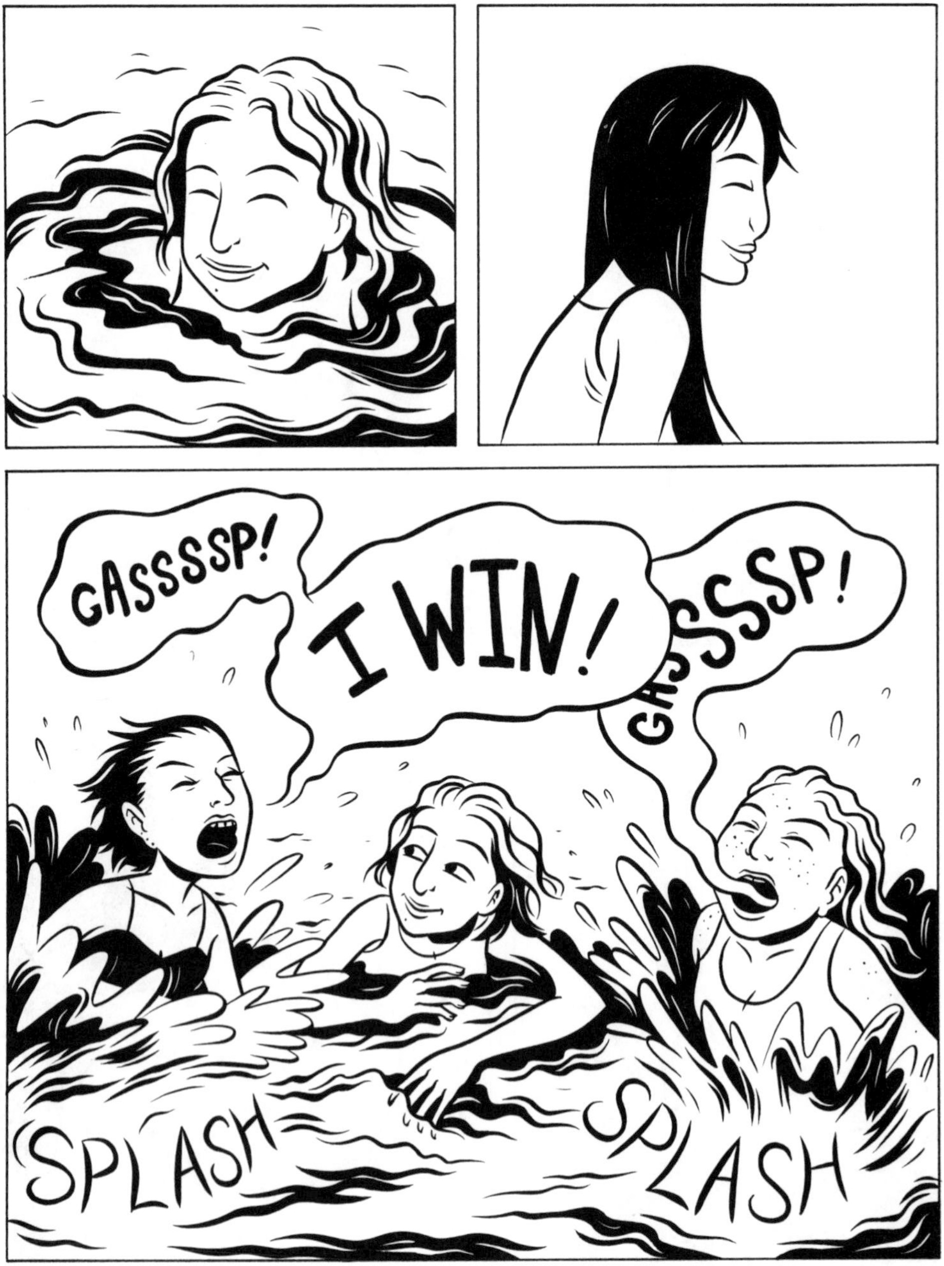
GASSSSP!
I WIN!
GASSSSSP!
SPLASH
SPLASH

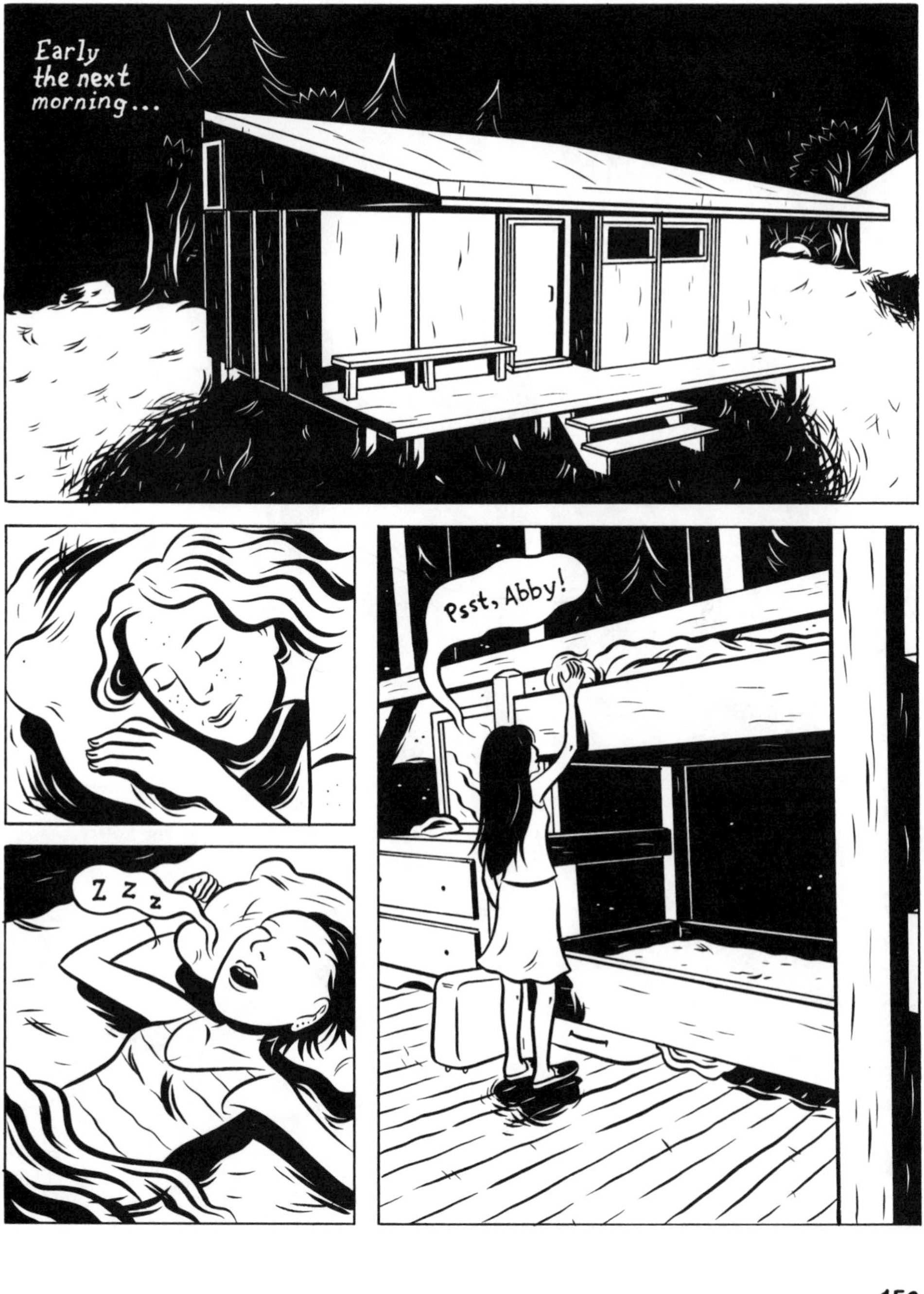
Early the next morning...
Psst, Abby!
Z Z z

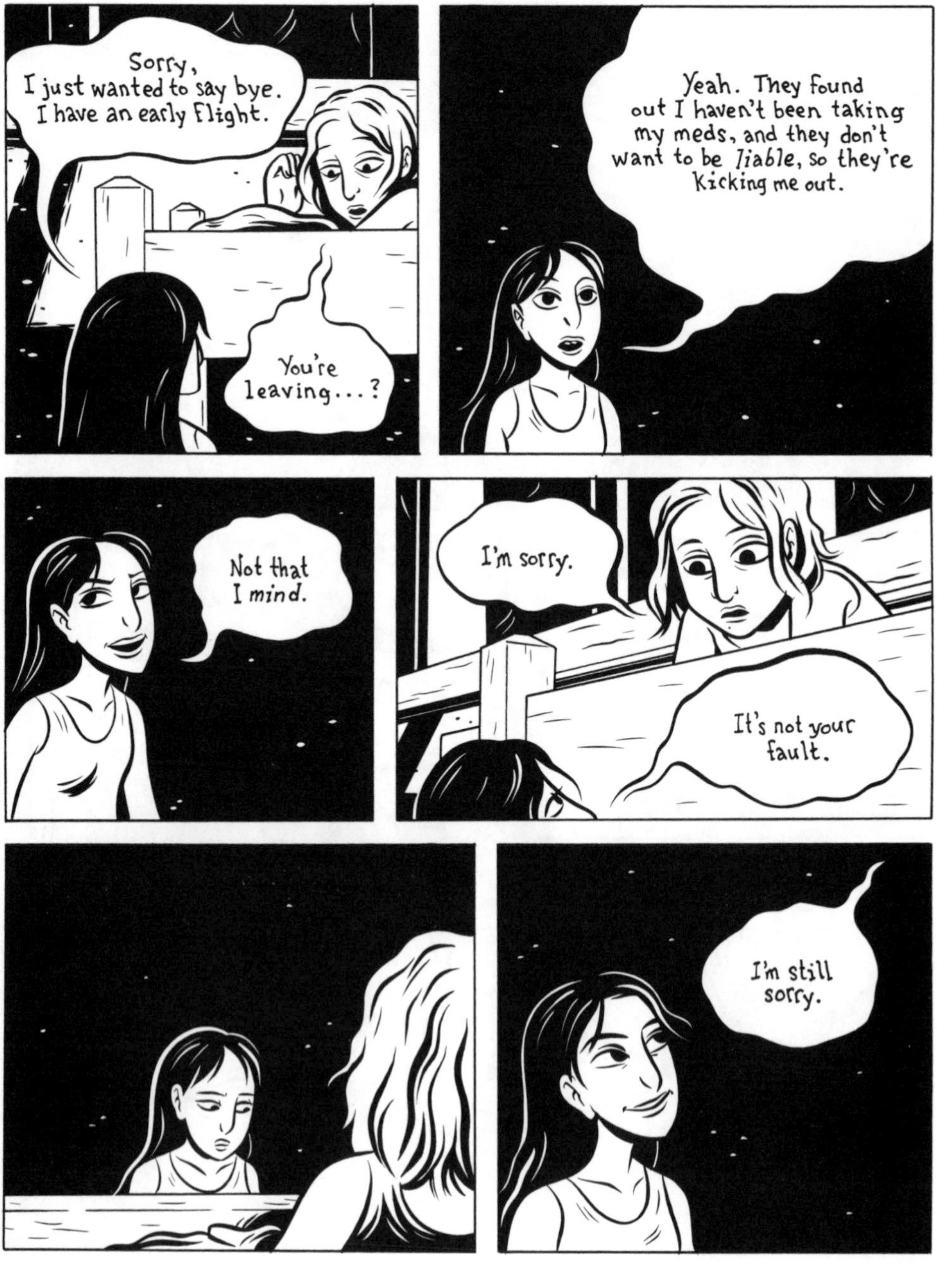
Sorry, I just wanted to say bye. I have an early flight.
You're leaving...?
Yeah. They found out I haven't been taking my meds, and they don't want to be *liable*, so they're kicking me out.
Not that I *mind*.
I'm sorry.
It's not your fault.
I'm still sorry.

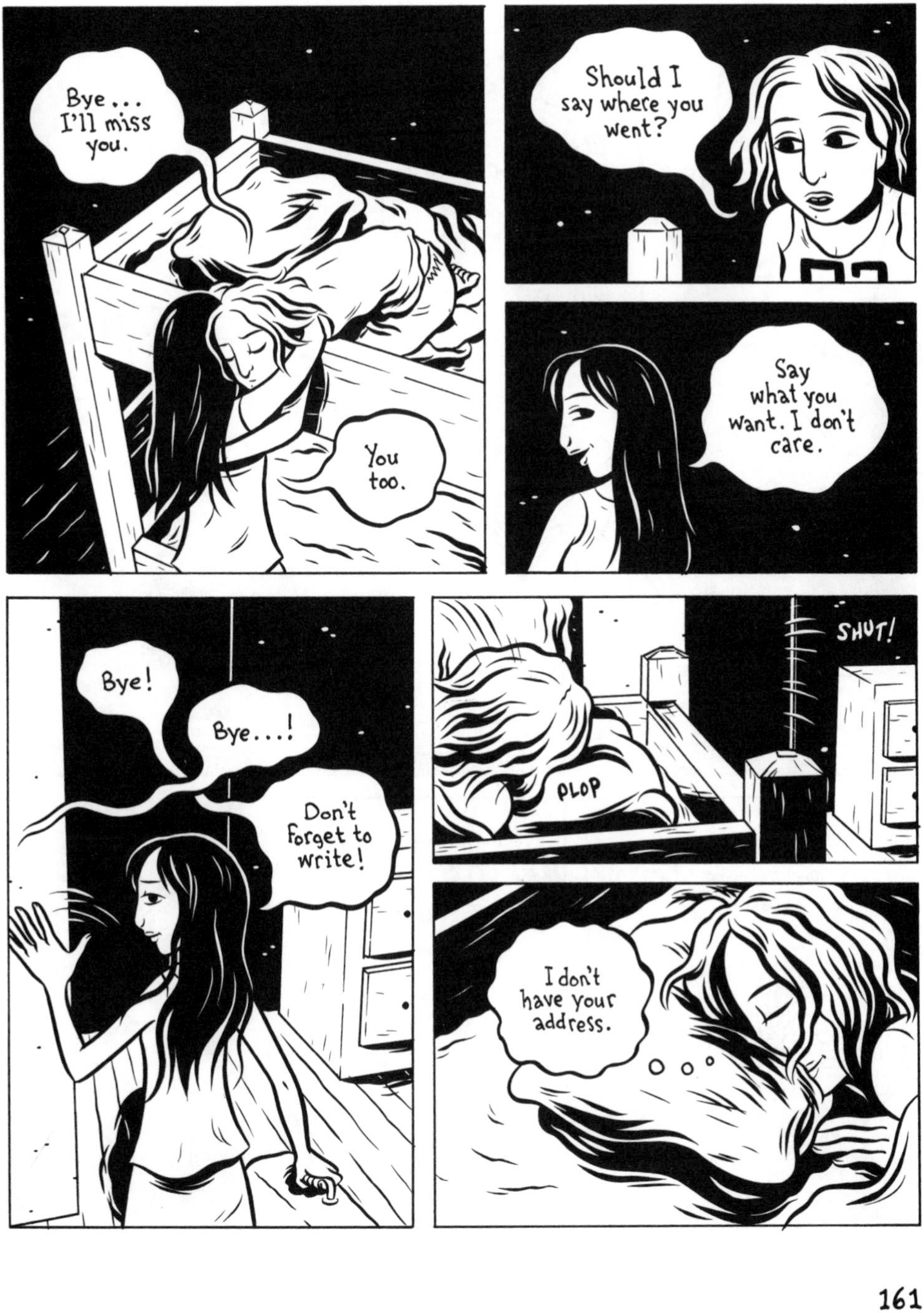
Bye... I'll miss you.
You too.
Should I say where you went?
Say what you want. I don't care.
Bye!
Bye...!
Don't forget to write!
SHUT!
PLOP
I don't have your address.

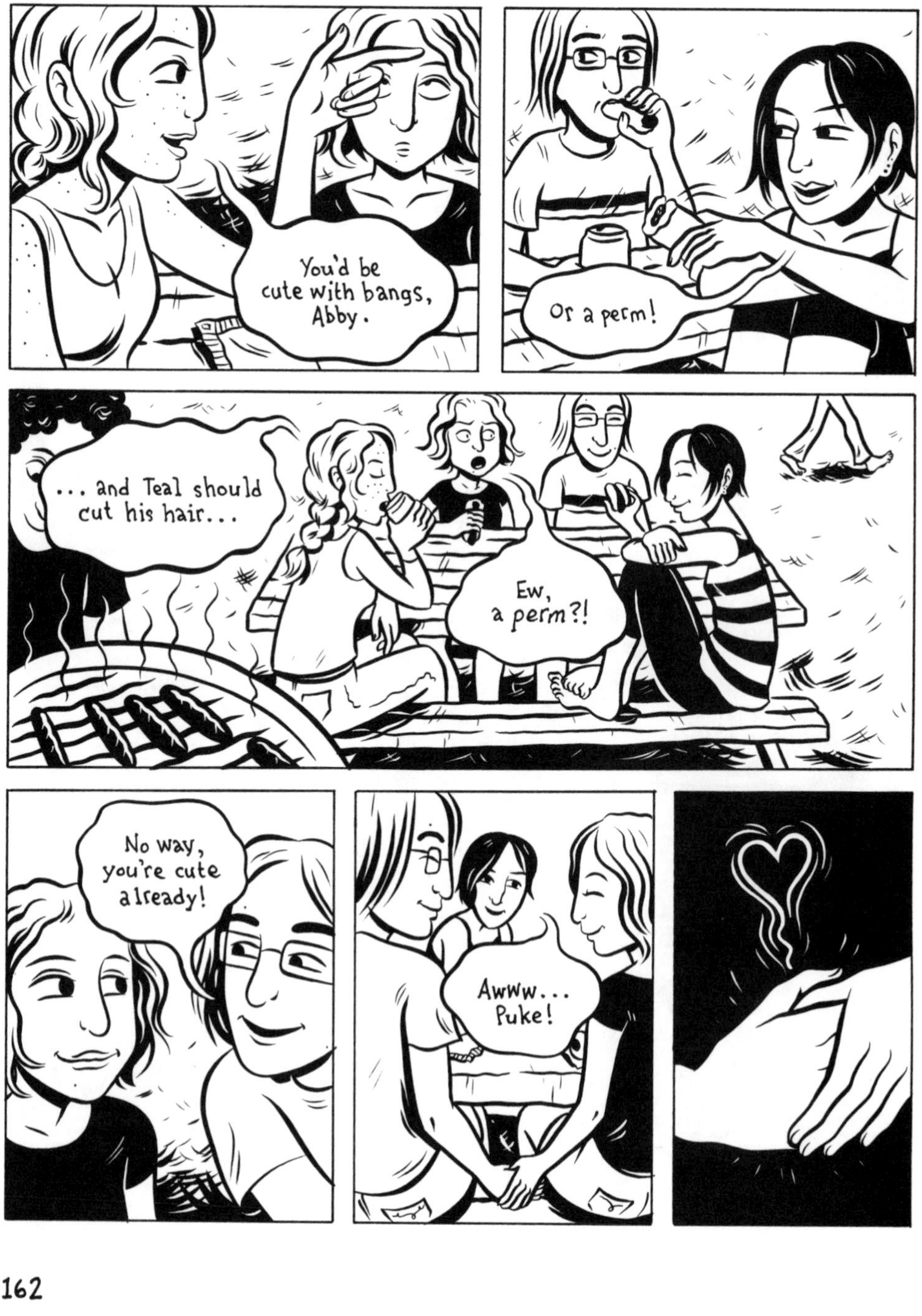
You'd be cute with bangs, Abby.
Or a perm!
... and Teal should cut his hair...
Ew, a perm?!
No way, you're cute already!
Awww... Puke!

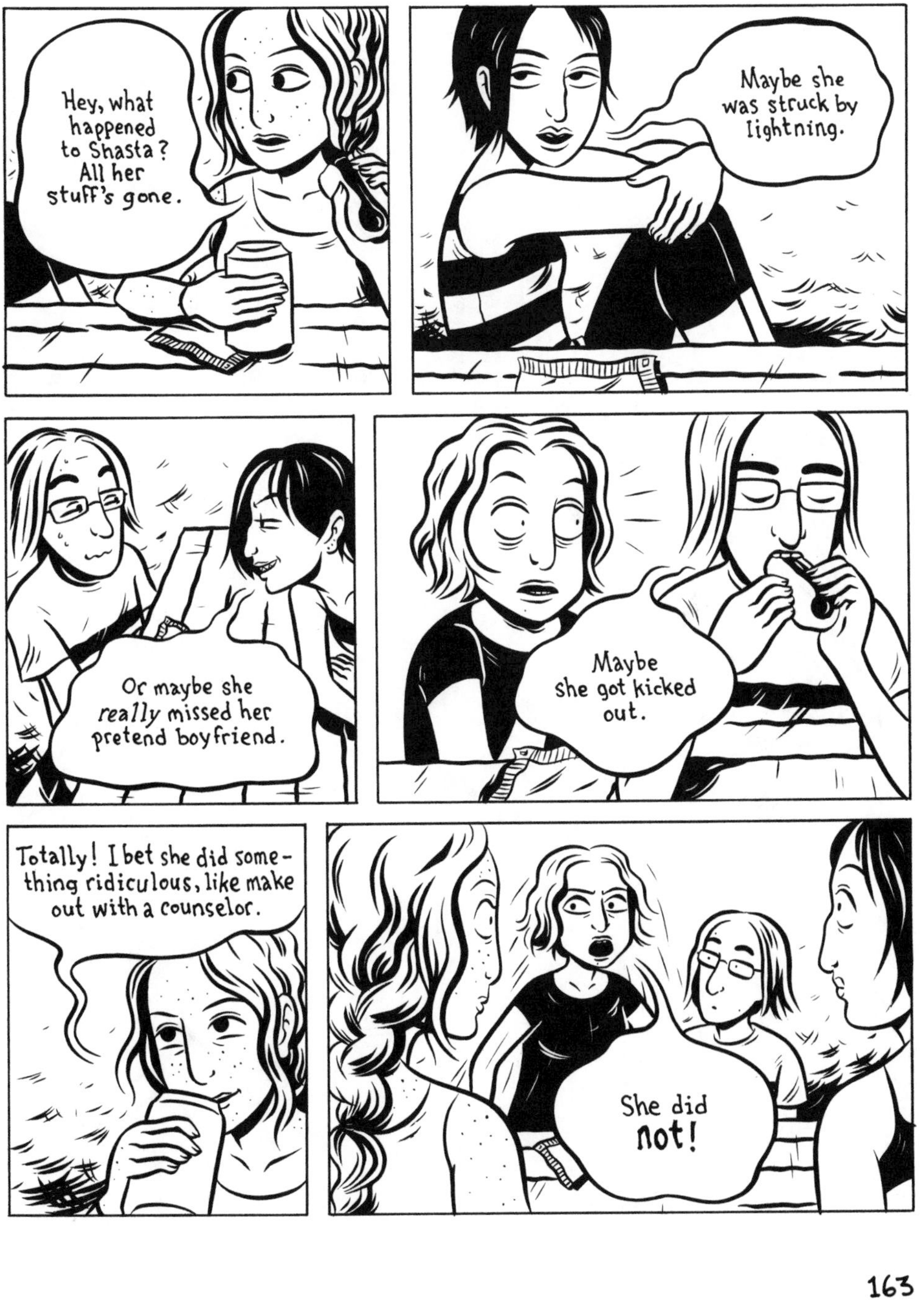
Hey, what happened to Shasta? All her stuff's gone.
Maybe she was struck by lightning.
Or maybe she *really* missed her pretend boyfriend.
Maybe she got kicked out.
Totally! I bet she did something ridiculous, like make out with a counselor.
She did **not**!

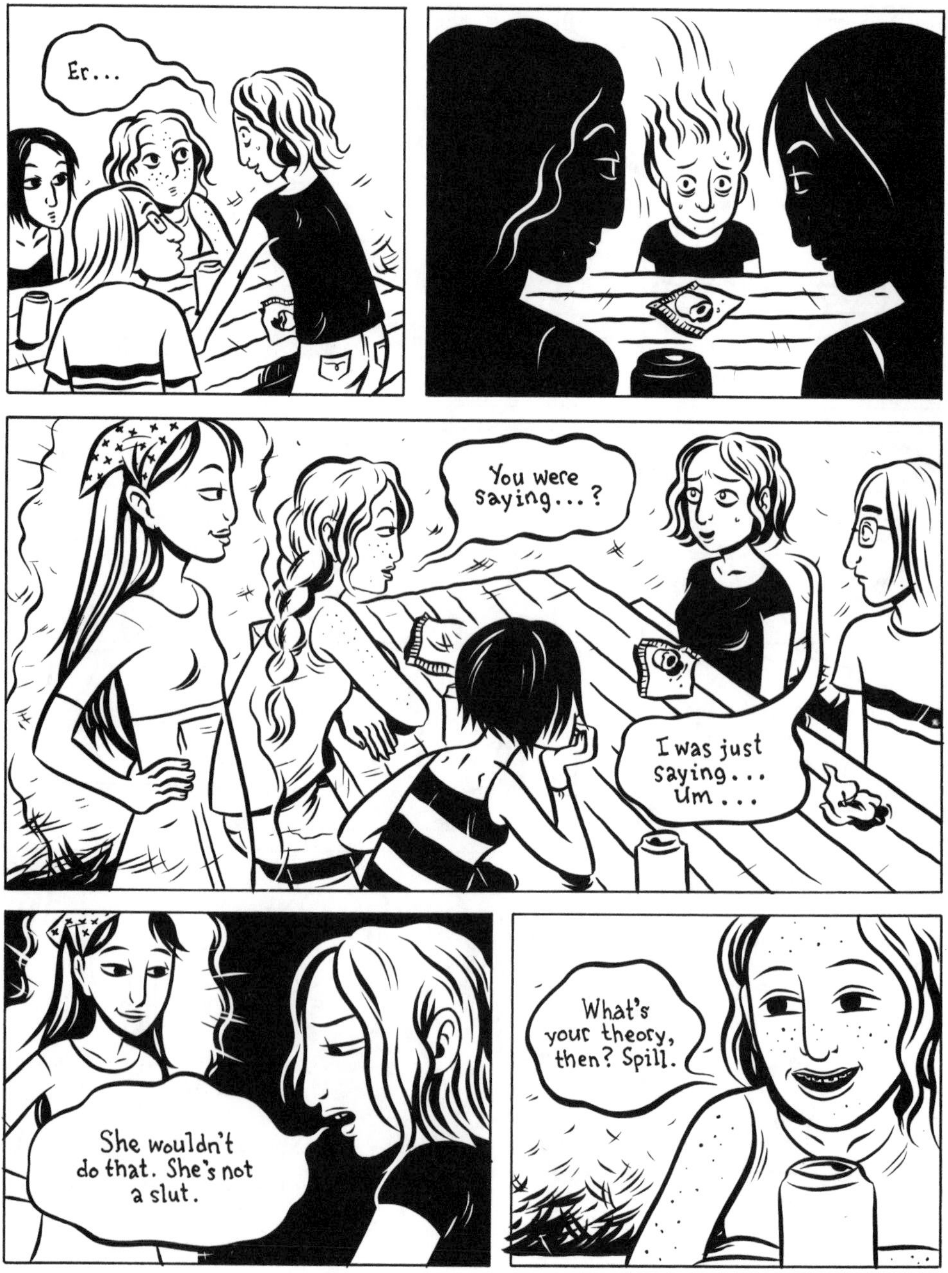
Er...
You were saying...?
I was just saying... Um...
She wouldn't do that. She's not a slut.
What's your theory, then? Spill.

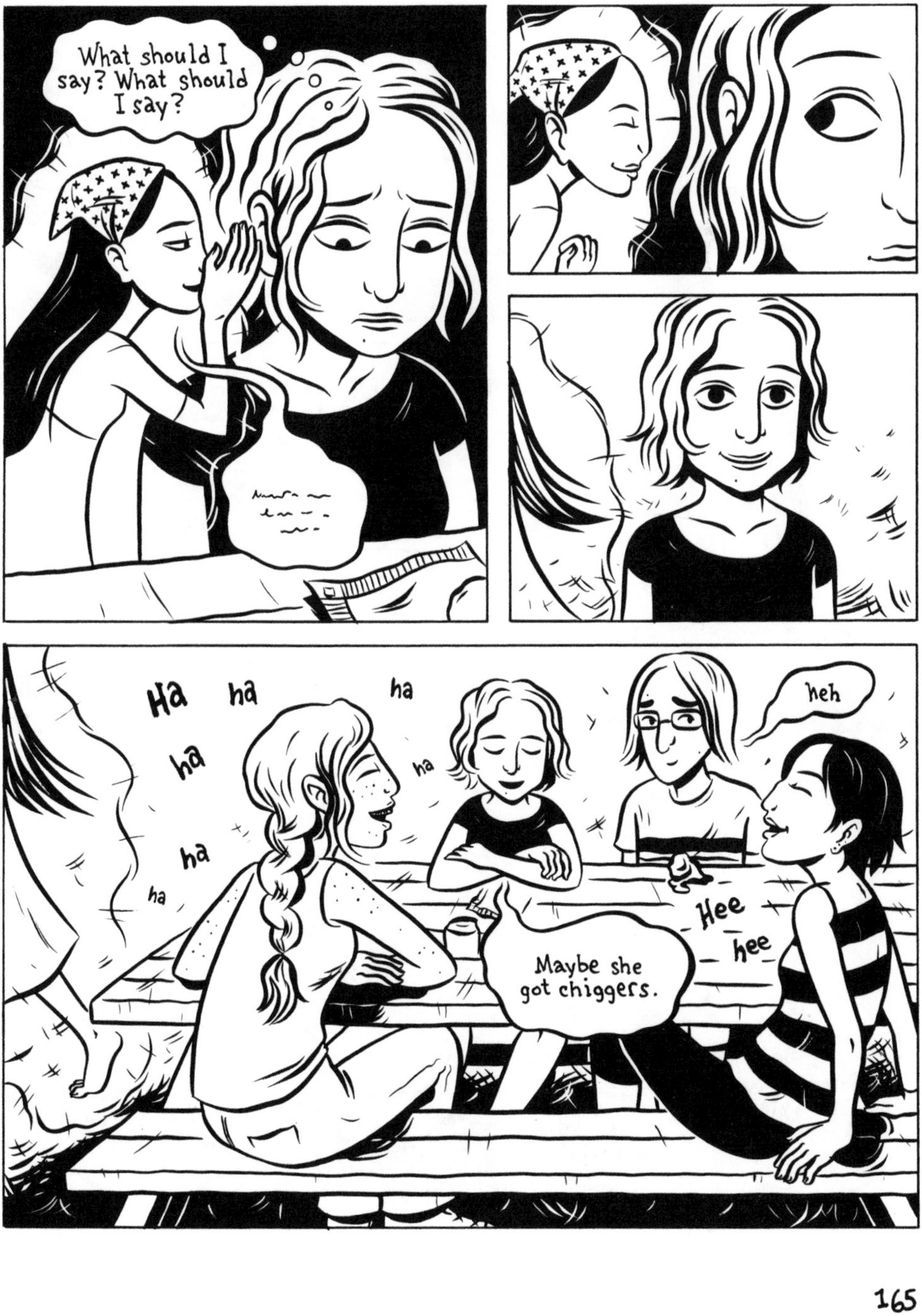
What should I say? What should I say?
Ha ha ha
ha
ha
ha
ha
heh
Maybe she got chiggers.
Hee hee

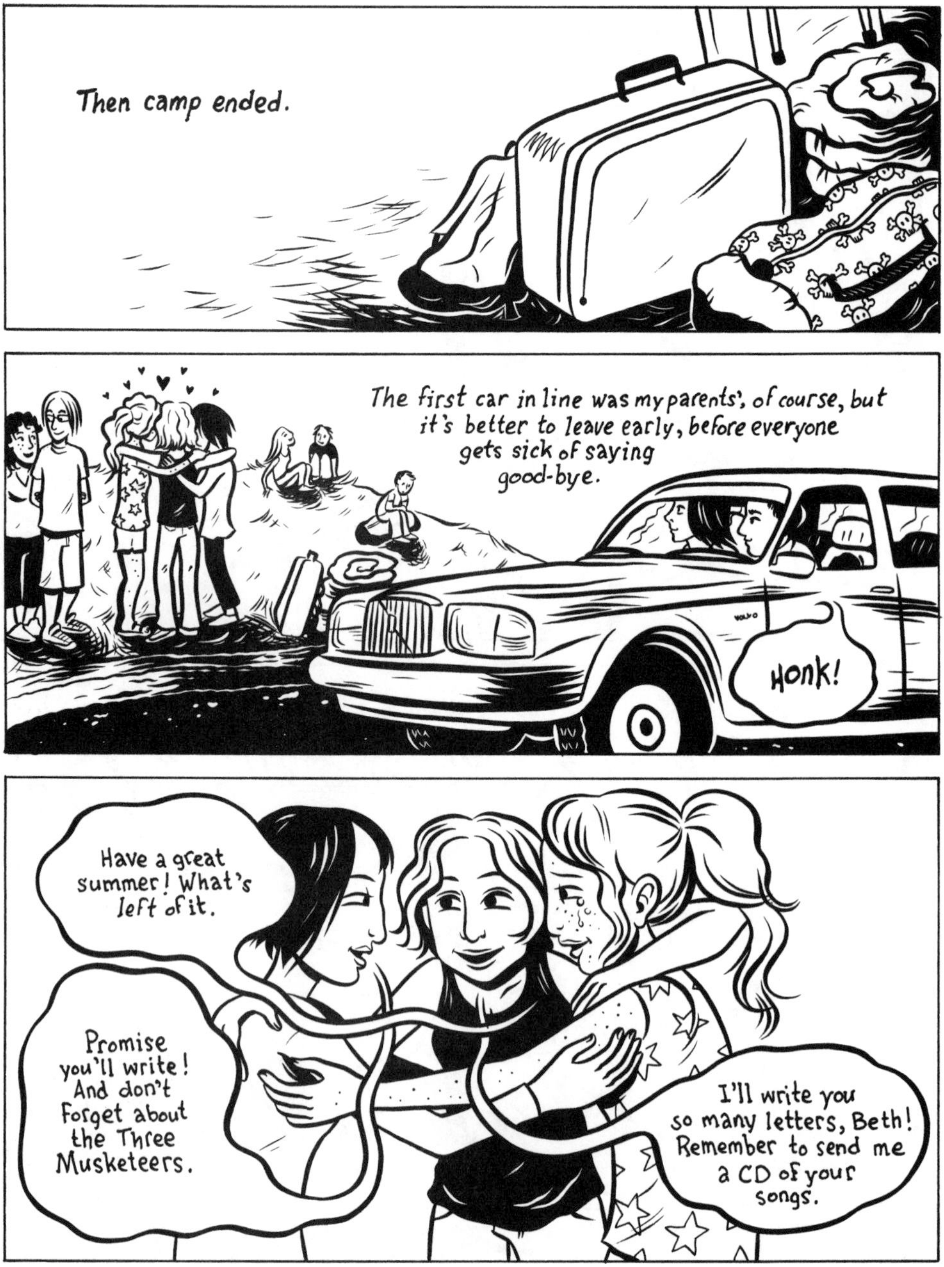
Then camp ended.
The first car in line was my parents', of course, but it's better to leave early, before everyone gets sick of saying good-bye.
HONK!
Have a great summer! What's left of it.
Promise you'll write! And don't forget about the Three Musketeers.
I'll write you so many letters, Beth! Remember to send me a CD of your songs.

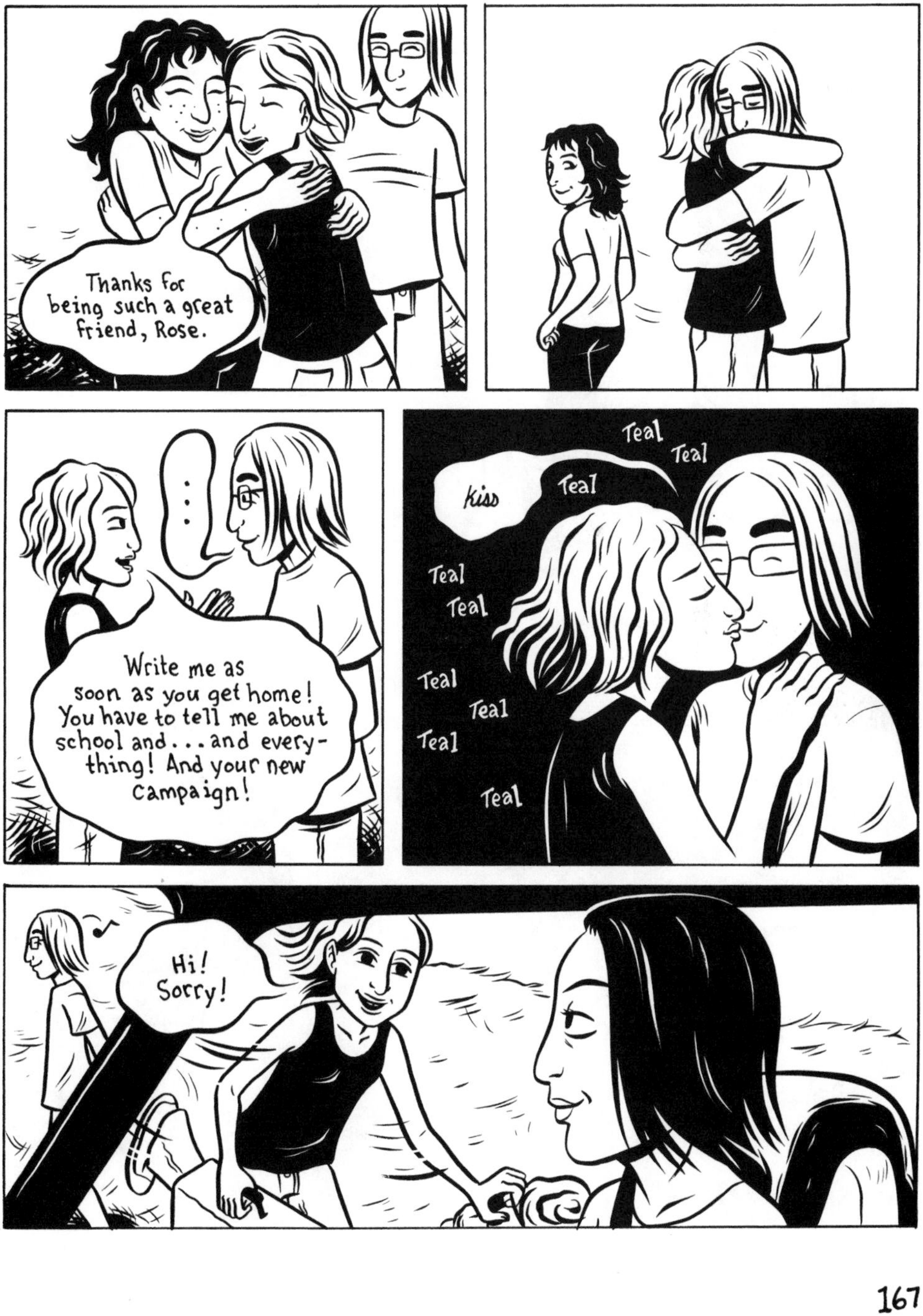

Thanks for being such a great friend, Rose.
...
Write me as soon as you get home! You have to tell me about school and... and everything! And your new campaign!
kiss
Teal
Teal
Teal
Teal
Teal
Teal
Teal
Teal
Teal
Hi! Sorry!

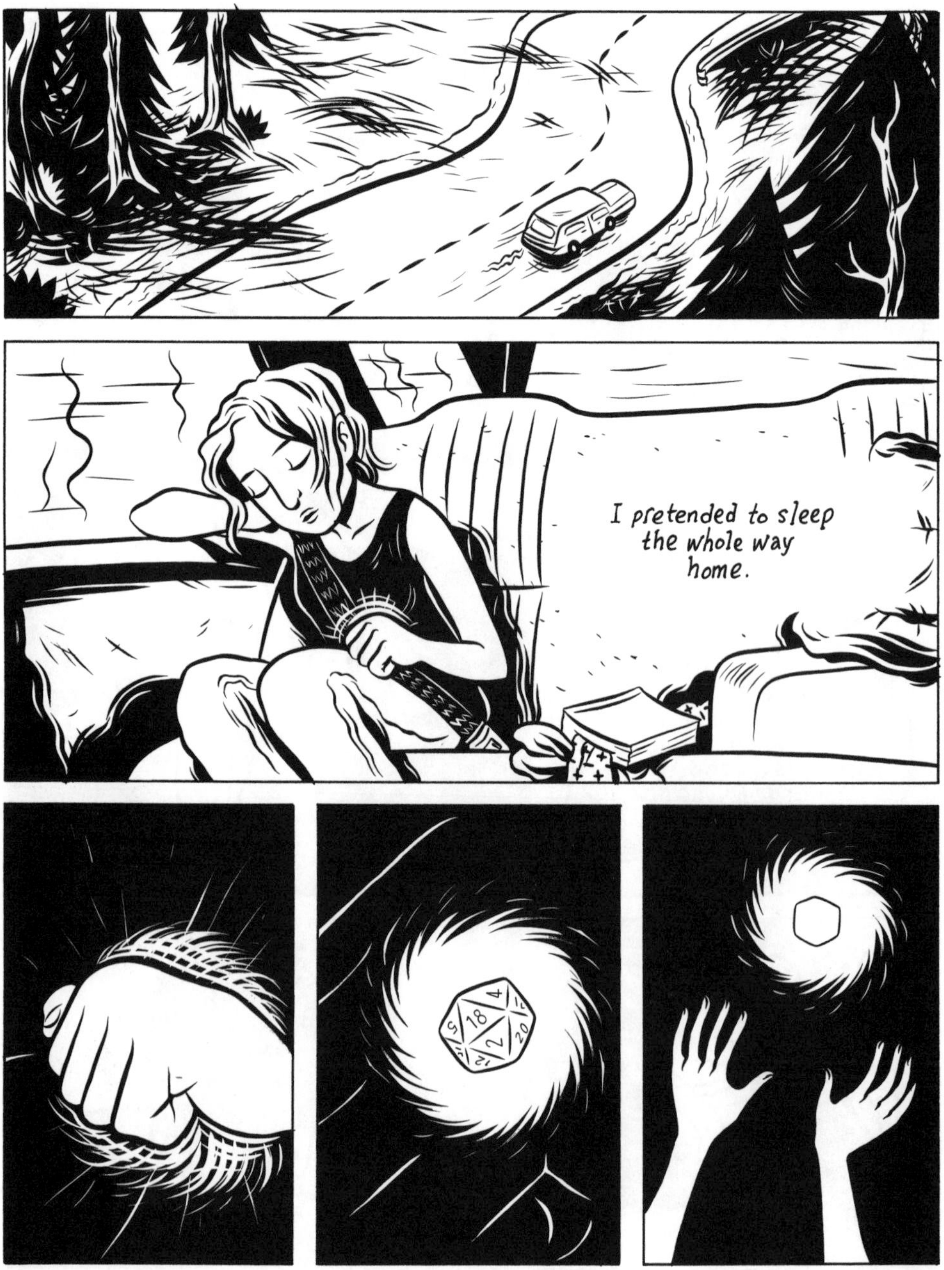
I pretended to sleep the whole way home.

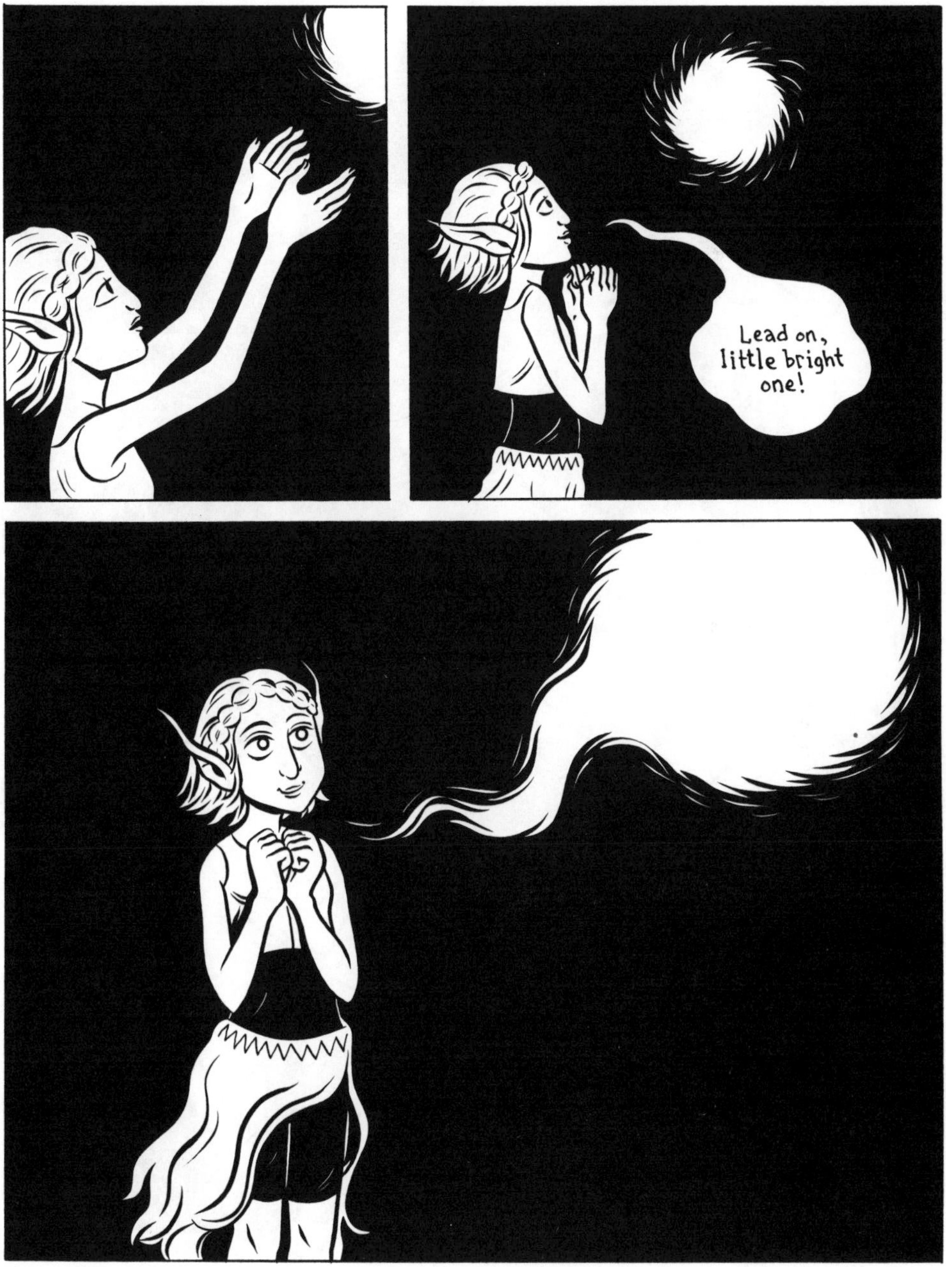
Lead on, little bright one!

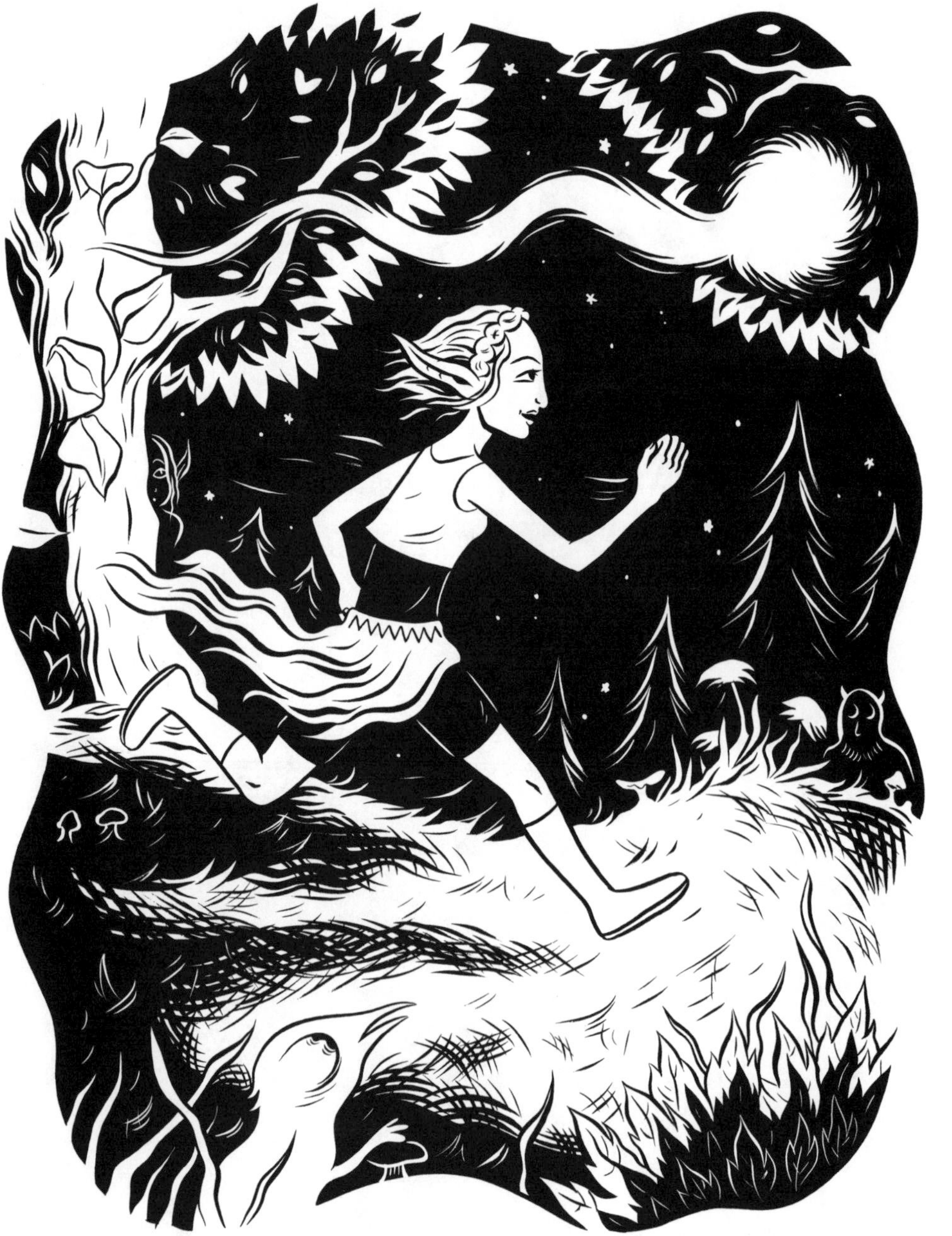

For a while I used Shasta's bandana
as a bookmark.

I don't know where it went
after that.

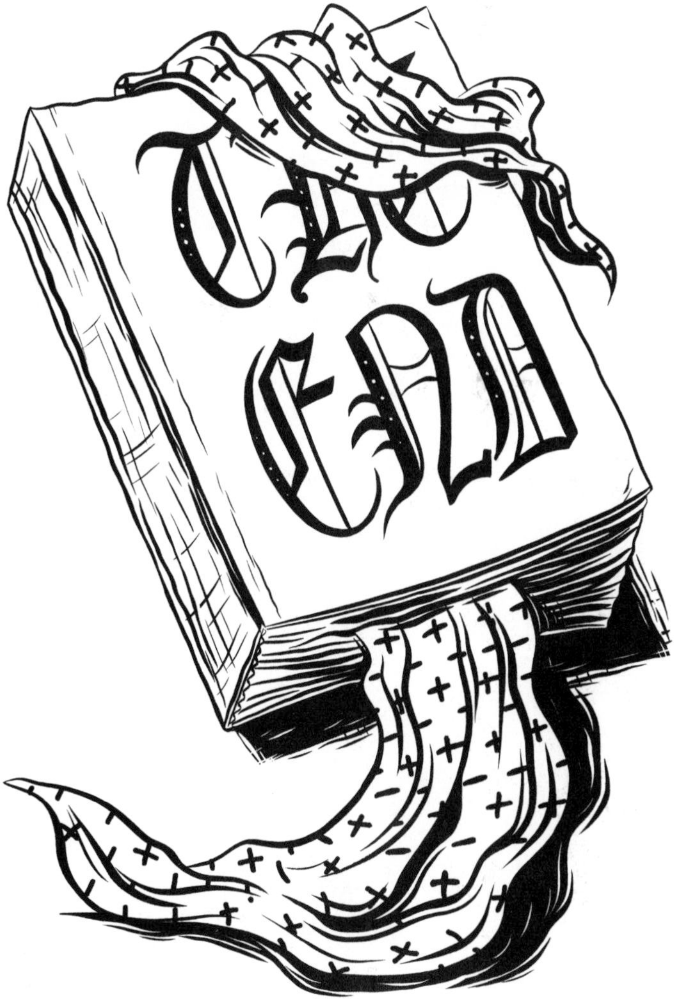
The End